COPPER
PRINCESS

JENNIFER ALLIS PROVOST

SPENCER
HILL
PRESS

ISBN
Paperback: 9781633921139
Ebook: 9781633921146

For inquiries about volume orders, please contact:
Spencer Hill Press
27 West 2oth Street
Suite 1103
New York NY 10011

Published in the United States by Spencer Hill Press

Distributed by Independent Publishers Group
www.ipgbook.com

Book design: Mimi Bark
Cover design: Lisa Amowitz

Printed in the United States of America

PROLOGUE

Sara

"Is that a kelpie of sorts?" Micah asked.

"It's the creature from the Black Lagoon," I replied. "You know, the guy from the title."

"Why is the lagoon black?" Micah pressed. "Is it cursed?"

"No, just dirty. Now hush; it's starting."

Micah and I were doing the most Mundane thing imaginable in the Mundane realm: taking in a matinee horror movie at the Promenade Market's vintage theater. I'd waxed on about my old Picture Vision so many times that Micah decided to learn what all the fuss was about and took me on a date to the movies. While it was a bit run-down, the theater hadn't lost any of its charm. Heavy velvet drapes framed the screen, and the walks were covered in vintage woodwork. The gilded ceiling and crystal chandelier rivaled the Raven Compound's atrium, even if the paint was flaking in spots.

I hadn't known how my silver elf would react to being in a movie theater, not to mention doing things like purchasing tickets and hitting up the snack bar, but he took everything in stride. Then the preview reel started, along with the questions.

Micah picked up a single piece of popcorn and scrutinized it. "I cannot fathom why you eat this."

"Says the man who's eaten half the bucket."

He scowled, then popped it into his mouth and went back for more. "Far too salty. And greasy."

Since my head was resting on his shoulder, I looked up into his blue eyes. That's right, they weren't his usual silver; for this latest journey into the Mundane realm, Micah had crafted us a set of completely new glamours. It was a good idea, since we'd worn our previous glamours so often the Peacekeepers had caught on to our true identities. So much for secrecy.

These new glamours made us look pretty good, if I did say so myself. Micah was still tall and lean, but his silver hair was darkened to coal black while his silver eyes were now a brilliant shade of blue. As for me, Micah had made my copper hair blonde, my green eyes brown, and added a few inches to my height. My actual form was still much shorter than Micah, but we appeared to be the same height to both onlookers and mirrors alike.

"Have I ever claimed that Peacekeeper food was anything other than vile?" I countered. "Why do you think I moved in with you? Better food."

Micah snorted. "And here I thought you loved me."

"Nope, just Shep's cooking."

We cuddled and talked through the entire movie. The theater was almost empty, and no one complained about our bad manners. After the end credits rolled, Micah and I left the theater, blinking as our eyes adjusted to the bright sunlight. We headed toward the main aisle of the Promenade and strolled among the stalls. Just like he'd done the first time I'd brought him to the market, Micah surprised me with a bouquet.

"Thank you," I said, sniffing the tired daisies. "We should get some for Mom, too. Daisies are her favorite."

"Then we shall." Micah paid for a second bouquet and we walked off hand in hand. The market was busy that day, with customers looking over everything from used shoes to pre-war books and music discs. Just like the Goblin Market in the Otherworld, anything could be had at the Promenade as long as you were willing to pay the price.

"Let's pick up some books for Sadie," I suggested, tugging Micah toward the booksellers. "And maybe a few newspapers for Dad and Max."

Of course, Micah agreed, and we spent the next half hour sorting through boxes of frayed paperbacks until we'd found a few leather-bound tomes, since nothing but the best would do for the Inheritor of Metal's library. After we paid for the books, we turned toward the newsstand and froze. Emblazoned across the *Capitol City Daily* were the following words:

ARMSTRONG DEFEATS OPPONENT IN PRELIMINARY ELECTION

"Great," I said. Based on that headline, Mike Armstrong, the man responsible for experimenting on Elementals and creating an army of monsters, was a shoo-in for Pacifica's next president.

"Sara, read the next headline," Micah whispered.

I did, and felt all that yummy popcorn become a concrete ball in my stomach.

ARMSTRONG CLAIMS ELEMENTAL RESEARCH COMPLETE, PLANS PRESS CONFERENCE TO SHARE FINDINGS

"Double great." I grabbed a copy and dropped some coins into the seller's palm. "Dad will want to read this."

"Yes," Micah agreed. "I imagine he will."

"Your father's a fan?" the seller asked, lifting his sharp, curious eyes.

"What was that?" I replied, bracing myself for the worst, and the seller nodded toward the newspapers in my hand. "A fan of Armstrong's?" I prompted.

"Yeah." He glanced around, then leaned closer to me. "Most of us here," he gestured to encompass the

Promenade, "are not his biggest supporters."

"Oh." I felt my heart racing; was this man for real, or was he trying to flush out dissenters? "We're not either. Not really."

The seller nodded, and I detected a softness in his face: relief. "Good."

"What do you plan to do about him?" Micah asked, leaning in and keeping his voice low.

"Vote against him," the seller replied matter-of-factly, his mouth tensing, his brow furrowed. "I fear it's all I can do."

Micah clapped him on the shoulder. "If everyone follows their conscience, it will be enough."

We wandered about the stalls for a bit longer, but our happy mood had shattered. Shattering it even further were the Peacekeeper recruitment posters plastered onto every flat surface: "Serve Your Country," they said, or "Protect Humanity." Last I checked, I was human, but not human enough to warrant their protection.

I'd learned a long time ago to protect myself.

It wasn't long before we left the market altogether and went toward that static portal that would bring us from the Mundane realm to the edge of the Whispering Dell.

"Sara, we will stop him," Micah said once we had stepped through the portal and into the Otherworld. "Your father is a brilliant tactician. He will not allow his home to be overrun by those monsters." He cupped my face in his hands and our glamours dissolved. Once again, I was gazing into the silver eyes of the man I loved. "Nor will I allow it. My love, so long as I breathe, I will protect you and yours."

I forced a smile. "I know." We looked at each other for a long moment. Then I drew away. "Let's go home."

Micah draped his arm around my shoulders and we walked down the hill toward the manor. I was glad we'd had our movie date, since I knew it was likely the last calm day we'd have for a while.

Maybe as soon as tomorrow, we were going to war.

1

Sara

Micah and I entered the manor and found Dad and Max, my brother, sitting at the kitchen table with heaps of paper spread before them. Dad was as neat and organized as ever, from his neatly trimmed hair and beard—Corbeau copper, of course—to his meticulously labeled and annotated paperwork. Even his lunch was neat, consisting of a sandwich split into two perfect triangles. Since Max wanted to be like Dad in all ways possible, he was also neat and organized, with the exception of his hair. It erupted from his head like flames from a campfire, and no amount of gel or brushing could tame it.

After we exchanged greetings, I placed the newspaper on the table in front of Dad.

"What's this?" he asked.

"It's a front-page article about our nemesis positioning himself for victory," I explained.

"So dramatic, my eldest daughter is," Dad murmured as he scanned the headlines. He frowned, his frown deepening when he moved on to the second article. "Max, read this," he urged, pushing the newspaper across the table.

"He's calling what he does research," Max growled after he glanced at the page. "It's more like genocide and legalized torture. Just one more reason we need to get going on these plans."

I peeked over Max's shoulder. He'd drawn a sketch of a few tents surrounded by a fence. "What's that supposed to be?" I asked.

"I'm making a map of Jovanny's resistance headquarters."

"Oh, *that* glorified campground?" I sat across from Max. A silverkin appeared at my elbow and deposited a cup of coffee before me; how I loved those little guys. "Dad, when you led the resistance, was your home base a field of tents? With no modern amenities?"

He scratched his beard. "No, we operated out of a warehouse on the southern side of the Promenade. It was not as primitive as what you have described as Jovanny's base."

"'Primitive' is one word for it," I muttered, remembering the tired old cots and musty blankets we'd slept on, and the lack of indoor plumbing. "Why are you making a map of Jovanny's place? Are we planning a tent raid?"

"I am planning on visiting them," Dad replied, "and I would like to have as much information about the location as possible to review beforehand. I do not like surprises."

"The biggest surprise there was Aregonda's coffee," I interjected. "It was really good, and she always made sure we had some." I nudged Max with my elbow. "I think she had a thing for Max."

Max dropped his pencil. "*Seriously?*" He snorted. "She's old enough to be my mother."

"She was always bringing you extra coffee, and little plates of food—"

"Food I couldn't even digest "

"*She* didn't know that!"

"You have established that Aregonda is an excellent hostess," Dad interrupted. "Sara, Max has also laid out a map of Armstrong's research facility." He spoke these last words as if they dirtied his mouth. "Please, would you look it over?"

He slid the sketch toward me, and Micah sat beside me as we scrutinized the drawing. It was a fairly detailed rendering of where Armstrong created cheap copies of Elementals by forcing raw materials into Mundane humans.

"It's all here," I confirmed, feeling my own face pinch with disgust. Max had labeled the five courtyards, each according to the element they were forcing into the hapless victims. The yard for metal Elementals was full to bursting, while the area for water victims was nearly empty. Apparently, most who had attempted to become water Elementals ended up drowning from the inside, though Armstrong kept trying to make those abilities stick. *No, good citizens of Pacifica, Mike Armstrong isn't a psychopath at all. Definitely vote for him in the next election.*

"An abomination of our inborn talents," Micah muttered. I pointed to the largest courtyard.

"This is where they kept the metal ones," I said. I could not, would not, call them "Elementals." "It seems that metal is the most easily assimilated of all the elements."

"In all my days, I've never encountered anything so evil," Micah whispered. "This Mike Armstrong makes the Iron Queen seem as innocent as a spring lamb."

"Which is why we will stop him," Dad declared as he stood. "I will fetch Mama. Then we shall pay a visit to the resistance. Would you like to accompany us?"

"*Hell* yeah!" Max exclaimed, standing.

"I shall as well," Micah added. "I desire to see this base with my own eyes."

"What about Sadie?" I asked. "Shouldn't she come with?"

"She's hiding in her library, pretending that none of this is happening," Max answered, direct as ever.

Dad gave him one of those withering looks only a parent could give. "Max, that is hardly how I would describe it."

Max shrugged. "I call 'em like I see 'em."

"You'd think Sadie would want to be in the Mundane world, away from Oriana and the threat of pledging to the Gold Court," I said. "Has anyone brought that up to her?"

"We can leave the kid out of it for now," Max insisted, motioning toward the library with a lift of his chin. "Juliana's keeping her company."

I pursed my lips, wondering how Juliana felt about babysitting the Inheritor of Metal. "All right, then," I said, glancing between their attentive, determined faces. "When do we leave?"

It wasn't long before the five of us—me, a re-glamoured Micah, Dad, Mom, and Max—portaled from the Otherworld to the woods beyond the resistance's camp. Max had wanted to show up right in the center of the ragged old tents, but Dad insisted on checking out the perimeter defenses on the way there. What he found left him rather unimpressed.

"Two sentries, no more," Dad remarked as he shook his head. "They didn't even think to cover the compass points."

"There's three if you count the one sleeping," Max added, shrugging.

"I do not," Dad said. He gestured to the camp's location in a valley. "And who chose this location in the first place? Easy to find, difficult to defend. The enemy could have them surrounded before they knew what was happening." He frowned. "The Jovanny I worked with is better than this."

"Like I said, these guys are not big-league potential," Max explained, leaning closer to Dad as he spoke. "Jovanny's a good guy, but his people have a serious lack of talent."

"I think there are magical defenses, like perimeter wards," I interrupted, the pit in my stomach sinking, growing heavier. "I felt something magical the last time we were here." I *hoped* they had *something* more going on than a few lazy sentries. If not, the resistance and all Elementals were surely doomed.

"There's nothing I can sense," Mom quickly countered, shaking her head. "Perhaps the magic handlers who once worked with the resistance are no longer available."

"You mean they're dead or captured?" I asked.

"Not necessarily," Dad clarified. "They may be stationed elsewhere."

"Or perhaps our people are spread too thin," Mom offered.

Dad sighed—maybe it was more of a groan—and

ran a hand through his hair. "All right, let's head down and speak to Jovanny."

We picked our way down the hillside, Dad leading the way while Micah and I brought up the rear.

"This operation is most unimpressive," Micah said under his breath.

"You've got that right," I replied, ducking under a low-hanging branch. "It's almost like they want to get caught."

"Perhaps there was more working against them than merely the shapeshifter," Micah posed, his tone tentative. "Perhaps that man you were associating with is, in fact, a Peacekeeper."

Micah was referring to Jerome Polonsky, the resistance double agent who'd rescued Max, Sadie, and me from prison. Mind you, after his daring rescue we'd just ended up in another prison, but it was the thought that counted. Jerome had also claimed to be the last Inheritor of Air's secret son, but Mom insisted that due to a childhood accident Avatar was incapable of fathering a child. We hadn't seen or heard from Jerome in weeks, and I imagined he was having a few serious discussions with his mother.

Or maybe Micah was right, and Jerome was just another traitor.

"Nothing would surprise me," I muttered.

We reached the camp, and Dad strode directly to the central tent. A woman wearing khaki jeans, a dark shirt, and a bomber jacket stood outside the tent flap. I understood the resistance's need to appear unremarkable, since I'd once gone out of my way to be a boring, bland woman and nothing more. The more you stood out in Pacifica, the more attention you got from Peace-keepers, and no one wanted their attention.

"Commander Corbeau," the woman said as she saluted. Based on Dad's bemused face, I figured that "commander" was a title the shapeshifter had come up with for his false identity. "We haven't heard from you in some time. I trust you are doing well?"

"I am," Dad replied, composing himself. "Is Jovanny available?"

"Of course," she answered, holding aside the flap. We filed into the darkened tent and found Jovanny Lopez seated behind his card table, shuffling papers and taking notes. Per usual, he wore faded green fatigues, which complemented his olive skin and salt-and-pepper hair. There was a communication device in his ear, and several radios were set up on a crate to his left. We'd caught him in the midst of planning something.

Jovanny looked up at the light streaming in from the open tent flap, leaping to his feet once he recognized Dad.

"Baudoin! So good to see you," he greeted warmly. "I had no idea you were coming here today. We haven't heard from you since just before the Phillips rally." Max chose that moment to step out from behind Dad.

14

"And what a rally it was," he said with a mischievous grin.

Jovanny's eyes narrowed. "Aregonda informed me of what you did at the rally," he said. "You're lucky you didn't get anyone killed, boy."

"Do not reprimand my son," Dad admonished, his eyes flashing. "In fact, I am here in part to discuss the events surrounding that rally. You believe the last time we saw each other was what, a scant two weeks ago?"

"More like three," Jovanny replied, glancing at his calendar. "What are you getting at?"

"Today is the first time I've been in your presence in more than five years, Jovanny," Dad explained tersely, meeting his old friend's gaze. "Until shortly after that rally, I'd been imprisoned in the Otherworld by Peacekeepers."

"Impossible," Jovanny scoffed, quirking an eyebrow. "Is this some kind of joke?"

"If this is a joke, it is not very funny," Dad answered, his voice low and dangerous. "The individual you were interacting with was a shapeshifter working for Mike Armstrong."

Jovanny sat heavily; by looks of the emotions skating across his face, he'd had a few doubts of his own about the Baudoin Corbeau he'd been dealing with. "You—*he*—he said he'd been captured by Ferra in the past. He said that after she was killed, he escaped the Iron Court."

"That much is true," Dad confirmed, the edge having left his voice. "I enlisted Ferra's aid to rescue my son, but she betrayed me and handed me over to the Peacekeepers. My wife only recently liberated me."

Jovanny's gaze snapped to Mom. "Maeve?" he asked, and she nodded.

"Pleasure to see you again, Jovanny," she acknowledged, curt.

Jovanny nodded, then his eyes narrowed. "How do I know *you* aren't a shapeshifter?" he demanded. "For all I know, I'm being played for the fool now."

"There is my wife's presence here, for one," Dad countered. "Did you not notice that Maeve never once accompanied the shifter? In the past, when have I ever made decisions of significance without her?"

"He . . . said you two had parted ways . . . " Jovanny murmured, wincing when he glanced back toward Mom. At the insinuation that she and Dad had broken up, her back straightened and her eyes flashed, and for a moment I thought Jovanny had uttered his last words. Then Dad put his hand on her back and drew her against him.

"I *never* willingly part from Maeve," he declared. "Not once since the day we met. These years separated from her were the worst of my life."

As Dad spoke, Micah wrapped his arm around my shoulders. I placed my hand over his and smiled at him; I hated being separated from him, too. Our movements drew Jovanny's attention, and he scowled at Micah.

"Baudoin, who is this?" he asked, his tone conveying that he didn't appreciate unknown individuals popping up in his tent.

"This man is Micah, my son-in-law," Dad replied. "Micah, this is Jovanny, the man who helmed the resistance in my absence."

"A pleasure," Micah said with a nod.

"Why don't you show Jovanny who you really are?" Dad suggested.

Micah dropped his glamours and stood before Jovanny in all his elfin glory. I know men aren't usually referred to as "radiant," but Micah practically shone in the dark tent. "I am Micah Silverstrand, Lord of Silver and the Whispering Dell," he introduced.

Jovanny started at Micah for a moment, then said haltingly to Dad, "You have the Inheritor of Metal *and* the Lord of Silver in your family?"

"And the—" I was going to add "Seelie Queen," but a sharp look from Mom silenced me. It seemed the resistance was on a need-to-know basis about the Corbeaus. Okay. I liked that.

"And the what?" Jovanny prompted.

"And me and Max," I finished. "We're pretty powerful, too, remember?"

"I do," Jovanny agreed with another sidelong look at Max. He stood, came around the table, and offered his hand to Dad. "Forgive me, Baudoin, for allowing myself, and the entire operation, to be led astray by an imposter."

Dad gripped his hand firmly. "No apology is necessary, my friend. The shifter's purpose was to deceive, and he did an admirable job." Jovanny grinned. Then Dad ruined the mood. "You do realize that we will need to completely relocate the operation, no? Change access codes, passwords, everything?"

The color drained from Jovanny's face. "Ah. Right."

"That shifter was working for the Peacekeepers," Dad continued. "We have no way of knowing what information he has long since relayed to our enemies. Best to be safe rather than sorry."

Jovanny glanced from Dad to the heap of paperwork on his table, then swore. "That . . . that would be best." He grabbed a manila folder and thrust it toward Dad. "That doppelgänger of yours drew up these plans to attack the Presidential Estate in Portland. We can split the force and use the attack as cover while the rest of the operation relocates."

Dad flipped through the folder, his brows lowering as he scanned the plans. If they were the same plans Max and I had reviewed, they were less than awesome. "How far along are your preparations?" he asked.

"We can strike by the end of the week."

"Good. Don't." Dad handed the paperwork off to Max.

"Seen it, hated it," Max said as he passed the folder to Micah. "Ask Sara. I knew these plans weren't your work."

"Would it not behoove you to disable this Mike Armstrong's research facility first?" Micah asked as he scanned the documents. "Since he appears to be counting on his force of monsters to turn the tide in his favor, disabling that operation would not only serve the resistance's cause; it would also positively impact the welfare of all Elementals."

"Maybe we can even rescue a few prisoners," I chimed in. "I really don't think any of those Elementals are willing subjects. I bet most of the Mundanes aren't, either."

"You have information about what the Mundanes are thinking?" Jovanny asked.

"Not really," I began, wincing as I considered whether or not that spark of hope we'd encountered in the market was anything to believe in. "But we were at the Promenade earlier, and we talked to someone who made it seem like most Mundanes aren't happy with Armstrong."

"The individual indicated that most would vote against him," Micah added.

Jovanny nodded slowly. "Interesting. In one fell swoop we could rescue many of our brothers and sisters and increase our standing with Mundanes."

It was Dad's turn to nod. "We are in agreement."

Jovanny rubbed his eyes. "Good, because we have plenty of work to do." He dropped his hand and eyed Micah. "Do you know anything about drawing up battle plans?"

The corner of Micah's mouth curled up, but he didn't reveal that he had once served as the Gold Queen's general. "I am somewhat familiar with the practice. Is there a map I may mark up?"

Jovanny rifled through his papers, then muttered, "I should get Aregonda. She'll want to be involved with this." He glanced at Dad and added, "She'll want to know we were compromised."

"I'll find her," I said, sliding out of Micah's arms. Since I knew pretty much nothing about battle plans, I figured that was the best way to make myself useful. "Coming?" I asked Max.

"Sure," he said with a shrug. "Maybe I can score some of that coffee."

"Be safe," Micah murmured, his thumb gliding across my cheek. Lowly, so only I could hear him, he added, "I do not trust this place, or these people. If you are not back soon, I will find you."

"I'm counting on it." I kissed the underside of Micah's chin. Then I followed Max out of the tent and into the harsh sunlight. The other residents of the camp regarded us with suspicion, and some of them glared at us with outright animosity. I guess we'd earned that after what had happened at Langston Phillips's rally.

"The natives are restless," Max observed. Good, he noticed the blatant hatred, too. "Let's get out of the line of fire."

I agreed, so we headed down the slope toward the waterfall and adjacent pool. We found Aregonda kneeling at the water's edge, rinsing out a pitcher. Her long rosy-brown hair was tucked behind her ear, and her rolled-up sleeves revealed tanned skin from many hours working outdoors. Even though she was kneeling, her long limbs betrayed her height and athletic build. For all that it seemed like Aregonda was usually in charge of domestic duties, she was built like a warrior.

"Hi, Aregonda," I called to her. "Are you busy?"

"Sara, Max," she greeted, looking over her shoulder at us, a small smile on her lips. "What a lovely surprise. I'd been expecting you, but not so soon."

Aregonda had been expecting us? *So* not good. "Our father—our *real* father—is talking to Jovanny," I said.

"*Real* father?" Aregonda repeated, her eyebrows raised. "Have you a false one as well?"

"The man you'd been dealing with was a shapeshifter," Max explained. "He's since been removed, and we found the real old man."

Aregonda's eyes clouded. "I suspected the Baudoin that contacted us some months ago was not the real man," she said, her voice bitter. "Still, we wanted to believe it was him. We needed a Corbeau to rally around."

I nodded, surprised to be agreeing with Aregonda on anything. "Yeah, we felt the same way."

"Is Sadie here as well?" she asked.

"Um, no." I looked down and saw that Aregonda wasn't actually rinsing out a pitcher. It was a silver bowl with a heavy, incised lip around its edge, and a handle on one side. I couldn't help asking, "What's that?"

"A bowl," she replied with a wink. "I burn herbs in it."

"Oh, for cooking?"

Aregonda laughed. "Not at all. For spellwork." She scooped some water into the bowl, then sat cross-legged with it before her. "Sit, and I'll teach you both a trick or two."

Max and I sat, both of us looking expectantly at Aregonda. She smiled at us. "I understand that you're both metal, as I am, but have you ever wished to experience a different element?"

"Yeah," Max said while I asked, "Experience how?"

"Why, experience as an Elemental would." Aregonda pushed the bowl closer to me and Max, then murmured, "Eau sacrée, venez à moi en tant que métal fait. Aimez-moi comme métal fait. Sers-moi que le métal fait."

"What in the world does that mean?" I demanded. Any Elemental worth her salt knew to never repeat a spell she didn't understand. I'd learned that right after I'd learned not to accept fruit from strangers.

"It's French," Max replied. "Means something like, 'Water, come to me like metal, love me like metal, serve me like metal.'"

I eyed my brother, skeptical. I didn't remember everything from when we were kids, but I did remember how often he skipped school. "You speak French?"

He was unfazed. "Dad taught me." He turned to Aregonda and added, "I thought spells were usually recited in Latin."

"They are said in whatever language the caster chooses," Aregonda clarified. "My first language is French, so it is the one I choose. Now, repeat after me and concentrate."

I glanced at Max, still nervous. "What do you think?" I whispered to him.

He shrugged. "It's just a bowl full of water. Can't be too dangerous."

I frowned, but nodded. Aregonda repeated the incantation, and Max and I repeated after her. I don't know what I'd been expecting, maybe a rainstorm or a miniature tsunami, but all the water did was sit in its bowl and shimmer at us. Then, it moved.

It *moved*.

It was sloshing around on its own in the silver bowl as if it were an animal pacing the length of its cage. Then it reached out and touched Max's hand.

The water frickin' reached out and touched Max.

"Hey," he said, jerking his arm away. "That was weird."

"Is it not how metal strives to be one with you?" Aregonda asked.

"I guess," Max mumbled.

"What about you, Sara?" Aregonda turned to me, but I was busy concentrating on the water. I imagined it leaping up, coiling around my wrist like my silver mark.

And then it was.

The entire bowl's worth of water reached out and wrapped itself around my wrist, flowing over my mark as if it were a riverbed. I laughed at the coolness of the water, at the amazing sight before me, and at Max's totally freaked-out face.

"Very good," Aregonda praised me with a brief nod. She flicked her fingers and the water obediently unwound itself from my wrist and flowed back into the bowl. "Now, I'm sure each of you has a heart's desire," she continued. "Speak these words, and concentrate on the water's surface: 'Montrez-moi ce que mon cœur veut, mais ma tête nie?'"

Without question, we repeated the words. Max and I gazed at the water in the silvery bowl. "What are we waiting for?" I asked.

"Your heart's desire to be revealed," Aregonda answered.

I shrugged, then caught a glimpse of something on the water's surface: a flash of silver, a blur of movement. Slowly, the colors coalesced into Micah, striding out of the manor's front doors to greet me. He was smiling, his arms outstretched as if he were happier than he'd ever been. Then I handed off a small bundle to him, and my heart swelled as he accepted it.

"Sis."

Max bumped my shoulder with his, thus ending my vision. "What?" I asked, my voice thick, as if I were waking from a dream.

"I think we should be getting back."

"Very well," Aregonda sighed. She took the bowl and emptied it into the stream. "Return to your plans. Please tell Jovanny I will be there directly."

Once Max and I were out of earshot, he whispered, "That heart's desire thing was a trick. She just wanted to get a peek inside our brains."

"How do you know?" I asked. "All I saw was—"

"You handing Micah a baby," he finished.

"I was *not* handing him a baby," I snapped, then stopped short. "How do you even know that?"

"I saw it," he replied. "Right next to my own vision, yours was playing out."

Great. If Max had seen my vision, Aregonda likely saw both of ours. The idea of that woman having a window into my psyche did not sit well with me. "What was your vision of?" I prompted, curious.

Max quirked an eyebrow at me. "Not Micah."

I snorted. "He'll be so disappointed." I glanced at my brother. "Seriously, what was it?"

He only hesitated a moment. "Like yours, only I was on the receiving end of the package."

It took me a second to realize he was serious. "Really?"

"Really."

2

Max

Sara gave me a long look, then shrugged and kept walking back to Jovanny's tent. She knew better than to ask me for any details. I wouldn't admit anything to her.

Hell, I wasn't sure I could admit it to myself. Not even seeing it, right there in the water, was enough.

I had no idea how Aregonda had performed that little trick and gotten my thoughts to play out like a movie on the water's surface. The only good thing about it was that Sara had been so distracted by her and Micah's dream baby that she hadn't seen my "heart's desire," if that's what you want to call it.

My vision had been—well, let's not get into that. What mattered was that Aregonda had managed to reveal both my and Sara's deepest wishes. How had she even done that? More importantly, why?

I glanced back at Aregonda as she carefully dried the bowl. I wondered what her deal was. Of all the things she could've possibly wanted to know about me, that vision was probably the least useful. All it really did was remind me that I was living on borrowed time.

See, when I was fifteen, I got wind that the Peacekeepers were looking for the Inheritor of Metal. That person just happened to be my youngest sister, Sadie. She was only seven years old at the time, and there was no way I was letting those government goons get their hands on her. My grand plan to thwart the Peacekeepers was to turn myself in, claiming to be the Inheritor they were searching for.

I was positive I was doing the right thing. With me in custody, Armstrong and the rest had no reason to suspect Sadie was the true Inheritor. My sister—both of my sisters—would be safe.

I was *also* positive that I would only be in Peacekeeper custody for a few weeks, a month at most, before I escaped. Chalk it up to the arrogance of youth, but I was shocked when the Peacekeepers transported me to the Otherworld and incarcerated me at the Institute for Elemental Research. I was in a whole different dimension, and in a place specifically designed to nullify my powers and keep me there. By the time I hit my sixteenth birthday, I'd been caught trying to escape a dozen times, and for every attempt they ramped up my punishment accordingly. I'd long since made peace with living out the rest of my days at the Institute by the time Juliana arrived.

Juliana isn't an Elemental or a government goon. Her uncle, Mike Armstrong—yeah, *that* Mike Armstrong—got her an internship so she could earn credits toward her psychology degree. When she learned what really went on at her uncle's facility, she spent every waking moment trying to free me and the others. No one had ever put themselves on the line for me the way Juliana had. She was good, and kind, and wicked smart, and she gave me a reason to hope again.

Until Langston Phillips started practicing his most sadistic torture routines on me, which culminated in my becoming his lab specimen, repeatedly shocked, dissected, and exploited in every way possible. When Sara first dreamwalked to me I was sure I'd hallucinated her, and when she and Micah freed me, I prayed for the first time in my life, thanking any and all gods who could have possibly been listening.

So, yeah, I'm still in shock that I'm not dead. That's going to have to wear off before I start planning anybody's future.

Sara and I entered Jovanny's tent and found him scowling at Micah. His Silverness had that typical look of disdain on his face, a look that was usually directed at me and always raised my hackles. Since Ma and

Dad were looking on with neutral expressions, I bet Jovanny deserved it.

"If you think you can just waltz into this place and—" Jovanny was saying, then clammed up when he caught sight of me and Sara. Seemed that he didn't want to argue in front of the kids.

"We have explained what we need to do," Dad said, then he picked up a stack of papers and slid them into a folder. "I shall finalize these plans and have them back to you in less than a day. In the meantime, make ready to strike. If all goes well, we shall move in two days' time."

"But—"

Dad held up a hand. "Please, Jovanny. No one holds you responsible for the shifter, or its actions. Let us move on."

Jovanny nodded. "Agreed, Baudoin."

With that, we left Jovanny sitting behind his table, buried in maps and file folders, and strode out into the sunlight. Those who'd been glaring at me earlier gaped at me walking beside my father; yeah, folks, you just showed some serious attitude to the son of the actual leader of this operation. Commence sucking up, ASAP.

We portaled back to the manor, all of us in relatively good spirits. The visit had gone better than expected: Sara and I learned some magic tricks, and we confirmed that Jovanny and Aregonda were still jerks. Speaking of Aregonda . . .

"Ma," I said, "Aregonda worked some kind of mojo on Sara and me."

Ma stopped dead in her tracks. "What did she do to you? Gods below, all women with that name are evil incarnate."

Dad gave Ma a look; Aregonda just so happened to be Meme Corbeau's given name. "Remember when you first met *maman*, and she said you were a she-devil come to steal her son?"

Ma smiled, and it was simultaneously reassuring and terrifying. "Max, what did Aregonda do?"

"At first, she taught us some spells," I replied. "She had Sara calling water like it was metal."

Ma and Dad stopped looking at each other and turned toward Sara. "You called water?" Dad asked.

"I didn't even know I was doing it," Sara said with a shrug. "She said the spells in French and we repeated them. I was concentrating so hard on pronouncing the words correctly I was hardly paying attention to anything else, and all of a sudden the water jumped out of the bowl and wrapped itself around my wrist."

"You did that when you were a baby," Ma murmured. "Beau, remember when she didn't want a bath and would send the water out of the tub?"

"I do." Dad chuckled.

"I don't remember that," Sara said. "And why would I start doing it again over twenty years later?"

I scoffed. It was just like Sara to forget her magic. I had to wonder if she'd spent so much time trying to hide it from other people that she reflexively hid it from herself, too. While I'd honed my Elemental magic (under not-so-great circumstances, yeah, but it was still practice), hers had just been suppressed, when it wasn't running absolutely wild. "You've called water since then," I insisted. "Remember when you drowned the Iron Queen with a tsunami?"

"The Bright Lady gave me a charm," Sara stammered. "I—I just used it."

Micah gave me a pointed look (defensive much?) and set his hands on Sara's shoulders. "Are you sure you are the one that called it? Could Aregonda have enchanted the water?"

"Maybe," Sara said. "Then she had us repeat other stuff, and we saw images in the water."

"Images?" Ma repeated. "What kind of images?"

I waved my hand and rolled my eyes. "Aregonda said they were our hearts' desires, but I don't know if I buy that. She probably could have made anything appear in front of us."

Before I could go on, Sara tugged my sleeve and nodded toward the manor's front door. I turned and saw Juliana standing there in the sunlight, outlined in gold. *Nope. Stop. Don't do this to yourself.*

I immediately looked back at Sara. "Yeah? And?" I growled, unable to keep the frustration out of my voice. I saw Juliana all the time, and when I did, I walked the other way. She'd made it clear that she wanted nothing more to do with me, and I was trying to respect that. It hurt, but it was the right thing to do.

"Max, look at her," Sara whispered.

Hesitantly, I sighed and turned back to Juliana. I hadn't noticed before, but it was obvious now how tense she was, and she was wringing her hands. The only time I'd ever seen her wring her hands like that was when Langston had forced her to sit in on experiments at the Institute. If she was doing it now, something big had happened. And that was something I couldn't ignore.

"Hey," I called out to her.

She turned around, and I lost my breath. Thanks to her Moroccan mother, Juliana's hair was all rich chocolate waves that shimmered gold when they caught the light. It wasn't nearly as long as it had been when we first met, now falling just past her shoulders, but there was still just enough for me to tangle my fists in, assuming she'd ever let me get close enough to do that again. Her eyes were the same deep brown as her hair, flecked with gold and emerald. With her smooth skin and perfect, curvy frame, she looked more like a goddess than a girl who'd ever be caught dead talking to me. I wasn't sure how that'd ever happened before. I wasn't going to question it.

Realizing I was staring, I coughed. "Hey," I repeated louder, trying to read her face from so far away. To see if there was something, anything I could do to help her, other than just ignoring her.

"Hey to you, too," Juliana replied, lifting her chin toward me in acknowledgment, cryptic as ever.

Damn it. I'd barely made peace with avoiding her, and now I have to make sure she's all right. I can't take these yo-yo emotions. I gritted my teeth and strode toward her, outpacing Sara and Micah and the others, the manor looming over me.

"What is it, Jules?" I asked when I was close enough, keeping my voice low so the others couldn't hear. "You okay?"

"I'm fine," she replied. Which was a lie, but I let her get away with it. "I just . . . needed to get out of the house."

"Let's take a walk," I suggested without thinking, then paused and reconsidered. "If you want. I don't have to come with—"

To my surprise, she nodded once. "Sure. Come on." Before I could even attempt to comprehend why she agreed, she'd already tossed her dark hair over her shoulder and made her way toward the gardens, glancing back once to make sure I'd follow. I nodded to her, flinching when I felt someone's hand on my arm.

It was Dad, of course, halting me. The rest of the family had managed to catch up. "Ask her about the shapeshifter," he said quietly, his face turned away from Jules as he spoke.

I rounded on him instinctively. "What? Now? She's already upset about something."

He quirked an eyebrow, unfazed. "If we don't know what the shifter's reports were, we'll all be upset."

Surprise, surprise, Dad had a fair point. I took a slow breath to relax and shook my arm loose. "Got it," I told him, and I couldn't bite back the rest of what was going through my head as I jogged after Juliana, careful to keep a fair bit of distance between us. "One interrogation, coming up," I muttered.

As I followed her along the path to the gardens, I realized this was the first time Juliana and I had been alone with each other since the day we made bread together in the kitchen. We'd talked and laughed so easily at first, our hands covered in flour while we kneaded the dough, and I'd let myself hope that things were good again between us. I wanted nothing more than to keep what happened in the Institute in the past and move on.

So I tried to take things further—not a lot further, but a bit—and she shot me down. Hard.

That had hurt.

Ever since, we'd been sickeningly polite to each other, and we navigated the manor specifically to avoid being alone together. If Juliana wanted space, I'd give it to her. As far as what I wanted, it didn't seem like I'd be getting it. Life sucked, but whatever. I was used to that.

But now, it seemed like she wanted me around, if only just so she wouldn't be out walking in the garden on her own. Something was clearly on her mind, I wanted to try to help her without crossing any boundaries, and as if that wasn't enough to juggle all at once, Dad had to come in and have *me* be the one to ask her how badly the resistance's operation had been compromised by the shapeshifter. Wouldn't you know it, I'd been called to duty. A soldier always carries out his orders. Even if he's still nursing his bruised ego.

Whatever. I knew I needed to get over what had happened in the kitchen. If Juliana and I were going to work together in any capacity, I needed to accept things as they were, not how I wanted them to be.

Juliana didn't seem to mind my thoughtful silence. We'd wandered all the way to the back orchard, and I took stock of our surroundings just soon enough to realize we were dangerously close to the Wood Witch's forest.

"Jules," I called. "Stay away from the forest demons."

"As if there are really demons," she snarked, but she did move away from the trees pretty quickly.

"You never know around here." I found a nice spot away from the forest and sat on the ground, motioning for her to join me. "Tell me what happened."

She did, sitting gingerly across from me before

reaching back to pull all her hair over one shoulder. Before she spoke, she took a breath to steady herself. "While you were gone, gold warriors stopped by. The Gold Queen wants to talk to Micah."

I snorted. "Interesting." Oriana's gold warriors were much like Micah's miniature servants, the silverkin. They weren't sentient beings, although Sara repeatedly made a case for the leader of the silverkin, Shep, being a "real boy." Instead, they were hunks of metal sculpted to look like real warriors that carried out their creator's wishes. "Did they say why?"

"Yeah. She's decided that looking for the scroll is a waste of time." Juliana bit her lower lip. "Max, the ones in the back were talking about Sadie. I think Oriana is going to force Sadie to pledge."

"Frickin' great." I eyed her tense shoulders. "Is that all that happened?"

"Isn't that enough?" She shuddered. "Those walking, talking mannequins are terrifying."

"I'm surprised you can still get scared, after everything we've seen." I paused, noticing that she'd relaxed a little bit. *Might as well get this over with.* "Dad wants me to ask you a few questions."

Juliana frowned. "What sort of questions?"

"The shapeshifter, for starters," I began. "How much did he report back on the resistance movement?"

"Not very much," she replied. "He was so concerned with pretending to be your father, he missed quite a few details, and the ones he did remember were inaccurate at best." Juliana rearranged herself so she was sitting cross-legged, and she tore at the grass absently. "He wasn't the best spy."

"I'm surprised they didn't get another shifter," I said.

"Believe me, they tried. Once word got out that Mike wanted a shifter to impersonate Baudoin Corbeau, it didn't matter how much money or how many pardons Mike was offering. Only a true scumbag would betray your father."

"He sure was a scumbag," I agreed. "So, did he give over any details? Locations, names, anything?"

"He supplied the coordinates for seven locations," Juliana explained, crushing the grass between her fingers and sprinkling it into her lap. "One was valid, though it was an unmanned outpost. As for the other six, three were vacant caves, two were government-run schools, and one was a field just past the southern edge of the Promenade."

I laughed through my nose; leave it to my family to get duped by the worst spy in history. "Was anything learned at the outpost?"

"No usable information was gleaned from the site. It looked like it hadn't been used in months, and while all the information within was accurate, it was also outdated." She looked up, the sun setting fire to the green and gold flecks in her eyes. "It's why Langston set him up with the plans to attack the Presidential

Estate in Portland. He figured if the shifter was incapable of gathering information, he'd flush out the
resistance another way."

"Those plans were awful," I said, smiling and shaking my head.

"I know." Juliana grinned. "Who do you think
wrote them?"

I stared at her for a moment, then we both burst
out laughing. "You came up with the big idea of seven
Elementals making a frontal assault against an armed
company of Peacekeepers?" I asked. "Man, Jules, I
thought you were the smart one."

"It's why I wrote in not to proceed without the
Inheritor," she said, wiping her eyes. "I knew you'd
never let Sadie go along with it. At least I hoped you
wouldn't."

"Hey, I'm much more responsible these days," I
teased.

"Yeah, you were wicked responsible at Langston's
rally. What the hell were you thinking?" she demanded.
"If you'd publicly executed Langston, that could have
destroyed all the progress the resistance has made.
Elementals would have looked like exactly what Mike
and Langston try to make them out to be: common
thugs."

"Truthfully, I wasn't thinking." I stood and walked
to the edge of the orchard. "All I knew was that I was
there as an Elemental, with no lab or drugs hinder-

ing me, and that the person I hated most was on that stage." I spread my hands before me, studying them. "I really wanted to kill him."

"I almost wish I hadn't talked you out of it."

I glanced over my shoulder. "I thought you wanted me to be the better man."

"You are the better man, for all that you're an idiot," Juliana said as she got to her feet. "You could kill a hundred Langstons and still be the better man." She dusted off her jeans, then looked me in the eye. "All right. Let's go."

"Go where?" I asked.

"To the manor. You were sent to get information from me, and believe me, I want to share it. It will be easier if I just tell everyone at the same time. We also need to discuss the message from the gold warriors, and Mike's press conference."

"What about his press conference?"

"I read the newspapers Sara and Micah brought back," she replied. "Attending it would be the best way to gather additional data."

"Yeah, I guess it would," I said, falling into step beside her. We were walking together. Talking again. We'd laughed. I couldn't believe it. We were actually . . . all right. I took a deep, slow breath, relieved. "I'm glad you're on our side."

"I always have been." Juliana took a few steps, then stopped, forcing me to stop to stay beside her. She lifted her eyes to meet mine and spoke slowly, deliberately. "Max, I'm really not a spy."

She'd said it so seriously, it was like she thought I believed she was one. That was ridiculous. The words came out of my mouth before I could even consider them. "I know. I believe you, baby."

She tensed, her lips pulling into a thin line. "I'm not your baby, either."

"Right." *Crap. Back to square one.*

Juliana turned and headed off toward the manor. I followed a few steps behind, wondering what I was getting myself into.

3

Sara

Once Juliana told us that Oriana was more interested in obtaining Sadie's pledge than finding the scroll—which contained the lineage of those of copper, who happened to be my relatives *and* the royal family that existed before Elementals ruled the Otherworld—Micah and I knew what we had to do. We hopped onto the metal pathway and sped toward the Gold Court, and I was clutching Micah's arm so hard I must have bruised him. I was still rattled from my encounter with Aregonda, and that vision from the water. The last thing I needed was a visit with the Otherworld's most insane resident.

"What if we can't distract her again?" I asked when we stepped off the path. "What if Her Battiness won't accept no for an answer?"

"Then we will talk to Sadie," Micah said. "If she still refuses to pledge to the queen, we will hide her."

"Hide her where?"

"I do not know just yet, but we will find a place." Micah kissed my fingertips. "Worry not, my Sara. I will not allow one of mine to come to harm, not even by the hand of the Gold Queen herself."

Since Micah was trying to reassure me, I didn't mention all of the gold warriors at Oriana's disposal who were more than capable of marching up to the manor and hauling Sadie away. Micah was powerful, but he was just one Lord of Silver. Even with the addition of Sadie's abilities—if we could get her to fight, that is—and me, Max, and Dad, we were still outmatched. Although we did have one weapon unlike any other: my mother, the Seelie Queen.

If we unleashed Mom on the Gold Court, that just might mean the end of the Otherworld.

The Gold Court loomed in front of us, and the pit in my stomach got impossibly deeper. According to Micah, the main palace had been constructed by various monarchs across the ages, each of them adding a tower or crenelated detail to ensure their own legacy. The high golden fence was the last addition, and was installed by the last Gold King, Eurwyn, in a last-ditch attempt to hold back the Iron Queen. He'd failed and then perished in Ferra's onslaught, and his queen, Oriana, had changed *quite* a bit in her subsequent time as a prisoner of the Iron Court.

As far as I knew, Oriana hadn't made any additions to the Gold Court. Maybe that was for the best.

A set of warriors—flesh and blood, not the creepy metal ones we usually dealt with—ushered Micah and I into Oriana's receiving chamber, and we found the Gold Queen perched on her throne. Oriana's mark was on her hands, and golden ribbons of her element twisted around her fingers and up her arms. Whenever Micah touched the copper raven on my back, it generated instant arousal. I often wondered if Oriana's mark was a pleasure to her, or more of a nuisance.

Awkward marks aside, Oriana was the picture of royalty. Her long blonde hair shone like polished metal, and it cascaded over her left shoulder. She wore a white gown that left her arms—and her mark—bare, and it was cinched at her waist with gold chains. When the now-deceased Gold King had ruled beside her, the two of them must have shone brighter than the sun.

Ayla, Inheritor of Fire and Oriana's current favorite, stood next to her. She was rough where the queen was refined, with her tomato red hair and orange dress singed to black in places. I'd never seen Ayla's mark, but it was rumored that flames erupted directly from her flesh.

After we'd done the requisite bowing and greeting, Oriana explained why she'd summoned us.

"While your idea of searching for the scroll had merit, Micah," she began, "Ayla has pointed out a few flaws in your plan."

"I assure you, my lady, I meant nothing but to assist you," Micah said.

"Of that I have no doubt," Oriana continued. "However, my dearest has shown me that issuing a royal bull for all and sundry to search for an item that may or may not exist is a waste of my precious time."

"Time that can be better spent ruling her lands," Ayla added. Oriana squeezed Ayla's hand, and the two gazed at each other.

After a small eternity of their googly eyes, Micah said, "A sound decision, my lady. How would you have me proceed?"

"Oh, you need do nothing," Oriana replied. "I've already rescinded the bull and declared the scroll non-existent. I merely wanted to inform you of this change in person, as a courtesy. The search was your idea."

Yeah, an idea that Micah had come up with on the spot to distract Oriana from the rest of the goings-on in the Whispering Dell. I kept my thoughts to myself, and both Micah and I thanked the queen for her graciousness. Since our business appeared to be concluded, we turned to leave.

"Lady Silverstrand," Oriana called after me.

"Yes, your majesty?" I replied, turning to face her.

"Your sister," she began. "She remains in the Otherworld?"

I debated lying, but that never ends well. "Yes. She is setting up her library at the manor."

"Good. That pleases me." Oriana descended the dais, coming to stand directly before Micah and me. "I want her pledge. No tricks, no subterfuge. I want the Inheritor of Metal's blood oath, and I want it now."

I opened and closed my mouth like a fish, but Micah kept his wits about him. "We have not spoken with Sadie about the matter since you commenced searching for the scroll," he explained without a moment's hesitation. "Will you allow us a brief respite to speak with her, and convince her that pledging you her loyalty is her best option?"

"All she has had is time to consider," Ayla countered.

Oriana glanced over her shoulder and purred, "Ayla, Micah was once my most trusted general. My dearest hope is that one day soon he will return to his position." She faced us and continued. "Ten days, I will grant you. Ten days, and I will have the Inheritor's pledge, or she will leave the Otherworld and never return. Perhaps her family will be sent along with her." She stared at Micah, her blue eyes boring into his silver ones. "Ten days. No more, no less."

"We shall confer with Sadie at once," Micah said. "Thank you, my queen, for your most generous patience."

Oriana nodded curtly, then returned to her throne. Micah laced his fingers with mine and we left the Gold Court in silence. We may have been granted a ten-day reprieve to convince Sadie to pledge herself to the Gold Queen, but I was starting to think that the

Otherworld would be better off without Oriana leading it. The only problem with my theory was that the
next person in line for the throne was none other than
Micah Silverstrand.

Our return to the manor was tense. Oriana had
threatened that a continued lack of pledging on Sadie's
part would result in her banishment from the Otherworld, including all of her relations. Now, it wouldn't
be so bad for us Corbeaus to return to the Mundane
realm—we could always hang out with the resistance,
or reclaim the Raven Compound from Armstrong's
Peacekeepers—but the Otherworld was all Micah had
ever known. If we yanked him away from where his
family had lived for untold years . . .

Well, that would be remarkably similar to how my
entire family had ended up in the Otherworld.

Still, I wanted Micah to be happy, and I didn't
know if he could be happy away from the Whispering Dell, not to mention the silverkin and the manor.
That meant that we needed to get Sadie to pledge her
undying loyalty to Oriana as soon as possible.

Once the metal pathway had deposited us before
the manor's front door, Micah grasped my hands.
"Sara," he began.

"I know," I said. "She needs to pledge."

"Actually, I was going to suggest we locate the scroll.
Did you not say you believe it to be here?" he asked,
gesturing toward the manor.

"Yeah," I replied. "But even if it is, shouldn't Sadie pledge herself to Oriana anyway?"

"We should talk to her about it, yes," Micah agreed. "But regardless of Sadie's decision, I would like to read this scroll for myself."

"Me, too." Of course, talking to Sadie directly about pledging would be like showing a turkey an electric carving knife a few days before Thanksgiving. Instead of plainly informing my sister of her obligations, I knew that subtlety would be my best bet. Too bad I sucked at subtlety.

"I'll start that conversation now," I said once Micah and I were inside the manor. "Wish me luck."

"Luck," Micah murmured.

I headed up to the library and to find Sadie sorting through boxes of books.

Sadie was the youngest and most delicate of us Corbeau kids, both in physicality and personality. She was the shortest and the slimmest, and her hair fell in a straight curtain of pure copper without a hint of curl. When we were kids, Max and I caused trouble in the house until Mom banished us outdoors. We'd spend hours in the nearby woods, climbing trees and searching caves for treasure. In the meantime, Sadie remained in the Raven Compound's library with her nose in a book. If it weren't for our strong family resemblance, no one would suspect she was related to us ruffians.

Aside from her petite stature, the only real difference between Sadie's and my appearance was a sprinkling of freckles across her nose. Max had an identical batch of freckles, whereas I had none. I'd definitely gotten the short end of the stick in the freckle department.

"Whatcha doing?" I asked, even though it was obvious.

"Just going through these donations," Sadie replied. The silverkin had crated all the books we'd received and hauled them up to the library. "I don't think I'm ready to shelve them yet, but I do want to get them sorted."

I looked over the dozens of boxes. "I thought Juliana was helping you."

"She was, but after the gold people showed up, she was too nervous to do much. She went for a walk to calm down."

"Micah and I were just there. At Oriana's."

Sadie froze in place, a book shaking in her hands. "Oh."

"Can I help with the books?"

"Sure."

I sat before one of the crates and started picking through the tomes. There were thick leather-bound books, delicate parchment scrolls, and I even uncovered a heavy clay tablet that looked to be about a billion years old. Since none of these were what I was looking for, I organized them by material, hoping the tablet wouldn't get too lonely all by itself, and moved on to the next crate. And the next. When I started rummaging through the fifth crate, I found it: the scroll in question. It was just as I remembered, with fancy copper endcaps and secured with a silky blue cord.

"Check this out," I said to Sadie, holding it up.

"Check what out?" she asked, rubbing at her nose— sorting books is dusty work. Even though she'd never seen it before, she knew exactly what it was. "Oh. That's it, isn't it?"

"It is." I moved to open one of the end caps, but Sadie stayed my hand.

"We should have Mom or Dad do it. Otherwise, who knows what we might unleash."

She had a point, so we brought the scroll downstairs. While Sadie rounded up our parents, I found Micah in his study. After explaining to him that we may have found the scroll everyone was talking about, the five of us convened at the kitchen table. Mom and Dad performed a cursory examination of the scroll, then Mom shrugged and nonchalantly popped off one of the end caps.

"Be careful!" Sadie squeaked, grabbing me by the arm and squeezing. "What if it's cursed?"

"It's been here for weeks now," Mom replied. "If it hasn't cursed us yet, like as not it won't."

"Like as not," Sadie muttered, her grip relaxing *just*

a bit. Dad unrolled the parchment and spread it on the table.

"It's in pretty good shape for ancient paper," I remarked.

"It is not ancient," Dad corrected, "it is enchanted." Before I could ask what he meant, he withdrew a black feather from the tube. "At some point in time, someone obtained one of the Raven's feathers and charmed it to reveal his bloodline."

"How would that have happened without us knowing about it?" Sadie asked.

Dad shrugged. "The feathers do not degrade. This feather may have been acquired by one of our own ancestors."

"How many feathers does that bird have?" I wondered aloud. We were always plucking out his feathers for one reason or another, but he didn't have any bald spots.

"Respect, *ma chère*," Dad said. "The Raven long ago decreed that his feathers would be enchanted to assist his descendants, no matter the type of help needed. As long as we, his children, exist, so do the feathers." Thus admonished, I leaned against Micah while Dad deciphered the scroll. After an excruciatingly long pause, Dad announced, "It is written in French."

"Shocking," Mom deadpanned.

Dad glanced up at her, his green eyes glinting in a way that made me think of the scrappy Beau that Mom used to reminisce about. "Too bad it's not Irish.

Perhaps it would detail how a queen might steal her neighbor's cattle in the dark of night."

"Can you read it?" I interrupted, trying to keep things on-topic. Watching your own parents make eyes at each other is just weird.

"Of course," Dad said, grinning. He focused on the parchment, while Mom stood behind him with her hands on his shoulders. "It is indeed a lineage, and it begins in the sixth century when the Raven met Aregonda."

"Aregonda?" I repeated, thinking about the resistance commander who pretended to teach Max and I more about magic when she really just wanted to peek inside our heads.

"Is that the same Aregonda who was a Merovingian queen?" Sadie asked, ever the scholar.

"One and the same," Dad confirmed. "We are descended from them, you know. My mother was named for her."

Sadie lifted her chin, triumphant in her knowledge of obscure facts, while I wondered how she knew anything about sixth-century France. And how cool was it that we really were descended from royalty?

"So, Mème Corbeau was right," I murmured. Mom rolled her eyes. Mème and Mom had never gotten along.

"This lineage," Dad continued, "begins with the Raven and Aregonda's issue."

"Wait," I said. "How did Aregonda and the Raven, um, have an issue? What with him being a raven and all."

"The Raven was a shapeshifter from the Otherworld," Dad replied. "Surely you remember the stories I told about our history, Sara." He glanced up and finally noticed my furrowed brow. He frowned and gestured toward the chair across from him.

"You were probably too young to remember. Sit, and I will tell you now." Sadie and I sat while Micah remained standing, his hands on my shoulders, thumbs tracing circles on the back of my neck. Mom perched on the table next to the scroll and ruffled Dad's hair.

"Aregonda lived a great many years ago, when France was called Gaul. She was a second wife; history says that her husband married her out of pity, for she walked with a limp. Still, she was a queen, and most said she was a kind and gentle woman. What they did not know was that she was an Elemental as well as a sorceress.

"The Raven, himself a member of the Otherworld's royal family, had the occasion to visit the Merovingian court, and was entranced by Aregonda's beauty. Since he could not act on his desire, he cured her limp instead. Soon afterward, Aregonda's husband died, and the Raven returned for her. She sensed that he was a greater sorcerer than she, and she consented to marry him on the condition that he would guard their children throughout time. He agreed and gave her his name. And so, the Corbeau line was begun."

"Wow," I murmured. "That's a pretty intense family history."

Micah cleared his throat and asked, "Do none of you find it odd that the woman casting spells with the resistance has the same name as two of your relations?"

Mom looked at Dad and raised an eyebrow. "It is a common enough name for a metal Elemental," Dad explained, shrugging. "Many families look for legacy names."

"And this new Aregonda is of copper as well," Micah continued. "You must admit, Baudoin, it is an interesting coincidence."

Dad looked at Micah and frowned. "And I do not believe in coincidence. What are you saying, Micah?"

"I do not know," Micah replied, "but I believe it bears closer inspection."

Dad nodded and looked at me. "Sara, can you attempt to learn more about this Aregonda? Where she is from, her family and such?"

I could think of a million things I'd rather do than hang out with her. "Sure."

"*Merci.*"

"Beau, the scroll," Mom prompted. "You were saying it shows the Corbeau lineage."

"It certainly does," Dad said. "And this scroll lists every last descendant, down to you two and your brother."

"How is it so linear?" Sadie wondered. "After all this time, you'd think we'd be somewhat . . . I don't know, diluted."

Dad shrugged. "Perhaps a strong bloodline is an aspect of the Raven's protection? Truly, I do not know. What I do know is that the scroll says that forty generations after the Raven's death, one would be born who is equal in both old and Elemental magic. I am the thirty-ninth generation, and, since I have no siblings, the fortieth generation consists solely of my children."

"And the fortieth generation suddenly has old magic?" I asked.

"I believe that has to do with me," Mom said.

"Oh." That made sense; Mom wasn't an Elemental, never had been. Her magic was fae in nature, as old as the earth itself.

"*Oui*, you both and your brother are more than mere Elementals," Dad said.

He let that sink in for a moment. When I figured it out, I gasped. "You mean Sadie's like a chosen one?"

"But you don't know that it means me!" Sadie squeaked, reddening. "It just lists our names. It doesn't say who has the most old magic, just that we have some."

"But *you* are the Inheritor of Metal," Dad said, his eyes shining. "*Ma chère*, it must be you."

"I'm surprised it's not Sara," Mom murmured.

"Um, what?" I asked.

"Agreed," Micah added, squeezing my shoulders. "Of all your children, Sara has the strongest affinity with old magic."

"First of all, Sara's right here," I snapped. I hated being spoken of like I wasn't in the room. "Second of all, what about Max? He's the one that builds portals and sets fires with his mind."

"Yes, I remember the fire in the orchard," Micah remarked, but Mom shook her head.

"Max knows a few tricks," she corrected, "but you, Sara, can work true magic."

Since I had no idea how to respond to that, I said, "Be that as it may, I'm no Inheritor."

"Perhaps you don't have to be," Mom said.

Dad smiled at Mom, then rolled up the scroll. "No matter which of our children are the most magical," he began, flashing Sadie and me a smile, "we do have more pressing matters. We need to burn the resistance's current plans, and craft something else that will work." He stood and rapped his knuckles on the tabletop. "I will locate Max and get to work."

Not long after we'd reviewed the scroll, we all went our separate ways. Micah went off to deal with village business, Mom took the scroll with her for more study, and Dad, Juliana, and Max grabbed a few maps and made notes about Armstrong's upcoming press conference. I admired their practicality. A lot had happened today and I was beat, so I grabbed Sadie and retreated to the kitchens to indulge in coffee and some of Shep's finest cookies.

Out of the blue, Sadie said, "You would be a much better Inheritor than me."

"Of course I would," I said dryly. "Who would want the brilliant girl who was on track for two master's degrees as the Inheritor when you could have a failed office worker as your leader?"

"As if you've ever failed at anything," Sadie retorted. "You just never made an effort after Max was gone."

"Yeah, well." She was right; after Max had been arrested, I spent my life keeping my head down and fading into the background. Then I met Micah, and he reminded me of who I really was.

"So, what's your plan?" I asked, changing the subject. Sadie stared blankly at me, so I added, "We all know you don't want to lead anything. Are you just going to lay low, pretend you're not special?"

Her eyes brightened at the thought. "Would Dad really let me do that?"

"Of course he would," I assured her, and it was the truth; he absolutely would. I chewed thoughtfully for a moment. "You know what would totally help you? Pledging to Oriana."

Sadie shuddered. "I *so* don't ever want to see her again."

"Me neither. But the best way to look like you don't want to be a leader is to commit to being a follower. It's what this failed office worker did."

"Sara, I didn't mean—"

I held up a hand. "I know. But you have to admit, it makes sense. A lot of sense."

"Yeah, it does." Sadie sipped her coffee. "Maybe . . . maybe I can ask Micah to send her a message and set up a time for me to see her and be thoroughly apologetic."

"He will. I'll ask him."

Sadie shrank down in her chair, gripping her cup with both hands. "Thanks." After a moment, she asked, "If I go through with it, do you really think Oriana will leave me alone?"

"Honestly? All I can say for certain is that she's nuts. But she wants you to pledge, so at least if you do that, you'll be obeying your queen."

Sadie shuddered. "How exactly is obeying her any different from obeying Peacekeepers?"

"I . . . I guess it's not."

"That's part of the problem," Sadie continued. "We're expected to blindly follow that nutcase, all because she happens to be gold and therefore a queen. There's no vetting process to ensure she's fit to rule, no checks and balances to make sure she doesn't start some stupid war."

"You don't sound like someone who doesn't want to rule," I said.

Sadie slumped in her chair. "I don't. I just don't think Oriana should. There's got to be a better option."

"Right now, she's our only option." I gave my sister a good, long look. "You're not going to pledge, are you?"

"I don't want to," she admitted. "But what else can I do?"

"You have a few days before you need to do anything. Think about things, come up with a plan."

"I will. There must be a better way than following that lunatic."

"And if you don't find a better way . . . ?"

"I'll pledge," Sadie finished. "If I can't come up with something all of us can agree with, I'll pledge." She sipped her coffee.

I sighed, considering both options. "I hope you come up with a good plan."

She managed a small and familiar smile, tentative but reassuring. "Me, too," she said softly. "Me, too."

4

Max

The next day, I woke up in a foul mood.

Talking with Juliana had been nice, sure. But it was also confusing.

Our walk in the garden reminded me of the old days when she spent her weekends at the Institute as the newest intern. Her assignment had been to observe how us Elementals interacted with each other. The day I met her was the first time I slipped into one of her dreams, not that we did that anymore. Juliana had kicked me out of her dreams a long time ago. I suppose it shouldn't have been surprising that she wanted nothing to do with me while she was awake, either.

Except it wasn't that simple. Back at the Institute, long before that time in the kitchen—*man*, was I trying to forget that—Juliana didn't act like she was avoiding me. Whenever we ran into each other, she'd smile and ask how I was doing. She always was sincerely happy to talk to me, and I remembered plenty of times when she brushed off Langston or one of his goons so they'd leave her alone. We were close.

Talking and laughing yesterday, it'd felt just like back then. Sure, I'd overstepped. "Baby" was too much. But she'd still asked me to walk with her. Maybe all of this tension was only in my head.

Maybe all of this tension would drive me nuts, and I'd end up in a whole different type of institute.

I didn't want to bite anyone's head off for no real reason, so I decided to let off some steam by jogging around the orchard. The only thing I'd ever enjoyed at the Institute (other than seeing Jules) was the well-equipped gym. I'd work out, and sweat, and feel like I was accomplishing something other than being a punching bag. That all ended when Langston figured me out and decided to turn the gym into a torture chamber.

He took a lot from me, but not the simple joy of a good run. I had some things to be thankful for.

After I'd circled the trees a few times, I headed back to the manor. I was halfway there when I heard someone calling my name. I turned around and saw Sadie and Juliana wandering up the road from the village.

"What's the news, ladies?" I asked, catching my breath as I jogged up to them.

Sadie looked over my sweaty clothes and scowled. "You stink," she declared before stalking inside the manor.

"Nice to see you, too!" I called after her. My gaze drifted toward Juliana. "You gonna run in after her?"

She surprised me by smiling. "I'm used to you being a sweaty mess."

Of course she was; she'd been there when Langston put me through all those exercises. "Yeah, I guess you are." I rubbed the back of my neck. "Did you two have a good time down in the village?"

"Um, yeah." Juliana looked toward the manor and bit her lip.

That was my cue to hit the showers. "All right. See you later."

"Max, wait." She chewed her lip some more, then whispered, "Can we take a walk? I need to talk to you."

"Sure."

We wandered among the trees for a while, and I didn't ask her to speak before she was ready. Hell, I was just happy that Juliana and I were alone together a second time. If this kept up, we might even be friends again. Not exactly what I wanted, but being friends was much better than nothing.

After we'd walked to the far side of the orchard, Juliana finally asked, "What does Sadie know about magic?"

I shrugged. "As far as I know, not much. Why?"

"We spent the morning in the village," she began. "Sadie said she wanted to get some more books for her library. She was especially interested in books about magic."

"Is that really surprising?" I asked. "What other kinds of books would she come across in the Whispering Dell?"

Juliana smiled tightly, considering it. "Good point." Her smile slowly became a frown.

"All right. What else is there?"

"It was like she was looking for something. Something . . . " Juliana paced back and forth, thinking. "I have no idea what. But the way she was asking questions . . . " She suddenly stopped moving and looked me in the eye. "Something's up with her, and I can't put my finger on it. Can you find out why she thinks she needs those books?"

"Why ask me?" I countered. "Why not Sara? Hell, why not ask Sadie yourself?"

"Sadie looks up to you," she replied. "She always has. Besides, you know more about Elemental magic than Sara."

"Dad knows way more than me," I said. "Micah, too."

"I don't think Sadie is going to have a heart to heart with *Micah* anytime soon, and if she was going to ask your dad she would've done so already."

"So what if there *is* something up with her? I can't stop her from doing anything." I linked my hands behind my neck and stared at the sky. "Who knows if she'll even listen to me."

"She will, because you can keep her safe better than anyone in the world," Juliana replied. "This world, or the one we're from. You're a professional sister saver, Max Corbeau."

I laughed through my nose. "Yeah, I guess I am." We looked at each other for a moment. I didn't want to push my luck. "Well, I'll go find her."

Juliana nodded. "Okay."

I turned to go, but I felt her touch my arm. "Thanks for listening."

Maybe being friends wouldn't be so bad. We'd started out as friends, before. "Anytime, Jules."

I jogged up to the manor and didn't once look back at Juliana. I was pretty proud of that. I found Sadie in her library, setting up her books. "Baby sister," I greeted. "Jules told me all about your trip down to the village. Sounded fun."

"It was," Sadie replied primly as she looked me up and down. "Did you shower yet?"

"Nah. I'm perfecting my natural musk." Sadie pinched her nose and turned back to the shelves. I chuckled. "Meet a cute guy in the village? Or a cute girl?"

"If I did I sure as hell wouldn't tell you about it," she replied.

I clutched my chest. "You wound me." She laughed

over her shoulder, and I grinned. It was nice, making her laugh. "Back in the day you told me everything."

"How far back are we going? When I was five?" Sadie moved on to the next shelf. "Since you're so *curious*, I went to get more books. They'll be delivered this afternoon."

I looked around at the stacks upon stacks of books that took up all of the shelves and most of the floor space. "Really."

"Yes, really." Sadie approached her desk and grabbed a notebook. "I've been putting the books into categories, and my stock for some of them is sorely lacking." I must have looked pretty confused because she then went on to explain, "You know, categories . . . like a real library? Did you ever go to school?"

"Yes, I went to school," I snapped. "Which departments had this glaring omission? Let me guess, magic?"

"Exactly! I mean, we're sitting ducks here in the Otherworld, and we have hardly any books on magic."

I picked up one of the books and flipped to the title page. "This one isn't even about magic. It's about Norse mythology."

Sadie smacked my hand and snatched the book from me. "It's a rare volume of the complete works of Snorri Sturluson, and *you* are getting your *sweat* all *over it*."

I had no idea who that guy was. "Sorry, Snorri," I said, snickering at the rhyme as I flipped the next pile of books on its side and read the spines. Sadie had picked up volumes on astral projection, transmogrification, and ritual cleansing. I picked up a book on summoning and realized it wasn't actually a new acquisition. Sadie had already been through it, and she'd made notes. Lots of notes.

"Will you take your sweaty paws off my books?!" she screeched, grabbing the book and snapping it shut.

"Why do you want to learn about stripping away someone's magic?" I countered.

She pouted, clutching the book to her chest. "I don't."

"You had the whole section highlighted."

"I—I just want to learn."

"Don't you think between Ma and Micah we've got plenty of magical knowledge around here?"

She ducked her head. "What if they weren't here? What if Juliana needed magic and no one was here to help her?"

I scowled. "That's a low blow, bringing Jules into this."

"I think she misses you."

I blinked, startled. "You think?"

"I do. I think you miss her, too."

"Wait. When you left us alone together, was that you meddling?"

"Not exactly. You really do stink." Sadie shelved the book. "But I do think you two need to talk. Maybe you should be telling her how you feel instead of messing up my library?"

I bit the inside of my cheek to keep from smiling. "Listen, if you need any help with these magic books, just ask me. If there's anything I don't want, it's you trying to pull off all kinds of magic without me."

Sadie hugged the notebook against her chest and smiled. "I will."

I left the library, pleased that I'd done a good thing. I'd listened to Juliana, and then I'd talked to Sadie—all things a good big brother should do. Even better, Juliana's fears were unfounded. All Sadie wanted was the best-stocked library in the Otherworld, and she deserved nothing less.

If she came up with any questions about magic along the way, she'd know where to find me.

The next morning came fast, and it was bright and sunny, without a single cloud in the sky. It was also the day of Mike Armstrong's press conference to announce his research findings, so it might as well have rained.

Only three of us would be attending the press conference: Sara and Micah, both wearing new glamours that might actually fool people this time, and Mom, who would be there as the magical heavy in case anything went awry. She'd also be wearing her true face, having declared that she'd be glamoured "over her dead body." Since arguing with her was the kind of thing that never ended well, everyone agreed.

Juliana had wanted to be our fourth, but I expressly forbade it. Which went over well.

"Who are you to *forbid* me?" Juliana demanded while my entire family watched her hand me my ass. "For that matter, why should I ever look to you for permission?"

"You called me out for my behavior at Langston's rally," I shot back. "Don't pretend for one single second you wouldn't take him out if you had the chance."

"And what if I did?" she pressed. "Don't act like the world wouldn't be better off without him."

"It would, and it will," I replied, lowering my voice, trying to calm both of us down. "But we need to do this the right way."

Juliana stood there glaring at me like a tiger. She was right, of course; the world *would* be better off without Langston in it. The world was *also* a better place with her alive and kicking and far away from him and her uncle. I knew how badly she wanted them dead. Badly enough to compromise the mission. Badly enough to compromise her own safety. I couldn't let her do that.

She was a better person than me, and I was a better person when she was near me.

I squeezed my eyes shut and took a breath. I tried to

come up with the right words to tell her how I couldn't lose her again. Preferably, words that wouldn't humiliate me in front of my entire family. Before I could say anything, Sadie spoke up.

"Ignore Max," she said, waving her hands. "I need to go down to the village book shops again. You should come with me. We can make a day of it."

"You can't *possibly* need more books," I said, remembering the stacks upon stacks upon stacks I'd seen in her library.

"Sadie can have all the books she wants," Sara retorted, getting right back to business. "Anyway, this family debate has been fun and all, but the real reason it's not a good idea for you to go," she turned toward Juliana, "is because all the Peacekeepers know *exactly* what you look like. Good glamours take time, and we can't swing one on the fly."

Sara elbowed Micah. Juliana hadn't seen it, but I did. "Yes, flying glamours are very difficult to construct," Micah said haltingly, quirking an eyebrow at Sara, who squinted at him, disappointed. I couldn't help chuckling.

"No matter what kind of glamour it is," she clarified, "it takes a lot of effort and patience to cast one."

Juliana visibly deflated. "Oh, sorry. I hadn't realized that."

"Most people don't," Sara said, patting her on the shoulder. "I'll tell you everything when we get back."

Juliana nodded, glancing once at me before moving to stand beside Sadie, who readily took her arm. "Remember to tell the truth. No matter what, no matter who asks," she urged, glancing between Sara, Micah, and Ma. "Truthmages don't wear uniforms like magic sniffers do."

"We'll be careful," Micah reassured her.

"Not talking at all might be your best bet," I offered, pointedly looking at Sara and my mother. "Really. *You're* bound to slip up, and *you're* not even going to bother trying."

Even Juliana laughed a bit at that. There was no way Ma would be caught dead mincing words with some Peacekeeper Truthmage. That's how we'd know she'd been replaced.

The lot of them set off toward the static portal, and their mission. After they were out of sight, Sadie perked up and tugged on Juliana's arm.

"Come on, the village book shops are opening soon!"

"You never answered me," I said. "Why do you need more books?"

Juliana's eyes widened, but Sadie just huffed and rolled her eyes. "Max, I *am* a librarian."

There really wasn't much I could say to challenge that. The two of them walked off arm in arm, chatting about books, presumably. "Something is going on," I said to Dad as I watched them leave, "and I am going to find out what."

Dad clapped my shoulder. "Do not begrudge your sister her books. They are her first love, after all."

I nodded, my eyes fixed on the back of Sadie's head, and I hoped Dad was right.

5

Sara

Much like the political rally we'd attended a few months ago, the press conference was set up on an outdoor stage in the middle of a field. Either Mike was expecting a large turnout, or he was so paranoid he wanted a clear line of sight in all directions. When I realized how many of those in attendance were armed Peacekeepers, I figured it must be the latter.

"Are all Mundane events so well enforced?" Micah asked. To our left, a woman was being searched, her bag upended, and the contents dumped onto the grass.

"Look eastward," Mom said. Pressed up against the fence were at least a dozen people holding up signs and shouting that Mike Armstrong was a fraud.

"Are they Mundanes?" Micah posed, squinting at them. "Perhaps we should stand with them."

Mom snorted. "Like as not that lot will be in jail by nightfall."

"Let's steer clear of them right now," I said. "Remember, we need to tell the truth, no matter what we're asked." The Truthmages would likely roam the crown engaging others in conversation, hoping to ferret out those who didn't share Mike's views.

"And why would I tell a lie?" Mom asked. "I have nothing to hide."

I blew out a breath and looked at Micah. He shrugged, and we wandered into the crowd.

The emcee called for our attention. Everyone around us quieted down and faced the stage. We did, as well, and right on cue, Mike Armstrong made his grand appearance. He didn't look like an evil man hell-bent on destroying Elementals. Instead, his pot belly and graying comb over made him look like a low-level manager, or harried public school teacher.

"Macroeconomics," I said, recalling Donald Coffin from my college days. Not only had that been his real name, but he was missing two fingers on his right hand. Macroeconomics was rougher than I'd realized.

"Pardon?" Micah asked.

I jerked my chin toward the stage. "He reminds me of my macroeconomics professor."

A woman behind me hushed me. Since we were there to blend in, I smiled over my shoulder and paid attention.

Mike surveyed the crowd for a moment, then raised his right hand. The crowd burst into applause, and Micah and I followed suit. So did Mom, after I elbowed her in the ribs.

"Thank you, everyone," Mike said once the applause died down. "I can't thank you enough for being here on this most important day. Did you know I'm running for president?"

Renewed cheering and clapping thundered across the field. I was silent for a moment. Then I threw my hands in the air with the rest. The woman who'd shushed me touched my shoulder.

"It does make you emotional, doesn't it?" she asked. When I stared at her, she pointed to my cheek. "He brings me to tears sometimes, too."

"It's not the first time," I said as I dashed my wrist against my cheek. She patted my arm again, and we both resumed cheering. Micah took my hand.

"Strength, my love," he whispered.

"You're probably wondering why I think I'd be a good president," Mike continued. "After all, I'm not a politician. I'm a scientist. But as a scientist, I have dedicated my life to studying the Elemental threat, and no one—*no one*—can protect Pacifica's good citizens as well as I can. In just a moment, I'll share my discoveries with all of you, but here's the most important bit: I have created a team of super-soldiers to defend all of us against Elementals, and whatever else is out there. My people, we now have our own force of element-wielding warriors!"

"He means the made." I turned to Micah. "Do they even want to be soldiers?"

Micah's response was lost to the crowd's roar. The audience was eating up Mike's every word. My heart sank. *Maybe we should all just stay in the Otherworld.* Elementals clearly weren't wanted here.

Micah leaned toward me and said, "Look to the western side of the stage."

I did, and my heart sank further. Jerome Polonsky was standing there, holding a plastic gun and wearing full Peacekeeper gear.

"What if he sees us?" I asked.

"He won't," Micah said. "Trust me, my love. He won't."

I did trust Micah, but that wasn't the point. Peacekeepers were full of tricks. Before I could figure out a covert way to ask Micah how ironclad these glamours really were, I heard a male voice speaking to my mother.

"Have you followed Mr. Armstrong's career for long?" he was asking her.

"Oh, since before the wars began," Mom replied.

I turned and saw that the man talking to her was wearing bland gray and brown clothes, had nondescript gray hair, and a forgettable face.

You know who's bland and forgettable? Any Peacekeeper, that's who.

I wrapped my fingers around Micah's bicep and squeezed. The man talking to Mom was a Truthmage, he had to be. I hoped she remembered not to lie. Not that my mother is known for lying, but we were undercover, and who knew what the Truthmage would ask her. I was straining my ears to hear their conversation and didn't notice the cloaked figure on our right.

"They're using magic." The mage pushed back his hood and pointed at Micah and me. In mere moments, we were surrounded by Peacekeepers.

"What? W—we aren't magic users," I said, doing my best to appear intimidated and innocent. "There must be some mistake."

"No mistake." The mage stood directly in front of us and took a deep breath. Wow, they really were magic sniffers. "These two fair reek of spells."

"Wait." Micah rummaged in his jeans pocket, eventually producing a silver bangle bracelet. "I got this earlier at the market. The stall was filled with magical-seeming items." He dropped the bracelet in the mage's hand. "It's, um, supposed to make the wearer love you."

Playing the part, I placed my hand on Micah's chest and gazed up at him. "You got me something?"

"It *is* our anniversary," he drawled.

"This is enchanted," the mage snapped. "Where did you get it?"

Micah gave the Peacekeepers a description of a basic vendor stall at the Promenade Market, and I stepped back toward Mom. "Isn't it sweet that he got me something?" I asked her.

"Lies," said a male voice, and I froze.

The Truthmage was right behind us.

Mom glanced over her shoulder and asked, "Pardon?"

"Lies," he repeated. "That bracelet was not purchased earlier today, and it is not your anniversary."

"So maybe he bought it on a different day," I said. "And it's not our wedding anniversary. We've only been married a few weeks."

The Truthmage's brows lowered. "Then what anniversary falls upon today?"

I leaned closer to him, and replied, "Honestly, I have no idea. He always gets his dates screwed up. I just go along with it. Keeps him happy, you know?"

The Truthmage's frown deepened. Finally, he turned to Mom and said, "You are obviously acquainted with these two. What do you make of all this?"

"Whatever's going on with them is none of my business." With that, Mom tossed the Truthmage her most withering glare. "Sara, collect Micah. I feel we can find a better, less noisy spot on the other side of the field."

I smiled and turned toward Micah.

"Sara," the Truthmage repeated. "Sara Corbeau?"

I paused, a fraction of a second too long. "That is not my name," I said, and that was not a lie.

"But it *was* your name," the Truthmage pressed. "Micah Silverstrand?"

Micah ignored him, but the Truthmage was on to us. "Sergeant! These people are fugitives!"

"Bollocks," Mom said. A moment later, she was wielding a sword and round shield, and her casual sundress and sandals melded into an armored bodice, battle skirt, and tall boots. She sighted the Peacekeepers down the length of her blade.

"Step away from my son-in-law, or die where you stand," she growled.

The sergeant barked an order, then columns of metal erupted from the ground and coiled around the Peacekeepers like tentacles. Micah walked toward me, his glamours dissolving.

"There's a vein of silver under here?" I asked.

"Aluminum," he replied. "Bauxite, actually."

"Wow, and you tore the element from the ore *and* refined it that quickly?"

"Children," Mom snapped over us. "Enemies approach."

"We should portal home," I said, but Mom shook her head.

"This is a splendid time to assess the enemy's strengths," she explained.

"Agreed," Micah said. He raised his hands and the aluminum rippled across the field toward him.

"Show-off," I teased. He smiled, then we turned to face the Peacekeepers.

But the people advancing toward us weren't Peacekeepers. They didn't wear body armor or uniforms, and they weren't armed. Instead, they wore identical gray pants and loose, sleeveless brown shirts. Each person had a large "E" emblazoned over their left bicep.

"What does the 'E' mean?" I wondered aloud. As if to answer me, the marchers raised their arms as one, and huge earthworks erupted all around us.

"I'd wager that it stands for 'earth,'" Mom said, stabbing a mound with her sword.

Micah sent a length of aluminum through the earthen mounds, shattering them. As I ducked behind him, I studied our opponents. They were expressionless, their eyes dull.

"They're the made," I said just as I realized it. "Mike sent the made after us!"

"He wishes to set an example," Micah added. "Of them or us, I do not know."

"They're like zombies," I murmured, watching their slow movements. "What did he do to them?"

"Don't feel sorry for them," Mom shouted to me. "They're the enemy!"

"I'm not so sure about that." I stepped around Micah and past the heaps of earth, and I looked one of the made in the eyes. "We don't want to hurt you," I said.

He faltered. Then he blinked, and said, "Bad."

"No. Good." I placed my hands over my heart. "Friend."

He nodded. "Friend."

The earthen mounds flattened, blowing away as if they were dust. If the made were upset over their creation being destroyed, they didn't show it. Instead, a brown-cloaked Truthmage emerged from behind them.

"You will not break thrall!" he screeched. The made's eyes glazed over, and he advanced.

A hand grabbed my shoulder. A moment later, Micah, Mom, and I were standing in the manor's kitchen.

"You can move between worlds without a portal?" Micah demanded as he swiveled to look at my mom.

She shrugged. "Within worlds as well. Sara, how did you take control of the made?"

"I don't know if I did," I replied. "I just talked to him."

"It was more than talking," Mom said. "That lot were enthralled to the mage, and while you didn't break it completely, you allowed them free will."

"I have no idea how that happened," I replied, wracking my brain for some explanation.

"No matter," Mom said. "Happen, it did."

"Regardless, two things are clear," Micah said. "We must stop this Mike Armstrong. The sooner the better."

I nodded. "And we have to rescue the made."

Micah glanced at me. "Are you certain they want to be rescued?"

"Would you want to live that way?" I countered.

"No, but perhaps they do. Many appear to have volunteered for that . . . that . . . *procedure*."

"Just because they volunteered—if they even *did*—that doesn't mean they're happy now."

"Our purpose is not to ensure every living being's happiness," Micah began. Then Mom stepped between us.

"Why don't we tell the rest what happened, and we can all discuss it over dinner?" she suggested. "Bickering about those enthralled fools won't help us, or them."

She was right, of course. But I'd made up my mind. We *would* discuss it.

By the time we got inside, the silverkin were setting out lunch. After we'd washed up and took our places at the table, I said, "The press conference was interesting."

Everyone's head turned toward me. Micah and I told everyone about Mike's terrifying speech, the zombie-like made and their enthrallment to a mage, and our daring escape. We specifically did not mention how Mom made the rookie mistake of calling us by our real names and blowing our cover. Some things were better left unsaid.

After we'd told them everything, I said, "I've done some thinking about the made."

"Have you," Dad said, setting down his fork. "And

what have you concluded?"

"I want to rescue them."

"Is that a smart move?" Max asked. "We're already in it up to our necks. Let's stop Armstrong first, worry about the made later."

"I think we should worry about them now," I said in a rush. Dad watched me with his endlessly patient gaze. I didn't look at anyone else. I swallowed, and continued, "Before we decide one way or another, shouldn't we do some research on them first? There's a lot more going on with them than we thought. None of us expected them to be handled by a mage, for one."

"Agreed, but where would we find such research?" Dad asked. "I thought Armstrong kept it well guarded."

My knee bounced under the table. Micah placed his hand on my leg to calm it. "Maybe we can infiltrate one of his outposts and take whatever research we find. Maybe it would tell us how he's holding them, what kind of guards he's posted, things like that."

"That is a good idea," Dad said. I let out a breath I hadn't realized I was holding. Dad's approval meant so much to me, and he wasn't one to acquiesce just to spare feelings.

"It shouldn't be that hard to get the information," Juliana offered. "Mike did a lot of his early research here in the Otherworld, and those locations were abandoned a few years ago."

"All of them?" I asked, and she nodded. "Why'd he

do that?"

"When Mike allied with the Iron Queen, he thought it best to be around her as little as possible," Juliana replied. "It would ruin his Peacekeeper image if he were seen with a powerful Elemental. The easiest way to hide their relationship was to move almost everything to the Mundane realm."

"I suppose he did not care about the prisoners, which is why we were left behind," Dad mused, and I remembered how we'd found him in that run-down Peacekeeper prison. Before the mood got too heavy, Dad grinned. "But we ended up turning that to our advantage, *non*? As we shall use this, too, to our advantage."

Micah shoved back from the table and stood. "I have maps of nearby Peacekeeper facilities in my war cabinet. I'll fetch them now."

Sadie leaned toward me. "Look at you, being all leader-like, with plans and suggestions."

I turned my attention back to my food, feeling an unfamiliar swell of pride in my chest. "Look at that."

The combination of Micah's maps and a list of Juliana's stolen passcodes did the trick, and a few hours later we set out to raid the two closest Peacekeeper facilities. Dad and I took the location west of the manor, while Micah and Max took the one to the south. Mom stayed behind to protect our home base, along with Juliana and Sadie. It was a smart move to split us and Mom up; since Micah, Max, and I were all Dreamwalkers, if we got captured, we could slip out and notify the others, and if no one came back Mom would be able to find us. What made things interesting was that my husband and my brother were not each other's biggest fans.

"I really hope Micah and Max don't kill each other," I said to Dad as we trudged toward the western base.

Dad laughed through his nose. "Micah is too wise to jeopardize a mission with petty squabbles, and Max can behave when he chooses to."

"The question is, will he choose to," I muttered.

We fell into an awkward silence; at least, I felt awkward. Dad marched on as if our lack of conversation didn't affect him in the slightest, and for all I knew, it didn't. This mission was the first time I'd been alone with my father since before he left for the war over sixteen years ago. Adult me had no idea how to interact with him. But I didn't want my dad to be a stranger.

"What was it like?" I asked. "When you were gone, I mean."

"Some times were good. Others were not so good," he replied. "Soon after I left for the war, most of my regiment was either captured or killed. Avatar and I rallied those who remained and we went into hiding. Those times were hard, and very, very lonely."

"You were hiding by yourself?"

"Others were with me, but not my family. I missed

you, all of you."

"We missed you, too." I swallowed the lump in my throat. "And then the Iron Queen betrayed you?"

"*Oui*. It was some years later, but yes, betray me she did. I never should have gone to her in the first place, but I was desperate to rescue Max. I should not have worried, since you rescued him for me."

Dad smiled at me, and I felt my cheeks warm. "It wasn't just me. Micah helped, and Juliana, too, though I didn't know it at the time."

"But you dreamwalked to Max, *non*?"

"I did."

"You are the one who freed him, *ma fille*, when no one else could."

"I still can't believe that worked." Dad said something in French that I didn't understand, and I shook my head. "You know what's funny? I'd forgotten how much French you work into conversation. The shapeshifter never said one word of French. I—I can't believe we never noticed."

"His job was to deceive, and he did it well," Dad replied. We stepped out from under the canopy into the late afternoon sun, and it lit up his copper hair like a firebrand. I considered how alike Max, Sadie, and I were, and how much we looked like Dad.

"Was Mom mad when none of us looked like her?" I asked.

Dad stopped walking and stared at me, then

laughed. *"Non, ma fille.* The copper is what gives us these features, not any genes I did or did not pass on. Maeve understood." He paused, and added, "What your mother did give you was a tendency toward leadership."

"You're a leader, too."

"C'est vrai, but your mother is a queen." Dad halted. "Can you feel the location?"

"Feel it?"

"Oui. We are in a natural area, but the facility has many metals inside it. It should feel off, almost unnatural to you."

I closed my eyes and listened to the forest around me. It was calm, but not quiet; there were birds singing, and leaves rustling in the wind. The forest was a happy place.

I pushed my awareness out farther and found a patch of emptiness. No birds sang in that spot, and even the wind avoided it. Then I felt it—metals that shouldn't belong.

"We're almost there." I opened my eyes, saw Dad smiling. "Maybe half a kilometer, a little less."

"Very good," Dad said, and we resumed walking. "Also, you did notice the shapeshifter's strange behaviors, and not just that his speech patterns were off. If you had not, he would be here with you, and I would still be imprisoned."

"You're wrong about that. That shifter was a jerk,

and I wouldn't have gone anywhere with him. He was so horrible that I wondered if all my memories of you were implanted in my brain by an evil mindwitch."

"Well, then. I hope the real me does not disappoint you. I believe we are here."

We reached the derelict Peacekeeper facility. According to the legend on Micah's map, it had been abandoned more than five years ago, right after Mike and Ferra got cozy. Vines crawled up the walls and over the roof, and the undergrowth was so dense that Dad and I had to hack our way through with machetes formed from our own copper. When we reached the entrance, we found crumbling cement steps and a rusted door.

Dad hacked away more vines until he revealed a keypad. "Do we think this is still operational?" he asked.

"Only one way to find out." I withdrew a paper and entered the passcode Juliana had written down. A moment later, the doors slid open, revealing a dark, musty corridor.

"*Es-tu prêt?*" Dad asked. He withdrew a fey stone from his pocket and held it aloft.

"I'm ready. Let's go."

He tossed me a second fey stone and we entered the building. The stale air was thick with dust, but thankfully that was the only smell we encountered. We followed the main corridor until we reached an auditorium. At the far end of the space was a door labeled "Data."

"That must be it," I said as I started across the room.

"Sara, wait!" Dad called out as the ceiling buckled and collapsed. Ceiling tiles crashed onto the concrete floors, ripping loose whatever piping and electrical systems had been installed above them. Thick, gray dust enveloped me like a filthy blanket. Tears streamed down my face as I coughed. When the dust settled, I took in the damage.

Nothing seemed to have hit me. I looked up and gasped; several huge metal panels were hovering in midair. "Dad?"

"Please, get out from under there," he said. "Holding the ceiling aloft is not as easy as it looks."

I backed away. When I was next to Dad, he released the panels. They clattered to the ground, creating another wave of dust. We covered our mouths and squeezed our eyes shut against the airborne grit.

"Half the ceiling was rigged to fall," I said when I could breathe again. "How did you catch it in time?"

"I will never forget the traps that Peacekeepers are so fond of."

I shivered. "Thank you."

He wrapped an arm around my shoulders and squeezed me. "I did not endure years of imprisonment to end up watching my eldest daughter get squashed flat like a pancake," he joked, and I laughed. "Now, then, let us see what we can retrieve about the made."

6

Max

While Sara and the old man hit up the Peacekeeper location closest to the manor, Micah and I went to the next closest. Even though we had to travel farther, our abandoned building was situated near the metal pathway, which made getting there much faster. We hopped on the path, and a few hectic minutes later we stepped off near the building's front door.

"Whoa," I said, waiting for the scenery to stop spinning. I'd only been on the path a few times, and it was more like a roller coaster each time. "That is some ride."

"The path is quite useful," Micah replied. Not a single silver hair of his looked out of place. "Do you not have these where you're from?"

"No, we do not." I crouched down and scooped up a few handfuls of pebbles. "Closest thing's probably an escalator . . . and that's not even that close. Magic's outlawed where I come from. I thought you knew that."

"Of course I did." I'd spent enough time around Micah to realize he didn't mean to sound as pretentious as he seemed, but his tone still just came off so damn *smug*. "What are you doing?" he asked as he watched me gather small rocks.

He didn't have to know everything all the time. "You'll see," I answered.

Micah's lip curled, but he didn't question me further. He knew better than to start a pointless argument. We approached the building, which looked pretty unremarkable, like any dilapidated warehouse. Well, the last dilapidated-looking Peacekeeper facility I'd been inside of was the state-of-the-art prison that held my father. Nothing about Peacekeepers was the truth, especially when it came to appearances.

We reached the entrance and entered our passcodes from Jules. The door slid open and Micah immediately moved to enter, but I blocked him. "Easy, big man," I said, which *definitely* made his brow crease. I tossed a few pebbles down the corridor. Hidden lasers promptly fired at the pebbles as a series of trapdoors opened in the floor.

"Motion detectors," I explained, looking for any trace of surprise in Micah's fine-featured face. There, of course, was none to be found. Go figure. "Peacekeeper facilities are full of traps. Now we know where they are."

Micah sighed. He raised his hand to rip the laser guns unceremoniously from the walls like so much scrap metal. "And now they're disarmed."

"Show-off."

We entered the corridor, skirting the edges of the trapdoors. Micah moved to close them, but I grabbed his forearm.

"Hey, we have plenty of floor left to walk on," I said as he stared at my hand like it was a cockroach. "Besides, we don't know if closing the doors will trigger a different set of traps."

Micah frowned and shrugged away from my hand, but thankfully he left the trapdoors alone. I found the research division's control panel easily enough; it looked just like the ones back at the Institute. The Peacekeepers had screwed a sheet of plywood over the controls, which did a decent job of securing whatever intel this panel held in its circuits. Unfortunately for them, they'd used metal screws. They always forgot something.

"Stand back," I said, reaching out with my ability to first find all the screws, then unfasten them from the board. One by one, they spiraled outward and fell onto the concrete floor, their pinging punctuated by the loud slap of the plywood.

"Your control is much more refined than Sara's, or Sadie's," Micah remarked. It was probably the closest thing to a compliment I'd ever get from him. "Why is that?"

"Because of these guys," I replied, gesturing at our surroundings. I held my fey stone between my chin and chest, and felt around the edges of the control panel. "Langston—he's Mike's second in command—used to put us through these endless drills. He wanted an extensive catalog of what our abilities could and could not do." I paused. "You know, I guess that was the beginning of the made."

"Perhaps it was." Micah stepped forward and scrutinized the controls. I wondered if he'd ever seen a computer before. He probably hadn't, but he could still make it look like he knew exactly what he was doing whenever he did something. "How ironic that the very abilities the Peacekeepers helped you hone will now contribute to their downfall."

How did my sister ever have a conversation with this guy? Micah was like a walking, talking fairytale prince. I found the panel's release lever and popped it. "There we go."

"Why are you removing the entire module?" Micah asked. "Were we not instructed to take only data?"

"We were, but what will we read the data on? A silverkin computer? If we bring the data *and* the control panel, we can read everything at the manor. Way more convenient than portaling to the Mundane realm and finding a computer that's not monitored by the government. Although . . . " I eyed the panel, thinking. "I don't know how we're going to get this powered up."

To my surprise, Micah grinned. "Leave that to me."

We left the facility, hopped on the metal path, and sped back to the manor, Micah and I combining our powers to haul the data panel inside and set it on the foyer floor. "Guys, we got something!" I yelled, glancing around to see who'd come running in first.

Micah winced. "The silverkin would have retrieved everyone. Quietly."

I shrugged and offered him a wink. "My way works, too."

Soon enough, Ma, Sadie, and Juliana joined us; Sara and Dad didn't seem to be back yet. When Juliana saw the data panel and the attached system, she crouched down to examine it.

"You took the whole thing?" she asked, shaking her head. "Damn. It must weigh a ton."

"S'alright. I'm strong," I reassured her, flexing my bicep.

"We did not need to lift it. The item contains a significant amount of metal, and our abilities allowed us to levitate it," Micah explained, throwing me under the bus with absolutely no hesitation at all.

Juliana raised an eyebrow, and Sadie actually laughed at me. "Hey, I'm still strong," I insisted.

"Sure you are," Juliana said. She went back to examining the panel. "This must contain all sorts of information, but why did you take it? We can't activate it without electricity."

Micah cleared his throat. "The manor has electricity." When the four of us just stared at him, Micah elaborated. "There is an outbuilding that contains solar panels behind the stone fruit orchard. My father set up the facility many years ago, intending to implement an automated watering system. Sadly, he passed before such a thing could come to fruition."

"Does it still work?" Juliana asked.

"Oh, yes," Micah replied. "The silverkin perform regular maintenance on it."

"Wait." Sadie held up her hand, her eyes wide. "You mean to tell me . . . this place has electricity? All this time I've been reading books by candlelight, but I could have had a real frickin' lamp?!"

"Are the candles not sufficient?" Micah asked, tilting his head. "Perhaps it is your eyesight that's failing. I will summon the village healer."

Sadie went beet red. "I. Do. Not. Need. A. *Healer*."

"Sadie's eyes are fine," I said hurriedly, placing my hands on her shoulders and squeezing them gently. "Any way we can get this electricity wired into the library?"

"I don't see why not," Micah replied.

"Great! I'll pick up a lamp next time I'm at the Promenade. Okay?" I gave Sadie a meaningful look, and I could see the boiling anger in her eyes starting to subside at the thought of her soon-to-come electrically-lit library. Micah knew a lot about a lot of things, but he sure could dig himself into a deep hole when it came to all the Mundane stuff he didn't know. He had no idea what kind of trouble he would have been in just then.

Let alone the trouble to come . . . I thought of Sara, considered what *her* reaction would be when she discovered that the manor could have had electricity this entire time, and my grin widened. Oh yes. Micah had a whole 'nother thing coming.

I levitated the data panel and swiveled it toward the rear door. "No time to waste. Let's fire this baby up."

When Dad and Sara returned to the manor, they found us out back in the shed, clustered around a Peacekeeper computer.

Make that a *working* Peacekeeper computer.

"Hey, guys," Sara greeted, eyeing the computer with a healthy dose of skepticism. "I see both missions were successful."

"Is that a computer?" Dad asked, approaching the screen. "It is. Is it on?"

"Yes, it is operational," Micah said. "At Max's insistence we liberated a complete computing system rather than just the single data panel. He appears to have had a sound idea, for once."

Ouch. I shrugged that one off, waiting for the

news to sink in. "For once, nothing. Check this out." I motioned to the monitor.

Sara approached the computer, her eyes widening when she saw all the information scrolling across the screen. "I take it you grabbed a battery pack, too."

"Oh, no, no batteries here," I said. "You may be surprised to know that Micah has been, ah, holding out on us."

"What? How?" Sara glanced around the small interior of the shed. It was filled with typical gardening equipment like shovels and pails, and of course, the incongruous computer. "Micah wouldn't do that."

"Really? *Really?* He wouldn't?" Sadie practically squeaked as she grabbed Sara's arm and dragged her outside. I, of course, followed them both, because Micah was about to get in trouble, and I'd been waiting for that moment since the day we met.

Sadie pointed at the roof, and the solar panels that covered it.

"See *those*?" Sadie asked. "This place has electricity. Electricity! It's a complete solar array!"

"Electricity?" Sara looked around until she found Micah leaning against the doorframe. "Why didn't you ever mention this?"

"I thought electricity was only useful for your Picture Vision," he replied, completely and utterly clueless. "I know of no such stations that broadcast in the Otherworld."

"But we could have had lights!" Sadie yelled. "Lights to read by!"

"Sadie, I *am* concerned about your eyesight," Micah retorted, causing the youngest Corbeau to throw her hands in the air and stalk off toward the manor.

Sara folded her arms across her chest and regarded Micah with a look that was evocative of Ma. "Frail humans like us *like* having electric lights," she said dryly. "It's a comfort thing. Maybe we could set up a water heater, too. Hot showers are nice."

Micah shook his head. "I had no idea these intangibles were of such importance."

To my absolute chagrin, Sara didn't shout or scold or snap. Her eyes softened, and she patted his arm. "We are a complex species."

And that was it. Discussion over. "Aren't you mad at him?" I asked, dumbfounded.

"No," Sara replied. Behind her, Micah smirked. "It was just a misunderstanding. Come on, let's see what we can get out of this contraption."

I watched them go back into the shed, still awestruck. Sara had been living like a monk with candles and cold showers for the past year, all because Micah never mentioned this little solar outpost, and she *wasn't mad*. She wasn't even irritated!

If I'd kept vital information like that from Juliana for just one *day*, she would have ripped me a new one, figuratively and (if she could catch me) literally.

Then again, I had kept something big from Juliana once. When we first met, she didn't know I was a Dreamwalker. I thought she'd figured it out after I popped into her dreams a few nights in a row, but wouldn't you know it, she actually liked dreaming about me. When she learned the truth, she'd been furious with me, and I swore I'd never keep anything from her again, not even for her own good. I thought about all the things I could've purposefully kept from her, me being under the impression that her having less information would somehow make her safer. I would've been wrong about each and every single one.

I reentered the shed. Everyone but Juliana had already left by the time I did. She was poring over the data the computer was spitting out, taking notes as fast as her fingers could move.

"If I lied to you, how would you feel?"

"Is this a new lie, or one I've already caught you in?"

"That's harsh."

She blew a lock of hair away from her nose and regarded me. "Omission of the truth is a lie by a different name. We've had this discussion."

"I know. I remember." I raked a hand through my hair. "Forget about all that. What if I lied to you now? How would you react?"

"I guess it would depend on why you did it. And what you lied about," she answered. "You really wanted Sara to give it to Micah about these solar panels, didn't you?"

"No. Maybe." All this self-exploration was giving me a headache. I jerked my chin toward the computer. "Why are you taking notes? I made sure the printer was attached."

"Yes, and it's fully functional. But there's no paper."

"I'll go get you some," I said hurriedly, as if my bringing Juliana a ream of paper would somehow erase all my past sins.

"Get ink, too." Juliana scribbled something into her notebook, then tore off the scrap of paper and handed it to me. "That kind. They sell it at the Promenade, over by the old hangar. Get as many cartridges as you can."

"On it." I stuffed the paper into my pocket. "Need anything else?"

She smiled. "Not right now. Thank you, Max."

"Anytime, Jules. Anytime."

The day after our dual raids, I went downstairs and found Dad having breakfast alone. The long table was heaped with maps and charts, and piles of printouts and handwritten notes taken from Armstrong's stolen research.

"I guess I got the right paper." I sat across from

Dad. "Where's Ma?"

"Still sleeping, as is the rest of the house," Dad replied. "Also, we will need more paper."

"Juliana used all of it?"

"She did," Micah said, entering the room carrying his own stack of papers. "She presented Sara with this stack last night. She referred to it as 'homework.'" Micah frowned at the papers. "They both thought it was quite funny."

I could have cracked a joke about Micah's cluelessness, but I wasn't up to it before having my coffee. "I'll get more paper," I told him, grabbing a stack of notes. "What are we looking for?"

"Anything that might be useful," Dad replied. "Do not be too selective. If you think we can use the information, now or in the future, make note."

"Yes, sir."

While we pored over the printouts, silverkin scuttled around the room, sweeping up crumbs and delivering coffee to me and Dad. Micah drank tea, of course. The caffeine had just started kicking in when Sara and Juliana joined us from the hall.

Sara sat beside Micah and peeked at his notes. "How's it going?"

"Quite well," he replied as he selected a map of the outskirts of Capitol City from the pile in front of him. When we were kids growing up in the Mundane realm, the city was called Portland, and it hardly qualified as a city. I wondered what we'd call it if—when—we dismantled the Peacekeepers. "Based on the information we retrieved, it appears that the made are held near the eastern perimeter of this facility." He circled the location on the map with his pencil. "Logic would dictate that any Elementals would be close to them. Our first strike shall be a rescue mission."

"First strike?" I turned toward my father. Micah may have been a general, but Dad was the master-mind of this operation. "We're planning on doing this multiple times?"

"Perhaps, perhaps not," Dad said. "My priority is to retrieve as many of our Elemental brothers and sisters as possible. If we destroy the facility in the process, all the better, but if we do not, we will need to return and finish the job."

"And the made?" Sara pressed. She'd told me how the mages had mind-controlled them, which was just sickening to think about. She worried they were worse off than Elementals, and honestly, so did I. Nobody deserved to be forced into using magic, or forced to fight. They were experiments, and more than likely unwilling ones. *Kinda like me.*

"Sara, as you said, I highly doubt they are there of their own choice," Dad replied. "By rescuing them as well, not only will we be doing the right thing, but our cause may receive, how do you say it, good press."

Sara smiled, relieved. "A twofer, then."

Dad smiled back. I realized how alike they looked. "A twofer, indeed."

"What about getting Mike's research?" I asked, glancing at Juliana, who was sat across from me. "That should be prioritized."

"I thought we grabbed his research yesterday," Sara said.

"What you got is helpful, but it's outdated." Juliana replied. "And there's more than just the made. In addition to making Elementals, Mike's been studying Dreamwalkers for decades."

An icy ball formed in the pit of my stomach. I felt Sara's gaze on me, but I didn't look at her. I knew she was seeing me as she found me, a prisoner in a lab. "What has he learned about dreamwalking?" Sara asked.

"Enough to make him dangerous," I said. "Mike's big goal is to make himself a Dreamwalker."

Dad set down his coffee. "That is preposterous."

"Yeah, well, he's nuts," I said.

"That's why we need to get into his current notes," Juliana added. "We need to find them and take them with us, if for no other reason than to keep others from trying to make themselves Elementals or Dream-walkers."

"Why not just destroy the notes?" Dad asked.

"Because we can use the research to counter what

Mike's already done." Sara looked up at Juliana as she spoke. "Can't we?"

"Counter it how?" I asked. "You really think you can unmake the made?"

"Sara and I already talked about it, and I think it's possible," Juliana said. "And it's the right thing to do."

"Is this something the made want, to be unmade?" Dad asked.

"If you had something like that forced on you, wouldn't you want it undone?" I asked, thinking about my own time in a lab. I didn't realize I was staring at the silver mark on Sara's wrist until she frowned.

"Listen, I don't mean something like your and Micah's marks," I explained. "These people were regular old humans, and in their eyes, Mike Armstrong has turned them into monsters. I'm with Sara. I think we owe it to them to undo the damage if we can."

Dad rubbed his chin. "Interesting. I do agree with your statements, but I must ask. Juliana, *ma chére*, do you think it is possible to reverse what has been done?"

"I don't know," Juliana replied. "What I *do* know is that I would give anything to undo what Mike did to me. If what was done to the made can be reversed, I'll help them, or I'll find someone who can."

"What if they don't want to change?" Dad pressed. "What if they wish to remain as they are?"

Juliana folded her hands in front of her. "Then I'll leave them be." She paused, then added, "There's also the fact that these records contain evidence of some of the most despicable crimes of the past century. If you want to prosecute Mike and Langston, this research can put them away for decades."

Dad raised an eyebrow. "Crimes other than what was done to Elementals?"

"For starters, there's murder. Of both Elementals and Mundane humans. He also dabbles in embezzlement, bribery of government officials, and basic theft," she replied. "Mike doesn't believe in raising money for his research. He thinks he's entitled to it, so he takes what he needs."

"Interesting," Dad said. "We will do our best to locate and retrieve this abominable research. Juliana, do you know where such information might be located?"

"Armstrong's office," I answered. "Wherever he's holed up, he brings everything with him."

Juliana looked at her hands. "Yeah. It would be there."

"Then it is settled." Dad stood and gathered up a few papers. "I must deliver our new plans to Jovanny. Max, would you like to accompany me?"

"Sure thing," I said as he stood. I paused behind Juliana's chair and leaned close to her ear. "We'll help them. I promise."

She nodded, and I squeezed her shoulder.

Dad cast the portal and we stepped through; it took

us directly to the resistance camp. Unlike last time, we appeared in the center of the operation, right next to the main fire pit. I bet Dad didn't want to be reminded of their lackluster defenses. One of Jovanny's cronies spotted us and ran off to find him while Dad and I waited in front of his tent.

"About Juliana . . . " Dad began.

"What about her?" I snapped.

Dad raised his eyebrows.

"Sorry," I said, taking a deep breath. "I get defensive about her."

"I see that," Dad replied gently. "Please do not bite my head off, but she is more than just a friend, *oui*?"

"She was, once. Now . . . now I don't know."

"Do you still trust her?"

"I'd trust Jules with my life." I motioned for Dad to step inside the tent, since I didn't want anyone over-hearing us. "Are you worried she's a spy?"

"Not if you are not," he replied. "If you have complete trust in Juliana, I do as well."

"It's funny, when I met Jules I thought she was a spy," I began. "Logical conclusion, what with her being Armstrong's niece."

"What changed your mind?"

"All he ever did was use her. First it was because she was friends with Sara, then he used her to hurt me. Or maybe he used me to hurt her."

"I remember when I saw you both at the Institute,"

Dad said, recalling his failed attempt to rescue me. No hard feelings on my part. It wasn't his fault that the Iron Queen betrayed him. "You saved Juliana from an iron warrior, then you grabbed her hand and ran across the yard to safety. During the chaos, you could have escaped, but you looked after her instead."

I laughed through my nose. "Escape wasn't even on my mind. I just had to get Juliana somewhere safe."

Dad smiled. "Perhaps you should ask Juliana if she is merely a friend."

I imagined Juliana's pointy glare, the litany of reasons she would give me as to why we were barely friends now, never mind something more. "Pretty sure I know how she feels."

"But what if you are wrong? Is it not worth asking?"

Aregonda entered the tent, coffeepot in one hand and two metal camp mugs in the other. "Wonderful to see you again so soon, Max." Aregonda set the mugs before us and poured. "Baudoin, do you take sugar?"

"Black is fine." Dad paused to have some coffee. "May I ask, is Aregonda a common name in your family?"

"As far as I know I'm the first Aregonda in my line," she replied. Jovanny entered the tent, carrying a notebook and a mug of his own.

"Fresh coffee always makes the afternoon better," Jovanny said. "Baudoin, Max, how goes it?"

"Well," Dad replied, "we have the plans set for attacking the prison." He handed a folder to Jovanny. As he flipped through the pages, Dad asked, "Have you made any headway on a new location?"

"We've begun packing up," Jovanny said. "However, we won't change locations until after we take down the made's prison. One thing at a time."

"Of course," Dad agreed. "Speaking of which, when did you last speak with Jerome Polonsky?"

"I haven't heard from him in some weeks, but that's not unusual," Jovanny replied. "He's never been one to check in regularly. It could blow his cover within the Peacekeepers."

"He was at Armstrong's event two days ago," Dad said. "Were you aware of this?"

"How does he avoid the Truthmages?" I asked.

Jovanny shrugged. "He either stays away from them or answers their questions very carefully, I assume."

I shook my head. "Sara said the event was crawling with Truthmages and magic sniffers. One of them detected Micah and Sara's glamours even in that huge crowd. How can one Mundane double agent evade that much magic?"

Jovanny's brows lowered. "What are you saying? You think he's a traitor?"

"Don't know," I replied. "But if he's not, then he's got more tricks up his sleeve than we thought."

"Keeping your true intentions from a Truthmage

would be more than a mere trick," Aregonda said. "And keeping that ability secret from the magic sniffers would require more power than most learned magicians or even Elementals can muster."

"Could you do it?" I asked.

Aregonda shook her head. "Perhaps for a short time, but not in the long term. If he is using magic to obfuscate his true intentions, he probably has help."

"But who would be helping him?" I wondered aloud. "The more likely scenario is he's been found out, and Armstrong's waiting for him to reveal something huge."

"We can't lose Jerome." Jovanny scribbled something onto some paper and handed it off to the guard outside the tent. "Those are orders for an extraction. I refuse to lose any more of my people to that monster."

"When he is returned, please advise me as such," Dad said. "If he is using something that renders him undetectable to Armstrong's mages, we should all have it."

Jovanny nodded curtly. "Safe travels, my friend."

"*Au revoir.*"

Dad cast the return portal and a moment later we were in the manor.

"I hope the extraction goes smoothly," Dad said.

"Me too," I agreed as I headed toward the kitchen.

"Where are you going?"

"To make some more coffee and think about our next move."

"Don't you think I should be involved in these plans?"

Shit. Dad was the leader. I stopped and turned to look at him. "Oh, I . . . I didn't mean I'd run off half-cocked without you," I began. "I just . . . need to be alone for a few and think about stuff, just me and my coffee. No offense," I added.

Dad shook his head, smiling. "None taken. I understand you are used to doing things on your own, but you do not have to." He set his hand on my shoulder. "You have me, and the rest of your family. We are all here for you." He leaned closer and said with a wink, "Even Juliana."

"All right, all right," I said, shrugging his hand off. "Enough about her. If she hears you, she'll flip out."

"And thus reveal her true feelings." He sobered. "I am serious, Max. You do not need to do it all yourself."

"I know, Dad. Thanks."

Dad gripped my shoulder, then we took off in opposite directions. Even though I'd just given him my speech about needing time with my thoughts, it was great knowing that I wasn't alone. Hell, if I yelled, my whole family would come running, not to mention a crap ton of silverkin.

Speaking of the silverkin, as soon as I entered the kitchen, the little guys sprang into action. They knew exactly what I wanted, and let me tell you, coffee in the Otherworld is a thing of beauty. The silverkin have this endless supply of beans that they just pull from a huge burlap sack, and while one of them started grinding the beans, another started boiling the water, and a third got a big mug ready for me. Who knew life could be this good? I'm sure Micah did, since he grew up with these metal servants waiting on him hand and foot. It's a wonder the guy knew how to put his own shoes on.

When the coffee was ready, I took it out to the garden. I took a long sip from my mug, leaned back, and stared up at the sky. Whether or not it was Jerome spying on us, information was being leaked. I just had to figure out how.

7

Sara

While Dad and Max met with the resistance, I helped Sadie out in the library, sorting through what seemed to be endless piles of dusty books. After an hour of shelving and organizing, I went down to the kitchen for snacks and found Juliana sitting alone at the table.

"I always find you here," I said. She nodded weakly, and I noticed that not only was she alone, but she wasn't eating anything either. "Are you hiding?"

"What? No. I just get bored sitting in my room, but I don't really know where else to go. It's weird hanging around someone else's house."

"Oh." I plunked down in the seat opposite Juliana. "I never really thought of that." She responded with a non-committal shrug, and I considered her situation. "You know, you're free to go wherever you want in the house and gardens. Just steer clear of the Wood Witch's forest."

She met my gaze. "The Wood Witch . . . I think Max mentioned her once. Is she for real?"

I sighed. "Unfortunately, yes. Even Micah avoids her."

We fell into an uncomfortable silence, both of us staring at the table. After a moment, I realized that Juliana was staring at my hands. Specifically, my wedding ring.

"Are you interesting in gemology?" I asked pointedly. When she gave me a quizzical look, I wiggled my fingers. "You're staring at my ring."

She blushed. "Sorry. I was just wondering . . . shouldn't your ring be copper?"

I couldn't help smiling. "Micah made it for me. That's why it's silver, like him," I said, stroking my thumb across the emerald. "I made his, too. His is copper."

"Does his have an emerald, too?" she asked.

Rather than describe it, I figured I'd show her. I leaned over to the bowl of pennies Max kept in the center of the table—he becomes more like a crazy cat lady every day—and selected a few. I closed my hand over the pennies, and a few seconds later I revealed a copper ring shaped like an oak leaf, nearly identical to the one Micah wore every day.

"It looks just like this," I said, placing the ring before her.

"Wow," Juliana said, picking up the ring and examining it. "That—*this*—is amazing. I can't believe you can do stuff like this."

I shrugged. "It's what I am."

"I know." Juliana turned the ring over in her hand. "Seriously, Sara, this is beautiful."

"You really think so?" I asked, and she nodded. "Keep it."

Juliana raised an eyebrow. "You want to give me a ring that looks just like your husband's wedding ring?"

I laughed. "Good point. Max might get jealous." I took the ring back and rendered the copper into a doughy clump, then smushed it around on my palm. It was delightfully, surreally soft.

"How did you meet Micah?" Juliana asked. I glanced up; when she drew back, I realized I was scowling. "I'm not trying to pry. It's just that I've never figured out how you crossed paths with an elf lord from the Otherworld. Before you met him, you hardly admitted to being an Elemental."

I forced a smile as I thought back. "I met him right in Real Estate Evaluation Service's parking lot," I said, naming the sham company both Juliana and I had worked for in Capitol City. "Remember how I used to go outside at lunch to warm up?"

It was Juliana's turn to laugh. "Yeah, I remember. That place was frigid."

"One day, I fell asleep in my car and had a dream about a man with silver eyes and hair. That man was Micah."

"So, you are a Dreamwalker like Max," Juliana said. "The shifter reported that to us, but we didn't know how reliable his information was, being that he tested negative for dreamwalking."

I felt the blood drain from my face. "You . . . you can test for dreamwalking?" Visions of Elementals having their heads cracked open like coconuts flashed before my eyes.

"It's a simple blood test," she replied. "Turns out there's a specific genetic marker for dreamwalking."

"Huh." I never thought I'd hear one of the most amazing abilities I possessed described so prosaically. While I contemplated how genetics interfaced with magic, Juliana came to a conclusion of her own.

"The day you had no panties at The Room!" she declared, slapping the table with her palm. "That was when you met him!"

"Um, yeah." All that blood returned to my face, and then some. My cheeks were so hot they could've melted butter. "That was the day."

Juliana laughed out loud. "One dream and he had you by your underwear? That has to be a world record."

"We didn't do anything," I insisted. "Even in our dreams, we only kissed."

"Uh-huh," she said, coy. "And later that night when you were screaming in your room? Were you two just continuing the dream?"

I glared at her, my mouth screwed up so tight my cheeks ached. Did she have to remember that? I hoped she hadn't caught a glimpse of my lavender nightie. *If she can dish it, she can take it.* "So, how do you know about all these Dreamwalker activities? Share any dreams with Max?"

Juliana shut her mouth with a clack and looked away. *Maybe not.* "Hey, Juliana, I'm not trying to be a jerk," I said, placing my hand on hers. "We were just talking, like we used to."

Her face brightened a little at that. "What, like Secret for Secret?" she asked, naming a game we used to play after school. Back then, our secrets consisted of me throwing out Mom's cooking and Juliana hiding her brother's sheet music so she wouldn't have to hear him practicing the same song over and over again. I remembered going to Corey's piano recitals. They were awful.

"Yeah, like that." I waved to Shep, and fresh coffees were placed before us a moment later. "I'll even let you go first."

"You do realize that my answers may potentially include your brother?"

"What makes you think I'll ask about him?"

Juliana sipped her coffee. "All right, then. In your room, how far did you and Micah go?"

I looked her in the eye and replied, "Kissing, no more. Once I figured out that he was more than a dream, we woke up together. I freaked out, being that my awake self had no idea why there was a man in my bed. Then you started pounding on my door, and Micah left."

"Oh." She sat back in her chair. "Sorry about that. But it really sounded like someone was murdering you."

"Thank you for your concern." I considered my question; based on past games of Secret for Secret, this wasn't going to last long before one of us was completely embarrassed, or completely pissed off. I decided to go for broke. "How did Max end up in the tube?" When Juliana only blinked, I added, "Come on, there had to be more to it than him giving you a metal flower."

"Honestly? Langston put Max in the tube because Max was too stubborn to die." Juliana paused, picking at the edge of the table with her fingernails. "Langston outdid himself creating tests, tortures disguised as exercises, anything he thought might harm Max and the other Elementals. Max not only survived them all, but he flourished. Nothing infuriated Langston more than Max's continued existence. Sometimes, I think the only thing that kept Max going was seeing Langston's disappointment over him not being dead." She was silent for a moment, swirling the coffee in its cup. "Once all the other Elementals were gone, Langston let his imagination run wild."

"Gone?"

"Dead. Once all the other Elementals were dead."

Juliana swallowed, then continued, "When he first showed me the tube and told me he was going to put Max in it, I ran from the lab and cried for hours. By the time I worked up the nerve to go back, they were already fitting Max with electrodes."

I blinked. "That's . . ."

"Horrific? Yeah." She drank more coffee. "Everything Peacekeepers do is horrific." She drained her cup, then asked, "So, you and Micah. When?"

"When what?" She gave me a look. "What, are we in high school? Why do you even want to know that?"

"My best friend ended up marrying elfin royalty," she said matter-of-factly. "I need details."

I took a deep breath and said, "The night I first breached the Institute, when Micah and I jumped out the window."

"And blew a hole in the perimeter," she added.

"Yeah," I said. "After we evaded the dogs and guards, we hid in an oak tree."

"An oak tree?" Juliana repeated. "Wasn't that a bit cramped?"

"Actually, it was really nice." I watched Juliana puzzle out how two adults managed to make love inside a tree.

"My turn."

Juliana's dark eyes went wide. She knew exactly what I wanted to know, but had the grace to let me ask it. "All right. Go ahead."

"You and Max," I began, choosing my words carefully. I'd heard and seen enough between my brother and Juliana to understand that whatever they'd had, it hadn't been one-sided. "How did you know he was my brother? We didn't meet until a year after he'd been arrested."

She sighed, her shoulders slumping forward. "Remember when I got accepted to Northridge's psychology program?" I nodded. "My uncle got me an internship at the Institute for Elemental Research so I could observe how Elementals interacted with one another. The first day I was there, this mouthy guy with red hair introduced himself as Max Corbeau." She met my gaze. "I never graduated."

I nodded. "How many Elementals were there, in the beginning?"

"When I got there, there were seven. Max, and six others that were murdered by my uncle and Langston."

"Gods." I set my elbows on the table and held my head in my hands. "That's horrible."

"It was." Juliana stared at the tabletop and traced the grain with her fingertip. "And you know what? If I hadn't been so hell-bent on getting myself and Max away from my uncle, maybe they all would have lived. Maybe one more would have lived, if I'd just outsmarted him."

"None of that was your fault," I said. "And you did save Max. That's got to count for something."

"I think all it did was inflate his ego." Juliana looked up. "And I didn't save him. You did. No matter how hard I tried, I couldn't save him."

"What I still don't understand is why Langston hates Max so much," I mused. When Langston had seen Max at the rally, he looked like he wanted to tear him apart with his bare hands. As for Max, he'd repeatedly affirmed his hatred of Langston. I remembered Max's reply when I asked what Langston had ever done to him: the worst thing a man can do to another man. Well, that could be anything.

Another shred of memory floated up, this one of something else Max had said at the rally: Langston had wanted the girl Max had given the iron lily to, and Max hadn't been pleased about that.

Juliana coughed, and I glanced up. "You're the reason he tortured Max more than the rest," I concluded. "Langston wanted you, but you wanted Max. When Langston hurt Max, he was hurting you, too."

"Yeah." She ran her hands through her hair, then propped her elbows on the table and supported her head in her hands. "Langston always was efficient, even with torture."

"You really had a thing with him?"

"With Langston?"

"No. Max."

"Define 'thing.'"

"You know, feelings."

"Yes, there were feelings. Lots and lots of feelings."

"Do you still have them?"

Before she could reply, of course, the man himself strode into the kitchen. He looked from Juliana to me, and demanded, "What's going on here?"

Deciding to save Juliana like any good friend would, I held up my blob of copper. "Oh, Juliana was just saying how awesome my Elemental powers are. I think she's jealous." Juliana snorted.

"Jules isn't jealous of you or anyone," Max said, striding toward the coffeepot and pouring himself a mug. "Jules's superpower is her mind, and we ain't got nothing on that."

Juliana's mouth dropped open, and I asked, "Her mind? Like telekinesis?"

"No, like she figured out how to tell you where I was without ever telling you," Max replied. "She can see through the cracks, find patterns where the rest of us only see junk. She's brilliant."

Max beamed at Juliana, so much that both of us were uncomfortable. Juliana excused herself and left. When she was gone, I asked, "'Brilliant'? Really, Max?"

"Well, she is," he replied, oblivious. "What the hell were you two talking about?"

"Girl stuff," I replied dismissively. "How'd it go with the resistance?"

Max's face fell. "Dad is worried the resistance has a mole."

"Well, shit. What do you think?"

Max leaned against the counter and drank his coffee. "I don't know. Jovanny keeps his people on a short leash. I don't really know how anyone could rat on him."

"Agreed. So, what are we going to do about that?"

"For now? Nothing. But after this caper with the made is all buttoned up, we need to take a long, hard look at each and every member. We need people we can trust, full stop."

The coffee roiled in my stomach. Max was right that we needed trustworthy people, but I couldn't help thinking that the more Dad worked with Jovanny, the closer he was to reclaiming his spot as resistance leader, and we'd just gotten him back. It was a selfish thought, but who could blame me for wanting to keep my father around?

"I wish this would just end already," I murmured.

"Me too, sis," Max sighed. "Me, too. When do you think it will be over?"

"You mean when do I think we'll stop the Peacekeepers, dismantle Mike Armstrong's shadow government, and mold Pacifica into a tolerant and inclusive nation?" I ticked off. "A week. Two at the most."

Max snorted into his coffee. "I like your gumption," he teased, his eyes catching on the kitchen's long prep table full of fresh ingredients. He loved to cook, even though he couldn't digest most of what he prepared.

Based on the gleam in his eye, he was trying to figure out what the silverkin were going to make for dinner. When he was in the kitchen, he looked focused, at ease, the way he typically looked when he was using his power over copper.

A power he could control much better than I could ever manage to control my own.

"Uh, Max?" I asked, snapping him out of his thoughts.

"What?"

"I . . . I think I need your help with something."

8

Max

Sara looked way too nervous for my comfort level.
What in the world could she need from me?

I set down my mug and faced her. "Help with what?"

"With my powers." Sara eyed the blob of copper in
her hand, which she'd kept at just about the consis-
tency of putty. "When I went to that old data center
with Dad, I realized how much more he can do with
his ability than I can."

"He's a lot older," I began to explain, but she shook
her head.

"You can do more than me, too," she said. "Micah
told me how you unscrewed that panel with your
powers. I can't do fine manipulation like that."

I spun a chair around and sat across from her.
"Micah could probably show you," I offered.

"He's way out of my league, too." Sara paused, setting down the copper blob on the table. "Besides, you're as strong as Micah. Maybe stronger than Dad."

"Hey, don't let the old man hear you say that." I didn't specify which old man I was referring to. Sara could puzzle that out for herself. After a long moment of considering whether or not I was cut out to be anybody's teacher, let alone my sister's, I decided to throw all caution to the wind. What the hell. "All right, let's get started. Put the pennies back in their original form."

She glanced between the copper and me. "Um, what?"

"They were pennies," I insisted, motioning toward my bowl of pennies, where she'd obviously taken them from. "Put them back." I picked up the copper blob, just to see what the metal told me. It wasn't much, but it was something, a brief story. I tried to explain it. "See, metal is unique in that you can reshape it dozens of ways, but it always carries the memory of what it used to be. If you get real good at listening, you might be able to trace that memory all the way back to when it was mined."

"Really?" Sara put her elbows on the table and leaned forward, scrutinizing the copper blob. "Do you think that's what Micah means when he says he's speaking to silver?"

I shrugged. Who knew what Micah meant when he said anything? Not me. "Yeah. Probably." I closed my hand around the copper. These coins were an older design from when pennies were actually made from copper; these days, they're mostly zinc. Still a good metal, but us Corbeaus prized copper above all others. "You're in luck," I told Sara, "since this copper went from the refinery straight to the coin fabricator."

"How does that make me lucky?"

"Fewer imprints on the metal means fewer steps to retrace." I set the copper on the table between us. "Do it."

She blinked. "Do what?"

"Put them back the way they were."

"Just like that?"

"Just like that."

Sara's forehead wrinkled. She touched the copper. It wiggled and shivered. Then the hunk of metal convulsed and broke into three pieces.

I grinned. "Good start." I picked up one of the pieces, verifying that it was one coin's worth exactly. Even better, all of the metal was from the same coin. If anybody was counting, I'd have to give bonus points for that. "Now flatten them down."

Sara frowned at the metal, then scooped the pieces together and slowly pressed her hand down onto them. I felt a shock travel from the copper bits through the silver table. She raised her hand and revealed three copper discs. "How's that?"

I picked one up, considering it, using my power to finely assess its shape. "They could be flatter, but we'll work on that next time. For now, restore the surface design."

Sara's brows shot halfway up her forehead. "From *memory*?"

"Ideally, yes. But since you're family, I can let you cheat a bit." I reached over the table toward the bowl of pennies. "Back at the Institute, if I'd been caught cheating it would have been the cattle prod for me."

Sara flinched. "What? They shocked you?"

"Did more than that." I heard a rattling sound. I looked toward it, and saw it was my own hand shaking in the bowl of coins. "A lot more than that."

I withdrew my hand from the bowl, then closed my eyes and took a breath. It had been years since I thought about the cattle prod, and even longer since I'd experienced it. Prods were crude weapons, and Langston preferred bespoke torture devices . . . but I remembered exactly what it felt like. A poke from one of those hurt enough to make your mind go blank, but it wasn't so bad it left lasting damage. It wasn't long before Langston started tinkering with the controls. Then there was the time he'd restrained Claire and set the prod against the back of her neck . . .

"Max!"

I blinked and straightened up. Sara was crouching in front of me. Was I on the floor? I hadn't even known I'd fallen over. "Yeah?"

"It's okay." She had a damp towel in her hands, and she used it to gently dab at my face. I touched my forehead and realized I was sweating like a pig. "There aren't any cattle prods here," Sara said softly. I focused on the sound of her voice, the cool feeling of the towel against my skin.

"I know." I took the towel from her and rubbed it up and down my arms. Gods, this was embarrassing. "I know. Remembering that stuff doesn't usually affect me, but sometimes it knocks me out."

She nodded. "I don't want you to help me if it's only going to open old war wounds."

"I've got wounds on top of wounds," I replied wryly. "Some of them aren't scarred over yet." I stood and stretched, then refilled my coffee. "Times like this, I really wish I could sample the hard stuff."

"Why don't you?" Sara asked. "If anyone could use a drink around here, it's you."

"Yeah, well." Since my panic attack had already humiliated me, I figured I might as well tell Sara all my secrets. "You know how the Institute's liquid nutrition destroyed my stomach lining?" She nodded. "I can barely handle a chocolate chip cookie. If I drank liquor, it might come out my belly button."

She eyed my full mug. "But coffee doesn't bother you?"

I raised my mug toward her. "No, because caffeine is proof that the gods love us and want us to be happy."

"Ha, ha." Sara crossed her arms across her chest. "You said your copper would heal all that, eventually."

"Hasn't yet," I replied. "Who knows if it ever will." There were a few lingering injuries on me and in me that showed no signs of healing, and aside from my digestive issues I'd managed to keep all of them to myself. Basically, anything that Langston removed from my body did not regenerate, regardless of how much or how often I sent my copper to the site. They were mostly small issues that didn't affect my quality of life. I took some small solace in the fact that he'd never decided to make me a eunuch.

I reclaimed my seat and pointed at the three copper discs. "Let's keep going. You're angry, and you can use that emotion to work the metal."

Sara huffed. "You're just trying to distract me."

"I'm trying to teach you," I snapped. "Don't you think I want you to know how to do this? Don't you think I want you to have a fighting chance against Langston? This isn't a game."

"I know it isn't." She sat and placed one hand on the discs and the other on my forearm. "I'm sorry."

"Don't be sorry. Be proficient in your ability," I said, the words just spilling out of my mouth without warning. It was exactly what Langston used to say to us when we failed at trials. I felt a fresh crop of sweat bloom on the back of my neck, and I willed myself to calm down. I did not need another panic attack right now.

What I needed was to get Langston out of my head before he finally drove me insane.

But Sara, she didn't know any of that. It was honestly more of a relief than anything else. She didn't hear Langston speaking to her in that moment: just her stupid older brother getting *way* too into this teaching thing. She grinned, then withdrew her hands and folded them in front of her. Before I could ask why she wasn't even trying to complete the coins, she jerked her chin toward them.

She'd done it. They were three round, shiny copper pennies.

I could breathe. Langston wasn't here, and he wasn't me. And Sara had actually done it. "Not bad." I ran my thumb over one of the coins. The image was perfect. It practically sang. "You've got potential. Not as much as me, but some." I flipped the coin over. She'd done both sides at once. Impressive for a first shot.

"I don't have potential. Just a good teacher."

I coughed and set the coins in the bowl with the rest. The last thing either of us needed was me getting all maudlin. "Okay, grab some more coffee. Lesson's not over yet."

"What's next?"

"I'm going to teach you how to make these pennies fly across the room."

Of course, *that* was when Sara's eyes lit up. "Cool!"

The next morning, we were all up before dawn, readying ourselves to attack Armstrong's research facility. We'd extracted every drop of information out of the stolen data panels, made plans, scrapped those plans, then drew up new plans. After we'd gone over *those* dozens of times, they were as airtight as they were going to get, and we'd *still* prepared contingency plans in case of emergency.

Who was I kidding? Before this was through, we'd probably burn through all our contingency plans and invent a few more on the spot. At least Sara could now send a penny flying into an enemy's eye, if needed.

As the sun rose, we assembled on the manor's front lawn.

"All right, so, we're doing this." Sara rocked back and forth on the balls of her feet and looked up at Micah. "We're really doing this."

"We surely are," Micah replied. "Why are you so nervous? We've gone into danger before."

"I'm not nervous," Sara countered quickly. I raised an eyebrow at her, and I wasn't the only one. She glanced between me and Micah and Dad, then sighed. "Maybe a little."

"Worry not, *ma chère*," Dad said. "While we are going into an unknown environment, I have the utmost confidence in all of you, my family. All I ask is that you have confidence in me." Dad withdrew a stash of portals from his sleeve and distributed them among us. "Having said that, if any of you feel unsafe at any moment, cast these portals. They will bring you directly to the manor."

"But what about the plan?" Sadie asked. Not only had she agreed to come on the mission, but she was even showing interest in participating. With any luck, things would go well enough that she'd want to be involved in the next one.

"Your safety far outweighs this mission," Dad replied. "Never forget the old adage of living to fight another day."

I clutched the portal Dad handed me, feeling the sharp edge bite into my flesh. A familiar voice rang out behind me.

"Can I have one, too?"

We turned and saw Juliana standing in the doorway. Her dark hair was caught up in a neat braid, and she was wearing a leather jacket over an olive-green shirt, along with jeans and thick-soled boots. It seemed that our raiding party had just increased by one.

"Are you sure you want to come with us?" I asked her, meeting her eyes. If she said no, I couldn't blame her. I remembered what we'd been through together. I couldn't imagine Juliana ever wanting to set foot in a Peacekeeper facility ever again.

"Do I *want* to? No." Her voice caught, and she began again. "No. But you need me."

"I don't know," Sara said, shaking her head. "Let us handle this. You've already given us a ton of information. Stay here where it's safe."

"No place is safe while Mike and Langston are alive," she said. "I've memorized hundreds of access codes to both bases and computer systems. I can get you through any checkpoint, virtual or otherwise, and into any room inside the facility." Juliana took Sara's hands in hers. "Sara, I can help."

Dad placed his hands on my and Juliana's shoulders. "Bringing Juliana along is the wisest course of action," Dad said. He handed her one of the return portals. "I trust you know how to use this?"

She nodded, but I saw the twinge of uncertainty in her eyes. "I do." She tucked the portal inside her jacket pocket, her hands trembling.

"Are you sure you're ready for this?" I asked her under my breath.

"For the mission, yes." Juliana rubbed her arms. "For the portal, no. I hate portal hopping."

"Wait, does it make you sick?"

"I mean, kind of. Stepping into a blackened void, being pulled this way and that by forces I can't control while hoping I land at the correct coordinates . . . It's not my idea of fun."

"So you feel pulled," I repeated. "Like you're going to come apart?"

Juliana shrugged and nodded. "It's uncomfortable.

It must be different for Elementals."

I didn't let myself hesitate or think too much about it. Whatever complications there were between us, I had to make sure Jules felt safe. I reached down and took her hand in mine. "It's okay. I've got you, Jules."

She bristled. "I don't need—"

"I know exactly what you need," I told her firmly. "Portals can screw with Mundanes. It can be like the world's worst acid trip. What you need is an anchor to keep you steady."

Juliana nodded, but judging by her frown and furrowed brow, this wasn't exactly the most ideal solution to her problem. Still, she laced her fingers with mine, and we all looked toward Dad.

"All right," Dad said as he cast the portal. "Now, we go."

The portal deposited us in the forested hills about a mile from where the made were being held. Juliana and I were the last ones out; I was none the worse for wear, but Juliana's face was ashen and she was sweating. As soon as she was clear of the portal, she shook her hand free from mine, dropped to her knees, and retched.

"Hey, hey, easy," I said, pulling her braid back from the danger zone and handing her my water bottle. "You okay?"

"Yeah," she managed to reply after swigging some water. "This always happens when I portal. It's like motion sickness, but it passes quickly."

Mom approached Juliana and touched her forehead. The confusion on Juliana's face was quickly replaced by relief. "Thank you," she said. "What did you do?"

"Teleporting once made me sick as well," Mom replied. "I learned how to combat the nausea years ago."

I turned away from Juliana and looked at the rest of our group. Sadie looked only slightly less green than Juliana, proving that some Elementals also don't do well with portal hopping, but Micah and Sara had come through unscathed. Why did portal travel affect some people but not others? I shuddered, wondering what the long-term effects of traveling between dimensions really were.

Mom left Juliana and stood back-to-back with Dad, and they scanned the ridgeline for signs that the resistance had arrived. We heard a loud crash, and Dad swore.

"Can they not manage silence?" Dad muttered. "Jovanny will be the death of me." He and Mom started toward the noise, but Juliana called after them.

"Did anyone bring the guns I asked for?" she asked. Dad faced her and frowned; since we Elementals were walking weapons, we weren't big on firearms.

"We did not have any at the manor," Dad admitted. "Jovanny is bringing them."

"Why do we need guns?" Sara asked.

"For the drones," Juliana said, indicating a few high points on the ridgeline. "Once the sensors detect us, the drones will go up. If we have guns—better yet, sniper rifles—we might be able to shoot them down before they get a proper scan of us."

"Are these drones not metal?" Micah asked. "Can we not merely pull them out of the sky?"

Juliana shook her head. "The sniffers will detect any magic used within a kilometer of the base, and we'll lose whatever element of surprise we have. Better to shoot them down."

"What about the portals?" Sadie asked. "They won't alert the sniffers?"

"Peacekeepers use portals all the time," Juliana said. "Sniffers aren't looking for portal activity."

Dad's frowned deepened, but he nodded. "Let us speak to Jovanny right away. Follow me." With that, Dad, Mom, and Juliana melted into the trees. I couldn't help it. I stared after her as she vanished from view.

"You're not going with her?" Sara asked.

"I'm supposed to stay with Sadie," I said, still looking toward the trees. She'd be fine. I just had to keep telling myself she'd be fine.

"I don't need a babysitter," Sadie said. "Go after her if you want. I'm fine."

"I am staying with you because that is where Dad assigned me," I insisted. "Okay?"

Sadie's nostrils flared and her fists clenched, but she didn't press me further. "Okay."

"We're going to meet Aregonda at the east check-point," Sara said to me. "Good luck."

"Yeah, good luck to you, too." I nodded to her. "Hopefully we won't need it."

9

Sara

Micah and I headed east and picked our way through the trees. We reached the checkpoint before Aregonda or any other resistance members, no surprise there. While we waited, Micah scanned the perimeter of the facility.

"So different, yet so similar to where your brother was held," Micah remarked.

"Really?" I peeked over his shoulder; the concrete and barbed wire fence looked pretty similar to me. "How is it different?"

"The Institute's main purpose was to ensure that Max was powerless," he replied. "This place is constructed in such a fashion as to enhance Elemental abilities. Look here." Micah indicated a section of wall that was a different color than the rest. "That portion is natural stone. And there," he pointed toward a stream flowing underneath a different section, "they are supplying fresh water to that section, which I imagine houses those of water. Also, I can feel metal surrounding us."

"I guess Mike really wants his experiments to flourish," I said.

"So it would seem," Micah agreed. "These aspects will also serve to enhance the abilities of whatever Elementals he has coerced to his agenda."

"How could any Elemental really be on his side?" I asked. "After what he and the rest of the Peacekeepers have done to us? I just don't get it."

"Sometimes people rebel for reasons known only to them."

"You're profound today."

Micah grinned. "Every day."

Jovanny joined us, with two of his people trailing close behind. "Where's Aregonda?" I asked, since she was supposed to be the one meeting us. And I was supposed to be learning her secrets.

"She is leading our reinforcements and will join us soon," Jovanny replied. "We've armed Juliana, and she's stationed near the drone huts. We will start with stone?"

"Stone," I affirmed. "Max said that the stones are the most powerful of the made, followed by metal."

Jovanny nodded. "Stone it is. Let's move."

Unlike my previous interactions with the resistance, Jovanny's people had come prepared. Just when

I'd written them off as the most incompetent group in history, they managed to surprise me.

While I stood there wondering how we'd get up and over the stone wall without setting off alarms, a resistance team had laid charges at a few predetermined points. Once everything was set, we retreated behind the tree line.

"One last check, then we'll blow the wall," Jovanny said. "Then we'll find out what's really going on here."

"Can't wait." I rubbed my palms against my thighs; all this waiting was making me more nervous than actual fighting.

"There's something else," Jovanny said. "I had a few people do some recon here, and at the Peacekeepers' main location in Portland. Armstrong might be at this site, but we have Phillips confirmed in Portland."

"Okay," I acknowledged, deciding *not* to mention that Langston Phillips being in the Mundane realm while were in the Otherworld was probably for the best. We did not need a repeat performance of Max going all psycho killer the way he did at the political rally.

"If we get Armstrong now, Phillips will be easy enough to catch," Jovanny continued.

"How so?" Micah asked.

"Armstrong and Phillips are tight," Jovanny replied. "If we capture one, we'll use that one as bait to trap the other."

Micah nodded. "That is a good plan. Perhaps once this operation is complete, we should send a small team into the Mundane realm and report Armstrong's capture."

"Yeah, we'll do that," Jovanny agreed. "Right now, let's blow the charges."

He left to confer with his people. Once he was out of earshot, I said, "You're always one step ahead of him."

"I merely see things from a different perspective," Micah said. "Jovanny is quite capable, but he is only one man. I wonder if the resistance wouldn't have achieved its goals long ago, had your father not been captured. The two of them working together must be quite formidable."

"If Dad had been free, everything would have been better." My words were punctuated by an explosion. The ground shook, but not too badly.

"Charges detonated," I said. "Let's see what the made are doing today."

The short answer was that the made weren't doing much of anything. Almost all of them had been inside their dormitories, many of them asleep. The few who were outside didn't put up much of a fight. Their blank stares and shuffling feet didn't seem anything like what you'd expect from the supposedly terrifying soldiers Armstrong had Frankensteined together. These individuals seemed tired and weak.

Their Peacekeeper guards, however, were quite active. They were decked out in full riot gear, and as soon as the explosives blew, they organized themselves into a defensive block and attacked us. That didn't go well for the guards since Jovanny's people were all Elementals, and more than half of them were metal. The Elementals split into two factions, with one side stripping the guards of weapons and communicators while the two stone resistance members created a circular wall trapping the guards inside. In less than twenty minutes, the bulk of the guards were disarmed and their communicators disabled before they could alert the rest of the facility.

"Should we take any of these back to headquarters?" one of the stone Elementals asked Aregonda, indicating the pile of weaponry.

"Reduce the weapons down to the raw metals, and leave whatever's left," Aregonda replied. "I do want the communicators." The Elemental nodded and set to work.

"This was easy," I remarked. Aregonda and I watched as the guards were removed from their circular prison and restrained one by one. Micah was inside the communications room ensuring everything had been properly destroyed.

"I agree," Aregonda said. "We were lucky to surprise this section. I do not believe we will be as lucky once we move on to the next."

"The next section is fire?" I asked, then a sudden pain stabbed my brain like an icepick dipped in acid.

I clutched my head as I doubled over, squeezing my eyes shut.

"Sara? Sara!" Aregonda crouched in front of me, feeling my forehead and cheeks. "What's wrong? Are you injured?"

"Hurts." My heart was racing and I could barely catch my breath. "Micah."

Aregonda stood and ordered two nearby soldiers to find Micah. Less than a minute later, one of them came rushing toward us.

"Micah's down," he said.

"Down how?" Aregonda demanded.

"We don't know," he replied. "He isn't bleeding, and no one touched him. All of a sudden he grabbed his head and dropped like a stone."

I heard the soldier speaking but I couldn't respond. The pain was so strong it was overriding the rest of my body, and my voice wouldn't obey. Since I was already deep inside my own head, I tried to pay closer attention to the pain.

It was intense, easily the worst pain I'd ever felt. What's more, it wasn't a physical pain; neither my muscles nor my bones hurt. This was mental pain, and it felt as if something—or someone—was trying to rip my thoughts out of my head. I tried pushing the pain out. When that didn't work, I mustered a mental shout.

Get out!

The pain grew stronger. My mental voice got louder. Gods, it hurt.

Get out!

Suddenly, I felt Micah in my mind. *Sara, remember my father's lesson.*

His lesson? A memory fluttered to the surface of my mind: Micah telling me about his youth. Specifically, it was a story about his father teaching him to shield his mind from other Dreamwalkers. It was one of Micah's few memories of his father, the grizzled war veteran teaching his son the delicate art of dreamwalking and how to protect himself while doing it.

He told me that I must build a wall brick by brick, Micah had said. *Slowly, strongly, surely. No one can breach such a defense.*

I visualized concrete blocks, huge ones at least a head taller than Micah, surrounding my mind like sentries. I created a mental mortar and fixed them together, laying the next layer, and the next.

It was an agonizingly slow process, but it worked. Once I laid the last brick in place, I could think again. I could breathe. The pain receded, and with Aregonda's help, I stood. I was still shaky, but I was upright.

"Take me to Micah," I said, stumbling, then catching myself against the nearest person: Aregonda.

With Aregonda supporting me, her arm around my waist, we found Micah. The pain had driven him to his knees, not flat to the ground as it had me. I knelt before him and pressed my forehead to his.

"I did what you said, just like your father taught you," I told him, aloud and in his mind. "Brick by brick."

"What . . . is . . . this . . . ?" he rasped.

"I don't know." I threaded my fingers through his superfine hair, then visualized his mind. I had half a row of bricks laid before he noticed my work.

"Sara, what are you doing?"

"I'm helping."

He turned his head and kissed my palm. "Thank you."

Together, it didn't take long for Micah and I to build the walls around our minds and fend off whatever was trying to invade our thoughts. Once it was apparent that we had this mental attack under control, Aregonda and her people moved on toward where the fire made were held and carried on the mission. The sounds of battle moved further away as our minds cleared.

"Are you all right?" Micah asked. He'd clutched his head so hard for so long his hair was flat against his head, and his skin was ashen.

"Now I am." I still felt a dull thud in my brain, but it was steadily receding. "Do you know what that was?"

"No. Nor do I know why we were targeted." Micah stood, then offered me a hand. "We should keep moving."

I let him pull me to my feet. "You're sure you're okay?"

"I am, because of you."

We started walking toward the center of the base. "Good thing you remembered your father's lesson," I mentioned.

"Agreed," Micah said. "When the attack began, I could hardly stand or even speak. Then I recalled what my father taught me about building walls to keep others out of my mind."

"I'm glad he knew what he was talking about."

"He was wise and strong, much like your father." We reached the corner of a building. Micah held out his arm, blocking my way. "The battle continues," he explained. "Are you ready?"

"I think so." I bit my lip. "I mean, I was ready before we were mind-attacked. I guess I'm still ready."

He smiled, then laced his fingers with mine. "All right, then. We go together," he said, and we rounded the corner into the center of the base.

It was total chaos.

Jovanny's people had laid additional charges around the fire made's boundary wall and blown holes into the concrete. We stepped through one of the holes and were met by guards running for their lives. From us.

"What is happening?" I asked. To the left of us were a half dozen guards huddled in a circle, cowering, while one of Jovanny's people reassured them we wouldn't hurt them. On the right side of the courtyard,

Dad and Sadie had corralled a group of people who I assumed were the made. Scattered everywhere were the rest of the Peacekeeper guards, trying to outpace those who were rounding them up.

"The soldiers appear frightened," Micah replied.

"This is just weird." Peacekeepers were well-trained soldiers, and pretty much all of them hated Elementals and would jump at the chance to attack us. The fact that the second-tier guards had been stationed here made me worry we'd picked the wrong location, or that maybe the operation had moved out. It wouldn't be the first time Mike had turned tail and run at the first sign of trouble.

And why were the guards around the fire made so much weaker than the ones guarding stone?

A scared man with a gun is still a man with a gun, and it took us a while to chase them all down and convince them we weren't there to kill everyone. Once everyone was disarmed and safely inside a holding area, Jovanny's team set up a perimeter while I checked on Sadie.

"How's it going?" I asked, jerking my chin toward the made.

"Fine, I guess." She frowned. "Most of them won't even talk to me. I—I don't think they believe I'm an Inheritor."

"Doesn't matter what they believe, you are what you are," I said. "Give them some time. They were prisoners until this morning. This whole situation is a lot to take in."

"I can calm them," Mom offered. She raised her hands, but Sadie jumped in front of her.

"Don't mess with their minds," Sadie pleaded. Mom's eyes flashed. Then she lowered her hands.

"I do not mess with people's minds," Mom said icily. "What I can do is lower their heart rate and other stress responses. Their thoughts remain their own."

"Oh. I . . . " Sadie covered her mouth with her hand and did her best to shrink into the ground. Luckily, Mom never held a grudge against her children.

"I will see about calming the prisoners," Mom said, then patted Sadie's arm and left. I guided Sadie to the edge of the courtyard.

"Why don't you sit," I said. "The stress is getting to you."

"I need to be with the made." Even as she said it, I could tell it was the furthest thing from what she wanted.

"You need to take care of yourself first," I said. "I'll come check on you in a bit."

Sadie nodded, and I left in search of Micah. On the way I passed by the Peacekeepers, who were now sitting on the ground patiently waiting for further instructions. Either Mom's calming mojo was working on the guards, too, or Jovanny and his people were more effective than I'd thought. So, yeah, I was betting on Mom.

Micah and I met up again at the entrance to the metal courtyard. Micah's arms were crossed over his chest and he was frowning.

"What's wrong?" I asked.

"This," he replied, gesturing toward the made. Sadie was trying to organize the metal ones again, since Dad was confident that having the Inheritor of Metal on hand would help gain the trust of both the made and the captured Elementals. "All of this. It is . . . wrong."

"I know." I looked over the bedraggled occupants of the metal enclosure, scared and filthy and so malnourished their bones jutted out, and my heart clenched. I wondered if Max had ever been forced to live this way.

"There's so many," I said. "I guess metal took better than the rest."

Micah arched a silver brow. "Took?"

I swallowed. "You know. Metal assimilates more readily into a Mundane subject than fire or water."

Micah's eyes searched my face. His fingers brushed my cheek. "I would have kept such sights from you, if only you'd let me."

"I wish I could've."

"Sara!"

I looked toward the voice and saw Aregonda rushing toward us, her long auburn hair streaming behind her. "What's up?" I asked.

"We've found some that were forced to assimilate water," she replied. "Hurry, they're this way."

Micah and I followed Aregonda to a long, rectangular room that reminded me of a hospital ward. There were rows of cots set up along the sides, along with privacy screens and rolling carts filled with medical equipment. Only three of the beds were occupied. On those three cots, the sheets and blankets were soaked, along with the men lying in them, the excess water having run off and collected into pools underneath the beds.

"How is there so much water? Is the roof leaking?" I asked. "We need to get them dry and warm."

"The water is coming *from them*," Aregonda replied. "They're the water made, and while they didn't drown like the others, they now have more water inside them than their bodies can handle."

I approached the person in the closest bed: a muscular man with a blond buzz cut. I wondered if Mike Armstrong had recruited soldiers from his own army. The man looked up at me with water-filled blue eyes.

"His eyes," I whispered. "They're . . . full."

"Sara, you must take the water from them," Aregonda urged.

"Me? How?" As I spoke, I remembered when the water leapt out of the bowl and coiled around my wrist.

"I showed you how," she replied. "Call the water to you. It will listen."

"What if it drowns her?" Micah demanded. "I will not let you lead Sara into harm."

"She won't drown." Aregonda grasped my hands. "You won't. Call the water. It will come."

I looked from the drowning people to Aregonda. "Why don't you do it?"

"Because you're stronger than I am," she replied.

"I—I don't remember the spell," I whispered. "Tell me the words again."

"The words don't matter. What matters is what you feel here," Aregonda touched my forehead, "and here." She touched my chest, right under the hollow of my throat. I looked at Micah.

"You'll stop me if it goes bad?" I asked.

"You will try this?" Micah challenged, his brow creased with worry.

I looked at the drowning people again. "I can't let them suffer, not if I can help. I have to try."

Micah nodded. I released Aregonda's hands and faced the patients. I was going to call the water and tell it to leave those people alone, of that I was certain. The water had listened to me once before. Here's hoping I could do it again.

"Um, water? You don't belong with them," I said. "You're killing them. Get out, go find a nice stream or something."

Nothing happened.

"I mean it," I said. "Water, be gone."

Still nothing.

"Water, I command you to leave these people *now!*"

The water *listened*.

All at once, a lake's worth of water poured out of the three men, as if each person was having his own private rainstorm. The three puddles coalesced into a river in the center aisle, then flowed toward me like a tidal wave. When it was a few paces in front of me, the wave paused. As if that wasn't weird enough, I heard— no, I *felt*—the water whisper an apology in my mind.

"I know you didn't mean to hurt them," I replied. "No one blames you. Go on, go be watery some- place else."

The wave crashed, and the water flowed away under the door and through the cracks in the floor. Aregonda nodded approvingly, then rushed toward the made and called for medical assistance. Micah cupped my face with his hands.

"The water spoke to you?" His brows pinched together while his eyes searched my face.

"Yeah," I replied. "It felt bad. It knew it didn't belong in those people, but it was forced inside them. It was sorry."

Micah's brows lowered and his silver eyes dark- ened. "I believe the water spoke to you the way silver speaks to me."

"I guess it did."

He rested his forehead against mine. "You are cer- tain you weren't harmed?"

"I'm certain." I covered his hands with mine. "I promise."

Micah looked at me for another moment, then stalked up to Aregonda, grabbed her shoulder, and spun her around to face him. "What have you done to Sara?"

"I haven't done anything to her," Aregonda replied. She wasn't shaken by Micah's roughness at all, and that was just weird. Micah was big and powerful, both magically and physically.

"You lie," Micah hissed. "The water communicated with Sara, yet she has never spoken to any metal, not even to copper. I ask again, what have you done to my wife?"

"I answer again, I have done nothing," Aregonda insisted, unmoved. She lifted her chin and crossed her arms, making a point of looking Micah directly in the eye. "I merely helped her unlock her potential. In time, and with practice, all the elements will speak to Sara."

"What?" I squeaked. "How is that possible?"

Aregonda reached out as if to touch my cheek, but Micah put his body between us. "You have an amazing gift, my child. You only need to learn how to use it," she said around him, her gaze catching mine just over his shoulder.

More of Jovanny's people rushed in, and Aregonda went to help them. I looked up at Micah and saw him staring at me as if I'd grown an extra ear.

"What did she mean by that?" I whispered.

"I have no idea," he replied. "When this is done, we will speak with Maeve." He stepped closer and tilted my chin upward. "You said you are unharmed and I believe you. However, if at any time that changes, please tell me."

I nodded. "I will. What should we do now?" The resistance medics rushed in and began moving the water made onto gurneys. Aregonda directed them while keeping an eye on Micah and me.

"We see to the people you rescued, and to the rest," Micah said. "For all the evil that was done here, there is still room for good."

10

Max

Sadie and I just stood around waiting while the others split off as planned. I swung my arms, clapped my hands, and rolled up on the balls of my feet. Waiting was boring, and I didn't do boring well.

"You look like an idiot," Sadie remarked.

"Usually I feel like one, too." I noticed her pursed lips, the way she rubbed her arms. "You okay, kid?"

"Why does everyone keep asking me if I'm okay?" she snapped. "I'm the super powerful Inheritor. I was born for this."

"You were born to run a library," I said. "It's okay to be nervous. We all are, each and every time. Well, not Ma, but she's different. Regular people like us are always on edge during these missions."

Her shoulders relaxed. "Really?"

"Really." I heard someone walking down the path and tensed. In another moment, Dad emerged without Ma or Juliana. "Where'd you leave the muscle?" I asked, referring to Ma.

"She is walking the perimeter, locating and disabling wards," Dad replied. "As for Juliana, she is watching for drones."

I grunted and scanned the tree line. "Good."

"You do not like that she's assisting us?"

"I don't like that she's alone," I clarified. "She is not like Ma. She's defenseless."

"Tell that to whomever is standing at the end of her rifle." Dad withdrew one of his portals and handed it to me. "Sadie and I will now head to the southern perimeter wall. Max, can you watch over the main road and alert me if any Peacekeepers approach? That portal will take you directly to me."

"Sure can," I agreed.

"I'm ready," Sadie said, and honestly, she looked it. "Let's get going."

"Very well." Dad nodded, then he and Sadie started toward the building's outer wall. After they'd gone a few steps, Sadie turned back and gave me a thumbs up. The kid was going to be all right. I was sure of it.

I'd resolved to be a good soldier, manning my post and watching the road, when I noticed movement a short distance down the ridgeline. Assuming it was a perimeter patrol, I skulked through the trees toward it. What I saw brought a smile to my face.

Juliana and her rifle were set up along the cliff's edge, and she was lying on her belly like a sniper. I leaned against the nearest tree and watched her as she concentrated on scanning the horizon, keeping our operation safe from the drones. Then I heard the barest rustle and swore under my breath. We weren't alone.

I spotted the patrolmen. They were behind me on the ridge and hadn't sighted Juliana. Yet. I crept up behind her, crouched down, and touched her ankle.

"Jules, it's me," I whispered when she flinched. "Quiet."

"Max, wha—"

"Quiet," I hissed. I put my hand on her back and portaled us, rifle and all, to the forest floor below the cliff. Once we materialized, I pulled her upright and dragged her behind some low, scrubby bushes. Juliana was perfectly still as she stood against me, not asking why I'd walked up behind her and portaled us away from her perch without a word of explanation. Even after everything that had gone down between us, she still trusted me.

A few pebbles rolled down the cliff face and bounced in front of us. Juliana stiffened, but otherwise didn't move. Then a drone flew by, and she twisted so her mouth was next to my ear.

"I need to shoot down that drone," she breathed.

"Let it go."

"Max, the others," she said. "If the drone sights them, they could be in danger."

I widened my stance so we were eye-to-eye. "If you shoot it now, those guards will track where the shot came from and find us."

"Then portal us away after I fire," she insisted.

I didn't want her to do it, but she had that look in her eyes that meant she wasn't budging. I nodded and stepped away, then Juliana took aim and shot. We were on the other side of the clearing before the noise was finished echoing.

"How can you stand that?" I asked, rubbing my ears.

"You get used to it." Juliana turned away from me and checked the skyline. All clear. "Aren't you supposed to be with Sadie?"

"She's with Dad," I replied. "I got worried about you being all alone with these creeps patrolling the area."

She glanced over her shoulder, her brows raised. "I'm not exactly defenseless. I have a gun."

"Would you have shot those patrolmen coming up behind you?"

"If I needed to." She faced forward and resumed scanning the horizon. "It's not like I've never shot anyone before."

I stared at the back of her head, wondering who she'd been shooting at. "Ever kill anyone?"

"No, but you're on the fast track to be the first." Juliana took aim and shot down another drone, then looked over her shoulder and grinned. Seemed like we could joke around with each other again. "When do we move in?"

I looked at the sun. "Any minute now, Jules. Any minute."

"You don't have to call me that."

"That mean I get to call you 'baby' now?"

Juliana fixed me with a glare so icy I almost shivered. Okay. Joking was a bad idea. "Brave words, especially when I'm the one with the gun."

"That gun can't hurt me."

"I'm willing to give it my best shot."

"Ha, ha."

Before we could continue either flirting or trying to kill each other—honestly, with Juliana and me it could be either—I heard a pop. It came from Mike's "dungeon of doom." "That's our cue," I said as I cast the portal and pulled Juliana along behind me.

We emerged at the perimeter. "Come on," I said, grabbing her hand and leading her along the outer wall. "They should have breached it over here."

"Who's getting the prisoners?"

"That's Dad and Sadie's gig. He's hoping that once they know she's an Inheritor, they'll be more trusting of us."

"As if Inheritors haven't betrayed Elementals before."

"Sadie's not like that. She's a born protector." I

grabbed Juliana's elbow. "I'm sorry I called you 'baby.' I didn't mean anything by it."

"Thanks," she said, and it took me a moment to realize what Juliana *wasn't* doing.

"Hey, you're not sick. You just portaled twice in a few minutes, and you're not even woozy."

"Yeah, you're right." Juliana touched her forehead. "Do you think your mother fixed my motion sickness permanently?"

"You never know with Ma," I replied. "She's capable of all sorts of stuff."

A gust of wind came out of nowhere, pelting us with sand and other debris. "Weird," I said when it passed.

Juliana seemed less perturbed and more curious. "I wonder if that wind means Auster's here."

I looked at her. "Auster?"

She bit her lip. "Crap. You didn't know? I told Baudoin, but I didn't know if he'd be here."

"Know what about who?" When her eyes widened, I continued. "Jules, I've never heard of anyone called Auster. Why should I know that name?"

"He's the Inheritor of Air," she replied. "He's been working with Mike Armstrong since he came into his abilities. We, um . . . We didn't talk about him at the Institute."

"What the hell else have I missed out on?" I demanded. "Are you the Inheritor of Stone?" Juliana swallowed hard, and I felt like a jerk. It wasn't her fault I hadn't known who Auster was. It also explained why no one knew who had become the Inheritor of Air after Avatar was murdered. The next Inheritor was a damn traitor.

"Sorry," I said. "We should let Dad know there's another Inheritor on-site." I moved to withdraw a portal, but she touched my arm.

"Max, Auster is Galen's son."

I froze, remembering Galen Vasquez, the air Elemental I'd done time with at the Institute. He was Avatar's brother, and he was more like a college professor than a warrior. If not for Galen, that place would have driven me crazy.

And now his kid was on Armstrong's side.

"Are you sure?" I asked.

"Positive," Juliana replied. "Just like you let them take you to keep your family safe, Galen went in for Auster's sake."

"Why did Auster turn?" I asked.

"After his mother died, Langston made himself his guardian. He grew up around Peacekeepers."

I took a deep breath and looked at the sky. "I never even knew Galen had a kid."

"He probably didn't want to jeopardize his son's safety." Juliana squeezed my forearm. "Galen was always your friend. Don't forget that."

I gently took her hand off my arm, then laced my fingers with hers and squeezed. "I don't forget the people who matter to me."

Her cheeks darkened as she withdrew her hand from mine. "We should let the others know Auster may be on-site."

Juliana slung the rifle across her shoulder and we walked in silence to the base. We found the blown-out portion of the wall, and Juliana moved to step inside. I caught her arm. "Listen, Jules, I don't want you to do anything crazy in there."

She looked at me, her lips pressed in a thin line. "Crazy?"

"Like I was at Langston's rally," I replied. "Even if we don't get Mike and Langston here, we will get them. I promise."

"You've promised me that before," she said.

"And you promised you'd get me out of the Institute, and you did. Looks like we both keep our promises." When she remained silent, I continued, "I know you want to leave us in the past, but I am staying with you every step of the way in here. I want them gone as much as you do, but not if it means you getting hurt."

Her strong, expressionless mask wavered for just a moment. "You mean that?"

"Which part?"

"About staying with me."

"Yeah." I slid my hand along the back of her neck and drew her closer. "No matter what happens in there, I'm gonna be right beside you."

"I wouldn't want it any other way." She moved closer, and asked, "Will you stay with me if I deviate from the plan?"

Dad hated it when his orders weren't followed to the letter. "Deviate how?"

"There are more than enough resistance members here to take out the guards and free the Elementals and the made," she replied. "I want to go after Mike and Langston."

It was a bad idea, but I wanted both of them punished, by my own hands if possible. "I'm in."

Juliana and I crept around the edge of the made's glorified prison and slipped inside the outer wall of concrete and barbed wire. We skirted the guards, and even our own people, since we had one thing on our minds: finding the main office and capturing the two men in charge.

"This way," Juliana said as she turned down a hall. "Mike has panic rooms built into all of his facilities. It will be in the center of the property, and most likely underground. That's where the research will be."

"Will he be there?" I asked.

"Yeah. He and Langston would have retreated there as soon as the alarm sounded."

"Great." I flexed my fingers and made a fist. "Can't wait to say hi."

The corridor ended in a reinforced steel door. Juliana struck it with her fist. "Damn it!"

"Don't worry. I got this." The door opened as soon as I told it to, further proof that the on-site metal Elementals were pretty lame. Even a weak Elemental, or one who was still a child, could convince a metal door to only open up for certain people.

The door opened into an office, and the far wall was covered with computer panels and video screens. Juliana approached the panels, her fingers dancing across the keyboard as schematics and other information scrolled across the vid screens. She paused on the building's blueprints.

"Is the research here?" I asked, trying to decipher the flurry of characters and images as they appeared, but they moved too fast. I focused on the blueprints. Juliana, on the other hand, seemed to have comprehended everything on the screens in a matter of moments.

"Most of the research on the made is here, along with the dreamwalking protocols," she replied, then swore. "Max, there's a portal chamber and a tunnel that leads right to it. Both of them are right underneath us."

I looked around the room, but I saw no way to access either. "You think they skipped?"

"It's the logical play if you're under attack." Juliana clenched her fists. "They're always one frickin' step ahead."

"Then let's step around them," I said. "They're not here. So where are they?"

Juliana took a deep breath, then turned to a third screen and tapped it with her index finger. A map came up, and she traced a route. "They're this way. If they took the tunnel, we might be able to catch them."

We left the panic room and turned down a narrow corridor. A smaller tunnel veered west from the main track, and we followed it. Midway down the hall, there was a wooden door painted to look like metal.

"Why custom paint an escape hatch?" I wondered aloud.

"Ever since Sara freed you, Langston's been terrified you'd come after him," Juliana replied. Every time she talked about him, her eyes darkened—it was like her mind went to a different place. "I think it's the only reason he kept me alive, so he could use me as a bargaining chip when you came to kill him." She ran her fingertips across the panels. "There should be a combination lock. Help me find it."

I felt along the walls and, sure enough, found a false panel. I pulled out my utility knife and used it to pry the plank free. Beneath the panel was a set of wooden tumblers.

"A wooden combination lock," I scoffed. *Now I've seen everything.* "Any idea what the magic numbers are?"

"Yeah." Juliana slid the tumblers. Her hands were shaking so badly it her took three tries to get the code right. Then the tunnel door creaked open. Without a word, she pulled a flashlight out of her pocket and plunged into the darkness, but I paused to check out the lock. The winning combination was zero-four-two-two.

Juliana's birthday is April 22.

I'm not going to kill Langston. I'm going to hurt him so bad he'll wish he was dead.

I followed Juliana into the darkness. The tunnel was damp and cold, and thanks to its dirt walls and floors our footfalls were nearly soundless. We reached the end and found another door. Since this one was real metal, I used my ability to push it open, only to immediately stumble back and cover my mouth and nose.

Inside the room was a heap of corpses.

The stench from the bodies made us gag. Juliana bent over and retched. I placed my hand on her back, but I wasn't far from puking either. I worked her flashlight out of her hand and pointed it into the room, catching flashes of metal among the limbs and a glimpse of stone.

We were looking at what was left of the Elementals.

"Oh, my God." Juliana covered her mouth with her hands.

"I guess we found them." One of the corpses looked fresher than the others. Wondering why this guy was the last to go, I hooked his shoulder with the toe of my boot and turned him over. It was Sara's friend, Jerome Polonsky.

"Hey, buddy," I said to the corpse. "Sorry it went down like this." I looked over the other bodies. I saw enough marks to verify that most if not all of them were Elementals, which begged the question why Jerome, a Peacekeeper, was with them.

"You think they caught on to him being under-cover?" I asked Juliana.

"Maybe." She pulled her shirt up over her nose, then crouched beside Jerome's head. "Look at this."

I crouched beside her and saw the dried blood clinging to Jerome's ears and nose. Mixed in with the blood was a green fluid that I recognized all too well: Langton's version of truth serum, one of the worst tortures he'd ever devised. The serum was injected directly into the muscle, where it burned like acid and made you feel like your bones were on fire. It had never worked on me, supposedly because I'm a Dreamwalker. Langston had injected me with it at least a dozen times just to make sure.

Mike and Langston had interrogated Jerome with this garbage. Then they'd murdered him.

I pulled Juliana out of the room and away from the bodies. "Come on, Jules." I shut the door. "There's nothing we can do for them now."

She swallowed hard. "What about Mike and Langston?"

I looked at the closed door. "If they were here, they're long gone now."

"No. *No!*" She lunged for the door. I grabbed her around the waist and hauled her away. "Put me down!"

"So you can do what? Stomp around a bunch of corpses?"

"It's not fair!" She moved to hit the wall. I grabbed her fist. She deflated. "It's not fair."

"It's not," I agreed. "It's awful, it sucks, and life hates us. But if you keep punching metal doors, you're gonna break your hand, and then everything will be worse."

"Why aren't you punching doors?" she asked, and it was a good question. It was no secret that I wanted Mike and Langston to suffer for what they'd done to me and everyone at the Institute, especially Langston. Any other time, I'd be ripping this place apart, razing the walls down to the studs to find the smallest clue as to their next move.

"I've got to take care of you," I said, the words just falling out of my mouth. "You're more important than them."

"I can take care of myself."

"Says the woman going head-to-head with a one-ton door." I released her and stepped back. Juliana ground the heels of her palms against her eyes, though I couldn't tell if her tears were due to the stench, sorrow for the dead, or frustration at losing the big fish.

When she finally spoke, her voice was low and certain. "You're right. Let's go back up, see if we can help the rest."

I wanted to make a joke about her saying I was right, but she was hurting. "This isn't your fault."

"I know. Doesn't make it any easier."

I took her hand. When she didn't pull away, I understood how upset she really was. "We'll get them."

She met my gaze, her dark eyes hard. "We will."

11

Sara

We gathered in front of the main entrance, and what a sight we were. Dad looked tired but happy, as did Jovanny with his satisfied smile. Sadie seemed irritated, but she wasn't saying anything, so I had no idea what her deal was. Mom stood over her like a mother hen, which almost certainly was contributing to Sadie's sullen attitude. Micah, still frazzled from the mental attack we'd endured, glared at Aregonda as if she were his sworn enemy. As for Aregonda, well, she ignored him.

I have no idea what I looked like, other than awful. I certainly *felt* awful.

Despite everyone's bedraggled state, Jovanny's people had come through again. They sequestered the guards in one of the courtyards and set the made up with some medical attention in a separate area. The only thing we were waiting on now was for Max and Juliana to report in.

"I would say this was a success," Dad declared. "I am glad we have rescued so many, but I do wish we had apprehended Armstrong and Phillips as well."

"Perhaps neither of them were here," Micah suggested. "We have verification of Phillips in the Mundane realm. The incompetent guards stationed here suggest all of this could've been a ruse, or perhaps a ploy to draw us out. Armstrong is far too cunning to hand over such an easy victory."

"Here comes an Armstrong now," Jovanny muttered, jerking his chin toward the building. I followed his gaze and saw Max and Juliana exiting the facility, their grim, tense expressions signaling that whatever news they had, it wasn't going to be good.

"Hey," I snapped, narrowing my eyes at Jovanny, "Juliana is on our side. If you have a problem with her, you have a problem with me."

Dad's gaze flitted between Jovanny and me. "In addition to Armstrong and Langston's absence, where are the Elementals?" he asked, ever diplomatic. "There must have been at least a few stationed here, or the made would not exist."

"We found the Elementals, what's left of 'em," Max answered. "Me and Jules went to the main office and grabbed all the research we could find, then we tracked Mike and Langston down an escape tunnel.

They killed the Elementals and left them in the portal chamber. There's at least a dozen bodies down there."

My heart sank. "They're all dead?"

Juliana nodded—she looked pale and shaken. "Yeah. All of them."

I leaned against Micah's shoulder. This was supposed to be a rescue mission, and I couldn't help wondering if Mike had killed the Elementals because of our arrival. I did not want to be responsible for their deaths.

"What about Armstrong?" Jovanny demanded.

Max shook his head. "Gone. Based on the state of those bodies, they've been gone for a while."

"Only Armstrong," Micah corrected. "Apparently, Phillips remains in the Mundane realm."

"Really?" Juliana asked. "That's unlike him."

Dad said something in French; based on Sadie's shocked face and Mom's laughter, I assumed he swore. "There is nothing more to be done here. Jovanny, we will return to your operation with the wounded. How soon before we have transport available?"

"Soon." Jovanny withdrew a communicator and barked a few orders into it. While he was out of earshot, I spoke to Max.

"Was it really that bad?" I asked, searching his face.

"It was horrible," he replied matter-of-factly, but I could tell there was something else. Something he had to steel himself to say. "Sara," he added, lowering his voice. "Jerome was down there. I checked, but there was nothing I could do."

"Oh." My hands started shaking, so I clasped them behind my back. "I guess this means he really was on our side."

"Guess so. At least he isn't suffering anymore." Max paused, then added, "From the looks of it, he was tortured for information."

"What?" I shuddered—they would likely have been interrogating Jerome about us. "You'll tell Dad?"

He squeezed my shoulder. "I will."

Of all the people I'd expected to die today, Jerome wasn't one of them. Had he been executed because he tried to help me? Was he really better off now? I thought about the made, all of them either dead or in various states of injury, and the guards who'd been captured along with them. Did any of them think they'd be better off dead?

"Hey," Max barked, and I felt myself jostle as he took my shoulders. "Snap out of it."

I opened my eyes. I hadn't realized I'd closed them. "Sorry."

"S'okay. I get it." Max paused before asking, "Did Auster make an appearance?"

"Auster?" I repeated, but before Max could explain, Dad whipped his head around.

"You know something of Auster?" he demanded. "Did you see him?"

"I think we felt him," Max replied. "Like a small tornado, trying to keep us away from the fence."

"So, he's air?" I offered.

Juliana swallowed hard. "Auster is the *Inheritor* of Air. He's also working with Mike and Langston."

"Auster has not been seen in public for over a decade," Dad mused aloud. "Yet he makes an appearance today. Why?"

"To ensure Armstrong's escape?" Micah posited.

"This day gets better and better," I muttered.

Once the facility was secured, and Jovanny left a contingent of his people behind to keep an eye on the grounds, the rest of us transported the made we'd rescued to the resistance base in the Mundane realm. Aregonda worked with tireless efficiency to get them set up with cots and rudimentary medical care. In no time at all she had them tucked away in a tent of their own, with two guards standing watch at both entrances. Even though we were pretty sure that the made were innocent victims of Mike's delusions, taking precautions was smart.

"Aregonda has only posted the bare minimum amount of guards," Micah observed as we walked past the mades' tent.

"You're just mad she didn't back down earlier."

Micah's gaze slid toward me. "Regardless, I prefer caution. I will speak to Baudoin about adding more guards."

"How many guards do you really need for a tent full of sick people? Most of them can barely walk."

"Perhaps they just want us to assume as much."

"Perhaps we just doomed them to a slow, painful death," I said. "Did you see all the medical equipment they had back at the facility? Can we even keep them alive out here?"

"It would have been foolish to rescue them, only to watch them perish." When I remained silent, Micah moved in front of me and set his hands on my shoulders.

"I am sorry about your friend," he said.

"Are you? I know you hated Jerome." I blinked and turned away—there had to be dust in my eye. "The one time you met him you threatened to kill him."

"I did not hate him," Micah murmured as he pulled me into his arms. "I merely wanted him to stop touching you. Only I get to touch you." I leaned into him, letting him comfort me as only he could.

"I can't help wondering if we should have taken him to the manor," I whispered, remembering how Jerome had been left behind after our second prison break. "Maybe he'd still be alive if we had."

Micah tilted my chin upward. "Do not torment yourself with what might have been. We did what we thought was right, and we had no way of knowing what might befall him after we parted ways. There is also the fact that had you insisted I bring him to the manor, I would have done so."

"Really?"

"Of course. I would do anything for you."

I rested my forehead against his chest. "You're my rock."

"Does that make you the wave that batters me?"

I tilted my head up, saw his smile. "You know it."

Aregonda called everyone to the center of the site near the main brick fire pit. She was again in her element—ha, ha, element—as she bustled around the fire, overseeing the preparation of food and drink for the rest of us. Once everyone had been served, Jovanny spoke up.

"It's too bad we didn't get our hands on Armstrong," he said. Again. "You said he was already gone when you got to the control room?" he asked Max.

"Long gone," Max replied. "Those bodies had been there for days."

"Not necessarily. They could have used a decomposition agent," Juliana offered.

"Decomposition agent?" I repeated, wincing. "Is that as gross as it sounds?"

"It speeds up decay in organic matter," Juliana replied. "It's how they used to dispose of bodies at the Institute."

At Juliana's frank description of how Peacekeepers dealt with those who'd died while on their watch, reactions ranged from disgust to outrage. She realized what she'd said and ducked her head. I stepped closer to her—I, too, was an expert at sticking my foot in my mouth, and I wasn't going to let her face the consequences alone. Jovanny, like a shark scenting blood in the water, went after her.

"Maybe it's all right that we didn't get Mike Armstrong," he began, smoothing his moustache like a cartoon villain. "We've got us an Armstrong right here. Mind telling us a bit more about your uncle?"

"I've already told Mr. Corbeau everything I know," Juliana replied tersely, refusing to meet his eyes.

"Do you know where Armstrong went?" Jovanny pressed. "Where he would hole up?"

"If I knew where he was, that's where I would be, not sitting around a campfire roasting hot dogs," Juliana shot back, her voice shaking. Juliana wasn't just mad, she was furious, and she only ever got that mad at herself.

"Well, isn't that convenient." Jovanny paced in a slow circle, eyeing Juliana. "You're the one who claims to know all this classified information, and you're the one who says your uncle got away. Seems like we have to take your word for it."

"I was there, too," Max said, his voice low, dangerous.

"You probably saw what she wanted you to see," Jovanny countered. "She didn't mention that Armstrong has an Inheritor on his side, not until it was all said and done. This could have all been a set up. It *seemed* like a set up."

"Hey," I snapped. "Back off. Juliana's on our side."

Jovanny's brows lowered. "Is she?"

Dad stood up and got in Jovanny's face. "Stop this line of inquiry," he commanded. "If not for Juliana, I would still be a prisoner."

Jovanny's eyes softened, but he stood his ground. When he spoke, his tone was direct. "Maybe that's part of her plan."

Dad crossed his arms. "Maybe you feel like a fool because *she* is the one who found me, while *you* followed a shapeshifter for months."

"We don't know if we can trust her," Jovanny insisted. He looked at Juliana, then at the rest of us, the Corbeaus, once separated and now united for the first time in a long time. "Blood is thicker than water, Baudoin!"

"My uncle is nothing to me," Juliana said, her voice stronger now. "If you knew how he'd treated me, what he did to me . . ." She pushed back her hair and looked Jovanny in the eye. "Yeah, I do know some classified information. I learned it to stop my uncle. And before you say anything else," she continued over Jovanny's attempt to cut her off, "know that I don't care if you believe me or not. I'm the one helping you here, not the other way around."

Juliana stalked away from the fire pit, Sadie trailing after her with a somber look directed toward me. Dad watched her go, then turned back to Jovanny.

"That girl is like a daughter to me," he said after taking a deep, slow breath. "I understand your caution, Jovanny, and your suspicion. Truly, I do. Perhaps you will note how we *all* trust Juliana and consider trusting her just as you trust in us."

He took Mom's elbow and they left the circle. Jovanny moved to follow, but Micah blocked his way.

"If you harass Juliana again, you will deal with me," he declared.

"You're on her side, too?" Jovanny shook his head. I almost felt bad for him. His disbelief was palpable—he really thought Juliana was behind everything, and it couldn't be further from the truth. "Why? She's nothing to you."

"She is my wife's friend, therefore she is my friend. I look after those who are mine," Micah calmly explained. With that, he walked out of Jovanny's circle of followers, and Max and I went with him.

"Thanks," Max said, glancing between us. "For sticking up for Jules."

Micah shrugged. "I only spoke the truth. Jovanny had no cause to attack her. She has shown us nothing but help and courtesy."

"Jovanny's an ass and an idiot," I muttered. "He couldn't lead the resistance out of a paper bag."

Micah sighed. "He worries for his people. Hopefully, no matter how worried he is, he will heed Baudoin's advice."

We came upon Juliana and Sadie sitting beside the stream. Mom and Dad were standing a little ways away, their heads close as they whispered to each other. I sat next to Sadie.

She fiddled with the ends of her hair, glancing once shyly at me before fixing her gaze pointedly on the rippling water. Her voice was soft when she spoke. "Earlier today, when you helped the made. Everyone saw it."

I blinked. "Saw what?"

"That you're powerful." Sadie tossed a pebble into the water. "Why aren't you the Inheritor? I'm just a librarian."

"Hey, don't talk like that," I said, rolling my eyes. "Remember our old school librarian, Mrs. Fintra?"

"Of course I do."

"She used to say that librarians were the gatekeepers of knowledge. Sounds like a pretty important position to me."

Sadie grinned. "She did teach us the magic of an interlibrary loan."

"See that? No matter what I inherited from who, there is no way I can make just the right book appear before me. That's something only you can do."

"*You* found the scroll."

"Yeah, because Aregonda sent it to the manor and I saw it, picked it up, and promptly put it back down." I bumped Sadie's shoulder with my own. "You know you're a great Inheritor, just like you're a great librarian."

"I guess. I just feel so useless sometimes."

"Welcome to real life. We all don't get to be fairy queens, lounging around our castles."

Sadie giggled. "You know Mom didn't have a castle."

"I like to picture her that way. Rapunzel in her tower, waiting for Dad to rescue her."

"Yeah, right. If anything, Mom's the one that rescued Dad. Our mother is the original self-rescuing princess."

"That she is." I eyed Sadie and remembered all the scrapes we had gotten out of by the skin of our teeth, even before we came to the Otherworld. "You know we're just like her, right? We're both strong and smart enough to get past anything. Even Oriana."

Sadie sighed. "I hope you're right."

The sound of footsteps piqued our interest—Sadie and I turned to see that Aregonda had joined us, tentatively glancing between all of our faces.

"Please don't hold this against Jovanny," she said to no one in particular. "He only wants what's best for the resistance."

"Questioning someone's loyalty like that really isn't cool," I countered. "It was more like public humiliation."

"God knows I've had enough of that," Juliana muttered.

Aregonda frowned, upset that her apology went

largely unaddressed. I saw my opportunity to do as Dad asked. I motioned for Aregonda to approach me. "Does Jovanny always freak out like that?" I asked her, keeping my voice low. "I get that he wants what's best for his people, but Juliana's done nothing but help us."

"No, he doesn't usually behave that way, and I agree with you about Juliana," Aregonda replied promptly. "She's given us more information in a few weeks than we normally obtain in a year." She looked back at the resistance camp and bit her lip. "Things have been so hard for us ever since Baudoin was captured, especially for Jovanny. That's not an apology for him," Aregonda said when I raised my eyebrows. "He can make his own amends."

"He seems to rely on you for a lot," I told her. "Like, a lot."

"What exactly are you implying?"

"Jovanny may be the leader, but you keep the resistance running." I recalled the many times Aregonda had organized meals, made sleeping arrangements, and all the other small tasks that allowed Jovanny to sit in his tent and plot out campaigns. Only, Aregonda wasn't anyone's lackey. Now that we were standing close to each other, I could feel power coming off her in waves. "If he's the brains of the operation, you're the heart."

She smiled and ducked her head. "Thank you. I do what I can."

"What I can't figure out is why you joined the resistance in the first place."

"Why? Well, I joined for the same reasons you all did," she replied, tilting her head. "Elemental equality."

"But you seem like more of a sorceress than an Elemental," I observed aloud. "How did you learn how to call other elements? And teach others to call them?" I paused, then added, "And why do you think I can call them?"

"You yourself are more than just an Elemental," Aregonda said. "You merely need to unlock your potential."

"Why are you so concerned about Sara's potential?" Mom's question was sudden—one minute she was talking quietly with Dad, and the next she was coming to join us.

Aregonda blinked. "All Elementals have a propensity for magic. Is it wrong that I've helped Sara tap into hers, as I have my own?"

"You've more than tapped into it," Sadie remarked, standing a little behind Mom. "You toss magic around like cheap confetti. You're like Sara-powerful."

Everyone looked at me. "I—I have no idea what you're talking about," I stammered, glancing between their knowing faces.

"Yes, you do," Sadie insisted. "You've always been powerful, even when we were kids. Sometimes it's like you're more powerful than even Mom."

All eyes then turned to Mom, the Seelie Queen, who'd been in hiding since she ran off with my father. Sadie's face went completely red when she realized what she'd nearly let slip, and she slid completely out of view behind my mother. "Have you some talents, Maeve?" Aregonda asked almost *too* innocently, her eyes sparkling.

Mom smiled sweetly, which had always been her final warning before all hell broke loose. "Why, yes. I'm an excellent cook."

Aregonda smiled back with similar vehemence. "As am I. We should trade recipes."

"Set foot in my kitchen and I'll pluck out your eyes."

"What was that?"

"We should get back to the main camp," Dad interrupted, his voice cutting the tension immediately as he stepped between Aregonda and Mom. "Jovanny has been left to stew long enough. For all that he has no manners, today was a victory and I mean to treat it as such."

"I think I'll go back to the manor," Juliana told him, wrapping her arms around herself. "I've had enough hospitality for one day."

"I'll take you," Max offered.

I watched Max cast the portal and pull Juliana out of this world. I turned to Micah. "While I am one hundred percent on Juliana's side, Jovanny has a point. This operation does seem like a set up."

"Agreed," Micah said. "Our infiltration of the mades' prison was laughably easy."

"What do you think went wrong?" Dad asked, raising an eyebrow.

Micah frowned. "In my experience, whenever the leaders of an organization leave the moment before their pursuers arrive, they were warned."

Dad rubbed his chin. "It is my turn to agree. Someone in our organization is working with the Peacekeepers." Dad regarded Aregonda. "Or perhaps not. We have cause to believe Jerome Polonsky was interrogated for information."

"That would be a problem," Aregonda said, shaking her head. "A very big problem. Jerome knows . . . knew . . . almost as much as Jovanny and me. How certain are you?"

"He is certainly dead," Dad replied. "And Max mentioned seeing traces of truth serum on him. What we need to establish is exactly what he knew, and who or what could be compromised. Aregonda, will you speak to Jovanny and the rest, discover as much as you can?"

"I will. And Baudoin," she added, "please know that we're all glad you've returned to us. The resistance needs you."

"*Merci*, Aregonda," Dad said.

Aregonda nodded and returned to the main camp.

Once she was out of earshot, Mom said, "Important job for someone we hardly know."

"It's important we learn if we can trust her," Dad clarified gently. "We will see what she reports back. How much she reveals about the others will help us understand where her loyalties lie." Dad turned to me and asked, "Do we think Jerome is the only one who revealed information?"

"I don't know," I answered, my voice stilted as I tried not to think about Jerome, dead, pumped full of truth serum. I pushed the image from my mind. "No one else has been captured, at least not recently."

"One does not have to be captured to reveal information," Dad reminded us. "We must find out if Armstrong has other ways of divining our secrets."

"How else could he do that?"

"We will find out."

With that, Dad and Mom headed back toward the main camp. Micah and I moved to follow, but Sadie caught my arm.

"What do you really think of Aregonda?" she whispered.

"Tall, righteous, a bit old-fashioned," I ticked off. "And someone who doesn't need to know about Mom's prior royal status."

Sadie went beet red. "I just meant that Mom's powerful, not—anyway, that's beside the point. Have you noticed how familiar she is with all of us? It's like she knows us, only . . . she doesn't. Does she?"

I thought about how invested she was in my family, from being a stanch supporter of Dad to all the times she made sure Max, Sadie, and I were fed. "She is rather friendly."

"Is she a relation?" Micah asked. "She is of copper, and has the same name as your grandmother."

"That's just a coincidence." I glanced at Sadie, who shrugged. "Okay, maybe it isn't a coincidence. We'll figure it out?"

"How?" she asked.

"Not sure," I said. "But we will."

After yesterday's raid on the Armstrong facility and all the arguing and accusations that had happened afterward with the resistance, Micah and I spent the next morning lazing away in bed. He was lying on his stomach while I stroked the silver tendrils of his mark that arched across his shoulders and down the sides of his back. He was also pretending he was asleep. I didn't call him on the ruse; plenty of times I'd kept my eyes closed while he stroked the copper raven that marked me as an Elemental, enjoying the sensations for as long as possible. Besides, I liked petting him.

"I believe Sadie is correct," he said, revealing his wakeful state.

"Correct about what?"

Micah rolled onto his back, and I tucked myself against his side. He grabbed the hand that had been stroking him, glanced at it and said, "Let me have your other arm."

He meant my left arm, the one with the silver mark wound around its wrist. I took my time sliding across his body, settling myself against his right side while I extended the requested limb. Micah grasped my wrist, gliding his thumb across the ribbon of silver that marked the thin inner skin.

"You are not just an Elemental. You possess gifts unlike any Elemental I've ever met." When I just stared at him, he continued, "These marks we share are more than unique. To my knowledge, nothing like this has ever happened before."

"What about what Armstrong's doing, making Elementals?" I asked, remembering the crude marks that had been incised onto the mades' bodies.

"That is the work of a madman forcing an element where it does not belong. Elementals do not mark one another, nor do we share our elements willingly."

"Really?" I'd never heard of an Elemental marking another either, but I'd assumed that was because we didn't talk about magic where I came from. "I've always thought that our marks happened because I stayed underneath the silver with you." My spine shivered as I remembered how badly Micah had been injured, how the silverkin had buried him in silver in order to save him. "I bet people don't get buried in metal caves very often."

Micah shook his head. "Being immersed in one's element is a common enough tactic to heal a grave injury, both here and in your home world. Do you not recall your moving picture?"

I blinked. I knew which movie Micah was referring to since he'd only ever seen one, but I was still confused. "*The Creature from the Black Lagoon*?"

"Yes, the cursed waters," Micah replied. "What they referred to as a 'creature' was clearly a water Elemental. At the end of the adventure, he returned alone to the water's depths, ostensibly for healing. You would think that the Mundane scientists would have tried preventing that to keep him from menacing others."

Micah needed to watch more old movies. With critiques like this, he could run a killer review column. "You're saying that injured Elementals don't usually have company while they're healing?" I asked.

"Yes, exactly," he said, "and that is because one of another element is unlikely to survive such an ordeal. That caution extends to metal Elementals being buried in metals that are not their own." He pressed his lips to my silver mark. "You, my love, not only survived being buried in silver, but you marked me as yours with something beyond mere Elemental abilities. And you marked yourself as well."

"Well, you are mine, just like I'm yours." I laid my left wrist against his right one, silver mark aligned with copper. Since I didn't really agree with his or Sadie's opinions of my abilities, I changed the subject. "If we have a baby, will it be both copper and silver, since that's what we are now?"

Micah quirked a silver brow. "I thought children were not on your agenda."

I felt myself smile. "Lately, I've become more amenable to the idea."

"Have you?" Micah propped himself up on his elbow, then rolled me onto my back. "I can think of only one way to find an answer to your question."

"Oh?" It was my turn to quirk a brow. "And what way is that?"

"We make one, and in less than a year the babe himself will reveal the truth," he replied, trailing his lips across my jaw.

"Himself?" I said.

Micah nipped my jaw. "Or herself. I would love a daughter just the same."

"Almost a year is such a long time to wait," I said. I brought his right wrist up to my mouth and kissed his copper mark. "What if we don't make one right away?"

"Then we try again," he insisted, kissing his way from my neck to my breast. "And again, and again if need be."

He reached a ticklish spot and I giggled. "Don't take this the wrong way, but I like the idea of trying again and again."

"Do you?" Micah murmured, pressing a kiss between my breasts. "Good." He nudged my thighs apart with his knee and slid inside me. I wrapped my legs around his waist, and hoped we'd have to practice at least a few times before we got it right.

12

Max

The day after the raid on the mades' camp, Dad and I turned the dining room into a research office. Dad arrived armed with the heap of maps and notes that followed him wherever he went, while I brought my plucky attitude and biting wit.

"Tell me again how you found the Elementals," Dad prompted after we'd eaten. The silverkin had made me my usual plate of soft-boiled eggs with a cup of hot chicken broth, the only proteins I could handle without disastrous side effects. Still, I needed to find something more calorie-dense to incorporate into my diet before I wasted away to nothing.

"They were left behind like so much garbage," I replied.

"How many were there?"

"At least a dozen, along with Jerome." I watched Dad take notes. "Keeping a count?"

"*Oui*. Perhaps we can find their names and locate their families. While we cannot bring their loved ones back, we may be able to offer some closure."

"It is terrible, not knowing the fates of those you love," Ma said as she entered the room, Sadie following close behind. She wrapped her arms around Dad and glanced at his notes. "If you find their names, I might be able to fashion a locator spell for the next of kin."

Dad kissed her knuckles. "Always the soft-hearted one."

"Yeah, Mom's wicked soft," Sadie added wryly as she took the seat next to mine. "We can check the address logs, too."

"Magic is way more fun than an address log," I said, then Juliana entered the room and claimed the chair on my right. She brought her own pile of paperwork, and she looked like she hadn't slept a wink.

"Morning," I greeted. "You look exhausted."

She flashed me a quick smile. "Nothing caffeine won't fix. Can you look through these reports and flag anything that might relate to the made?"

She shoved a tower of paperwork at me. I eyed it warily, but eventually met her eyes and nodded. "Sure thing."

Sara and Micah made their way downstairs sometime after noon. "Nice of you two to join us," Dad commented, glancing only briefly up from his work.

"Planning for more war?" Sara asked, looking over the heap of maps and notes scattered on the table. "Shocking."

Dad smiled. "You sound like your mother."

They sat, and Shep delivered two plates filled with eggs and toast, and cups of coffee and tea. Sara ignored the food and went straight for the caffeine— no surprises there. "Are we still calling yesterday a victory?" she asked. I was interested in knowing how Dad would answer that one.

He leaned back in his chair and sighed. "I would like to. I wish we had known about Auster's where-abouts beforehand, if for no other reason than to keep Jovanny from holding it over us."

"Sorry," Juliana offered, and she really did look sheepish as she looked between Dad and Sara and me. "Langston hasn't deployed Auster in years. Still, I should have mentioned him."

"No apologies are necessary," Dad said, to my relief. "You have already given us so much information, and you cannot be expected to know the Peacekeepers' every move."

"Auster or no, can Jovanny really hold anything over you?" I asked. "I always thought *you* were the one in charge of the resistance."

Dad laughed through his nose. "Perhaps I was, once. However, with me being in the Otherworld and Jovanny remaining on-site, he is in a better position to be the sole leader, and that is for the best. He has kept our people alive and out of Armstrong's hands all these years. I could not have done any better. So yes, I consider yesterday a victory, and Jovanny worthy of his role."

"Something weird happened to Micah and me yesterday," Sara began. "While we were at the prison, we both got hit with these incredible migraines at the exact same time."

"Migraines?" Juliana repeated. "But Max didn't have one."

"What does Max have to do with it?"

"Uh, hello, I'm right here." I waved my hand in front of Sara's face and she rolled her eyes, swatting it away.

"Hang on." Juliana got up from the table and left the room.

Sara raised her eyebrows and motioned toward where Juliana ran off to. "What's that all about?" she asked me.

I shrugged. "Jules must have a lead on what happened."

Juliana returned carrying a tablet, a battery pack, and a bunch of cords.

"Where'd you get all that?" I asked.

"I've had the tablet for months, and the cords are from the solar set-up out back," she said as she plugged everything in. "I stole a few battery packs yesterday.

And this," she plugged in a data cartridge, "is Mike's research." While the tablet read the data, she scrutinized Sara and Micah. I scrutinized the battery packs. I'd been watching Jules like a hawk, and I never saw her lift those. When did she manage to do it?

"These headaches were painful?" Juliana prompted, her eyes flitting away from Micah and Sara to fleetingly skim the screen.

"Beyond painful," Sara replied. "It felt like someone was ripping my brain in half."

"Agreed," Micah said. "I have never experienced the like."

"That's because you've never been in range of this." Juliana tapped a few commands, then turned the tablet's screen toward us. It held an image of a fitted cap with a chin strap, and the sides and top were covered with electrodes.

"And that is?" Sara asked.

"Mike's dreamwalking helmet," Juliana replied.

"Huh." I angled myself so I could get a better look at the image. "The old bastard really did it."

"Sort of," Juliana clarified. "Mike's goal is to become a Dreamwalker, but he can't figure out how to do that. The helmet lets him tap into other Dreamwalkers, sort of like a mental spy."

Micah put his hand on Sara's as she spoke, her eyes wide. "Someone really was trying to rip our brains apart . . . Wait, did Mike read our minds?"

Juliana shook her head. "Probably not. He figured out how to send information, like pain, but the helmet's not good at receiving from a distance. You would have to be within a few feet of the helmet for the wearer to discern any thoughts."

"Oh, good," Sara said halfheartedly. "We *probably* weren't compromised."

"Why wasn't I affected?" I asked.

"I think Mike used the helmet while we were in the underground offices," Juliana replied without a moment's hesitation, seeing me tense and shift toward her in as subtle a warning as I could manage much too late for it to make any kind of difference. Ah well. She was honest. A good trait more than a bad one, to me.

"Underground offices . . . ?" Dad narrowed his eyes at Juliana, who went a lovely shade of red as she realized her mistake. "Was that part of your assignment?"

"My fault." I spoke up so quickly it was obvious that it had been Juliana's idea to not follow the mission. I couldn't stop myself. There was no way I was going to just sit and watch Dad tear into her. "All my fault. I was hoping we could catch Armstrong."

Dad eyed me, but he tactfully let the matter drop. For now. "You were saying, Juliana?"

"The helmet doesn't have much of a range," she continued, frowning a bit, thinking. "It also means that while we were looking for him in the tunnels, Mike was above ground, escaping."

"Are there many Dreamwalkers in the resistance?" Sadie asked. "We all think someone's leaking information, but maybe no one betrayed Jovanny. Maybe Mike snuck in their dreams and stole information."

"Maybe that's what happened with Jerome," Sara offered. "The Truthmages knew he was lying, but Mike kept him around until he learned all he could from him."

"That would explain his death," I said. "Armstrong left his body as a warning."

"Is there a high mortality rate with this helmet?" Sara asked Juliana.

"Very high," she replied, her voice getting soft. "Well over half of Mike's test subjects perished. I know of two who went catatonic."

I swallowed hard. Of all the tests I'd tried to forget, the helmet was one of the worst. Being a Dreamwalker meant I'd been inside other people's minds many times, and had them in mine, but we Dreamwalkers always kept our presences away from the host's thoughts. When Mike used the helmet on me, he'd forced his way into my brain, ripping apart memories and rending my sense of self. It was far worse than any of Langston's physical tortures, and it hadn't left a visible mark on me.

Juliana glanced at me, and whatever she saw made her turn the helmet schematics over. "Only the strongest Dreamwalkers survived," she said, nudging my foot under the table. I nudged back.

Dad swore in French. "He is using our own minds against us, and we sit here eating brunch. We should be searching for him now. I should have remained in the Mundane realm until he and his assistant, Phillips, were captured."

Mom slid her hand across Dad's shoulder. "Perhaps we should consider going home."

"We are home," Sara began, but she abruptly stopped, reading our faces. The manor was home for her and Micah, sure, but not for me. Not for Mom and Dad, or for Sadie and Juliana either, we were all just hiding out here from a madman.

Micah drew his hand along the back of Sara's neck. "All of you are welcome to stay as long as you need to," he insisted. "And once you reclaim the Raven Compound, I hope you will consider Silverstrand Manor your second home."

"Thank you, Micah," Dad said. "That means the world to me."

"If you're all going back to the Mundane world," Sara interjected, trying very hard not to sound bitter, "maybe that means Sadie doesn't have to pledge to Oriana at all."

"Sounds good to me," Sadie piped up, shrugging her slender shoulders.

"What I don't understand is why Oriana's so bent on Sadie, but not Dad or Ma," I said. "No offense, Sadie, but Dad's got way more pull than you do."

"None taken." Sadie smiled tightly. "I think she only wants my pledge because it will give her an ego boost to have another Inheritor as her subject. Although, you'd think that would make her go after Mom, too."

"Oriana, go after me?" Ma posed, her lips quirking upward as if she were just about to laugh. "I would like to see her try."

"Can I ask a question?" Juliana ventured. "I mean, you guys already know everything about me."

"Of course," Dad replied. "I was not exaggerating when I told Jovanny that you are like a daughter to me. Please, Juliana, ask away."

Juliana pursed her lips, glancing between Sara and me. Finally, she turned to Ma. "*What* are you?"

Ma cocked her head to the side. "Pardon?"

"You're obviously powerful, more so than Micah and even Sara," Juliana continued. "Powerful enough to keep the patriarch of the Raven clan in check."

Dad looked positively pleased by that description.

"And you're not an Elemental, or any kind of magical creature I've ever studied," Juliana continued. "You're something different, something more than all the rest. Am I correct?"

Ma looked at Juliana for what felt like forever, then said to me, "You did say she was brilliant."

"I might be a fool, but I can see what's right in front of me," I responded, motioning toward Juliana.

"You've known me for years, Juliana," Mom continued. "Why ask me about this now?"

"For one, there's much less of a threat of Mike torturing me for information about your family," Juliana explained, curling in on herself a bit while she did.

I set down my coffee. "Did that really happen?"

"Yeah. A few times." Juliana looked back at Ma. "There you have it, I bled for you and your children. Does that get me into the secret club?"

"Gods, Mom, just tell her," Sadie urged.

"I am a queen of Connaught," Ma said, drawing herself up. "And of other places, as well."

"She's the Seelie Queen," Sara added. "Dad snuck into her fairy castle and stole her. Dad, you should tell that story after dinner."

"Perhaps I shall," he murmured. "And I went *underhill* for Maeve, not to a 'castle.'"

"Wait," Juliana gasped suddenly. "Are you the same Maeve that defeated Eleanore?"

Ma smiled. "Why, yes. You've heard of me?"

Juliana looked from Ma, to me, and finally Dad. "Why are you even bothering with the resistance? She alone has the power to level the Peacekeepers!"

"I'm not nearly powerful enough to dismantle an entire organization," Ma scoffed. "While I am formidable on the battlefield, I'm still only one woman."

"Also, this is not truly her fight," Dad replied. "We Elementals have been trying to bring about change in

Pacifica for decades, since long before I met Maeve. This fight belongs to Elementals, and we need to win it on our own terms."

Juliana nodded. "I get that. Still, what a fantastic ace in the hole to have."

Ma leaned back in her chair and regarded Juliana. "While I do let my husband and our children fight their own battles, rest assured that I will no longer remain on the sidelines as I once did. Now that my family is reunited, I mean to keep us together."

Sara placed her hand on top of Micah's and squeezed. She understood exactly how Ma felt, and so did I. Now that Dad was back and we were a complete family again, there was no way I'd let anyone change that.

I slid my gaze toward Juliana. She was shuffling through her massive stack of papers, always working, always trying to make the world a better place. We all considered her family. I hoped she felt the same about us.

One of the silverkin brought Micah a message. "I have business in the village," Micah said. "If you'd prefer that I remain here with you, I will send another."

"We'll be fine," Sara told him. "Will you be back for dinner?"

"I plan to return long before then." Micah kissed Sara's temple, then nodded toward the rest of us. "Send for me if you need anything."

"We will," Sara said.

Dad stood. "I promised Jovanny I would stop by. Max, you said you wanted to come with?"

"That I do." I looked at my sisters. "Either of you want to head over to the resistance with us?"

"Sure," Sara agreed just as Sadie blurted out, "Not really."

Sara glanced at Sadie. "Want me to stay here?"

"Go," Sadie insisted, poking at Sara with a finger. "I'll be fine in the library."

I glanced at Juliana. "Want anything from the Promenade? Wait, let me guess. More ink?"

"Ink *and* paper," Sadie corrected me. Her smile lit up her whole face, and it made me want to smile, too. I'd bring back whatever she wanted to keep her that happy. "Maybe some pens, too. And magazines?"

"Magazines it is," I confirmed. "Let's see what's happening with the resistance today."

"I wish Micah was here," Sara grumbled as we trudged down the hill toward the resistance camp.

"Miss him already?" I teased.

"I don't trust these guys, and Micah doesn't either." Dad glanced over his shoulder when he heard her, and Sara pointedly added, "Well, can you blame me?"

"No, I cannot," Dad said. "Trust must be earned. If Jovanny has not earned your trust, that is his failing, not yours."

"Do you trust him?" I asked. "And what about Aregonda?"

"Once, I trusted Jovanny with my life," Dad explained, sighing. "I still want to, but as you know, I am a paranoid old fool. As for Aregonda, she is a new commodity for me."

I mustered every ounce of my sarcasm. *"That bodes well."*

We reached the edge of the camp. Unlike previous visits, no one asked us our business or scowled at us. If anything, they made way for us. It seemed that no matter what Jovanny thought about yesterday's mission, his followers considered it a success.

"Baudoin," Jovanny called as he walked toward us. He was wearing yet another set of military fatigues. I wondered if he was once in the Mirlanders' army. "Am I glad to see you!"

"Good morning, Jovanny," Dad greeted, the corners of his mouth quirking into a grin. "Although you're only ever happy to see me when you have a problem for me to solve."

Jovanny simultaneously laughed and grimaced, but he didn't dispute Dad's claim. "It's the made. They're recovering well, but we don't have any sort of long-term plan for them."

"Are the elements leaving them?" Sara asked.

"Not all of them," Jovanny replied. "Only the water made have truly reverted. Some are not faring well at all. Would the two of you like to visit them?"

Sara glanced at me. I shrugged. "Um, sure."

"Go ahead," Dad said. "I will catch up."

Jovanny gestured toward a large tent near the center of the camp, and Sara and I made our way toward it. "He didn't waste any time getting rid of us," I said to her.

"Fine with me," Sara replied. "He creeps me out almost as much as Aregonda does."

Guards were still posted at the entrance to the tent—whether to protect the made from the resistance or the other way around, I didn't know. One of them held aside the flap that covered the entrance, and Sara and I were soon among those we'd rescued only a day prior. A chalkboard was set up near the entrance; it listed the made we'd rescued, grouping them by element. There were seventeen metal, five earth and stone, five air, three water, and one fire.

"Thirty-one made," I muttered. "I thought there were more."

"There were."

Sara and I turned toward the new voice. He was a burly guy with a blond buzz cut, and he looked more like he should be on a Peacekeeper recruitment poster than hanging out on resistance grounds.

"What happened to the rest?" Max asked.

"They were fire, and they burned up from the inside out," Buzz Cut replied. "Right in front of us, they turned to ashes."

"There's got to be some way we can help," Sara said. "Max, didn't Juliana think she could reverse what was done to them?"

"*You* can reverse it," Buzz Cut said to Sara. I opened my mouth to ask why he would even think such a thing, but Sara spoke up first.

"You were one of the water made," she said.

"Yes, and you fixed us," Buzz Cut insisted, and it didn't seem like Sara had anything to say to contradict him. I looked over at her, surprised. She was always doing some wild thing or another with her power that nobody could predict, and of course it was always when I wasn't around to try and help. Go figure.

Buzz Cut pressed on, his brow creased, and as he came closer to Sara I moved a bit in front of her. "Can't you do the same with fire?" he asked.

"I don't know," Sara replied. "I don't even know how I did it with you." He frowned, and I realized that he wasn't just asking for help. He was begging.

I took him by the shoulder and met his eyes. "What's your name?"

"Noah," he replied. "The other two water—well, those who *were* water—are Alexander and Finn."

"And the fire?" I prompted. "What's his name?"

"Eddie." Noah glanced over his shoulder toward a screened-off area on the far side of the tent. "Can you at least have a look at him?"

I looked at Sara, and she shrugged. "Of course."

Noah led Sara and me toward the back of the tent. The fire made, Eddie, wasn't lying on a cot like the rest, but in a tub of ice water. Someone had thought that cooling him down was the way to fix him.

"That's not gonna work," I said, shaking my head. "Get him out of the water."

"The water's the only thing keeping him from burning up," Noah countered.

"The ice is making him burn hotter!" I moved to grab Eddie, but Alexander and Finn blocked me. I felt my heart rate quicken and my body instinctively brace for a fight, but that wasn't going to help anything. It took a second, but I managed a deep, slow breath.

"Listen, I was born an Elemental," I began. "I know a thing or two about how this works. Fire craves heat. Warm him up, get him near some flames. That's what he needs."

Noah looked at Sara. "Come on, there's a fire outside," she said, beckoning toward the tent flap.

Finn and Alexander hoisted Eddie out of the tub and carried him out of the tent and toward the central fire. Per my instructions they laid him right on the edge of the fire, so close that ashes smeared across his still-wet legs.

"Are you sure this is going to work?" Sara whispered to me.

"When I was in the Institute, there was a fire Elemental," I replied. "She taught me a lot about other elements. Hell, she taught me about metal."

"Was she an Inheritor?"

"I don't know. The less we knew about each other's lives, the longer we tended to live." I kept my voice neutral, calm and still as a lake. Inside, I was a mess. The Elementals at the Institute, we'd been our own family. And we were torn from each other one by one.

"What was her name?" Sara asked.

"Illyana," I answered. "Illyana Petrovsky."

"You two were friends?"

I laughed through my nose. "Not even remotely. When I got to the Institute, she'd already been there for years. Most of them got there before me. It was like Langston was trying to create a perfect set of Elemental abilities. I remember him saying I was the only metal who'd survived the initiation process."

"Initiation? Like into a club?"

"Like into hell." I kicked up a few pebbles. "Anyway, Illyana was tough. She wasn't friendly, or nice, but she was the toughest, smartest person in there."

"You miss her?"

I cleared my throat. "Every day."

We turned our attention to Eddie as he lay next to the flames. It wasn't long before it was obvious that I was right. As the heat of the fire burned off the excess water, Eddie's limbs went from a pallid gray to healthy pink.

"Turn him around," I directed. "He needs the heat on his arms and his chest."

Finn and Alexander sat Eddie up. I noticed that Eddie's blond hair had a half inch of orange roots; he'd dyed it so he wouldn't look like a fire Elemental. Sara once told me that she and Sadie used to dye their copper-colored hair dirt brown and hide their marks. Maybe the made and Elementals and even Peacekeepers weren't so different after all.

Huh. How ironic that Eddie had naturally orange hair and Armstrong tried to make him into a fire Elemental.

In no time, Eddie's eyes were open, and he looked like he might make it.

"Thank you," Alexander stammered, first looking at Sara, but then remembering I was y'know, *there*. "Both of you. You saved the three of us, and now Eddie. Thank you."

"You're welcome," Sara said. She glanced at me. I frowned and shook my head. We moved out of earshot from the rest.

"That was a damn fast recovery," I told her in a low voice.

"You acted like you thought that would work," Sara said.

"I did, and it did," I began, "but it shouldn't have worked this fast. Remember when Micah was buried in silver? It took him weeks to fully recover, and he's way more powerful than one of Armstrong's people."

I looked toward Eddie, who was sitting up and smiling, and his recovery made even less sense. After Micah had dug himself out of the silver cairn, he'd been so weak he'd needed the silverkin to carry him around the manor. Even drawing on the vein of silver that ran beneath the Whispering Dell had hardly strengthened him. Yet here was Eddie, all healed up and fresh as a daisy.

"I think we need to keep an eye on Eddie," I muttered. "The rest of the made, too."

Sara nodded. "I think you're right."

After Eddie was settled and resting peacefully, Sara and I sought out Noah.

"How are you doing?" I asked him. "Are there any, ah, aftereffects from the water?"

"Not yet," Noah answered. "Who knows, though? Maybe a wave will come crashing out of my ear or something."

I glanced at Sara, unsure if that was a joke or if Noah really was worried about water gushing from his head. I cleared my throat and said, "Elements don't really work that way."

"Thank frickin' God." Noah rubbed the back of his neck. "Listen, thanks for helping us yesterday, and

Eddie today. When we signed up for this, I had no idea I might drown in my own body."

"You actually signed up?" I said, surprised. "Is that how you ended up at the facility?"

"We were recruited, just like the rest of the squad," Noah replied. "You've seen the posters. 'Serve your country. Pacifica needs you.'" He smirked. "Maybe you two didn't pay much attention to those."

"No, we didn't." I took a deep breath, the wheels turning in my mind. "Are you saying that Mike recruited you from Peacekeeper ranks, and then he experimented on you?"

"Yeah, but he didn't say he'd make us into freaks. No offense," he added.

"None taken," I said. "Then how did he convince you to do this?"

"He said we'd be super-soldiers," Noah explained. "He said we'd be an elite squad, no other Peacekeepers like us. That we could protect all the innocent citizens from Elementals."

I gave him a good, long look. I was no stranger to prejudice directed at Elementals by uninformed Mundanes, but I was unaccustomed to having polite conversations with the people who had actively sought my death. "How does it feel that one of those freaks saved your life?"

"Do you know how it feels to drown inside your own body?" Noah shot back. "The water . . . It was everywhere, in my lungs, my mouth. So much was in my eyes that I couldn't see straight, and it was up in my ears. Every time I opened my mouth, it was like a river poured out of me. It was everywhere. And then you took it." Noah looked Sara in the eye. "You saved me, when you had no reason to."

"You needed help, so I helped," she said simply. I felt a swell of pride in my chest. *That's my sister.* "What will you do now?"

Noah shrugged. "I guess whatever you tell me to do."

"Why would I tell you to do anything?"

"Haven't we been captured?"

"We don't take prisoners," I clarified.

Noah's mouth became a grim line. "Then why did you bother with all of this? Why not just let the water finish me off?"

I laughed. "We're not executioners either. Once you've recovered, you and your buddies are free. Live your life, hate on Elementals. Whatever."

"I never said I hated—" Noah began.

"But if I were you," I spoke over him, cutting him off, "I'd think long and hard about what just happened over the past couple days. Think about who hurt you, and who saved you. And I'd think about maybe joining the good guys."

Noah glanced from Sara to me and nodded. "I will. I'll talk to the others, too."

I nodded, then we left Noah alone with his thoughts.

"You want to recruit the made?" Sara asked once we were outside. "Is that a good idea?"

"What we need are people who know firsthand how evil Mike is," I told her. "People who can go out and sway others to our side. Until now, we had only me, Dad, and Jules. But if word gets out that Mike did this to his own men, it could change everything."

"I guess it could." Sara looked back at the tent. "It's a good way to keep tabs on them, too."

"Mmm hmm." I cracked my knuckles. "Something's not right about them. I mean, nothing's right about any this, but there's something else. Something deeper, and we need to figure out what's going on."

"Do you think Mike used that Dreamwalker helmet on any of them?"

My jaw tightened. "I sure hope not."

"I noticed something else. The earth made we rescued are not the same people from the rally. Mike has at least one more group out there, maybe more."

"I'll talk to Jules, see if she can dig a location out of the data she's been working on. Don't worry, Sara. We'll find them all, and we'll help every single one that can be helped."

Sara's face brightened, just like I knew it would. "That's right. We will."

After Sara had checked in with all of the made—all that was left of them, anyway—we met up with Dad and portaled back to the Otherworld. Sara and I had agreed not to mention our conversation with Noah near Jovanny. I didn't know how Jovanny really felt about the made, and I didn't need him shooting down my ideas before I'd had the chance to fully explore them.

"Sara and I had some fun with the made," I began as we stepped into the Otherworld. By the time we'd reached the manor, Sara and I had told Dad everything that had happened with Noah and his friends, and how we'd helped Eddie.

"Interesting," Dad said once he'd heard everything. "Neither one of you knew that Armstrong was conscripting his own people for these experiments?"

Sara shook her head. "I've never heard a word about it. Back when I was a cubicle monkey, everyone thought becoming a Peacekeeper was an honorable path to take, like you were protecting people."

Dad snorted. "I suppose, if you choose to protect some and not all. Max, were any of these experiments done at the Institute?"

"Yeah," I confirmed, wincing. "There was a pretty high failure rate, especially in the beginning. Mike either got lucky with this batch, or he made some major advances in research."

Sara shuddered. "Failure rate? That's horrific."

"It was."

Dad patted Sara's arm. "Max, how well do you remember those early attempts?"

"Permanently burned on the backs of my eyelids. Why?"

"I want you to consider becoming a liaison between the made and the resistance."

Sara laughed—until she realized Dad and I weren't laughing with her. "Seriously?"

"Who better than Max, one who suffered directly at Armstrong's hand, to help others who were oppressed?" Dad posed. "Both Mundanes and Elementals need to work together to save Pacifica."

"Actually, that's a good idea," Sara agreed. "With Max as a figurehead, he can appeal to both sides. He's been away so long that no Mundanes remember who he is, other than how Peacekeepers took him when he was still a kid. It could work."

"What do you think?" Dad asked me. "Will you consider such a role?"

"I can do that," I said with my usual bravado. My stomach was doing cartwheels. "In fact, I've got some ideas."

"Already?" Dad prompted. "Please. Tell us."

"Start with the made," I began. "Once we have a solid plan for helping them, they are the ones who can recruit more members. No offense, Dad, but going after only Elementals isn't the way to beat Armstrong."

"Juliana's one of our best assets, and she's Mundane," Sara added.

"Damn right, she is," I said. "That's the thing—there are way more Mundanes than Elementals, and they don't seem to like Peacekeepers much, either. For as long as I can remember, the resistance has been working against Peacekeepers but avoiding Mundanes entirely. Imagine what we could accomplish if we worked together."

"Victory," Dad declared. "Victory, and an end to this conflict. *Mon fils*, you make me proud."

"Yeah, well. It was Sara's idea, too."

Sara swatted my arm. "Take a compliment, for once."

"There are two other things," Dad continued. "For one, Jovanny still suspects we have a mole."

"You think someone in the resistance ratted us out to Armstrong?" I said. "Who would even do that?" Dad gave me a long look. I clenched my fist. "That bastard accused Juliana, didn't he?"

"He did," Dad replied. "I defended her. Not only do I not doubt Juliana's character, but the simple fact is that she had no opportunity to alert Armstrong, or anyone else, about our plans. It isn't as if she could have picked up a telephone at the manor and called them."

"You sure Micah doesn't have a stealth phone company behind the solar panels?" I teased, elbowing Sara.

"We can all agree Juliana's innocent," Sara said as she gave me some side-eye. "Did Jovanny name any other suspects? What about one of the made? What about the creepy dreamwalking helmet?"

"What about Jerome Polonsky?" Dad countered.

"Oh, Sara's boyfriend?" I asked. Sara smacked my arm. "Ow!"

"You deserved that for speaking lies about the dead," Sara snapped. "I guess we really don't know what Armstrong got out of him."

"We do not," Dad said. "Sara, I would like you to write down everything you know about this Jerome. Perhaps if we can establish a list of his known associates, we can determine what information may have been compromised."

"Okay," Sara replied, nodding. "I'll start on that now." She hurried toward the manor while Dad and I hung back.

"So, you are going to recruit the made to our cause," Dad offered. "A noble task."

"It is, isn't it?" I asked with a chuckle that hopefully seemed more self-assured than nervous. "I'm kind of shocked I came up with it. I don't know, though. Might be too big a cause for a guy like me."

"You will not be alone," Dad insisted. "You will have your family, the resistance, and your Juliana helping you. If we can bring even one to our side, it will be a great win."

I felt my face heat up. "Yeah, uh, she's not 'my' Juliana."

Dad clapped my shoulder. "Even so, I have every confidence in you."

We stood there for a second, smiling like fools. Then we walked the rest of the way to the manor. It felt good to be praised by Dad.

It felt even better to have a cause I could really get behind.

13

Sara

Despite Dad's specific request, I didn't write down any-thing about Jerome. I know, bad daughter. Instead, I decided to work on calling other elements.

It all started when I went to the kitchens for a snack. The silverkin kept the fire going in the hearth day and night, and I paused to watch the flames. The fire was this beautiful, unbridled energy, and I got to thinking: weren't all elements forms of energy? Granted, fire was pretty blatant about it, whereas metal and even stone fell under *potential* energy, but it was energy all the same. If the same energy was present in each ele-ment, then why couldn't I control them all? I mean, I had controlled water more than once.

"Only one way to find out," I muttered. I called to the fire . . . and accidentally incinerated the stool I was sitting on.

I'd wielded enough control over the fire to keep myself from being burned, and Shep assured me that the stool wasn't a priceless family heirloom. Then he presented me with a plate of cookies and shooed me out to the garden. The help had kicked me out of my own house.

I spent the rest of the afternoon wandering among the hedgerows and manipulating a few bits of stone I found in the garden; working with fire was great and all, but I needed better control before I tried handling living flames again. Since Max had done such a great job teaching me about metal, I approached working with the stones the same way. It took a long time, and the entire plate of cookies, before I'd flattened the rounded stones into three smooth discs.

And now what do I do with them? Deciding I needed to confer with someone who knew more about Elemental abilities than me, I pocketed the stones and set out to find Micah. He found me first, walking up the lane as he returned from the village.

"Have you been back long?" he asked.

"Not super long," I replied. "I've been trying to work with other elements."

"Have you? Which ones have you worked on?"

"I made some flat stones." I presented him with the three smooth, cool discs, and specifically did not mention my escapade with fire. I hoped the silverkin had swept away all the ashes.

Micah turned the stones over in his hands. "This is very good work," he said at last. "Most would never know these stones weren't naturally flat."

"Most? Who would be able to figure it out?"

He grinned. "Me, for one. I feel the essence of you on them."

"Oh." I'd never thought about my essence or anyone else's, and I'd certainly never felt one. Or had I? Micah's fingerprints were all over the manor, and everything inside and out reflected him. I'd always felt safe inside its silver walls, but now I wondered if I'd been sensing Micah all along.

Micah pressed the stone discs into my hand. "Which element would you like to work with next?"

I blinked. "You don't think it's weird I can do this?"

"On the contrary, I think it is fantastic."

"Oh. Um." I hadn't been seeking Micah's approval, but I couldn't deny that it meant the world to me. "I'm not really sure what to try next. Want to take a walk and see what we find?"

Micah extended his arm. "I would love to."

I tucked my hand into his elbow, and we were off. As we walked among the roses and sweetbriars, I told Micah everything that had happened earlier, including how Max and I had saved Eddie from bursting into flames.

"Interesting," Micah murmured, thinking aloud. "As I recall, none of the fire made had such difficulties yesterday, yet all but this Eddie have now perished?"

"Supposedly, we barely saved Eddie," I said. "Now that I think about it, he didn't seem like he was about to spontaneously combust."

"A more pressing concern is why their abilities were affected today, yet were fine yesterday," Micah added. "An outside force must have acted upon them."

"Are you saying someone may have murdered the other two?"

"I am. But who would bother with such a ruse? Armstrong?"

"Maybe. Or maybe there really is a double agent in the resistance." I turned the facts over in my mind. "It makes sense that the fire made eventually burned up. Max said it happened often at the Institute."

"Then, what makes Eddie different?" Micah asked.

Suddenly, my whole body was chilled, as if a cold gust of wind had zeroed in on my neck and slithered down my spine. But the morning air was still without even a hint of a breeze . . . *Where did that come from?* I stopped walking and rubbed my arms.

"What is it, love?" Micah put his hand on my arm, only to flinch away from the coldness of my skin. Before I could answer him, we were hit by a shockwave. Completely silent, it packed the force of a hurricane as it pushed Micah against me and then threw both of us to the ground.

A moment later the wave was gone, having left behind no evidence save a few leaves fluttering to the ground and the gently swaying rosebushes.

"What was that?" I asked at the same time Micah demanded, "Why are you so cold?" We stared at each other for a moment, then I replied, "I don't know. All of a sudden, I was just . . . frigid."

Micah searched my face for a moment longer, then rolled off of me and into a sitting position. "That wave was magic," he said as he pulled me upright and began chafing my hands. "Powerful magic."

I nodded, my thoughts clearing as Micah rubbed warmth back to my limbs. If the wave was caused by magic, and it had pushed Micah into me . . . I looked behind him, my breath catching in my throat. "Micah, it came from the manor."

We were running in an instant, Micah muttering under his breath about Max's occasional experiments as we crossed the gardens. When we reached the door, we saw Max emerge from the orchards, which were in the opposite direction from the manor.

"What the hell was that?" Max shouted.

"We don't know," I replied, and we followed Micah into the manor. We'd just made it inside the atrium when Mom and Dad came running from the rear of the house.

"Was Juliana with you?" I asked Max.

"No," he replied. "I don't know where she is."

Dad pointed upward. "The magic came from above."

Mom's gaze skated around the room. Then she ran up the stairs. I was about to ask what she was looking for, when I realized who else wasn't accounted for. Sadie.

I was still on the stairs when I heard Mom scream as she flung the library door open. Then she started sobbing. Dad entered the room right behind Mom, shouting Sadie's name and begging her to open her eyes. Even with those warnings, nothing could have prepared me for what was in that room.

Sadie was in the center of her library, lying face up on the floor. Blackened soot streaked her face and hands, the skin underneath pale and dull. Even her hair looked faded, devoid of that shimmer I'd always been so jealous of. Mom had Sadie's head in her lap while Dad grasped her hands. It wasn't until Max shoved past me and the color drained from his face that I truly understood what I was looking at.

"What's going on?" said a voice from behind me. I turned around and saw Juliana coming up the stairs. "I felt the shockwave, and—"

"I think my sister's dead," I mumbled. Mom wailed even louder, as if my saying it had made it real. In a way, I guess it had.

"Oh, Sara," Juliana said softly, leaning to the side as she tried to see into the room around me. "Are you sure? If it was magic, then maybe—"

"Where were you?" I demanded.

"What?" Juliana countered. "You don't really think—"

"I don't know what to think!"

"Love," Micah murmured, drawing me against his chest and away from Juliana. "Do not lash out in grief at one who only seeks to give comfort."

I turned to face Micah, the grief in his own eyes speaking to mine. It was then that I noticed how much I was trembling, chilled for reasons other than the cold. I let him wrap his arms around me and struggled to tamp down my tears. There would be time for crying later. First, we had to figure out what did this. If there was any way to fix it.

"I'm sorry," I whispered to Juliana. "I . . . I didn't mean that."

"I know." Juliana touched my hand. She entered the library and stood beside Max. Micah and I followed her, me trying and failing to not look at Sadie's body.

Gods. Sadie's *body*.

"What happened here?" I rasped. "How did someone get in here to cast a spell?"

"I do not think anyone did," Dad mumbled, his voice thick with grief. Without looking away from Sadie, he held out his hand. I slipped out of Micah's arms and knelt beside him, letting him wrap an arm around my shoulders while he kept a firm hold on Mom with his other hand.

"Look," Dad said, nodding toward Sadie's right hand. In it was a tightly clutched a piece of paper with Sadie's writing scrawled across it. "Whatever this spell was, she cast it herself."

I looked around the library, Sadie's library, and saw that Dad was right. There was a circle set with candles and little dishes of herbs on the floor, though the blast had flung some of the props out of the pattern. Whatever Sadie had called up, it had been too strong for the circle to contain.

"Why did she do this?" I whispered. "Sadie didn't want anything to do with magic." A tear rolled down my cheek and splashed onto Sadie's sooty hand. "If she had to use magic for something, why didn't she ask one of us for help?" I wiped at the clear track on my cheek with the back of my hand.

Why?

Mom and Dad tried every trick they knew to reverse whatever Sadie had done, but nothing helped. Their biggest obstacle was that since Sadie had acted alone, none of us knew what she was trying to accomplish, and therefore we didn't understand how to reverse it. When dawn broke, Mom admitted that whatever Sadie had done was beyond her ability to fix. But that didn't mean she was admitting defeat.

With Dad's assistance, they brought Sadie's body to her bedroom. Mom cast an inertia spell over the room so everything would remain unchanged while we investigated what had happened. No one was ready to give up on Sadie.

After the spell was cast, we all went out to the gardens; it was too much to stay in the manor with a corpse, even if that corpse happened to be my sister. We ended up in the rose garden near the memorial for Micah's mother.

"Should we bury Sadie next to your mother?" I asked, my voice wavering.

"Hush." Micah wrapped his arms around my waist and kissed the back of my neck, two acts that normally would have made me melt into his arms, or at least lean into his embrace. I couldn't even move. "We are not there yet."

"What else can we really do?"

"I don't know, but we will find out. We will try everything, and once we've exhausted all measures here in the Otherworld we will move on to the Mundane realm, and any other realm needed. We will not give up."

I stared at the statue of Selene Silverstrand. Micah had lost his mother so young, and even with all of his power and influence as the Lord of Silver, he couldn't bring her back. What was the point behind all of this—Elementals, the Raven's feathers, all of this magic—if we couldn't even save the people we loved?

"I feel like I'm going to shatter," I croaked.

"You won't," Micah murmured, tightening his arms around me. "I will hold you together."

Behind me, my brother laughed. "What exactly is funny?" I demanded.

"Nothing. Nothing at all." Max's back was rigid, his fists clenched at this sides. "You know what's really not funny? I've spent my entire life trying to keep her safe. I did everything I could think of to protect her. I scared off bullies. I went into the goddamned Institute for her," his voice had gotten louder and louder, until his yelling echoed across the grounds, "and now she's dead anyway!"

"Maybe we can—"

"Maybe nothing." Max dragged his sleeve across his face. "It's over. It's all over."

Juliana put her hand on Max's shoulder. He pulled her against him, his face buried in her hair as his shoulders shook. I glanced to my left and saw Mom weeping against Dad's chest.

"Why is it over?" I said, to no one. To everyone. "It can't be."

Juliana maneuvered around Max so she could see me and grabbed my hand. "I'm so sorry," she offered, giving my hand a gentle squeeze. "I would bring her back if I could."

"I know. I know you would." Max looped his arm around me so I was mashed against him and Juliana. I hated it when my big brother cried.

After we stood that way for a few minutes, I said, "I can't stop wondering why she did it."

Juliana glanced at me. "You really don't know?"

Max stepped back and scrubbed his face with his hands. "None of us do. Sadie never, not once, worked with any magic beyond her own abilities. What I really don't understand is why she would have worked a spell this complex without asking one of us for help." He blew out a breath. "Damn it. I should have asked her more questions about those books she got from the village."

Juliana shook her head and leaned against me. Micah looped his arm around us. All of this love was stifling. If Micah and Max actually hugged my head might explode.

I just wanted to hug my sister.

"Sadie was a research geek," Juliana commented, looking back at the manor. "She had one of the most brilliant minds I've ever come across."

"Yeah," I agreed, because it was true.

"She wouldn't have gone into this without some careful planning," Juliana continued. "That must have been what she was doing with all of the books she got from the village. She read about whatever she'd wanted to do, probably took notes—"

"Notes we can read," Max and I finished at the same time. He glanced at me, and I nodded.

"Jules, will you help me?" Max asked. "Will you help me find out what happened to my sister?"

Juliana looked up at him, her dark eyes shining. "I will."

The day after we put Sadie in stasis dawned as gray and as cold as my heart.

After I dragged myself out of bed, I went downstairs and found Mom and Dad sitting at the kitchen table, thumbing through spellbooks. There were empty coffee cups and wine glasses strewn between them, and I didn't know if they were trying to drink their pain away or caffeinate themselves beyond reason.

Not that I blamed them. Nearly every choice they had made over the last twenty years had been about keeping Sadie safe. Not only because she was the Inheritor of Metal, but because she was their daughter. Their baby. My sister.

I left my parents to their own devices and had Shep bring some tea and toast up to my room. Micah and I settled on the window seat that overlooked the formal gardens and Selene's grave.

Gods. This window would soon overlook *Sadie's* grave.

"Love, you should eat," Micah urged; my ignored toast had gone cold. I started to say that I couldn't imagine eating anything ever again when Micah touched his fingers to my lips. "Please. For me."

It wasn't his words but the tremble in his voice that reached me. I smiled at him, probably the most pathetic smile in the history of facial expressions, and let him feed me a crust, my favorite part of the bread. "For you," I said after I swallowed.

We resumed staring out the window, nibbling at our toast and sipping tea.

"When do you think we'll know who the new Inheritor is?" I asked.

"Leave it, for now," Micah answered. Though he hadn't said as much out loud, I know he wondered if Sadie was beyond help. I was starting to think that was the case. "A new Inheritor will emerge soon enough. Until then, we should take the time to heal."

"I don't know if I can." I turned into Micah's arms, my cheek against his throat. "It hurts."

Micah didn't say anything, not that he'd ever been one to offer empty words of comfort. Instead, he tightened his arms around me and wiped away my tears before we both drowned in them. At least it was just tears this time, not the violent, wracking sobs that had kept both of us awake last night.

Once my tears slowed and my vision cleared, I peeked out the window and saw Max sitting on the ground next to the rosebushes. Poor Max, who'd told the Peacekeepers that he was the Inheritor of Metal and let himself be taken prisoner just so Sadie could have a normal life. Normal for us, anyway.

As I watched Max, another figure came into view: Juliana. She stayed about six feet away from him, and a little behind, but Max's suddenly rigid posture told me that he was well aware of her presence. After a few minutes, he said something over his shoulder. Juliana nodded, then they walked back toward the manor and out of my view.

"What was that about?" I wondered. "They acted like they were planning something."

"A memorial, perhaps," Micah posited, but then I heard Max and Juliana speaking in hushed tones as they walked down the corridor and passed our door. That meant that they were headed toward the far end of the manor, and the wing that housed Sadie's library. That, and Max's bedroom.

"I'm going to go see what's up," I said.

"Would you like me to accompany you?" Micah asked as I slid out of his arms.

"No. I'll yell if I need you."

I left the warmth and safety of Micah and followed Max and Juliana down the corridor and to the library. I stood in the cold, lonely hallway for what seemed like eternity, staring at the closed library door. The last door that Sadie had walked through while she was still alive.

What was the point of all these gods people pray to if they let my sister die?

I could hear Max and Juliana speaking inside the library, but not well enough to understand their words. Eventually, I scrubbed my face with my hands, took a deep breath, and shoved the door open. I have no idea what I was expecting to find, but Max and Juliana seated on the floor amid piles of books and papers was not it. They both looked up at my clumsy entrance, Juliana blowing a lock of hair out of her eyes.

"Um." I stared at them, my despair replaced by confusion. "What are you doing in the library?"

"We're trying to figure out what happened here," Max explained.

"We know what happened," I began, but Max shook his head.

"No, we know what the end result was. I want to know what came before." Max gestured at the books, and at a small pile of tchotchkes beside him. "This was not Sadie. Sadie did not cast spells, and she sure as hell didn't touch dark magic." He picked up something from the pile; it was an inscribed plate covered in ashes. I remembered the soot on Sadie's hands.

"Where did you get that?" I asked.

"Me and Jules rounded up all the magical implements we could find in the library, and in Sadie's room," he replied. Based on the size of the pile, Sadie must have been on a supernatural shopping spree.

"What makes you think she used dark magic?" I asked as I sat next to Juliana. "Maybe it was just a spell gone wrong."

Max frowned. "Show her, Jules."

From somewhere to her left, Juliana produced a lidded clay jar. It was a nondescript gray color, and while it looked familiar, I couldn't remember having ever seen that particular jar. Although, there could have been a million reasons why Sadie needed a jar . . .

Then, just underneath the lid, I saw a glow.

"It's a soul jar," I screeched, making Juliana jump. "Sadie's soul is in the jar!"

"Sara, we don't know that," Max warned.

"Yes we do!" I leapt to my feet. "We need to put her soul back!" Elation flooded me; my sister wasn't gone. She'd be back, just as soon as we got her body out of stasis and reunited it with her soul. Just as I was calling for the silverkin to bring Sadie out of her bedroom, Max grabbed my shoulders.

"Sara," Max said. I looked at him, confused as to why he still looked so upset. Wasn't this the best news ever? "We don't know if that's Sadie's soul. And even if it is, we don't know why she sent it from her body."

Slowly, I turned from Max's face to the jar in Juliana's hand. "Who else's soul could it be?"

"I don't know, but we don't want to run off half-cocked and make things worse," Max replied.

Great, now Max had a sense of responsibility.

Juliana cleared her throat, and said, "I have all of Sadie's notes I could find. Once we know what sort of spell she cast, we'll better understand how we should proceed."

I nodded, sad and hopeful and really wishing I was the sort of person who could just go numb. "All right," I said. "But we need to move quickly. If that is Sadie's soul, I don't think her body can survive long without it."

"I do not like this," Dad said.

"Nor do I," Mom agreed.

"I concur," Micah added, and I'd heard enough.

"What is wrong with you people?" I demanded. We'd all gathered in the library, where Juliana brought the notes she'd found, and, most importantly, the soul jar. No one was impressed, or even excited, which made me wonder if I'd explained things properly.

"Don't you get it?" I continued. "We can bring Sadie back!"

"Sara," Dad began, "I wish it were so, but we cannot."

"We have her soul!"

"A soul is not a hat to be put on and discarded as you please," Mom snapped. "Once the soul leaves the body, there is no undoing the act."

"What about astral projection?" I pressed. "What about all those stories of shamans and mediums and—"

"Sara," Mom yelled. "Don't you think that if magic could fix this, I would have fixed it already?"

Mom's words left me speechless. Of course Mom would have brought Sadie back if it was within her power. Now the Seelie Queen stood in the middle of a library with tearstained cheeks, clutching a clay jar, unable to do a single thing about it.

"Can you sense anything in there?" I asked her, desperate. "Is it Sadie?"

Mom pressed the jar against her forehead. "Yes. I believe she's in there."

I looked from her to Dad. "What do we do now?"

"*Ma chère*, I do not know if there is anything we can do."

"No." I backed away from them, shaking my head. "No, no, no."

"Sara!" Max barked. "Ma just said she can't do it. Take a breath."

"I don't want to take a breath! All I want is my sister back!"

I clapped my hands over my mouth. I was mortified, angry, and so, so sad. Micah took a step toward me, but before he could touch me or speak, I turned and fled. Behind me, I heard Dad saying that I needed some time.

I didn't need time. I needed Sadie.

14

Max

A few hours after Sara stormed out of the library, I found her sitting in the back garden next to Selene's grave. The statue of Micah's mother loomed over us; this place was on track to be quite the family cemetery. *Maybe I should mark out a spot for myself.* With my luck, I'd need it soon enough.

I sat next to Sara and contemplated the mound of freshly turned earth over what would be Sadie's final resting place. The silverkin, efficient little workers that they are, had already gone ahead and dug the grave. My parents were talking with them about putting up a marker, but not until after the ground settled, assuming we all survived our fight against the Peacekeepers and whatever the Gold Queen threw our way.

"There really isn't anything we can do," Sara whispered. "Even though we have her soul, and her body is right frickin' there, that's it. It's over."

I opened my mouth, intending to point out how Sadie's body would have begun degrading from the moment her soul left, and that even if we managed to retether her soul to it, it would be in a compromised form . . . but instead, I stayed quiet. A speech about our possible zombie sister wouldn't help either of us.

"Dead is dead," I said. "If it was easy to reverse death, it wouldn't mean anything."

"Sure it would. It would mean plenty." Sara ripped up a handful of grass and threw it into the air. "This isn't fair."

I threw my own handful of grass in solidarity. "Welcome to life."

Sara flopped back on the grass. "How are you so complacent? You're a fighter. Why aren't you fighting to get Sadie back?"

"Believe me, if I thought there was a chance to save her, I'd be all over it." I laid back next to Sara and watched the clouds float on by overhead. "I've seen a lot of death. Pretty much every friend I've ever had is dead; some went fast, some took so long to die I almost killed them myself just to get it over with. None of them ever came back."

"That was all at the Institute?"

"Yeah. Mostly." Out of habit, I dragged my sleeve across my face. "The best thing we can do for Sadie is take time to grieve, then move on. We can honor her memory."

Sara laughed through her nose. "Next you're going to tell me the pain will get better in time."

"That's the thing. It won't. All we can do is learn to live with it." I searched for patterns in the clouds, a clue, something. Anything. The barest hint that would explain why we were here. Why we were *still* here, when Sadie wasn't.

I closed my eyes and breathed deep. The air was clean and the sun was warm. The ground underneath me was soft. I had a place to sleep, and I wouldn't go hungry anytime soon. Maybe the secret to life is hidden in all these little moments, and finding contentment within them. That's all I ever wanted for Sadie, and it was all I could do for her now.

"This is how we'll honor Sadie," I told Sara, taking her hand in mine. "By living."

I went dreamwalking that night, which was what I'd done every time I slept since the last bout of deadening drugs I'd been fed in a Peacekeeper holding cell had worn off. From what I'd learned over the years, most Dreamwalkers go out maybe once a week, if that. After all, if you stayed awake during your dreams, how would you ever get any rest?

I couldn't rest, though. I had to watch over Juliana.

Not that she wanted me looking after her. We had an understanding, she and I: I was not to enter her dreams ever again without her express invitation. I'd agreed to her terms years ago, and I'm a man of my word. Hell, the fact that we'd needed this agreement was all my fault. But that didn't mean I couldn't check up on her, which I accomplished by making a quick pass along the edge of her dreams each night before I turned in.

I never, not even once, entered her dreams. That meant I was keeping my promise . . . technically, at least.

Technicalities aside, I couldn't not look in on her. I'd gotten into the habit after I'd left the Institute, just to reassure myself that she was still alive. Even though I couldn't interact with her, at least I'd know she was breathing.

I didn't get to check on her this time, but it wasn't for lack of trying. I'd waited for hours, but I got no sense of Juliana in her dream state. Eventually I let myself wake up, though all I did was laze around in bed. If Juliana hadn't been dreaming, it meant she hadn't been sleeping. What had she been doing all night?

My gut clenched as I drew the instinctive conclusion; no, it obviously couldn't be that. Juliana was an adult and clearly capable of spending the night with someone, but her options were, to put it mildly, limited since she hadn't left the manor after Sadie had passed.

But then, what had she been doing all night?

I was still contemplating Juliana's nighttime activities when there was a knock at my door. After pulling on a pair of jeans, I opened it and found Juliana standing in the hallway. Her eyes were bright with excessive caffeine and her arms were overflowing with books and loose papers.

"Good morning, I guess," I mumbled as she shoved past me. Juliana had been reading. She'd been up all night reading. Words couldn't express how this revelation lowered my stress levels. Not that I'd *really* been worried she'd been with someone else. That would've been completely irrational. Impossible. Ridiculous.

And yet.

Juliana dumped the books and papers on my bed, then spun around to face me. "I figured it out," she said flatly.

"Figured what out?"

"Why Sadie cast the spell," she replied.

My gaze darted back to the heap of books. "You were up all night trying to figure out why Sadie . . . why she's gone?" I asked. Juliana's eyes narrowed; great, I'd just outed my protective surveillance activities. Lucky for me, it seemed like she was willing to overlook my latest transgression.

"Look at this," she said, shoving an open book under my nose. I looked down and read the first few lines of a ritual intended to temporarily transfer one's skill with magic to another.

"You can lend your abilities to someone else?" I remarked as I read. "Who would even want to do that?"

"Sadie, for one." Juliana dug through the pile and presented me with a sheet of notebook paper covered with my sister's messy scrawl. "She rewrote the spell—a few times, actually—to make it permanently transfer her Inheritor ability."

"What?" I scanned the page, and, yeah, that had apparently been Sadie's intent. "But you're born the Inheritor, just like you're born an Elemental. The spell she based it on is for a learned magician to lend a few tricks to a friend. You can't send away a part of yourself like that."

Juliana's gaze lowered to the floor. "I know. I think that's why her soul went with it."

I rifled through the papers and checked out a few more of the books. Then I dropped everything on the bed and rubbed my temples. "Gods. This sucks."

"Yeah. It does."

"Why didn't she ask one of us for help?" I continued. "If she hated being the Inheritor so much, I would have helped her."

"You would have helped divest her of her ability?" Juliana countered, lifting her chin. Sometimes she knew me better than I knew myself.

I shook my head. "No. I would have hidden her away and kept the world from knowing what she is. Was." My head fell forward, and if I'd still had tear ducts, I would have been crying. Langston had removed them years ago, just to see what would happen. Unfortunately for him, my element kept my eyes as healthy as the day I was born. Unfortunately for me, I could still cry, but without the waterworks. "I would have told her that all these spells wouldn't do anything but kill her."

I felt the most amazing sensation, like a feather brushing my cheek; Juliana was stroking the side of my face. "I'm sorry, Max," she said softly. "I wish she'd spoken up. At least we know . . . at least we know what she was trying to do."

"Yeah. There's that," I replied. I took Juliana's wrist. We looked at each other for a moment, then she lowered her gaze, coughed, and turned away. I looked down and realized that I hadn't fastened my jeans. *Oops.*

"Hang on," I muttered, turning my back as I buttoned up, then opened the top drawer to hunt for a shirt. When I looked up, I spied Juliana's reflection in the wall mirror. She was staring at me, her expression a mixture of fascination and . . . nostalgia?

"Is my butt really that nice?" I teased.

"Your mark," she explained, referring to the copper raven on my back. It was a raven in flight, and it stretched from my left shoulder to my right hip. It marked me not only as an Elemental, but also a Corbeau. "It's hard to look away from it."

The corner of my mouth curled up. "Remember the first time you saw it? Awake, that is."

She laughed through her nose. "How could I forget? I thought Greta was going to kill me when I touched it."

My smile became a grimace and I pulled my shirt over my head to hide it. Greta had served time with me at the Institute, but never made it out. Shirt on, I faced Juliana. "You've gotta admit, though, my butt is pretty awesome."

There was that pointy-browed glare I knew and loved. "Yeah, I can hardly keep my thoughts in order while sharing the same space as your posterior of perfection," she deadpanned. I smiled, then bit back my next comment. This was the most Juliana had opened up to me since she'd arrived at the manor, and I knew better than to push my luck. Juliana was like a wild animal, distrustful and easily spooked.

For now, I stepped toward my bed and picked up Sadie's rewritten spell. I concentrated on the words, rearranging them in my mind, hoping I could reverse what had been done. No such luck. Juliana had once called me a professional sister saver, and it seemed I'd failed miserably.

"It really is her soul in the jar," I confirmed aloud. Not that I'd doubted Ma, but this was just more proof.

"Her soul, and the Inheritor's power," Juliana clarified. "She . . . she wanted to give it to Sara."

Shit. I sat on the bed and held my head in my hands. Why did Sadie hate her power—herself—so much?

Was it because we hadn't told her until she was an adult? Was it somehow my fault?

Most of my life I wouldn't change. Yeah, I'd had some seriously bad times, but they all led me to where I am today: a free man, a complete family, Juliana free of her uncle's influence. Of course, Juliana and I weren't as close as we used to be, and my family bore a gaping hole now where Sadie had been.

Regardless, if I could go back in time and change things, I wouldn't change our decision to not tell Sadie she was the Inheritor. Would it change the way our lives had played out? No idea, but a guy had to hope that he'd done the right thing.

"What makes you think she wanted to give it to Sara?" I questioned, not looking up. Juliana shoved another scrap of paper underneath my nose.

"She wrote it down, for one," Juliana replied. "Sad it wasn't you?"

"Sad my sister's gone." I grabbed the paper and realized Juliana was right. It was as close to a suicide note as I'd ever seen, with Sadie explaining exactly why she thought Sara would be a better Inheritor. As if Sadie hadn't already been born the best person in the world. "Glad you're here, though," I added, glancing up at Juliana.

Her cheeks darkened and she looked away. "Yeah, I bet."

I grasped her hand; when she didn't pull away, I rubbed my thumb across her knuckles. "You're one of the few good things in my life, Jules. I am very, very happy you're here."

Juliana smiled, but she wouldn't meet my eyes. She also didn't take her hand from mine. "Come on, we should tell Sara."

15

Sara

My mind was reeling.

An hour ago, Max had found me and led me to the dining room table. Juliana had been sitting there with a heap of books and papers spread before her. Before I could ask, Juliana launched into an explanation of what she'd uncovered in Sadie's notes. She mentioned the spells Sadie had studied, the books on dark magic she'd been hoarding, and that final, damning note.

Sadie had wanted me to be the Inheritor instead of her.

I stared at the books and papers before me, wondering how I'd gotten to this place. *Why*—

No. It was useless to ask why. There was only the here and the now.

"I . . . I need to talk to Micah," I rasped. "And Mom and Dad, too."

"I'll get them," Max said, then disappeared through the kitchen doors. I looked at Juliana where she sat opposite from me.

"You and Max figured all this out?"

"Just me," she replied. "I found the original spell last night, then I backtracked through Sadie's notes."

I nodded, then looked at the evidence spread before me. "This is everything?"

"Everything I found."

"Are you doing this for Max?"

Juliana's gaze hardened. "I'm doing this for Sadie, who is probably the best person I've ever met."

I winced at that. "Sorry. I didn't mean to question you like that. It's just . . ."

"I know," Juliana acknowledged, softening. "It's horrible."

"Yeah." Before I could say anything else, Max returned with the others in tow. Micah stood over me, picking through the loose sheets of notebook paper. When he found one of significance, he held it out to my parents.

"This must be the spell she based everything on," Micah said. I wondered if he'd just divined that information by himself, or if Max had filled him in. "And this," he continued, finding the last thing Sadie wrote, "is why."

I couldn't look at my parents while they read that scrap of paper. It was my fault Sadie was dead, being that she'd seen me as a more appropriate Inheritor of Metal. As if I'd ever been the right choice for anything.

Once Mom finished reading, she squeezed her eyes shut and buried her face in Dad's neck. I wanted to do the same to Micah, but he stayed me.

"There is something else," he said.

"What else even matters?" I choked out.

"Oriana," he replied, "and the deadline for Sadie's pledge. Today is the tenth day. We are expected at the Gold Court within the hour."

Oh, crap.

We buried Sadie before we left for the Gold Court.

We should have waited. We should have left for the Gold Court immediately, being that Oriana had already granted us more than enough time to convince Sadie to pledge to her. Then again, Oriana's hounding of Sadie was a big reason why she'd resorted to collecting magic books and working with spells she didn't understand, so while I wouldn't call Oriana a murderer, she'd essentially contributed to Sadie's death.

For that, she could wait.

Dad and Max created a copper coffin for Sadie, a fitting resting place for the Inheritor of Metal. I had no idea where they found enough copper, but the finished casket was a thing of beauty. The sides were decorated with bookshelves, and the lid was engraved with an image of Sadie sitting in her library. She would have loved it.

Sadie was interred in the rose garden next to Micah's mother. As the silverkin lowered the coffin into the ground, Dad dropped one of the Raven's feathers onto its lid.

"We watch over our own," he said, "always and forever."

I watched the feather flutter into the earth. I was empty, emptier than I'd ever been, and I didn't know if anything could fill the void.

My sister was gone.

Micah, having finished directing the silverkin as they filled in the hole that now held my sister, stood behind me. "I'm so sorry, love."

"Yeah. Me, too." I wiped my cheeks. "Let's deal with Oriana and put this mess behind us."

When we arrived at the Gold Court, we were greeted by the same golden footmen and escorted down the main corridor to the royal receiving chamber. Oriana was already there, seated on her throne. Ayla, the Inheritor of Fire, stood beside her, with one of her hands resting on Oriana's shoulder. It seemed that these two had been getting steadily closer. *How nice.* When Oriana saw only Micah and me, her face puckered as if she'd sucked on a lemon.

"I still await your sister's pledge," Oriana purred by way of greeting.

"My queen, I am sorry to say that you will never receive Sadie Corbeau's pledge," Micah declared. Oriana's eyes narrowed and her nostrils flared, but before she could speak, he added, "She has perished. We buried her just this morning."

Oriana's gaze darted between Micah and me. "Is this true?" she asked. "Who would dare harm the Inheritor of Metal? And who has the strength to defeat her?"

"It wasn't . . ." I took a deep breath and began again. "It wasn't an attack. It was an accident." Oriana raised her brows, her unasked question forcing me to relive some of the worst moments of my life. "Sadie didn't want to be the Inheritor. She found a spell to release the power from her body, but it released her soul as well."

Oriana sat back in her throne. "Where is the power now?"

"What? Gone," I replied, cold sweat blooming across my neck and chest. Oriana couldn't know about the soul jar.

"The power passes from one Inheritor to the next in a heartbeat's time," Oriana explained. "No new Inheritor has surfaced. I'd have known if one did. I ask again, where did she send the essence of the Inheritor?"

What an excellent time for our queen to get in touch with her shrewd side. "Um, it's contained."

"Contained how?" Ayla pressed. "Is it in a soul jar?"

"Yes." I almost lied, but I didn't understand the jars and spells well enough to misdirect Ayla or the queen.

"Sadie used a soul jar."

Ayla whispered into Oriana's ear. The queen's face lit up, and she clapped like a little girl. "Wonderful," Oriana cried. "Bring the jar to me, and I will be the Inheritor."

"No."

Oriana's gleeful face turned to stone. "Pardon me?"

"I said *no*."

I glared at the Gold Queen, hurt and furious all at once. How could she care so little about Sadie's death? How could she think I would hand over the one part of my sister I had left?

"Micah, I grow weary of your family's defiance," Oriana said between her clenched teeth. "Bring me the essence of the Inheritor, and all is forgiven."

"My queen," Micah replied, resting his hand against my copper mark, "Sadie's intent was to bequeath her power to Sara. Should we not honor her final wish?"

Oriana scowled. "Honor a foolish child, and one who sought my throne, at that? I think not."

My pain got the better of me, and I ground out, "You'll have to pry that jar from my cold, dead hands." With that, I turned and stalked away from the throne. I wasn't surprised when gold warriors barred my way. Just like the footmen, they weren't human warriors, but animated metal. That meant I—or rather, Micah— could crush them.

"If you refuse to let me leave, you'll never know where it is," I called over my shoulder. "Keep me here and the essence stays trapped. There will never be another Inheritor."

"You dare threaten me?" Oriana demanded.

"No threats. Just truth." I turned around and saw that Oriana had descended the dais. She gestured and gold warriors surrounded Micah, cutting us off from each other. "The only two people who know where the jar is or what it even looks like are Micah and myself. Keep us here, and you'll never have it."

"As you wish," Oriana growled. "My guards will accompany you to the Whispering Dell and once there you shall hand over the essence."

"I'll die before I let you have the essence of my sister," I hissed.

Oriana smiled a cold, calculating smile; I'd thought many things about the Gold Queen before, but until that moment I'd never thought she was evil. "As you will. Rot in the bowels of my castle, as I once rotted for Ferra. Soon enough you will beg me to accept the jar."

Before I'd fully processed what Oriana was threatening, there was a blur of movement at the base of her dais. Micah disarmed the three human guards attempting to contain him, and the metal warriors crumpled in on themselves like so much used paper. He moved toward Oriana, but Ayla leapt in front of the queen, flames dancing on her palm.

"Think you to melt me?" Micah demanded, looking down at the fire Elemental. "Ask your lover what metal can do to fire."

"If my brother were here," Ayla began, but Oriana grabbed her arm and lowered it.

"This need not end in violence," Oriana interjected, cutting her off. "Surely we can come to an arrangement."

"Perhaps we can, but not today," Micah countered. "It is past time for my wife and I to depart."

"Micah," Oriana ordered, "honor your pledge to your queen! I demand it!"

Micah spun on his heel. "No," he declared. "I pledged you my loyalty, yes, but my oath to my wife supersedes that. Are you surprised at my displeasure when you threaten to take something that is rightfully hers? When you threaten to imprison her?" Micah shook his head. "You wished for the Inheritor's pledge, and now her power, to strengthen your claim to your throne, because you have no other way to reinforce it."

"I cannot do it any other way!" Oriana shrieked. "Micah, Sadie's followers still plot against me!"

"And why do they plot?" Micah retorted. "A land's king is its strength, but its queen is its wisdom. The Oriana Raintree I once served as a general was a wise woman, one who always looked to her land and people's well-being. You are not her."

Micah turned away, Oriana recoiling as if he'd struck her. Wisely, the gold warriors that had surrounded me didn't get in Micah's way. He placed his hand on my elbow, and we left the throne room and the Gold Court.

We reached the metal pathway, stepping onto it in silence. Once we'd arrived at the manor, I asked, "What are we going to do now?"

Micah pursed his lips. "I believe we need to meet with those of copper."

I nodded. Meeting with those of copper was a smart idea. They were probably the only group outside our immediate family who had a similar agenda to ours, although theirs had included replacing Oriana with Sadie. Despite Sadie's fears, none of her family had ever wanted that.

"We need to tell them about Sadie, too," I insisted. It's not fair for them to keep working toward getting her on the throne, when she . . . when she . . . "

Micah pulled me into his arms. "Yes, sharing the truth with them would be a kindness. Too few kind acts have been done of late."

I nodded against his chest. Me losing my sister was the least kind act of all. "How do we get in touch with them? They've always just sent weird messages to the manor. I don't even know if they're here or in the Mundane realm."

"Why don't we begin by speaking with Aregonda?" Micah suggested. "Not only is she of copper, but she has also been aware of the scroll for some time."

"I thought you didn't like her."

"I don't. But if speaking to her can lead to answers, I believe that is the path we should take."

Reluctantly, I slid out of his arms. "All right. Let's see what she has to say."

We portaled straight to the Mundane realm, not bothering to stop by the manor and tell anyone where we were headed. After all, if speaking to Aregonda was a bust, we would have to make a new plan anyway.

We arrived at the resistance's main location, but we didn't enter the camp proper. Instead, we skirted the tents and common area and headed toward the stream. Aregonda tended to linger there, and she was there as we'd expected, in almost the exact spot where she'd taught Max and me to call water. Interesting how that event had led to me saving the water made, and a whole host of other weird occurrences. The coincidences were definitely piling up with this woman.

"Hey," I called. Aregonda looked up and smiled.

"Sara, Micah, what a pleasant surprise," she greeted. If Micah's scowl affected her, she hid it well. "What brings you by today?"

"We came to see you, actually," I replied. I meant to say more, but the lump in my throat prevented me from making any other sounds. Micah squeezed my hand. I squeezed back, grateful he was there with me.

If Aregonda noticed my silence, she kept it to herself. "Well, then, how can I help you?"

"You're in pretty regular contact with those of copper, right?" I asked. "Not just the ones here at camp, but the ones who sent the scroll to the manor?"

"Yes, I am."

"Can you set up a meeting between us and them? By 'us,' I mean me and my family," I added.

"Of course I can," she said, smiling. "How soon should this meeting take place?"

Tears pricked my eyes. I bit the inside of my mouth. "The sooner the better."

"Sara, what's wrong?" Aregonda asked, her eyes softening.

"Nothing."

She held up a hand. "You are obviously upset. Even if I can't right whatever wrong you've suffered, talking about it will help."

I took a deep breath and looked at the ground between us. "My sister, Sadie. She died."

"What?" Aregonda drew back, shaking her head. "No, no, you must be mistaken."

"I wish I was," I said. "We buried her at the manor."

Aregonda, still shaking her head, clasped and unclasped her hands. "This makes no sense. How could Baudoin have let this happen?"

"Baudoin had nothing to do with it," Micah explained gently. "Sadie acted alone, and in secrecy. Had we known what she was attempting, we could have helped her, and likely saved her."

Aregonda cocked her head. "This was an accident?"

"Evidently so," Micah confirmed. "The items we found around Sadie suggest that she attempted casting a spell."

"A spell? For what purpose?"

"Sadie's ultimate intent remains somewhat unclear," Micah hedged. "Still, it matters little at this point. No matter what her intentions may have been, Sadie is gone."

"Her intent matters. It matters a great deal." Aregonda stood up so fast, Micah and I stepped back. Even though she was of average height, whatever was going on inside her head made her seem like she towered over Micah and me.

"Take me to Baudoin," she demanded. "I must speak with him about this . . . this problem."

"We can tell Dad you want to meet," I began, but Aregonda wasn't having any of my delay tactics.

"There will be no telling him," she snapped. "I must speak with the current head of the Corbeau clan immediately."

I paused, wondering why Aregonda was so upset. Sadie's loss was both terrible and heartbreaking, but Aregonda had hardly known her.

"Why are you so interested?" I prompted.

"You're asking why I'm upset she died?" Aregonda demanded.

"No, not—" I took a breath and centered myself. My stress levels were through the roof, and I needed to think before I spoke. "What I mean is, you didn't seem close to Sadie. You hardly ever spoke with her. I didn't think it would affect you this much."

Aregonda sighed, and for the barest moment I saw a bent old woman in a tattered gray cloak; the wise woman who ground herbs and sold simples in the village. I could even smell the scent of crushed herbs clinging to her. "I mourn the loss of all my descendants, no matter how far removed. Sadie's passing makes my heart ache."

"Descendants," I repeated, dumbstruck.

"Surely you figured it out long ago," Aregonda said. "Your mate did, right around the same time you first visited my apothecary. Am I right, Micah?"

"Not at once," Micah admitted. "It wasn't until you showed a special interest in Sara and her siblings and wanted to be their teacher. Your actions, coupled with Baudoin's stories of a sorceress and a raven, told me the rest." He frowned, then added, "I will admit, I did not realize until this moment that the owner of the apothecary in the Whispering Dell is also the progenitor of the Raven clan."

The facts clicked into place in my head, and I glanced from Micah to Aregonda. "You're *that* Aregonda? How is that possible? You should have died centuries ago!" Aregonda gave me a look. "Sorry. That was rude."

Aregonda—*the* Aregonda, apparently—shrugged.

"Immortality was one of the first gifts the Raven granted me. How else was I supposed to look after our children's well-being?" Her face clouded and she continued, "And for all our planning, I failed Sadie. Please, take me to Baudoin."

Micah's mouth was pressed in a thin line as he considered her request. "It is your choice, Sara," he insisted.

"I don't think there is any choice," I said. I turned and walked toward the spot where Micah and I had portaled in, Aregonda following close behind.

"So, if you're supposed to be watching out for us and all, why did you give me the queen's lace?" I asked, thinking back on the tincture of the herb that'd almost killed me. "You had to know that it wouldn't end well."

"I gave it to you because you asked for it," Aregonda replied, shrugging. "You would not be the first woman who came to my shop seeking to rid herself of an unwanted babe."

"That's not what I wanted," I snapped. "I was trying to *keep* from getting pregnant, not *end* a pregnancy."

Aregonda blinked, quirking an eyebrow as she examined my face. "You're an Elemental. You don't need birth control."

I stopped walking. "What?"

"Much as your element heals you, it can also hold your fertility in check," Aregonda explained. "Didn't Maeve teach you that?"

"My mother's not an Elemental," I replied. "She probably doesn't know."

"The things Maeve does not know are few indeed," Aregonda murmured almost coyly. "One would think she would have—"

"Keep talking about my mother, and you'll find out just how much of her temper I inherited," I snapped. "When are you planning to collect the debt I owe you for saving Micah? And why did you pull that heart's desire vision on me and Max?"

"Consider the debt paid," Aregonda responded matter-of-factly, unbothered by my threat. "As for the visions, you'd just told me that Baudoin had been impersonated by a shapeshifter. I needed proof that neither you nor your brother had also been com-promised."

"Did we pass?"

"We're still speaking, aren't we?"

We reached the portal site, and Micah withdrew a glass disc.

"Are we ready to travel?" he asked.

"Let's just get this over with," I muttered, still trying to reconcile the impossible truth of Aregonda being an ancient family member with the impossible truth of Sadie being gone forever. It seemed like I never would as I watched Micah drop the portal. I saw the Mundane realm vanish around us as we stepped through it.

16

Max

"You must be joking," Ma growled.

Aregonda's eyes narrowed. "Why would anyone joke about such a thing?"

Aregonda had just dropped the bombshell of a lifetime on us: not only was she a Corbeau, but she was one of the first. Technically the second. Add to that the fact that she'd been spying on us for months from her shop in the village, and I was seriously creeped out. A quick glance around the room told me that *everyone* was creeped out, except Ma. She was just pissed.

When Ma got pissed, heads rolled. Literally.

"Why have you not revealed yourself before today?" Dad asked. "You claim to be our guardian, but where were you while I was imprisoned? Where were you when Max was imprisoned?"

"A condition of my continued existence is that I not interfere with my descendants," Aregonda replied. "It's why I established the apothecary, so that I could lend wisdom but remain unknown."

"*Lots* of wisdom to be had there," Sara muttered. "And you're not exactly remaining unknown if you're hanging out with the resistance."

"True," Aregonda conceded. "I have played a more active role of late, but that was only because you needed my help."

"Now that you've blown your cover, what does that mean?" I asked, quirking an eyebrow.

Aregonda leveled a gaze so cold even Ma would have flinched directly at me. "Since I broke the bargain, I may lose my immortality."

"Oh. That's, uh, pretty heavy." Actually, it was nuts. The woman who'd cosseted me and brought me coffee was also an incredibly powerful, incredibly old sorceress. And now she'd likely have to face death like the rest of us. Wild. "Still, why now?"

"We've waited generations for an Inheritor in the Corbeau line," Aregonda answered bitterly. "And you let her perish."

"Watch yourself," Ma seethed, stepping toward her. "That's my child you're referring to."

Aregonda bowed her head. "Apologies, but you must understand. You need my help now more than ever."

"So how do we know it's you?" I asked. "I mean,

really you? You've got to admit, you're asking us to believe the most unbelievable thing ever."

Aregonda's eyes became slits. "What is so difficult for you to comprehend, boy?"

"Max isn't a boy."

All of our heads turned toward the voice; Juliana had just defended me. "What was that?" Aregonda demanded.

"Max is not a boy," Juliana repeated. "He's a grown man. You're only calling him a boy to belittle him. That's not fair."

"You dare scold me?" Aregonda demanded, but Dad raised his hand.

"Juliana's words are valid," he affirmed. "I have seen many amazing things in my time, but women nearing their second millennia are quite rare. I'm sure you understand our need for proof."

Aregonda's anger bled away, and she asked, "Is he here? My husband?" When no one answered, she continued, "Surely you would accept his word, even as you doubt mine."

"You want us to bring the Raven to you?" I clicked my tongue and grimaced. "He's . . . um . . . " I spread my hands, a preemptive and wordless apology for my bluntness. "He's pretty dead."

"He is not," Aregonda insisted. "A being such as he cannot die, only be reshaped." Her gaze softened, and she smiled. "Please, may I see him? It has been so long."

I looked at Dad, who looked at Ma. "I do not know if this is wise," she said, still glaring at Aregonda as if she could behead her with her gaze alone. Knowing Ma, she probably could.

"Only one way to find out," I said as I stood. "I'll get him." I waited for Dad's nod, then turned and headed toward the old basement.

"I'll come with you," Juliana called out as she rushed to catch up with me.

"Too weird back there?"

"A little. And I just told off what might be a two-thousand-year-old sorceress." Juliana shuddered. "Do you think she's for real?"

"I have no idea. Hopefully the Raven will clear all this up for us." I stopped at the end of the corridor, right in front of a painting of our favorite golden girl, Oriana. Micah must have been feeling patriotic when he hung it up. "There are a few things we haven't told you about the manor."

"Coming from you, that's nothing new."

I glanced at Juliana. "What can I say, old habits and all. Anyway . . . So, you know how we all relocated here and pretty much abandoned the Raven Compound?"

"That must have been terrible," Juliana murmured. "All of your family's history, just gone."

"Actually, it's all here."

I pressed a certain spot on the wall and Oriana's

picture slid away, revealing a wooden staircase that descended into darkness.

"You moved everything from home to the Otherworld?" Juliana asked as she peered down the steps. "That must have taken a billion portal hops."

"Not quite. This isn't the manor's basement. This is the old basement from the Raven Compound." I grabbed a couple fey stones from the bowl next to the entrance and tossed one to Juliana. "Let's do this, before Ma and Aregonda start throwing spells at each other."

We lit up the fey stones and started down the steps. Juliana was still trying to wrap her head around the old basement being attached to the manor. "How did you get part of the Raven Compound here? Wait, is the building in the Mundane realm an illusion?"

"Good guess, but the house is real," I replied. "The old basement is where we put all of our magical artifacts after the wars started. Peacekeepers checked the house over dozens of times, but they never found their way downstairs."

"Nice job," Juliana said, and we shared a smile. "I know they searched the place pretty thoroughly. Back in high school, I was there once when a contingent of them showed up out of the blue and started looking in and around everything. They even checked out the yard."

I stumbled; sometimes I forgot that Juliana and Sara had been friends for almost ten years, long before

Juliana and I met at the Institute. If it hadn't been for her friendship with my sister, Juliana might have been spared all of this. But if they hadn't been friends, I may never have met her.

Juliana put her hand on my elbow. "You got quiet," she said, her eyes filled with concern. It took me a second to say anything, seeing her looking at me like that.

"Just thinking," I managed.

I moved so my arm was looped with hers and we picked our way through the crates and heaps of other items. The basement had never been organized all that well, and after the shift between dimensions, things had really gotten jumbled up. There were stacks of ancient spell books, charmed jewelry and trinkets, and so many enchanted paintings that we could have opened a Corbeau art gallery. I ignored it all and walked straight toward the Raven.

Juliana, on the other hand, noticed a few things.

"What is all of this stuff?" Her head swiveled this way and that as she took in every bit of the treasure trove she possibly could. We passed a petrified troll, and I felt her shudder. "Is that what I think it is?"

"Depends on what you think it is."

She shuddered again and moved closer to me. "What I don't understand is why Sadie ever went to the village for books on magic. You already had Magic 101 down here, and I bet the Raven—whoever he is—would have kept her from hurting herself."

My spine straightened, but I didn't say anything. Juliana was only pointing out the obvious.
We reached the far end of the room, and I stopped
walking. In front of us was a leaded glass casket,
inside of which was the Raven. The guy who had
started all of this.

I don't know how long he had been dead or sleeping
or whatever he was doing in his glass coffin, and his
appearance didn't give me any clues. His feathers were
full and shiny, such a deep black that they absorbed
the light around them. His beak and talons were razor
sharp, a fact I knew well from reaching in for a feather
and accidentally slicing open my fingers.

Huh. Like Sara had pointed out a few days ago, we
were always asking the Raven for his feathers, yet he
had never developed a bald spot. Maybe Aregonda was
right, and he'd been alive all along.

"That's him?" Juliana whispered.

"Yes." I pushed up my sleeves, then handed Juliana
my fey stone. "Angle it so the light's in front of me."

"Okay."

I took a deep breath. I picked up the glass coffin
and its occupant . . . and found out that it weighed
nearly nothing. That explained why Sadie wasn't
stressed when she carried him over from the Raven
Compound. We hadn't trusted the spell we used to
push the old basement into the Otherworld to transport our ancestor unscathed, and having the Inheritor

of Metal carry him from our home to the Otherworld was the finest transport we could arrange.

Gods, I missed my sister.

While Juliana shone the fey light in front of us, I carefully made my way out of the old basement. I carried the Raven up the stairs and into the parlor, where Ma and Aregonda were still staring each other down. No one was dead or bleeding, so that was something.

I cleared my throat to break the silence. "Where should I put him?" I asked.

Micah left and returned carrying a small table. He set it in the center of the room, and I set the Raven's coffin on top of it.

"Open it," Aregonda urged, almost breathless. She'd forgotten about Ma the moment she saw the coffin. "Open his crypt."

I unlatched the glass lid, the ancient hinges creaking as I opened the coffin. Aregonda approached the Raven and stroked his head without a moment's hesitation.

"Come back," she whispered. "I miss you so."

The Raven twitched, then hopped up and stretched his wings. He stared up at Aregonda as a wave of magic rippled across the room. By the time the wave receded, the Raven was gone, and a tall man wearing old-fashioned clothing and a red cloak stood in his place.

"Bran," Aregonda croaked, her voice thick with emotion as she nearly fell into his arms. "Bran, Bran, how I've missed you."

268

"Aregonda," he managed as he pressed his face into her hair, "my beloved, why have you woken me earlier than agreed?"

"I had to wake you," she insisted. "The youngest of this generation has perished."

The Raven—Bran?—stepped back from Aregonda and surveyed the roomful of open-mouthed descendants. He had copper hair, green eyes, and a full beard that matched Dad's. "How can that be? Sadie's soul remains, along with her power."

"Her soul, yes, but not her body," Dad clarified as he stepped forward. "My youngest child is dead."

"How?"

Dad nodded toward me. I cleared my throat, and began, "She didn't want to be the Inheritor. She was scared of the power, scared of what she might have to do . . . So she tried to give her power away to Sara, but she didn't understand the spell she was using. She was so smart, but she just didn't know . . . "

My voice cracked and Juliana touched my arm. I grasped her hand and pushed myself to finish explaining how my baby sister had died. "Sadie didn't understand her abilities as well as she thought she did. When the power left her, so did her soul."

Bran's gaze went hard. "Why did she not understand? Why was she not taught?"

"These are difficult times," Dad replied, shaking his head as he spoke. "I was separated from my daughters for many years, as was Max. We could not teach them."

Bran glanced at Aregonda. "Perhaps you were right. Perhaps you should have made yourself known some time ago." Aregonda bowed her head, the most graceful "I told you so" in history. "Sara."

Sara went white. "Y-yes?"

"You will accept Sadie's gift and become the Inheritor. You will honor your sister's memory."

"I will," Sara said. "You have my word."

Bran's gaze swept about the room. "Please, my children, never hesitate to contact me. I fear I made a mistake in not remaining as close with this generation as much as I'd done in the past. You all have my deepest apologies."

"It's not your fault," I told him, thinking of the feathers the Raven had given us. "You've always helped us when we asked. Can't blame yourself for us not asking sooner." *I can only blame myself for that.*

Bran smiled. "Your youthful wisdom reminds me of my second son. Ari, you remember our Siegebert?"

"Of course," Aregonda replied. "Max is loyal and has a great heart, just as Siegebert did."

Juliana squeezed my hand, to my surprise. Maybe she agreed.

"Do you know of the Elementals' struggles?" Dad asked. "Is there any way you can help us?"

Bran bowed his head. "Of course."

I felt something between my palm and Juliana's. Juliana raised a black, shiny feather, and asked, "Where did this come from?"

"Him," I replied, nodding toward Bran. I looked at the others, and saw that Ma and Dad had a feather, and so did Sara and Micah.

"How can a feather help us against Peacekeepers?" Juliana asked.

"Think of it as a wish," Bran replied. "When the time comes, and you need a portion of my magic, use the feather. You will know when you need it."

"Thank you," Dad said. "Thank you for everything."

"Anything for you, my children." Bran extended his hand to Aregonda. "I must leave you now. I fear I cannot hold this form as long as I once could, and I would like to spend my remaining time with my wife. Baudoin, I trust you will inform me of how things transpire."

"I will," Dad promised. "While I was imprisoned, I missed our talks."

Bran smiled. "As did I. Farewell, children." He gathered Aregonda into his arms, and the two of them faded from view.

"We have been blessed," Dad sighed, gripping his feather. "Blessed more than I'd ever hoped possible. I always knew we could defeat the Peacekeepers, but I once worried that I would die before that came to pass. Now that we all have the Raven's blessings, I am confident we will live to see a better world."

"Of course you will," Ma insisted. "You think I'd let something as petty as death take you from me? We shall never be separated again."

Dad grinned. "Never."

"I guess you're going to be the Inheritor," I said to Sara. The courage I'd seen in her when she'd spoken up before had faded as quickly as it came. She flinched at the word "Inheritor" and wouldn't meet my eyes.

"I guess so," she said, her brow creasing. "I have no idea of how to do that."

I squeezed her shoulder. "Don't worry," I reassured her, motioning toward everyone, Ma and Dad together, Juliana beside me, then Micah, who stood over Sara like a sentinel. "You've got all of us to help you."

It was a relief to see Sara smile, small as the smile was. It was a start. "Yeah," she agreed. "I do."

That night, I stashed my Raven feather in a safe place and went out dreamwalking. I did my typical circuit of the Whispering Dell, officially making sure Oriana hadn't sent any gold warriors after us. *Unofficially*, since I'd accidentally told Juliana I checked in on her, I was trying to spend a few nights away from the manor, and her. Not like I could really be with her, anyway.

Once my tour of the village and the surrounding forest was done, I went back home. The manor was quiet and dark, as it usually was after sundown. I didn't get too close to my parents' or Sara's rooms (didn't want too much information on what went on in there) and entered the corridor that led to my room. As soon as I slipped inside, I felt it.

Terror.

Hopelessness.

Juliana was having a nightmare.

I snapped back into my body, threw on some clothes, and headed toward Juliana's room. When I heard her crying, I couldn't stop myself from going in.

I eased the door open and saw Juliana lying in bed. She was tossing and turning, her cheeks streaked with tears. Wondering the whole time if this was a good idea, I sat on the edge of her bed.

"Hey," I murmured, shaking her shoulder. "Wake up."

She blinked, then sat straight up. "Max? What are you doing here?"

"I was just getting back from the village—" *technically true* "—and I heard you crying." Juliana touched her cheeks, then stared at her wet fingertips. "Bad dream?"

"You could say that." Juliana pulled her knees up to her chest. "I have them all the time. I'm surprised you never noticed before."

"I have," I said. It was pointless to lie about it. "You never cried before. Not out loud." I found her foot beneath the blanket and squeezed. "Want to tell me about it?"

"What I want is to erase the last five years from my memory and move on with my life," she replied. That stung, but I knew she didn't want to erase me, too. At least, I hoped not. "No matter how far I get from him, he still finds ways to torment me. I'm an entire world away now, and he's making me suffer without even trying."

"Jules, we're gonna stop your uncle."

"Not him." She raised her dark eyes to mine. "Langston."

I didn't realize how hard I was clenching her foot until she frowned and pulled away. Juliana's dreams were haunted by Langston Phillips, the man who had gotten between us all those years ago. "You two seemed pretty tight for a while," I remarked, brusque. A cheap shot, but there it was.

"We never were. Max, I never wanted anything to do with him," she insisted, her voice catching in her throat.

Man, I hadn't wanted to hurt her. "How did he react to that?"

"Badly." Juliana crossed her arms on top of her knees and rested her head on them. "Very, very badly."

"Juliana." When she didn't look up, I moved closer and put my hand on the nape of her neck. "What happened? What did he do to you?"

"Less than he did to you," she mumbled. She raised her head and wiped her cheeks. "I really don't want to talk about it."

I nodded, since I didn't want to talk about it either. I just wanted to slice Langston's balls off and shove them down his throat. "When we go back to the Mundane realm, you don't have to come with us," I told her firmly. "Stay here at the manor, where it's safe."

Juliana met my eyes with a gaze so fierce I fell in love with her all over again. "I can't. If I don't see his dead body, I'll forever wonder what happened. And he *is* going to die."

I grazed my thumb across her cheek. "That's my girl."

"Max, the Raven," she interrupted, pulling her eyes away from mine. "Why did he give us a feather?"

I dropped my hand and blew out a breath. "The way I understand it—and I'll need to double check this with Dad—is that the Raven has different types of feathers. When we go to him for a feather, we usually end up with one of the smaller wing feathers; they're called secondaries."

"You know about types of wing feathers?"

"I *am* in the Raven clan. We're experts on all sorts of ornithological facts. Anyway, his feathers act like drops of pure magic. They add extra *oomph* to whatever we're doing."

"So, the feather is like a battery," Juliana said, and I nodded. "But the feathers we got were really big. Were they tail feathers?"

Noticing details was what Juliana was best at. "He gave us three of his primary wing feathers, the most powerful help he can offer. If the secondaries are drops of magic, the primaries are each a full jug's worth."

Juliana shuddered. "I'm glad you held on to the feather. But why was it one feather for two people?"

"Ah, they're really powerful. Probably takes two people to wield them."

"But why us?" she pressed. "It's not like I can use magic. And the other two were given to Sara and Micah, and your parents."

Juliana let the insinuation hang in the air but stopped short of saying that the Raven had paired us off. "The thing with magic is that it doesn't require skill," I explained, letting that implication lie, at least for now. "Not when you start off with it. What it needs is for the user to have a clear conscience, a strong will, and a good and noble heart."

"And you think I have those qualities?"

I touched the back of her hand. "I know you do."

We stared at each other for a moment, then the realization that I was sitting on her bed in the middle of the night hit me and I pulled back. The last thing I wanted to do was push Juliana too far and ruin the trust I'd rebuilt with her. Her trust meant everything to me.

"So, yeah, they're pretty powerful, but don't worry," I finished, confident. "You can handle it. The Raven wouldn't have given them to us otherwise."

"Why don't you ever call him Bran?" she asked.

"I've only ever heard him called the Raven," I replied. "I didn't even know until earlier that his name is Bran."

"Bran Corbeau," Juliana said. "Such a regular, forgettable name."

"Hey, there's nothing regular or forgettable about us Corbeaus," I countered with mock outrage. "Just try and forget me, baby."

"As if I ever could." Juliana yawned and glanced at the dark window. "Is it really late?"

"A little after midnight. Why? Got a one o'clock date?"

She smirked. "Funny. What I have is exhaustion, and I usually can't get back to sleep after one of those dreams."

I almost offered to stop her nightmares, but I stayed quiet. If I asked and Juliana refused to allow me back into her dreams, it would crush me. I'd been crushed enough already.

"Then we'll stay awake," I suggested instead. "I'll have the silverkin make us some coffee."

"You really don't mind?"

"I really do not mind."

Juliana smiled, then tossed the blankets aside. She was wearing a long-sleeved knit shirt and these little pajama shorts, and it was hard not to stare at her legs. "You know what this means?" she asked.

"What?"

"You're my one o'clock date."

I draped my arm around her shoulders. "I'll even walk you home."

"You have a good heart, too," Juliana said, then ducked her head.

I smiled. Rebuilt trust was a beautiful thing. "You know it."

17

Sara

I stared at that spot where the Raven and Aregonda had just been, clutching the feather Micah and I had been given. "What should I do with this?" I asked no one in particular.

"Keep it safe," Mom replied. "For now, we just need to keep them safe."

I nodded. "I'll put it in my room."

My mind was blank as I climbed the stairs and opened the door to my and Micah's chambers. I sat on the bench in front of my dressing table and spied the empty glass vial that had once held the tincture of queen's lace. Since I'd gotten it at the apothecary, and the crone had turned out to be my ancestor, I set the vial on the feather to hold it in place. That seemed appropriate.

Micah entered the room and sat on the bench beside me. I leaned against him. "How long have we known each other?"

"Less than a year," he replied. "I will admit, on occasion it feels like I first saw you only yesterday, while other times it's as if we married a thousand years ago."

"A thousand good years?"

He wrapped his arm around me and kissed my hair. "The best moments of my life have been spent with you."

"So much has happened in a year, and more is coming." I took his hand and traced the lines on his palm. "What was your life like before you met me? Was it this crazy?"

He laughed. "Hectic? Yes. Crazy? Perhaps." He paused. "Before I met you, I was busy. The demands of the manor, the Whispering Dell, and the Iron Queen were many."

"I bet Ferra made some interesting demands."

"That she did." Micah tilted up my chin. Up close, his silver eyes still made me catch my breath. "And while I was never without tasks, be they handling disputes in the village or fending off that madwoman, I handled them all alone. Now I have you."

"Does that mean I'm your sidekick?"

Micah's brows peaked. "If a sidekick refers to a much-loved companion, one I cannot fathom living without, then yes. You are my sidekick."

My head drooped, and I pressed my cheek against the bare skin below his throat. He was always so warm and comforting. "Will I be the same after I'm the Inheritor?"

"No, I don't think you will," he replied. "You will be stronger, and we do not know how your abilities will be enhanced. Perhaps not by much, as you are already very powerful. The addition of your mother's magic makes everything quite unpredictable."

I swallowed hard. "Will anything change between us?"

Micah hunched down so he was at eye level with me. "No. Nothing will ever change what I feel for you. You could be the most powerful Elemental in all the worlds or the least You could lose every bit of power you possess and become a Mundane human. My love will remain constant."

I closed my eyes and let out a breath, feeling a weight lift from my heart. "Thank you."

"Do you know how you can best thank me?"

"How?"

"By letting me off this bench."

I opened my eyes and saw that he was perched on the very edge of the bench and in imminent danger of sliding off. "Want to go swimming?"

Micah was always down for a dip in the Clear Pool. I still preferred showers to splashing around in a pond, and Micah had grudgingly accepted my "indoor waterfall," but there was something special about the Pool's water. It was always cold, but it left me feeling refreshed more than chilled. Micah claimed that the water was enchanted, and I believed him. More than that, my time as "regular" Sara was nearly over. I had no idea what would happen after I became the Inheritor, and I wanted one last good experience with Micah.

Of course, we were never alone in the Pool. The Bright Lady lounged on the far shore, combing her long teal hair and overseeing everything that went on in her waters. Micah and I waved in greeting, then ducked under the surface and swam toward the eastern shore. That part of the Pool had several underwater boulders arranged so the water reached our shoulders—or in Micah's case, his elbows. Micah sat on a boulder, and I sat on his knee. He steadied me with his arm wrapped around my middle, just in time to feel my belly rumble.

"I'll ask the silverkin to prepare us a meal," he said. He stood and moved toward the shore. One of the little guys was already waiting, and Micah explained what we wanted. Since he was occupied, I swam toward the Bright Lady.

"Hello, Sara," she greeted. "May I comb your hair?"

"Sure."

I sat in front of her, and she set to work on my hair with her pearl-handled comb. Having the Bright Lady of the Clear Pool tend to your hair was both an honor and a luxury.

"Sara, I am so very sorry about your sister," she said. "If there is anything I can do for you or your family, name it."

"Thank you." A tear rolled down my cheek and splashed into the enchanted water. "Now that Sadie's gone, I'm going to be the next Inheritor of Metal."

"Do you want to be the Inheritor?"

"I just want to live here with Micah." I watched him standing on the shore as he instructed the silverkin. I assumed that in addition to ordering food, he was telling them to man the manor's defenses and activate the wards against all things gold. Oriana didn't care that we were in mourning, and she'd be here sooner rather than later.

Despite our dire circumstances, I loved looking at him. The water had flattened his fluffy silver hair against his head, and droplets glinted on his warm brown skin; once, I'd said he was the color of caramel. Micah thought of himself as oak-colored. The moisture on his skin threw every muscle and sinew in sharp contrast, and I was left with one overriding thought: my husband was hot, and I was a very lucky woman.

"When will you take on your new role?" the Bright Lady asked, rousing me from fantasizing about Micah.

"Soon. The sooner the better, really." She finished my hair, and I turned to face her. "We have a lot going on."

"So I have heard." The Bright Lady replaced her comb, then checked her appearance in an abalone mirror. "I have also heard tell that you can wield more than just metal."

I blinked. "You hear about what happens beyond the Pool?"

"My dear, I know everything that happens on and in the water."

"It was so strange," I said. "I told the water what to do, and it listened. Metal doesn't even listen to me, but the water did."

"Perhaps metal has been speaking to you in a much more subtle manner," she suggested. "Water makes its will known . . . either as a babbling stream or a crashing wave, or anything in between. But now that you have listened to water, perhaps hearing the other elements will come more easily to you."

"Maybe. I did mess around with stone a bit."

"And how did that go?"

"Pretty well."

She smiled. "A good start, then."

I watched her arrange her combs on a polished slab of river rock. "You know, I don't even know your name. Unless it is just Bright Lady?"

She smiled, her cheeks round like apples. "My name is Shelliya."

"That's pretty," I said, and Shelliya blushed. Micah concluded his business with the silverkin and sat beside me.

"Apologies for taking so long," he said.

"It's all right," I assured him. "Shelliya and I were just talking."

"Were you?" he asked. "Tell me, Bright Lady. A year ago, could you have imagined a more perfect mistress of Silverstrand Manor?"

"Never," she replied. "But I never doubted you would find your mate."

After our time in the Clear Pool, Micah and I spent the rest of the day relaxing in our rooms and keeping the silverkin busy with endless requests for food. I wanted to taste everything one last time. What if all these flavors changed after I became the Inheritor? Research needed to be done.

Despite our late night, the next morning we were up with the sun. When we went downstairs, we found Max and Juliana sprawled out on the couch, fast asleep. Juliana was lying on her side with her head resting on Max's lap, while he leaned back against the cushions with his hand on her shoulder. The table next to the couch was littered with empty cups and plates.

"Looks like they had a late night, too," I remarked. I moved to shake Max's shoulder, but Mom entered the room and shook her head at me.

"Let them be," she whispered. "They've both had little enough peace of late."

I nodded. "They're always moving toward each other. I wonder if they even realize it."

"I think they do." Mom faced me then, her brow furrowed. "Beau placed the jar in Sadie's library."

"Why—oh." I swallowed. "You think I should do that now? Before breakfast?"

"I don't think putting it off will benefit anyone, least of all you." Mom's expression softened as she embraced me, her soft, golden hair tickling my neck. "You'll watch over her?" Mom asked Micah.

"Of course," Micah replied.

"Good." Mom drew back, pausing to touch my cheek. "Come find us afterward."

She left the room. I laced my fingers with Micah's and we climbed the stairs to the library together.

We sat in the middle of the library's floor and set the soul jar on the carpet between us. The library had been cleaned from top to bottom, and all evidence of Sadie's spellwork was gone. The silverkin had even shelved the remaining books. Sadie's library was complete, and she wasn't even here to enjoy it.

I stared at it, the soft glow emanating from under the jar's lid, wondering if I could do it. Wondering if I could release the essence within and let my sister's soul go for good. Wondering if I could be the Inheritor when Sadie couldn't.

"Love," Micah murmured, the first time either of us had spoken since we'd sat down. He'd always been patient with me, but I understood that this wasn't just about me. Time was of the essence.

"I know," I whispered. "I just don't know if I can do this."

Micah grasped my hands. "Of course you can. You are one of the strongest people I have ever met. You will be a fine Inheritor, just as Sadie was."

A tear fell onto my knee. "Okay." I wiped my cheek, then shook out my hands. "Okay. Let's do this." I moved to grab the jar, then hesitated. "Should you be here? I mean, will it be dangerous for you?"

Micah caressed my cheek, his hand coming to rest on the nape of my neck. "You did not abandon me in my hour of need," he said, referring to the time I stayed by his side while he was buried in silver. "I will not leave you in yours."

I leaned forward and kissed him, then grasped the jar. After a tense moment, I cracked the lid.

Nothing happened.

I opened it a bit further . . . still nothing.

"Um . . . Shouldn't something a bit more dramatic be taking place?"

"Truly, love, I have no idea," Micah replied. "I have never been present when a soul jar has been opened."

"Great." I stared at the dark interior of the jar, wondering if I needed to shake it a bit, or maybe tip it over so Sadie's soul could roll out. Were souls heavy? In the midst of wondering if souls were even visible, a blue orb made its way to the lip of the jar and peeked over the edge.

"It's shy, just like Sadie," I murmured. I noticed that the orb was tinged with whorls of copper, and I felt that lump in my throat again. "Is it still Sadie? Does she know we're here?"

In response, the orb floated out of the jar, hovering in place about eight inches in front of me.

"I would say so," Micah confirmed softly.

"Sadie?" I asked. The orb floated a bit closer. I cupped my palms together, and the orb nestled there. It was warm and tingly, like holding a ball of static electricity. "Oh, Sadie, I miss you so much." The orb quivered, then grew warmer. Was she trying to tell me something? "Were you really trying to make me the Inheritor?"

The orb floated upward until she was directly before my eyes. We looked at each other for a long moment, then I nodded. "Well, okay, if that's what you really want. But don't think we aren't having a talk about this when I finally reach wherever you are." The orb bounced up and down; had I just made a soul giggle? I laughed with her, only to have my heart clench when I realized this would be the last time I would laugh with my sister.

"I miss you so much," I said. "I had this whole speech planned. I was going to yell at you for not asking for help, for thinking you're not good enough. You were perfect, you know that? You were my perfect baby sister." The orb stopped moving. "And now that you're here, I don't want to yell. I just want to hug you and tell you how much I love you. We all love you, you know that?"

The orb floated toward me until she was against my jawbone. I moved so she was nestled between my face and my shoulder, which was probably as close to hugging an orb as I could get. What's more, I knew that Sadie hadn't meant for things to turn out as they had. She'd made a mistake, and she was sorry.

"It's okay. No one's mad at you. But if you could find a way to come back and visit us, that would be awesome."

The orb quivered, sending tingles down my arms and spine. She returned to hovering in front of me. "Of course, I'll still take the power," I said. "It's what you want, right?" The orb approached my cheek, and I felt warmth. Happiness.

"You're sure you don't want to give it to Max?" I asked. The orb stilled. "You're right. He's been through enough already."

"Sara," Micah began, hesitant. "Are you communicating with her?"

"Yeah. There aren't any words, but I know how she *feels*." The orb wiggled, and I laughed. "Sadie says she liked you from the get-go, even when you made her leave school and come here. She said you're a good man, and I'm lucky to have you."

Micah bowed his head. "And I am lucky to have known her."

"How much time do we have?" There was still so much I wanted to talk about with my sister.

"I am not sure, but I would imagine time is limited," Micah replied. Then he addressed Sadie directly. "Sadie, once you left the confines of the jar, your soul began to dissipate. Wait too long and you will not be able to transfer anything to Sara."

"This is it, then." I took a deep breath and said, "Okay, well, here I am, Sadie Grace. Power me up."

For a moment, the orb just floated in front of my face. Then she advanced, slowly at first, and disappeared through the bare skin at the base of my throat. I let out a breath I hadn't realized I was holding and looked at Micah.

"I guess that's it," I mumbled, then the full force of the Inheritor's essence hit me. Power pushed its way through my veins, my skin straining as if my mere body was too small to contain such forces. I could see nothing but blinding white light. I could smell and taste nothing but the light. Nothing else existed, only me and the power. The Inheritor's power.

My power.

It filled my throat and spilled out of my mouth, shimmered behind my eyes, seared itself into my bones. Its heat should have burned me, or at the very least choked me, but instead I laughed. It was just as the Raven had said: this power was *mine*. It recognized me, spoke to me, flowed through me. It belonged to me, and I belonged to it. It found the spark of the old magic within me and melded itself to it. I felt strong. Amazing. Invincible.

I was the Inheritor.

The light faded as the power settled deep within me, and a faint gleam danced across my flesh, the only lasting indication of my new abilities. My vision returned to normal, and I saw Micah sitting across from me. He hadn't moved a muscle, but his bloodless face and wide eyes told me that he'd watched, helpless, while I was overtaken by mysterious forces.

"Hey," I said, grasping his hands. "I'm okay. Really, I'm okay."

Micah nodded. "I see that, now."

"I guess I'm the Inheritor," I murmured, staring at my hands. I flexed my fingers, feeling the power shift and crackle inside me.

"No," Micah said, "you are so much more." He pulled me toward him, settling me between his knees. I pressed my forehead against his chest and felt the strong thump of his heart. "You are no mere Inheritor. Old magic flows through you as well; I can feel it as surely as I can feel copper and silver. You are a blending of the old and the new. My Sara, you have become a force unlike any other."

I peeked up at him. "What do we do now? Tell Oriana that I'm Super Sara?"

He shook his head. "I do not know if that would be wise. Let us confer with Baudoin before we act too rashly."

Micah and I stood, but when he moved toward the door, I remained rooted in place, clutching his hand. "What is it?" he asked.

I pulled him against me. "Thank you." When his only response was to quirk a brow, I elaborated, "For being here with me."

"Of course." I wondered when he'd gotten shorter than me, then realized I was floating. Micah reached up and pulled me back to the floor. "I could not let you deal with such forces alone."

I shook my head. "Not just this. You're always here for me, no matter what. Thank you for that, for picking me up when I fall, for barging into my dreams . . . Thank you for everything."

Micah smiled and traced my cheek. "My copper girl, you mean more to me than my life. I will always be here for you."

He embraced me, and we both floated toward the ceiling. "Whoa," I said. "Being the Inheritor has a learning curve."

"We shall learn it together," Micah assured me. We kissed, not as long as I or the new power inside me would have liked, but that was all right. We had work to do. There would be time for kissing later.

I thought heavy thoughts and we returned to the floor. I picked up the now-empty soul jar and said, "We've done as the Raven asked. Let's figure out what's next."

18

Max

I woke up on the couch with Juliana's head resting in my lap. I didn't even remember falling asleep.

What I *did* remember was trying my damnedest to make good on my word and stay up all night with Jules. The silverkin had helped, bringing us cookies and sandwiches and coffee by the quart. Juliana and I had hung out together for hours, talking and laughing about everything and nothing. We talked about our families, what it had been like for us growing up, and, eventually, about the Institute. I got to know her all over again, without the shadow of that hellhole hanging over us. Juliana was as amazing as she ever was, not that I had any doubts.

And now, here we were, snuggled up on the couch. Ever since the day we'd met, I wanted to wake up with Juliana. I never thought it would be like this.

I smoothed her hair back from her cheek. She

looked peaceful, as if all the horrors of the past few years had happened to someone else. If only they had.

Juliana stirred, then rolled onto her back and opened her eyes. "Hi."

"Hi." I kept stroking her hair. "Who do you think fell asleep first?"

"You did. I was going to draw one of those curly villain mustaches on you, but I couldn't find a marker."

Before I could snark back—and check a mirror—a shockwave rolled through the manor.

"What the hell was that?" Juliana was on her feet in an instant. "The last time I felt something like that—"

"Sadie died," I finished. I ran upstairs, taking the steps two at the time, hell-bent on reaching the library before I lost Sara, too. When I reached the library doors, I flung them open, and found Micah and a glowing woman standing in the middle of the room.

The glowing woman was Sara.

"What just happened?" I asked. Then I saw the soul jar in Sara's hands. "You did it?"

"I did." Sara leaned forward and crossed the room in a single step. "Whoa." She was as surprised as I was. Maybe more surprised, honestly.

I grabbed her elbow. "Relax, speed racer."

Micah took her other elbow. "There is so much power inside you, it doesn't know where to turn."

"It's overflowing, like the water was in the made. It's looking for someplace to go." Sara touched her face. "I wonder if this is how Mom feels."

"Let's go ask her," I urged, pulling Sara toward me. Ma was our resident expert on all things magical, and she needed to have a look at Sara before she exploded, or worse. "Think you can handle stairs?"

"Um, sure."

Sara and Micah went first, with him clutching Sara's waist and guiding her down the stairs. I wondered if he was trying to keep her from falling or flying away. The glow emanating from her skin bounced and refracted off the silver walls, making the manor look like a disco for fairies.

"Aren't you freaked out?" Juliana whispered.

"*So* freaked out," I whispered back.

Ma was waiting for us at the bottom of the stairs. Dad was right next to her, holding the now infamous copper scroll.

"I see it was a success," Ma began. Sara threw herself into Ma's arms. While they had their moment, Dad approached Juliana and me.

"The moment Sara became the Inheritor, the scroll changed," he told us.

"How do you know it changed the moment she did?" Juliana asked.

"Immediately after we felt the magic wave, the scroll began to glow."

"Strong indicator." I jerked my chin toward the scroll. "What's new?"

"It rewrote Sara's entry," he replied.

"How did it change?" Sara asked as she turned from Ma.

Dad handed the scroll to her. While she looked it over, he said, "The scroll proclaims Sara to be not only the Inheritor, but also equal portions of old and new magic. This is unprecedented."

"Unprecedented how?" I asked.

"It seems that she can be a true peacekeeper, pardon the term," Dad offered. "Sara can be the bridge between the old ones and Elementals, and perhaps also Mundane humans. Together, we can end the Peacekeepers once and for all."

"That's amazing," Sara said, looking at all of us in turn as she took a long, uncertain pause. "Exactly how would I do that?"

"If it was me," I posed, still thinking it through as I spoke, "I'd contact the most powerful old one I could find and have the rest rally around them." I turned to Micah. "Who's the most powerful old one in the village?"

"The Whispering Dell is not a place where those with power make their homes," Micah replied. "Those in my village look to me for protection."

"There must be someone nearby. Can't you ask another Elemental? Maybe someone in the queen's court?" I ventured, even though Oriana's people had never seemed to know much of anything.

"At the moment, I doubt any of us are welcome in the Gold Court," Micah countered, smug as usual. The guy just couldn't help himself. "We need the knowledge of one well-versed in the old magics, those creatures that have existed since the beginning."

"The beginning of what? Do we need a dinosaur?" Sara muttered.

As usual, Micah was right, and I knew it. "Then you mean not just old ones, but those with pure magics," I continued. "Earth spirits, people like that?"

"Yes," Micah agreed, not hiding his surprise at me actually knowing things. As if I hadn't grown up with the Seelie Queen in a house packed with magic. "That is exactly what I mean."

I looked at Sara, then we all turned toward Ma. Once she realized why we were staring at her, she rolled her eyes. "Bloody hell, *I'm* not an old one."

She had a point. "And while you are the Seelie Queen, you are not fae born," Micah clarified, making another good point. "The ancient lineages are held by those with pure blood." Ma sniffed, but didn't argue. It was the truth, after all.

"So, where do we find some pure-blooded ancient with old magic?" Sara asked. "The Magical Assisted Living Center?"

Micah didn't even raise an eyebrow; either he had no idea what an assisted living center was, or he'd built up an immunity to Sara's awful jokes. It was probably the latter. "I know of one such elder, but she is not likely to help."

"Why wouldn't she?" I demanded. "I mean, Sara can bring those of old magic on equal footing with Elementals. She can help them."

Sara immediately cut in. "Hey, hey, don't get ahead of yourself, Max, Sara *can't*—"

"You can," I interrupted, promptly cutting her off. I stared at Sara for a moment, then continued, "You can. You're already both, apparently the first being to ever be equal parts Elemental and old magic."

"I'm not sure any of the old ones will agree with that, but arguing about it now would be pointless," she conceded. "We can argue about it later, assuming we live through this."

"That's right," I said, then turned to Micah. "Well? Tell us the way to the old ones, silver man."

Micah ignored me, speaking directly to Sara instead. "Love, you must appreciate the danger she will put you in. She is not trustworthy. She would sooner sell her children's souls than commit an act of faith or trust."

"How bad can she be?" Sara sighed. "Is she a troll? An ogre?"

"Love, she is the Wood Witch."

Sara frowned. "Shit."

"Shit, indeed," I said. I didn't know much about the Wood Witch, other than that she was powerful and hated everyone outside her forest. Even Micah avoided her, and his land was arranged to intrude on hers as little as possible.

"Before you seek her out, you must gain a modicum of control over your new abilities," Micah urged. "If it appears that you cannot control your own power, the Wood Witch will deem you weak."

"She'll think I'm weak because I'm too powerful?" Sara asked.

"With the old ones, appearance is everything," Micah insisted. "You cannot behave as if this is a power newly gotten. You must exhibit enough control for her to deem you competent."

Sara stared at her hands. Flashes of light brightened and faded on her skin; if I hadn't known the power was a very deliberate gift from Sadie, I'd say it wanted out.

"I barely understand what's happened, and now I have to act like I've always been this way?" Sara took a breath and squared her shoulders. "How long do we have?"

Micah's brows lowered. "The sooner you learn to control these gifts, the better."

"Let me help you," Ma said. "Sara, let's take a walk outside. You too, Max."

"Me? What for?"

"You know slightly more about being an Elemental than I do." Ma turned toward the door. "Quickly, now."

I followed Ma outside. "Where are we going?" I asked.

"Far enough from the house that we won't damage it," Ma replied. We made it to the middle of the meadow, then Ma faced Sara. "All right. Show us."

"Show you what?"

"Everything."

Sara spread her arms wide, tilted her head back, and closed her eyes. The power cascaded out of Sara, threatening to take over everything around her. I could see it, hear it hum, and smell it like ozone after a thunderstorm. Sara's power surrounded Ma and me, pooling around our feet in an endless rainbow-hued wave. It was warm, and welcoming. The power loved being used, being free. It was happy.

The power noticed Ma and inched toward her.

"Enough of that!" Ma swatted away the tendrils of magic.

Sara opened her eyes. "What happened?"

"Left unchecked, this ability of yours would roll over everything, taking over minds and bodies by the dozen. Hundreds, maybe." The tendril reached again toward Ma. She shook her finger at it. "Don't you dare."

"How can I make it behave?" Sara asked.

"It needs someplace to rest when you're not using it. Someplace quiet and safe."

"Like its own room?"

"Yes, much like that. Imagine a box, small enough to fit in your hands. It must be dark, and safe, and have a tight-fitting lid."

"And a lock?"

"No lock," Ma replied, making a cutting motion with her hand. "If you need the power instantly, you don't want to be fumbling with keys and latches. A lid will do just fine."

"Make it like your dreamwalking shields," I suggested. "Strong and solid, but easy to roll back when you need to."

Sara thought for a moment. "This box should be like a soul jar?"

Ma nodded. "Aye. Like a soul jar."

Sara swallowed hard, then held her hands out like she was cupping water. A moment later, a clay jar appeared.

"Not a real jar." Ma touched her forehead. "One here, in your mind."

"Oh." Sara pressed her palms together, and the soul jar melted into her flesh.

"Did you just transfer the jar from the physical plane to the mental?" I demanded. "With a single thought?"

"Yeah," Sara replied. "It's sitting on top of my shields."

I stared at my overpowered sister, then said to Ma, "If she can move things between planes just by thinking about it, we're gonna need more than a couple hours of training."

"Be that as it may, a scant few hours is what we have," Ma said. "The jar is stable?"

Sara hesitated. "I think so. Now what?"

"Put the power in the jar. Don't rush it," I advised gently. "Take your time."

Sara gathered up the power that had stretched out across the grass, endless ribbons of blue and pink and green, red and purple, a few lengths of copper, and one wide stream of silver. She wound them up like skeins of yarn, like she was hurrying to pick up before company came over. Ah well. I'd tried.

"You'll want to separate those colors," I remarked.

Sara halted. "How do you even know what I'm doing?"

"You also need to work on your shielding," Ma added. "But focus on getting everything contained for now. We can refine things at a later time."

I could tell when the last dregs of power settled into the jar. Sara's shoulder's relaxed, and the lights stopped dancing across her skin. When she spoke, her relief was palpable. "Powers contained."

"Good," Ma said. "Now you need to keep others from knowing what skills you possess."

"Can't I just stash the jar behind my Dreamwalker shields?" Sara asked.

"A good idea, but no," I answered. "Dreamwalking already takes up a huge part of your inner world. If you keep the old magic alongside it, they might not get along well together." Panic skated across Sara's face.

"What?" I asked.

"Nothing. I just imagined old magic and dream-walking bickering inside my mind. That would definitely drive me nuts." Sara looked at Ma. "Have you ever dreamwalked?"

"No, but I have projected my senses elsewhere," Ma replied. "A similar technique, but one I learned instead of possessing it since birth. Now, let's see to those shields."

With Ma's and my help, Sara built a set of shields around her mind that would have kept out ten Iron Queens, a host of Peacekeepers, and hopefully one crotchety old Wood Witch. The shields, which were the mental equivalent of a twelve-inch-thick steel vault enclosure, had two key features. First, the length of it was hinged, so Sara could get at all her magic at once if needed. The second key feature was a small door near the center, good for offering quick glimpses at what she could do.

"Hopefully a glimpse is all the Wood Witch will require," Ma commented after we'd tested and re-tested Sara's shields. "Of course, you could always hit her with everything all at once. That would show her a thing or two."

"Wouldn't that kill her?" Sara asked, and Ma shrugged.

"Perhaps. If it did, would all her people be beholden to you?" Ma tapped her chin. "That may be the easiest way to get this done."

"Ma," I interjected. "Let's not make Sara a murderer."

"I'd really not like to add 'Wood Witch–killer' to my resumé," Sara added. "Am I ready to see her now?"

"Ready? No." Ma glanced at the sky; the sun was almost directly overhead, meaning it was near noon. We'd been at this all morning. "But I fear it's past time you got going."

Micah, Dad, and Juliana were sitting on the front steps of the manor when we returned. After Ma and I assured them that Sara had made good progress, we started planning her foray into the woods. That was when Sara realized she was going after the Wood Witch alone.

"Wait, I have to go by myself?" she asked.

"Yes," Ma replied, at the same time Dad said, "That is not smart."

Ma glared at Dad. "It is not," he insisted.

"What do we know about the Wood Witch?" Ma asked. "That she is powerful, and that she does not like to be disturbed. Better to send one person than bother her with an entire search party."

"We know more than that about her." Sara looked toward Micah. "Don't we?"

He swallowed, then began, "I know a bit more, but not much. Most importantly, I know that for as long as Silverstrands have lived in the Whispering Dell, we have avoided her wood."

"Why do you avoid her?" I asked. "I get that she's strong, but what does she do to trespassers? Turn them into bushes?"

"Max, if you are going to insult—" Micah began.

"Max didn't mean to insult her, or you," Sara interrupted. "And it's a legitimate question. What would she do to me?"

After tossing a warning glare at me, Micah replied, "Her ability lies in that of the wood, and those within. She could set a host of poisonous snakes after you, cause undergrowth to block your path, or draw down a cloud to obscure your vision. In her wood, you will be at her mercy."

"Okay, so anything could happen. Then why am I going alone?"

"To prove you understand the stakes," Juliana answered. "It's just like when you give your final dissertation. When you begin the class, you have tons of support from your teachers, classmates, reference material—but in the end, when you're standing before the academic committee and explaining your thesis, you're alone. You need to prove that you understand your subject inside and out, and that your research is sound. No one can do that but you."

"I didn't take a class," Sara said, but Juliana held up her hand.

"You didn't, but it's the same concept. I can tell people how powerful you are and what excellent control you have over your abilities are all day long, but it doesn't matter unless you exhibit those abilities and that control yourself."

Sara nodded. "All right, I'm going alone. Let me change and I'll set out."

She disappeared inside, and returned dressed for hiking in jeans, boots, and a hooded sweatshirt. I debated filling a canteen of water for her, but I didn't know how the Wood Witch would react to her bringing in water from outside her borders. Would she see it as Sara bringing a weapon? Better for Sara to be thirsty than unintentionally commit an act of aggression.

We gathered at the edge of the wood. Before Sara set out, we offered her a few last pieces of advice.

"Remember, you control the power, not the other way around," Ma advised. "It is strong, yes, but you are stronger. The power knows this, though it will try to test you. Be strong, be firm, and it will behave."

Dad added, "You are a Corbeau, but you are also a Connor. You are the best of all of us."

"You are a Silverstrand, too," Micah assured her. "Never forget how many want you to succeed. Draw from all of us if need be."

I punched Sara's shoulder. Lightly. "I always knew you were awesome."

Juliana surprised everyone by hugging Sara and whispering, "I'm so proud of you."

"Thank you," Sara said as she stepped back from Juliana, her eyes flitting between all of our faces. I wondered if she could tell how worried we all were, worried and proud all at once. If she could, I didn't notice. Her last words to us before she strode off into the forest were as confident as we could expect.

"Well, here goes nothing."

19

Sara

I walked out of the orchards and into the Wood Witch's forest, wending my way through the tall, densely packed pines. The ground was covered in fallen needles, making my footsteps as silent as a cat's. I wondered how long the forest would remain docile, and when I would come across the first bit of strangleweed or spray of venomous pollen. What I didn't wonder was how to find the Wood Witch. That wouldn't be a problem.

She will find me.

While my gaze darted about, searching for angry plant life and other undesirables, I noticed an utter lack of oak trees. That made me more nervous than the rest of the dangers put together. One of the reasons I'd so readily agreed to go to the Wood Witch was because of Micah's alliance with the oaks; surely, if I was hurt or captured, the oaks would let Micah know, and he'd rescue me. I now knew that wouldn't happen. I really was all alone, just me and a wacky new power I didn't fully understand or know how to control. Awesome.

I remembered all the well-wishes my family had offered. I wished all of them—or hell, just one of them—were here with me now.

The pine forest transitioned into a bog, and low, leafy green plants replaced the comfy pine needle carpet. Recognizing those leaves from a swamp I played in as a child, I found a stick and poked the soil between the plants; it was wet, but not unstable. Skeptical me threw the stick into the center of the plants, where it hit with a splash and sunk like a stone.

I'll just go around the bog. As the thoughts formed in my mind, I looked from side to side, then swore. Impossibly, the bog stretched as far as the eye could see in both directions. *Well, it's not like I thought that finding the Wood Witch would be easy.*

Despite my smug thoughts, I was pretty screwed. I could attempt to pick my way across firmer ground, but I had no way of knowing how much firm ground there was. And I was deliberately trying not to think about what was lurking in the mud, just waiting to nibble on my toes.

Think. The bog reminded me of the bedtime stories Mom used to tell Sadie and me; they were all about heroes facing trials and saving the day. This bog was my own trial, and I had to get past it to find the Wood Witch and save my family, the Elementals, and the entire Mundane realm. I was going to do this.

I took a deep breath and examined my surroundings. There were trees scattered throughout, and I briefly contemplated zigzagging from one tree to the next, or maybe swinging from one to the other like a jungle woman. Not that I had any rope, or the upper body strength to accomplish such acrobatics. In the midst of all this bad planning, I rubbed the mark on my wrist.

The *silver* mark on my wrist.

I'm the Inheritor of Metal, and there's a huge vein of silver hanging out below the Whispering Dell.

I laughed out loud, amazed I hadn't thought of it earlier. By the time my laughter faded, I'd sent out a ribbon of power and called a sizeable portion of the silver to me. Together, the power and I built a bridge that stretched across the bog. As I stepped onto the bridge and walked high above the muck, I laughed again. *If the rest of my journey is this easy, I'll be having tea in the Wood Witch's parlor any minute now.*

I spied movement in the bog and immediately crouched down. A few brown creatures splashed among the leaves. Otters, or maybe beavers? Only these animals didn't look like they could swim.

"Hang on, guys." I extended a hand, lowering the side of the bridge. As soon as the silver ramp reached the water's surface, all sorts of critters scrambled onto the bridge. There were chipmunks, kittens, rabbits, and other, well, Mundane animals. As I watched the parade of creatures shake the water from their coats, I realized that of all the things I'd expected to find in the Wood Witch's domain, regular animals weren't it. I'd been prepared for fairies, or ninja gnomes, or any manner of magical creatures trying to hinder me. The fact that she shared her home with squirrels and bunnies made me wonder if we weren't so different after all.

That was when the bees struck.

One moment was all it took for the previously empty air around me to turn black, the bees so thick around me I could feel their legs skittering across my flesh, their wings beating against me. I was covered in them, a living insect blanket that cut off my air and filled my ears. The wood hadn't managed to kill me with whatever was in the mud. Then it distracted me with bunnies and sent an air attack. If I lived through this, maybe I'd ask the Wood Witch to draw up a few battle plans for us to use against the Peacekeepers.

I crouched down, feeling the bees crunch against me as I folded myself into a ball. I steeled myself against the inevitable stings, the burning venom that would follow . . . but there was nothing. Just squashed bugs.

Is the old magic protecting me? I swept my hands across my body, wiping away the bees as if they were so much mud. The bees disintegrated as they hit the silver bridge, and a few moments later I resumed walking. *A vision of bees, then, unfriendly but not deadly.*

That didn't make any sense. Why bother creating a vision of bees that couldn't hurt or hinder me? It was a waste of energy, and no one as old or as experienced as the Wood Witch would behave that way. She would either ignore me altogether or send bees that could actually harm me. In the midst of my wondering, a large bee appeared and hovered in front of my face.

"Um, hello," I said. "Did you know those bees? I didn't mean to hurt them, but the swarm scared me."

The bee flew forward and perched on my shoulder. I remained stock-still, unsure if I should swat it, or run, or maybe dive into the bog. Then the bee touched its tiny leg to my neck, and I relaxed.

The bee wanted to help me.

"Sidekicks all around," I joked as I resumed walking. "I'm Micah's sidekick, and now I have a bee sidekick. We're superheroes."

Unsurprisingly, the bee remained silent. I reached the end of the bridge but hesitated before I stepped from the silver to the forest floor. I'd already endured two trials, and I figured these sorts of things often came in threes, which meant that I had one more task to accomplish.

I scanned the forest and noticed three paths winding through the trees; obviously, I needed to pick the right one to find the Wood Witch. The center path was wide and clear, and at the end sat a mimosa tree covered in fluffy pink flowers. The canopy was thin above the mimosa, and it was surrounded in bright sunlight. Birdsong wafted toward me, and the grass surrounding the tree was lush and green. It looked like an image of paradise.

Well, that can't be it. I turned to my left and saw a path that was as dark as the central one was light. There was a tree at the end, just like the light path, though this one was blackened and dead. Something that might have been a vulture, but was probably something much worse, glared at me from its perch atop the branches. The soil surrounding the trunk was bare and dry, as if the life had been sucked out of it. I really, really hoped that this wasn't the path I needed to take.

I looked toward my right and considered the remaining path. It wasn't exactly a path, more of a meandering trail, the edges overgrown with vines and thin, reedy trees. In addition to the vines, I spied thorn bushes and those smelly plants that grew near swamps. This path looked like a mess, in more ways than one.

At the path's end, there was a small evergreen shrub. When I say small, I mean downright miniscule; it couldn't have been more than two feet tall. Around the shrub was a scattering of green lawn, with a few violets and clover lending the grass a bit of color. Compared to the clearing with the mimosa, it was hardly worth a second glance. But I found it beautiful.

What are trees, if not understated beauty? I set off down the path, intent on reaching that lone shrub in the clearing. As I neared it, I saw it was small and squat, akin to a juniper, and my un-shut-off-able inner monologue started cracking gin-and-tonic jokes. A shaft of sunlight pierced the canopy, illuminating the shrub like a spotlight. The bee buzzed its wings, further confirmation that I'd made the right choice.

"I know it's you," I blurted out. It's not like I knew the proper way to address a Wood Witch. *"Your Woodiness," maybe?* "Please, show yourself. I need your help."

The shrub quivered, and the Wood Witch unfolded herself to her true height. She looked just the same as when I'd met her during our Beltane celebration at the manor, with her long, spindly limbs and bark-like skin. Her hair was a shining sheaf of yellow with violets woven into the strands, and her dress was a loosely woven mat of vines and leaves slung over her shoulder. Once the transformation from shrub to woman was as complete as it was going to get, she speared me with her sharp gaze.

"Help?" she repeated. "What could I possibly offer the Lady Silverstrand in the way of help?"

"You're one of the most powerful old magic beings in the Otherworld," I replied. "I need a patron to explain to others of old magic that I'm on their side. I want them to live as equals with Mundanes, equals with Elementals. I can make that happen. I can lead them."

The Wood Witch threw back her head and laughed. "You expect others of my kind to follow you, an Elemental? Are you mad, child?"

"I'm not just an Elemental." I stepped forward, holding out my hand, palm up. "I have old magic, too." With my other hand, I held up the Raven's feather.

The Wood Witch didn't move, save for a narrowing of her eyes. Was she looking into my soul? I could feel tendrils of magic poking at my brain, my mark, invading my sense of self and examining me down to the cellular level. As intrusive as it was, it was far less uncomfortable than the time Oriana had caressed my mark.

The Wood Witch frowned, and I felt the magic withdraw. "You speak the truth," she murmured. "How is this possible?"

"Basically, my family's been screwing around with magic for a few centuries," I replied. We didn't have time for me to explain the entire story, not that I even understood all the facts.

The Wood Witch's gaze landed on my shoulder. "You've allied yourself with the hive-dwellers?"

The bee fluttered its wings. I liked having allies. "I have. Will you help me?"

"What is your goal?" she countered. "Surely you're not merely altruistic."

"I want you to help me in the Mundane world," I replied. "I want your kind—*our* kind—to help Elementals stop the Peacekeepers. I want our people to walk freely in the Mundane world, like they used to."

The barest twitch of a woody brow, but it was there. Mirlanders, and the Peacekeepers that came after them, had long since eradicated old magic from Pacifica; the only reason Elementals had it any better was their belief that someday we'd serve as soldiers in their armies.

"What will we gain?" the Wood Witch asked.

"Freedom, for a start," I answered. "Once we've stopped them, you won't be oppressed in the Mundane world. You can do whatever you'd like there. Within reason, that is."

She scowled; maybe I should have phrased that a bit better. "We will take the matter under advisement."

"We're going to war literally at any second," I pressed. "I'd really like an answer now."

"And I do not speak for all of me and mine," she shot back. "Return to your cold metal home, little witchling. You shall have your response after we've considered your words." When I remained rooted in place, she raised her arm and pointed down the path from which I'd come. "Go."

Not wanting to gain firsthand experience of what a mad Wood Witch could do, I went. The way back was devoid of mad bees and suspicious wetlands, and I let myself believe that I'd (probably, hopefully) impressed the Wood Witch. Then again, maybe she was just waiting for me to leave her forest before she offed me, so my body wouldn't clutter up the place.

Near the edge of the wood, the bee on my shoulder took flight and hovered in front of me. "Thanks for going with me," I said. "It was good to not be alone back there. And if I hurt any of your bee friends, I'm sorry. I hope they're okay."

The bee landed on the tip of my nose, then buzzed off to make honey or do whatever bees did. I found Micah waiting for me at the edge of the orchards. Instead of calling out or saying a single word, he just folded me into his arms, tucking my head underneath his chin. I pressed my cheek against his chest and took all the comfort he was offering. It was more than enough.

"Did you find her?" Micah asked, as if he'd been holding his breath.

"Yeah. She's going to talk to her people, then her people will talk to my people." I leaned back and looked up at Micah. "She didn't seem too eager to help."

"That was to be expected," he said with a sigh, smoothing my hair back. "Still, nothing is lost by asking."

"What if they refuse?" I asked.

Micah pursed his lips. "Then we will find another way."

We broke apart and made our way toward the manor.

The long way, that is; I wasn't in a rush to report my failure, and Micah was content to wander around the orchard for a few hours with me, eating plums and talking about nothing. When we emerged, it was almost sundown, so we went inside and went to bed.

The next morning, we were woken by Max pounding on our door.

"Sis," he greeted, jerking his head toward the front garden. "You've got some visitors out front."

"I do?"

"Yeah. Like . . . a lot of visitors."

After we shooed Max away, Micah and I got dressed and went downstairs. When I opened the front door, what I saw made me stop dead in my tracks, causing Micah to bump unceremoniously into my back.

The Wood Witch was there, but she wasn't the only one. All factions of old magic were represented, from pixies to fauns to trolls. There had to be hundreds of them scattered across the meadow before the manor. Even Shelliya, the Bright Lady, was there, with Ash the Satyr blacksmith on her arm. And they were all looking at me.

"I believe you have your answer," Micah murmured. I took his hand and addressed the crowd.

"Have you come to a decision?" I asked, looking pointedly at the Wood Witch.

"We have not," she snapped. "We remain offended by your impertinence."

"Not all of us are offended," Ash cut in curtly. "We of fur and hoof and horn appreciate how Sara assisted us."

"I did?" I squinted at the gathering in the front lawn. It was hard to make everything out in the slanted morning light, but were there otters and rabbits among the fauns?

"She did not set out to rescue anyone," the Wood Witch challenged, but an otter stepped forward.

"But rescue us she did," he insisted, lifting his furred head. As the otter spoke, his torso lengthened, and his furry otter legs stretched into human limbs.

"Did you know there were otter-people out there?" I whispered to Micah.

"I did not," he replied, his eyes as wide as mine.

"You kept us in that bog for untold years," the otter continued. "Generations lived and died in that bog, having never known a life outside your borders. Yet when Lady Silverstrand noticed our plight, she did not hesitate to help us!"

"I disagree," the Wood Witch countered, because of course she did. "Sara crafted a bridge to see to her own passage. That you and yours also availed yourself due to her handiwork proves nothing!"

"It proves enough," Shelliya said. "I felt the plight of those trapped within your borders, and their relief upon escaping."

"*Plight*," the Wood Witch scoffed.

Shelliya's eyes narrowed. "Do you dispute what the water told me?"

Before the Wood Witch could either recant or dig herself deeper into a hole, a swarm darkened the skies. It was the bees, but they didn't attack as they had in the forest. The swarm hovered above the Wood Witch, something she did not enjoy very much.

"Hive-dwellers," the Wood Witch hissed. "Many bodies but one mind between you!"

The bee who had ridden on my shoulder appeared in front of me. Then a golden light obscured her. By the time it faded, the bee was gone, and a tall woman with honey-colored hair and insect wings stood next to me.

"Whoa," I said, taking a step back and bumping into Micah. He put his hands on my shoulders to steady me.

"We of the hive also stand with Lady Silverstrand," the bee-lady said. "You, Hedge Witch, attempted to set my hive against her. When she saw we meant no harm, she let us pass."

"Sara has always helped us," Ash continued. "All of us. From the moment she arrived in the Whispering Dell, she has sought to know our kind. She treats us as her equals and with respect. My kind stand with her as well."

"As do those of water," Shelliya added. "You would do well to remember, Wood Witch, that our kind is meant to work together rather than apart." She quirked an eyebrow and lifted her chin. "Perhaps *you* could learn something from the queen of the hive?"

The Wood Witch paled, her mouth screwed up tight. "Am I to take it you all stand against me?" she bellowed.

"I don't think anyone's against you," I said, shrugging. "Everyone's just expressing their opinions. And look, maybe we don't all have to agree. Maybe you can stay here in your forest while the rest of us fight together."

"Leave me behind?!" the Wood Witch screeched. "How dare you suggest that, you . . . you . . . inferior, second-generation—"

"Your insults demean only you!" Ash boomed, his voice reverberating off the manor's walls. The Wood Witch's mouth shut with a clack. "My kind stands with Sara!"

"As does the hive!" the transformed bee proclaimed.

"And we of water do as well!" Shelliya declared.

The Wood Witch glared at each of them in turn, knowing full well that they would cause her much more trouble than she could cause them on her own. She hissed and tossed her head. "Very well," she conceded. "It seems we will all follow you, little witchling. We will help you in your struggle against those who oppress our kind, and your Elementals."

I nodded, trying not to look as awestruck as I felt. Ash, Shelliya, and my new friends from the wood—

they stood up for me. If they'd each done it alone, the Wood Witch would have probably squashed their dissent, but together they were a greater force. And they wanted to lend me their help. My heart clenched. "Thank you," I managed. When they all continued staring at me, I pulled Micah close and whispered, "Now what do we do?"

"Sara!" Dad approached me from inside the manor, waving a scroll. "We have news from Aregonda! Those of copper will follow you!"

"They will?" I glanced from Dad to Micah. It had worked. Not only did we have old magic on our side, but all of those who had once backed Sadie were now with us, too.

"That's it, then," I said. "We can begin."

I put Mom in charge of making a roster of the magical beings. She did have the most experience in that area. Along with her notes, Dad listed those of copper and all of the resistance's resources, mortal and otherwise. It wasn't long before his tactician's mind had organized everyone into regiments fit for battle.

Juliana took one look at all he'd done and shook her head. "It's not enough."

"How could it not be enough?" I asked. "We've got the resistance, Elementals, and all of the creatures beholden to old magic. Centaurs, nymphs, you name it."

"I know. And I also know what the Peacekeepers have in the way of firepower. If you send a bunch of nature spirits at them, you're signing their death warrants."

I blew out a breath and scrubbed my face with my hands, imagining a herd of gnomes being blown to bits by heavy artillery. "Crap. You're right."

"What of the creatures with more violent tendencies?" Dad suggested. "Dragons, things of that ilk?"

"A sound idea, but those such as dragons are rare, even here in the Otherworld," Micah replied. "Those with what you call 'violent tendencies' tend to be solitary creatures."

I leaned back and looked at the ceiling. "Then what was the point of getting their support? So they can sprinkle pixie dust on the winner?"

"Sara," Micah admonished. "Our allies can bring much more to the table than just military strength."

"Yeah," Max mumbled, pushing back his hair with a hand. "Nothing like some cannon fodder that *sparkles*."

Micah's eyes flashed, but before he could speak, Mom cleared her throat. "Perhaps my redcap army could help," she said, fiddling with the hem of her sleeve.

I stared at my mother, who was clearly the most close-lipped being in history. "You have an army?"

I demanded. "And you were going to bring this up *when*, exactly?"

"Oh, they aren't *technically* mine," Mom explained, waving her hand. "They're the Seelie Queen's. The so-called current queen's, that is."

"Okay," I began, "and what kind of creature is a redcap?"

"Like a goblin, really," Mom answered. "Ugly little buggers. They're as nasty as the day is long. They fight with iron pikes and wear cold iron boots. As distasteful as they are, they're quite effective. Point them toward the enemy, and they'll decimate them."

"Why are they called redcaps?" I asked. "Is the cap part of a uniform?"

"Their caps don't start out red," Mom explained matter-of-factly. "They dip them in their victim's blood. The brighter the cap, the more kills to the wearer."

Not so long ago, such a declaration would have turned my stomach. Now I only nodded. "They sound like the exact kind of army we need. How do we convince them to join up?"

Mom grinned, and it was simultaneously heartening and terrifying. "Simple. I'll return to the *brugh* and reclaim my throne. The redcaps are beholden to the queen, whomever she may be."

I threw my hands in the air. "Right, yes. Very simple, Mom. And how do you plan on reclaiming the throne?"

She tilted her head. "By killing the sitting queen."

Only Mom and I went to the *brugh*; apparently you only need a small force to remove a queen and claim a throne as your own. *I must remember this the next time we visit Oriana.*

The *brugh* turned out to be a lovely little hill, blanketed in grass that looked ripe for haying. The hill was the lone elevated point in the meadow, which must have been convenient for all those late-night fae revels.

"So, this is where you met Dad," I commented, making a show of giving the place a once-over. "Most people's parents meet at school or work, have a first date at a museum or a nice restaurant."

Mom fixed her sky-blue gaze on me. "Luckily for you, your parents are exceptional. The entrance is this way."

I followed Mom around the base of the hill, thinking on my exceptional parents and their unconventional courtship. "Where was your first date?" I asked, unable to stifle my curiosity.

"I suppose that depends on what you consider a date. We spent the first night we knew each other drinking and carousing, but that was every night in my court. The next day, we went out for a bit of excitement."

"Excitement?"

"I took Beau to the Unseelie Court and marked its queen."

"Gods. You're both lucky you survived."

"As are you," Mom countered. "Here's the doorway."

What Mom called a "doorway" looked like a regular old stretch of hillside to me, but it called to the magic within me the moment I saw it. The grass and dirt wavered and disappeared, revealing a tunnel. Mom and I entered, and the tunnel led us to an area that looked like a pre-war historical romance movie.

We were in a long hall with exposed timbers on the walls and a layer of straw on the floor. There were two long wooden tables set lengthwise, the benches filled with people. Some were dressed as warriors, some as dancers, and some were obviously only there to have a good time. At the far end of the hall was a raised platform where a woman sat on a throne. She had long, slender limbs and a sheaf of straight dark hair, and she wore a sword belted at her waist. A gold circlet on her brow marked her as the current Seelie Queen.

"There she is," Mom said, jerking her chin toward the platform. "Eleanore."

"I thought the old queen's name was Eleanore."

Mom rolled her eyes. "Sara, there's *always* an Eleanore."

She strode down the aisle between the feasting tables, her head high and her arms loose at her sides.

When those seated at the tables saw Mom, they stopped what they were doing and stared. Just before Mom reached the queen's platform, a man blocked her path.

"Maeve Connor," he announced, as if everyone present hadn't already known who she was. "You've got some nerve to be showing your face here."

"Fergus, how lovely to see you," Mom greeted, her words as icy as the glint in her eyes. "Of course you think I have nerve. I've always had more than you."

Laughter rumbled across the hall, giving me the impression that Mom and Fergus had been more than casual acquaintances in the past. Red-faced, Fergus demanded, "Why are you here?"

"I've come for my army."

At that, the hall went dead silent. After a few moments of tension, Queen Eleanore cleared her throat. "That army is mine now."

"For the moment, yes," Mom replied. "We can do this one of two ways. Either you step down and give me the throne willingly, or I kill you. The choice is yours, Eleanore."

"Why would I step down?" Eleanore demanded, her voice going shrill. "And give my throne to you of all people? You, the queen who abandoned us to run off with a filthy human!"

"Hey," I interjected, but Mom shook her head.

"Let me, Sara," she said. She turned back to Eleanore. "I take it I'm to kill you, then."

Eleanore went white as a sheet, and Fergus drew his sword. It was bronze instead of steel, which I thought was both unusual and convenient. "Arm yourself, woman," he growled.

"This fight does not involve you," Mom told him. "Anyone may challenge the Seelie Queen for her throne, and no one will interfere. Have you forgotten your own laws, Fergus?"

"What if I kill you before you reach the queen?" Fergus countered.

Mom glanced at me, and a moment later Fergus's sword became a set of bronze manacles around his wrists. "What are you?" Fergus demanded, looking me up and down.

"I'm Sara," I answered, lifting my chin. "I'm good with metal. Threaten my mother again and I'll have to kill you."

Fergus's eyes widened. "You're his daughter," he said. "The one Maeve left with."

"Sure am. Now shut up." I clamped a bronze gag over his mouth and turned my attention back to Eleanore. "Last chance."

Eleanore stood and moved to draw her sword, but Mom ascended the steps in an instant and grabbed Eleanore by the throat. Eleanore clawed at Mom's fingers, gasping like a fish as her eyes bulged. When she went limp, Mom unceremoniously dropped her. Mom looked out over the hall.

It took me a second to fully comprehend what I'd just seen: my mother choking out the Seelie Queen. Actually, *former* Seelie Queen. "Is she dead?" I asked, tentative.

Mom glanced down at Eleanore. "Not yet. Why? Are you feeling merciful?"

I placed a hand on Mom's shoulder. "I don't really feel anything for Eleanore," I told her, "but I'd like it if you were merciful."

Mom smiled, her whole face softening. "You've a good heart, just like your father."

I smirked back at her. "Not like you?"

"I spent too many years in the *brugh* to have much of a heart left." Mom gestured toward Eleanore, and two people stepped forward and lifted her. "Bring her to the infirmary and see that she's cared for."

"You're not queen unless you kill her," someone shouted.

Mom didn't hesitate. "Who was queen prior to Eleanore?" she demanded, her voice ringing through the *brugh* as if the surrounding earth spoke with her. "*Me.* As you can see, I am not dead. Nor did I yield my throne. Therefore I have *always* been your queen. Have you any other questions? Are there any other challengers?" When she was met with silence, she sat on the throne and surveyed her subjects. "Wise choice."

"You weren't going to kill her at all," I whispered. Mom glanced at me and smiled.

A man stepped forward and went down on one knee. "How may we serve, Queen Maeve?"

Mom smiled. "For starters, you may call up my army."

The redcaps were terrifying.

They were no bigger than the silverkin, but their smallness only added to their air of evil. Every redcap wore a beard, be it long and white or short, scraggly, and brown, and their black eyes flashed as they glanced about their surroundings. Their boots had iron soles that matched the iron pikes they wore strapped to their backs. And yes, their red caps dripped blood down their necks.

"I thought the Seelie were the good fairies," I said to Mom. She'd assured me that the redcaps wouldn't attack except on her order, but I wasn't sure the redcaps knew that.

"Whoever told you that any of the fae are good?" Mom countered. "The Unseelie are a filthy lot, blatant in everything they do. We Seelie are just a bit more refined."

"By 'refined,' do you mean 'sneaky'?"

Mom grinned. "Aye, that we are."

Through a combination of Mom's magic and Dad's portals, we got the redcaps back to the manor. Micah was decidedly unpleased at having a company of murderous dwarves milling about the grounds.

"If any approach the village, they will be killed on sight," Micah advised Mom. "I cannot risk a redcap running amok among my people."

Mom shrugged. "They've been told not to break company under any circumstances. If one abandons his post and you don't kill him, I will. For disobeying orders."

She then walked off to speak with Dad, and Micah turned to me. "I will never understand how such a bloodthirsty woman gave life to you and your gentle sister."

My heart ached at his mention of Sadie, but I was getting accustomed to that pain. "But you understand how Max came about?"

The corner of Micah's mouth curled up. "Perhaps your brother took the bulk of his disposition from Maeve, and you are more like Baudoin."

"Perhaps." I surveyed the meadow, populated with redcaps and Elementals and scores of other types of creatures. "I hope I don't do anything during this attack that will change your opinion of me."

Micah shook his head. "Trust me," he began, taking my face in his hand. "That will never happen."

20

Max

Since my help wasn't needed to sort out the redcaps, I decided to head to the village. There was always something happening down there, and I was hoping to overhear some news from the Gold Court. Everyone knew how Sara and Micah told Oriana to pound sand, which meant golden retaliation would be happening. There was also an excellent bakery right in the village square, and Juliana had a sweet tooth.

She and I had been getting steadily closer over the past few days. We'd rebuilt a good deal of what we'd lost between us, which was great. What wasn't so great was that I didn't know if she saw me as a friend, or more than a friend. Hell, I'd even take *potential* more-than-a-friend status. As long as she wanted me in her life, I'd be content. I'd concluded that a steady supply of cookies could likely help with that. I was deep in thought about bakeries and ulterior motives when I heard the unmistakable sound of metal feet marching toward us.

I crested the last hill before the village and saw a company of gold warriors; most of them were standard animated metal, but the three in front were human. Can't say I was surprised to see them, but I was surprised that it had taken Oriana this long to send a response.

I slid a portal disc out of my sleeve, intending to return to the manor and warn the others, but the company's commanding officer sighted me, and I quickly slipped the disc back into its hiding spot. I didn't need these golden boys learning any of my tricks.

"Halt!" the leader commanded. He was tall and wiry, with perfectly polished gold armor that had obviously never seen battle. "State your name and your business."

"Why?" I exaggerated looking to the left, then to the right. "This isn't the Gold Court."

The leader blinked, then motioned two others forward. "Oriana is your queen no matter where you stand. State your name and your business."

I glanced at the other two warriors. Unlike the leader, their armor had seen some action. All three were gold Elementals, as evidenced by the marks on their arms and necks, but that didn't matter to me. Copper was harder than gold.

Now, the gold warriors behind the three humans could be a problem. They weren't sentient per se, but they were solid gold, like bigger, uglier versions of the silverkin. And there were a lot of them, more than even I would take on singlehandedly.

The three in front conferred with each other, betraying that these guys had no idea who I was. That gave me an advantage, and I was not going to waste it.

"Oriana may be *a* queen, but she's not *my* queen," I said, just to piss off the leader. "I'm not even from around here."

Leader-man spat at my feet. *Rude.* "Take him," he snarled.

I sidestepped the first two goons, but a third sucker punched me. I saw stars. I spit blood toward the leader's feet. They'd gotten the drop on me, but they didn't know who I was or that I was an Elemental. By the time I raised my head, my copper had already healed my mouth.

They struck first. I always struck last.

I clapped my hands together and two of the gold warriors slammed into each other. The noise echoed off the hillside; I bet the entire village heard the crash.

"Hey, I'm an Elemental, too. Looks like we have a lot in common." I spread my arms wide and flung the warriors to either side. "Is there, like, a club or something I can join?"

"Seize him!" the leader shouted. I held up my hand, and my ability held every bit of metal on the human warriors' bodies in place. They struggled forward, like mimes pretending to be trapped in molasses. As for the metal men, they may as well have been statues.

"Fun fact, I don't like being seized," I explained with a shrug, savoring the moment. These guys were fun.

The leader pulled himself free and drew his golden sword, and he beckoned the rest of his company forward. Knowing I couldn't take on that many at once, I dropped the portal and came out running in the manor's atrium.

"Gold warriors!" I yelled. "We have gold warriors approaching!"

Micah appeared in front of me. "Which direction are they coming from?"

"East," I replied, rubbing my healed but sore jaw. "At least thirty, maybe more. Most are metal."

Micah's eyes narrowed. "Sending so many gold warriors at once is an act of war. Oriana means to make an example of us."

Sara stood beside Micah and grasped his hand. "It's time to stop playing nice with her. I don't care that she's the queen. We can't let her get away with this."

"We can send the redcaps," Ma offered, as she sidled up beside Sara.

"Good plan," I said, grinning as I imagined the lead guard's face upon seeing a hoard of death-gremlins swarming him as he approached the manor. "I've already pissed off their leader."

"Shocking," Ma said.

"Save the redcaps," Sara cut in, sounding the most confident I've heard her sound since . . . well, since we lost Sadie. "I've had enough of Oriana's people pushing us around. They need to learn some manners."

Micah looked to Ma. "We may need to retreat in haste. Are the redcaps prepared to travel?"

"Aye," Ma replied. "I'll see to Beau and Juliana, and the rest as well."

Ma retreated deeper into the manor to finalize our escape plan. Sara and Micah headed toward the main entrance,

"Max, come with us," my sister said, meeting my eyes over her shoulder. "I want them to know they messed with my brother."

This was a Sara I could get used to seeing. "My pleasure."

She went out the front door and stood at the top of the steps, Micah and me flanking her. We watched the gold warriors approach, though the two I'd crumpled were nowhere to be seen. A scowl twisted the leader's face when he saw me.

"Lord Silverstrand," he began. "I am Rukmini, general and commander of the Gold Army. Queen Oriana demands that you remand yourself and your wife into our custody. And," Rukmini paused to glare at me, "we will apprehend that one, as well."

"No one is apprehending my brother," Sara countered. "Nor will anyone be 'remanding' anywhere."

"You allow your wife to speak for you, Lord Silverstrand?" Rukmini scoffed, not bothering to acknowledge Sara. Big mistake.

"My wife may speak for me, yes," Micah replied, his eyes narrowing to slits. "But if you need it said again in order to comprehend her words, she is disinclined to acquiesce to Oriana's demands, as am I. Max, do you concur?"

"Oh, I concur." There was a word I'd never said aloud before.

"This scoundrel you're harboring destroyed two of my gold men," Rukmini shouted.

Sara raised her eyebrows. "Only two?"

"Yeah, well, what can I say? I'm getting old." I rolled my shoulders and let my arms hang loose at my sides. "Can I help with the rest?"

"Sure."

Sara raised her hand. Suddenly, Rukmini and all of the human warriors were lifted off their feet and into the air, their legs working like cartoon roadrunners. She'd copied my move, but whatever. I'd tease her about it later. As for the metal men, Micah took care of the left side of the regiment while I decimated the right. In less than a minute, two dozen gold warriors were little more than shiny piles of rubble.

Sara crooked her finger and brought Rukmini forward, halting him a few inches in front of her nose. "As I was saying, we aren't going anywhere with you," she repeated dryly.

"The queen demands it," Rukmini sputtered. "You dare defy her?"

Sara flicked her wrist. Rukmini spun around, now facing his destroyed metal men and the human warriors still hanging in the air. "I'd say we look pretty defiant. So, here's what we're going to do."

"You presume to command me," Rukmini squeaked.

"Where do these guys learn to speak?" I asked. "It's like Shakespeare in the Park for the drama-obsessed."

"Maybe there's a gold finishing school somewhere." Sara giggled, then flipped Rukmini around to face her. "Mr. Rukmini, please advise her most gracious Goldilocks that if she wants to speak to me, or Micah, or anyone else here at the manor, she can bring her shiny gold ass here." She leaned forward and added, "And I want you to use those exact words. Tell Oriana to bring her shiny. Gold. Ass. Here."

Rukmini scowled. "Be warned, I shall return with the full force of the Gold Army."

"I feel duly warned. Micah, anything to add?"

Micah rubbed his chin. "Only that now, in hindsight, I realize that I should have returned to Oriana as her general. Truly, surrounding herself with such incompetents has hastened the queen's downfall."

Rukmini paled, then his face went red like a tomato. "Let's get rid of these guys before Ruk-man has a stroke," I suggested. "Bodies can be cumbersome."

"Sounds like a plan." Sara linked hands with me and Micah. "One, two, three!"

We shoved our abilities forward as one, thrusting the gold warriors away from the manor and as far out as we could get them. Thanks to the magical punch from my sister, they went pretty far.

"Don't hurt them," Sara urged. "Remember, we're the good guys."

"I know, I know," I said. Despite all my posturing, I didn't really have the stomach for violence. Destroying a few metal men was no big deal, but I'd never hurt a living person unless there were no other options. "That bought us some time, but I don't think Rukmini was kidding. We need to get gone before the rest of the army shows up."

"Agreed," Micah said. "Advise the others. I shall activate the wards around the manor."

"Will they hold against an army?" Sara asked.

Micah exhaled. "We shall know soon enough."

"Even if they destroy the manor, you can rebuild," I said. "You created this one, right? Maybe the next manor can be a full-on silver court."

"Very true," Micah said, and he seemed to seriously consider it. "A silver and copper court."

"Now you're talking."

While Micah and the silverkin activated the manor's defenses, Sara and I told the others what had happened with General Rukmini and the gold warriors. No one was surprised that Oriana had sent warriors to the manor, or that there had been metal warriors alongside Elementals. Luckily, Dad had already finalized our plan for attacking the Peacekeepers' main headquarters and was ready to move.

"With the addition of Maeve's redcaps, we Elementals and those of the old ways have the strength to take down our foes," Dad announced. "Now all we need is a way in."

That was Dad's plan in a nutshell: we infiltrate Mike Armstrong's main base, disable the defenses from inside, and take them down. The old man had a few more details than that, but that was the gist of it.

"And how do you suggest we infiltrate?" Micah asked. My gaze slid toward Juliana.

"Juliana knows a way," I said.

All eyes turned toward her. Juliana coughed, then said, "If I approach the main entrance with the proper access codes and a prisoner, I can get in."

"Can you?" Dad asked. "Peacekeeper facilities are notorious for not allowing anyone in or out."

"Jules is the master of breaking and entering," I boasted, and Juliana cringed. "I mean, in a good way."

Micah grunted. "How certain are you of success?"

"One hundred percent," she replied. "No one knows which access codes I've memorized, which means that no one has had cause to change any of them. What's more, my uncle and Langston don't know where I've been for the past few weeks. They have no reason to suspect I'd be working against them."

"They really don't know you're here?" Sara asked, surprised. "But you came here with the shapeshifter."

"I intercepted him before he gave his report, then I advised control that I had a mission that would take a few weeks to complete," Juliana explained. "If I go back with a prisoner and a report about you unmasking the shifter, it's just believable enough to get me in."

"Sounds legit," I agreed. "I'll be the prisoner."

Juliana made a cutting motion with her hand. "Bad idea. If you show up, you'll be shot on sight."

I couldn't help it—I grinned. "Really?"

As Juliana rolled her eyes, Dad said, "Take me, then."

"No offense, Mr. Corbeau, but they'll shoot you even quicker than Max."

"What about me?" Ma asked.

"Ah, they don't really know who you are," Juliana answered hesitantly. Ma's eyes flashed and Dad placed a hand on her arm. I exchanged a warning look with Juliana—implying the Seelie Queen was some kind of "nobody" was not smart. Juliana continued quickly, "You've been so low-key as the Seelie Queen that most think you're a Mundane woman who married an Elemental. For this to work, I have to bring in someone they've wanted for a long time."

"So me, then," Sara spoke up, leaning forward.

Juliana nodded. "You are who I had in mind."

"Why not me?" Micah demanded. "Your Peacekeepers know who I am. They've watched me attack their fortresses and foil their plans. I will go."

"They are not *my* Peacekeepers," Juliana snapped. "Now, think about your idea for a moment. I'm supposed to convince those people that I—one Mundane human—somehow overpowered the Lord of Silver? How exactly would I do that?" She shook her head. "There's no way I could capture you, and they know that. However, I can convince my uncle that I talked Sara into defecting to their side."

Micah sniffed. "As if an Elemental would ever side with Peacekeepers."

"Sara wouldn't be the first," Juliana said.

Micah opened his mouth, but I spoke first. "Elementals side with Peacekeepers all the time. Auster's been working with them for years. So did the Iron Queen. But the point is," I continued loudly when he tried to argue with me, "they've never dealt with anyone like Sara. She's smart enough to handle herself, and she's got the power to back it up."

Micah glared daggers at Juliana, his fists clenched. Before he said something he might regret, Sara spoke up.

"I'll do it. Juliana won't let anything happen to me. We can trust her."

"See that, big man?" I said to Micah. "Trust. It's a beautiful thing."

Micah gave me one last glare. A vein throbbed in his neck, which was new. I wondered if the Lord of Silver could have a stroke. "Juliana, you're certain?"

"I am." Juliana smiled tightly. "We just need to work out a few details."

Sara nodded. "Let's do it."

Sara, Dad, Jules, and I sat and worked out the plan for Jules and prisoner Sara to approach the Peace-keepers' headquarters and bluff their way inside. The whole time, Micah stood over Sara and scowled.

"Micah," I said under my breath, leaning toward him. "You have got to relax."

"I *am* relaxed," he bit off. *Okay, then . . .*

"The plan seems fairly simple," Dad confirmed. "Once they get past the gates, Juliana will disable the automatic defenses."

"And that," I added, "will clear the way for Dad's Elementals and Ma's creepy little goblins to breach the perimeter." I gave Juliana a long look. She dropped her gaze.

"What are Sara's duties?" Micah asked.

"Sara's job is to protect Juliana and take care of any wards or other magical defenses," Sara answered, then leaned back and regarded Micah. "I'm right here, you know."

344

"I know." Micah caressed Sara's hair. "How could I forget?" For all that I didn't understand what Sara saw in him, there was no denying that Micah cared for her.

"All right," Dad declared. "We all know our roles. Let's get to work."

He rapped the table, and everyone except me got up to prepare. We'd come up with a good plan, well thought out and everything.

Only problem was . . . it wouldn't work.

When Juliana passed by me, I touched her arm. "Hey," I began. "About this plan, you and a prisoner."

She squared her shoulders and faced me. "What about it?"

"You really think it'll work?"

Juliana blew out a breath. "Yes. Maybe." She looked at me, her brows peaked. "It's awful, isn't it?"

"I wouldn't say *awful*." I turned to the table and grabbed a fresh sheet of paper and a pencil. "But we can probably make it better."

Juliana sat across from me and watched as I sketched out the Peacekeepers' grounds. I knew from the look on her face that this was nothing she hadn't considered before, that she'd been holding this back on purpose, and for good reason. "You know that there's only one way this is going to work," I told her solemnly.

She swallowed, then nodded, resolute.

"I know."

21

Sara

Within an hour, all of us were ready to return to the Mundane realm and leave the Otherworld and Oriana behind. By "all of us," I meant the regular residents of the manor, the Elementals Micah had recruited from the village, the creatures brought by the Wood Witch, and Mom's redcaps. Jovanny's resistance forces were set to meet us in the Mundane world, along with others of copper.

"Is Maeve certain she can control them?" Micah asked. He was standing at our bedroom window, which just so happened to look out over the redcaps. Ever since their arrival, they'd hunkered down in the side garden and watched us, the moonlight reflecting dully off their iron pikes while their glassy black eyes darted from side to side. No, having that right outside the window hadn't interfered with my sleep at all.

"I guess so." I peeked around Micah's shoulder at the redcaps and shuddered. "They don't move or even eat unless she orders it." I looked up at Micah and frowned. "Really, I have no idea."

"I trust your mother implicitly, but I do not trust those creatures," Micah muttered. "Stay close to me."

I nodded. "Okay."

We went downstairs, and once the portaling logistics were worked out, the whole mismatched lot of us arrived at the rendezvous point in the Mundane realm. The Wood Witch's creatures blended into the surrounding forest, while the Elementals blended in with Jovanny's people. The redcaps followed Mom like loyal dogs at heel, snarling and snapping and scaring the crap out of those who were just now meeting them.

Dad called for a final meeting in Jovanny's tent. There was a map of the Peacekeepers' campus spread across the camp table.

"This is as close as we can accompany you," Dad said as he pointed to a location on the map. "From there, you and Juliana will approach on your own."

"Okay," I confirmed, trying to gauge the distance from Dad's finger to the Peacekeepers' front door. It looked awfully far. "We can do that. Right, Juliana?"

"Right." Her face was set, almost grim. "Are we going now?"

"I don't see why not," Dad replied.

We organized ourselves into a not-completely-awful formation and picked our way down the mountainside toward Peacekeeper World Headquarters. We whispered among ourselves as we marched, like my brother who just couldn't help muttering plans under his breath. Only the redcaps were silent, being that they hadn't yet been given leave to speak. As for me, I couldn't stop wondering what would happen when all this was over. And we still needed to deal with Oriana.

Eventually we ran out of mountainside and reached the road. It was the only paved road in the general area that was in good condition, and it led right to the campus's main entrance. While everyone else took cover in the trees, I looked up at Micah.

"Here's where I get off," I told him, offering what I hoped was a reassuring smile.

Micah set his hands on my shoulders. If he was reassured, he didn't show it. "Be safe, beloved."

I smiled at the pet name. "You've never called me that before."

Micah tilted my chin up with one long finger. "Be cautious, come back to me, and you'll be amazed at the many ways I will tell you how much I love you."

"Bet I love you more."

"I will take that wager."

I kissed him—not a goodbye kiss, just an I'll-see-you-soon kiss—then looked around for Juliana. Outfitted as she was, in an olive drab coat and jeans and with her hair pulled back, she looked like a soldier. "Ready?"

"Absolutely not." As she started toward me, Max grabbed her shoulder and squeezed.

"You'll do great, Jules," he assured her.

Juliana nodded, then turned toward the road. I followed her, and we headed into the dragon's den.

We marched straight toward the base, though I have no idea how I made it that far. I was so nervous my hands were shaking, and if I hadn't been walking, my knees would have probably knocked together.

We reached a checkpoint with an automated recording machine, complete with a keypad and a video screen. The machine was attached to a device that barred the road. While open fields stretched on either side of the checkpoint, I knew Peacekeepers well enough to know that those fields were likely littered with land mines.

Juliana keyed a code into the machine. After some beeping and a few flashing lights, the bar ascended and we resumed walking. "How many of those are there?" I asked.

"Just one more before the door."

We walked in silence to the second checkpoint. Juliana entered her codes, then there was nothing between us and the perimeter fence topped with barbed wire. The road led directly to a set of steel doors.

"Why aren't there any guards posted at the checkpoints?" I wondered. "Or drones?"

"Don't worry, they're out there," Juliana said. "The codes I entered indicated that I was bringing in a valuable prisoner." Her gaze slid toward me. "Funny, for all those years, they thought you were the Inheritor, and they were wrong. Now you *are* her."

I made a sour face. "Glad I worked that out for them."

Juliana turned back toward the steel doors. "A team of experts is currently verifying our identities and scanning us for weapons." Lucky for me, my weaponry was factory standard. While I contemplated how this all seemed just as easy as our raid on the mades' prison camp, Juliana took my hand. "Sara, I need you to know something."

I glanced sideways. "Is it a code or something?"

"No." She swallowed. She stopped walking and dragged me to a halt. "You really are the best friend I've ever had. Now that Sadie's gone, you're pretty much my only friend."

It was my turn to swallow. "Yeah, well, you were always there for me, even when I didn't know it."

"And Max," she continued. "I never got to fully answer your question, but yeah, there were feelings between us. Real feelings."

"I get that," I said. "He still has them."

Juliana cocked her head to the side. "You think?"

Wow, she really thought he didn't love her anymore. "I don't *think*. I *know*."

Juliana took my other hand. "I love you like a sister, Sara. I'm so sorry."

"Sorry?" I felt the prick, like a bumblebee had gotten angry with my palm. I withdrew my hand from Juliana's and saw the tiny syringe clutched in hers.

"Why?" I asked, staring from my palm to her face. "I . . . thought . . ."

A tear slipped down Juliana's cheek. "I'm sorry," she whispered as the steel door slid open and Peace-keepers filed out.

I passed out before I hit the ground.

When I woke, I was sitting upright in a chair, which was just weird. I couldn't remember ever having fallen asleep in a chair, and why I'd fall asleep in the uncom-fortable wooden contraption I was now sitting on was a true mystery. Then I felt the plastic cords binding my wrists and ankles to the chair, and my memory returned in a rush.

Juliana had betrayed me. Again.

Man, I am not *the smart one.*

"Wakey, wakey."

I looked up and saw a thin, pale, oily-looking man with bug eyes so huge I worried they'd pop loose at any moment. My captor was Langston Phillips, the man who'd spent years torturing my brother and other Elementals.

"Langston," I croaked. "I don't think we've been formally introduced."

"We have not," Langston said. "Though Juliana has told me all about you, Miss Corbeau."

"Actually, my name is Sara Silverstrand," I corrected. "Did your spies forget to tell you about my wedding?"

"I'd hardly call a dalliance with a lower being a proper marriage," Langston sneered.

I bared my teeth. "Insult my husband again and I'll kill you."

"You're in no position to make threats," he admonished. "Juliana has assured me that you'll be most compliant."

He smirked and looked over his shoulder; I followed his gaze and saw Juliana behind him, standing as far away from Langston as she could in the small room. "Yeah, I'm wicked compliant," I said, my narrowed eyes meeting hers. She immediately glanced away. "Always have been."

"Good." Langston moved to the side, and I saw a helmet covered in wires and electrodes perched on the table behind him. It looked an awful lot like the diagram Juliana had shown us of Mike's dreamwalking helmet. "Your brother was compliant, too, once he understood what was at stake."

"What *is* at stake?" I asked, not taking my eyes off the helmet.

"For Maximilien, it was Juliana's life. For you, perhaps the lives of your family members will encourage your cooperation."

Langston opened a cabinet and brought out a rather terrifying-looking machine balanced on a metal cart. It was covered with lights and dials and had long, curling cords attached to defibrillator paddles.

"What is that?" I demanded.

"Just something to help you talk," he answered matter-of-factly.

"You haven't even asked me anything yet," I challenged. "You're supposed to ask, and when I refuse to answer, *then* you torture. Seriously, it's in the villain handbook. Look it up."

Langston struck me across the face with one of the metal paddles. "You are not in control here."

The pain made me momentarily senseless. I opened my mouth, but instead of words, blood dripped onto my chest and leg. Despite the gore, I could already feel my fractured cheek bone knitting itself back together.

"Enough!" Juliana grabbed Langston's arm and pried the paddle from his grasp. "You've already incapacitated her. Hurting her now won't help you learn anything."

"She's hardly weak," Langston spat. "She's the Inheritor."

"She was never trained," Juliana shot back. "Now stop the unauthorized violence, or I'm getting Mike."

Langston narrowed his eyes at Juliana. "Interesting threat, coming from you." He switched off the machine and grabbed the helmet, calling over his shoulder, "Now, you sit tight until I return."

The door clacked shut, and Juliana was at my side. "How much does it hurt?" she asked, dabbing at my chin with a cloth.

"Not much," I said. Even though he'd hit me with everything he had, I could already feel myself healing, though I wasn't sure how.

"That's good. I can't give you back to Micah missing any teeth." She cleaned up the side of my face, but I wasn't falling for the best friend act again.

"What happened out there?" I asked. "Why was I unconscious?"

"I injected you with deadening drugs," she replied.

"You really are the worst friend."

"What else could I do?" she countered. "Deadening drugs are the only substance proven to quell Elemental abilities."

"What do you call it, the Max Special?" I sneered. Juliana winced, the only sign I'd gotten to her up to now.

"Max helped me come up with this plan," she murmured.

"With the two of you in charge, we'll be dead in no time."

"Think about it, Sara. What else could have been done, other than the drugs?"

With that, Juliana left me alone with my thoughts. They ran the gamut, from feeling pissed off, to stupid, to just too damn tired to deal with all of this. Eventually, I fixated on Juliana's wording.

Deadening drugs are the only substance proven to quell Elemental abilities.

Elemental abilities.

I wasn't just an Elemental. I was healing where I sat, and I finally knew how.

Tentatively, I sent out a few magic tendrils. My old magic was in perfect working order. Juliana had only incapacitated the Elemental side of my abilities, which meant it wasn't my copper healing me. It was pure old magic. It also left me with an ace in the hole. No Peacekeeper knew I could work any other sort of magic. Well, not unless Juliana had told them.

Somehow, I knew she hadn't. At least I hoped she hadn't, so I sent out a few more magic tendrils and completed what Juliana and I were supposed to have already done: one by one, I disabled the exterior cameras, then the drones, and the infrared surveillance. Finally, I unlocked every perimeter ward, and a fair few inside the building. I wondered what reckoning I'd unleashed.

Peacekeeper World Headquarters was a ticking time bomb. And I was sitting in the middle of it.

22

Max

I had to hand it to Jovanny; for all the missteps the resistance had taken along the way, they were handling this mission like trained soldiers. I liked to think it was because Dad and I had scrapped their old plans and drawn up new ones, but who knows. Maybe Jovanny had it in him all along.

After receiving their orders, the resistance broke into teams and disappeared into the landscape around the main Peacekeeper campus. The copper Elementals following Aregonda had done the same. Those of old magic had disguised themselves among the trees and undergrowth, doing what they did best. Even the redcaps were behaving. It was looking like we might actually pull off this mission.

During a calm moment, I approached Aregonda. "How's it going?" I asked.

"Well," she replied. "We've stationed stone around the perimeter, much like the last mission. We have also located the main water source for the base. I have water Elementals surrounding it to see what they can learn."

I nodded. "Are you doing okay?"

Aregonda blinked. "Me? I'm fine. Why do you ask?"

"After everything that happened with the Raven, I wondered if you'd gotten punished."

"Ah." Aregonda looked over her plans and shuffled a few papers. "You're concerned that by helping you, I've compromised my immortality."

"Have you?"

"Bran would never punish me, if that's what you're asking," she answered. "But I did break a magical contract. I'm sure any ramifications will make themselves known soon enough."

"I'm sorry," I said, and I was. It wasn't fair that Aregonda ended up suffering when all she'd done was try to help us.

She cupped my cheek. "Don't be. I've been flirting with punishments for a long time. First when I rallied those of copper, then when I joined the resistance. If anything, I should have made myself known to you earlier. We waited a long time for your generation, and I am beyond grateful I got to meet you and your sisters."

"We're lucky we got to meet you, too," I told her, and I meant it. "Still, working with magic can be a raw deal at times, can't it?"

She laughed softly. "It certainly can."

After my talk with Aregonda, I checked in with the rest of the factions. Just like she said, everything was going according to plan. Eventually, I glanced at my watch. Exactly thirty-three minutes had passed since Juliana and Sara had left us. "Sara's probably out by now," I announced. "Let's move."

"Out?" Micah repeated, looking down at me. "I understood that Sara and Juliana were entering the establishment."

"Yeah, well, that plan would have gotten both of them killed," I clarified, bracing myself for more disapproval. "Me and Jules modified the plan."

An instant later, His Silverness was so close I could smell his breath. "Modified in what way?" he demanded. I tried stepping back, but he wrapped his fingers around my bicep in a vise grip. "You will tell me, and tell me now, what is happening to Sara."

"Micah," Dad said, placing his hand on Micah's shoulder. "Be calm. I am certain Max would not endanger his sister, or Juliana for that matter." Micah glanced between me and Dad for a long moment before he released my arm.

"Max, *s'il vous plaît*, explain why you altered our plans without first discussing it with us," Dad pressed. Ma stood beside him, her arms crossed over her chest.

"Think about it," I began. "If Sara and Juliana had just wandered into the place, no matter their cover story, they'd be thrown into a cell. A cell that would be warded against Elementals and who knows what else. We did this whole song and dance a few weeks ago, and look how well it worked out then. For this plan to work, Jules had to make them *believe* that Sara had been captured." I paused for breath and looked at the three sets of eyes glaring at me. In hindsight, maybe I should have at least clued in Ma and Dad.

"And?" Dad prompted. "How will Juliana accomplish this?"

"At the first checkpoint, Jules will enter a code advising that the Inheritor of Metal has been captured," I replied. "At the second, she will enter that the prisoner is about to be incapacitated."

"Incapacitated how?" Ma demanded.

I looked at my mother and felt like I was gonna throw up. What kind of a brother sets up the only sister he has left for this kind of stunt? "Deadening drugs."

"*What?!*" Micah roared, grabbing me by the neck. This time, Dad didn't stop him. "What will these . . . these *deadening* drugs do to Sara?!"

"Block her Elemental ability . . . put her to sleep . . . nothing else . . . " I gasped as I tried to pry Micah's fingers from my throat. "Sleep of the dead, so . . . so she can't dreamwalk."

Micah let go of my neck so abruptly I stumbled. "You are a fool," he growled. "You think that making Sara helpless is the way to win this bout? You think that making her a prisoner is anything other than reckless?"

"Yeah, I do," I shot back. "Listen, I know Peace-keepers better than any of you. I was their prisoner for ten years. I know how they operate. There is no way—*no way*—Jules and Sara could get in there without one or both of them ending up a prisoner. This way, with Sara as the prisoner and Jules acting like a Peacekeeper, Jules can disable the defenses and get the rest of us in."

"I was also their prisoner," Dad said quietly. "It is not something I would wish on anyone, least of all my child."

"All of your children have been their prisoners at one time or another," I countered. "Stick to the plan, and this will be the last time Peacekeepers imprison *anyone*."

"How do they know that Sara is now the Inheritor?" Micah asked.

I met his gaze. "Jules already sent them a message letting them know."

Micah turned toward the Peacekeeper campus. "So, they are expecting them. Like as not, my wife is already in a cell."

"She's my sister, too," I snapped.

"And our daughter," Dad cut in. "Max, Micah is correct. This was reckless. You should have informed us of this change."

"Couldn't do it," I said, shaking my head. "Sara's every thought plays across her face; if she was a poker player, she'd be in debt up to her ears. She needed to believe the plan, which meant that you three needed to believe it as well." I looked from my parents to Micah. "C'mon, she's with Jules. She's as safe as anyone can be while they're with Mike and Langston."

"As safe as you were?" Micah demanded, his voice low and cold.

Ice slid down my spine as I remembered how Micah had first seen me: naked, unconscious, and covered in wires and electrodes. Still, I made it, the only Elemental who ever left the Institute outside of a body bag. I lifted my chin. "I'm still breathing, aren't I?"

Micah looked down at me with a gaze meant to humiliate and terrify me. I didn't flinch. I'd already survived worse than he could ever do to me. "If Sara is harmed, I will take it out on you in kind."

"Have a little faith in your wife," I countered. "Sara can handle this. Let her be strong and do what needs to be done."

Micah's face went from scowling to abject fury. He spun on his heel and stalked off.

"Max, inform the rest of this change in plans," Dad ordered. "Report back when that is complete."

Before I could respond, he and Ma walked off in the other direction. I sighed and headed for the stone Elementals. I knew no one would like the new plan, but it had to be done. Now I just needed Sara and Juliana to hold up their end.

After I'd clued the rest of the resistance in on my and Juliana's change of plans, me, Ma, Dad, and Micah climbed up to a ridge that loomed over the main access road. It gave us a good view of the base's building and the surrounding area. Micah and Dad kept in radio contact with Jovanny, and they directed the ground forces in tandem. All in all, it was a waiting game.

"The wards are down," Ma told us after a very tense hour. "All of them."

"Are you certain?" Dad asked.

She gave him a pointed look. "Of course I am. Our girl did exactly as she was supposed to do." Ma glanced at me, then turned and walked away. "I shall alert the redcaps," she called over her shoulder. She then descended the hill, which left me, Dad, and Micah standing on the ridge.

"See, guys?" I prompted. "Sara and Juliana know what to do. We'll be in and out of there in no time."

"For their sake, and yours, I hope so," Micah murmured, then turned to Dad. "Baudoin, shall we wait for word from the redcaps before moving further?"

"We will not have long to wait," Dad replied. I stood beside him and watched as the red-topped imps swarmed down the hillside and used their pikes to batter the concrete boundary wall into pebbles, all in less than two minutes.

"Those critters are going to demolish the place," I muttered.

"Yes, with your helpless sister inside," Dad shot back. "Maximilien, how did you obtain those drugs?"

"After we rewrote the plan, I portaled to the prison where you were held," I explained. "That place was stocked to the gills."

"Your first mission upon returning to the Otherworld is to destroy the rest of that poison," Dad commanded. "As for Sara, hopefully we can get to her before the Peacekeepers discover our little ruse."

"Sara's not helpless," I said, "and neither is Juliana." When Dad refused to look at me, I turned to Micah. "C'mon, you of all people understand what Sara is capable of."

"Just because Sara is powerful does not mean I wish her to be in harm's way," Micah replied, his words clipped. "But you are correct. Even bereft of her Elemental abilities, she is far from helpless." He eyed me, then added, "When she learns of your treachery, she will likely skin you alive, if she has not already taken out her anger on Juliana."

Man, I hadn't thought of that. Sara didn't lose her temper often, but when she did it was only a shade more manageable than Ma's, and I'd left Juliana right in the line of fire. Well, Juliana had been friends with Sara for years, and if there was anyone other than Micah who could find a way to defuse her anger, or redirect it toward the actual bad guys, it would be Juliana. *Juliana's smart, and Sara isn't stupid*, I thought as I saw the redcaps scale the rubble they'd created and charge into battle. *They'll figure it out. Together. And they'll get out of this alive.*

I realized my thoughts sounded something like a prayer, but the ensuing action below snapped me out of it. Those Peacekeeper scumbags had no idea what hit them.

Not only did we have a host of magical creatures and all five elements represented, but those redcaps were the real deal. They swarmed over the checkpoint and then the outer walls of the facility, leaving nothing but rubble in their path. Ma led them herself, and she was just as bloody and ferocious as the imps. She was a warrior down to her bones, and she fought like she was born on the battlefield. I hadn't seen her grin like that since Sadie was born.

"We should have been using redcaps all along," I remarked to Dad. We'd taken a new post near one of the downed checkpoints to direct the battle. It was the perfect spot, being that it offered cover and was elevated so we could observe and direct most of the action.

"Apparently so," Dad agreed absently. His gaze never left Ma, tracking her every move.

"Have you ever seen Ma fight before?" I asked.

"Oh, yes. Many times." Dad glanced at me and

grinned. "Is she not beautiful?"

"Kind of bloody for my tastes," I replied, before I realized I was discussing my mother's hotness with my father. And my future therapy bill just got bigger.

"Who is that?"

"Huh?" I followed Dad's gaze and saw a man standing on the highest point of the facility's roof. He was too far away for me to see his features, but I could make out his raised arms and the tiny whirlwind that grew between them.

"Auster," Micah said, coming to stand beside us. "The rogue Inheritor of Air your Juliana spoke of."

"That's Avatar's successor?" I asked. While I'd never really known Jorge Vasquez—the previous Inheritor of Air who'd gone by Avatar—I'd known his brother, Galen, almost as well as I knew myself. It hurt to think that his son was working with the enemy.

"The way he stands reminds me of Jorge," Dad remarked. Avatar had been one of his closest friends. "If Armstrong is setting Auster against us, he means to stay and fight."

"So do we," I said. "If we portal to the roof and flank Auster—"

"I will handle him," Micah declared. "Then I will find Sara."

"You're going up against an Inheritor alone?" I demanded. "No, man, I'll come with you."

Micah looked at me, his eyes harder than his metal. "No. I will do this alone. Afterward, I will see to my wife, as you should see to Juliana."

Micah strode down the road yelling Auster's name. The Inheritor noticed him immediately and threw little cyclones into Micah's path. Micah retaliated by raising a wall of silver in front of him.

"He's going to get himself killed," I growled.

"I am sure the Lord of Silver can withstand a bit of wind," Dad replied. "This is the perfect distraction. Max, go now."

"Go where?"

"As Micah said. See to Juliana, and your sister, too."

He didn't need to tell me twice. I portaled inside the fence and slipped through one of the many holes the redcaps had smashed in the walls. Once inside the main building, I climbed up to a mezzanine level and checked out the open area below. There was a mass of Elementals and made fighting each other, some wielding their elements better than others. When I scanned the crowd and didn't see either Juliana or Sara, I melted into the shadows and considered my next move.

Sara and Juliana were obviously free, but where were they? I remembered how Juliana said that all of these facilities were set up with identical floor plans, making it easy for Mike to move from location to location. That meant that his office was always in the same spot relative to the main entrance . . . and so was Langston's.

The only person Juliana had ever wanted to see dead was Langston. And Juliana wouldn't wade through this mess to get to him. No, she'd take the tunnels.

I found an elevator shaft and opened the doors; luckily, the car was already on the top floor. I held it there with my ability, just in case, and climbed down to the bottom level. Once I got out of the shaft, I found the tunnel entrance, turned due east, and ran.

23

Sara

I'd been alone in that room for who knows how long, strapped to a wooden chair while staring at Langston's cart of torture devices. Of course, I'd loosened the ties that bound me *much* earlier, right after I'd disabled the main surveillance systems. The only cameras working in real-time were the ones watching me, and other internal goings-on.

While my magic had been taking care of the surveillance, my brain had figured out that Juliana hadn't betrayed us. She'd gotten me exactly where I needed to be, and the Peacekeepers didn't suspect us. If nothing else, Langston had believed Juliana was on his side. I hoped the rest of the Peacekeepers believed it, too.

The last perimeter camera went dark. I'd done all I could do, and now I had to concentrate on staying alive long enough to find my way out of this place. In the midst of wondering how I was going to do that, Juliana entered the room.

"You okay?" she asked by way of greeting.

"I hate you," I said, playing along for the camera.

"I guess that means you're doing fine," she said, quirking one of her fabulously expressive brows.

"All those questions, asking me about how Micah and I met," I continued, "you were just fishing for information. You didn't care at all about me."

Juliana looked at me, then blinked and looked to the left, exactly where the room's surveillance camera was located. "Yeah, that's what you did," I added. Juliana blinked again and looked to the right; she wanted me to know that there was something significant there. I reached out with my old magic and felt a data panel hidden behind the wall. "Did you want me to think you were my friend again?"

"Yeah, I wanted that." She wrapped her arms around her waist and turned toward the control panel. "I told you, I only ever wanted to be your friend."

I rocked the chair legs against the linoleum floor. "You tie up all your friends? I never knew you were kinky."

"That's me. Kinky."

She turned sideways, her gaze moving from me to the concealed panel, then back to me. I knew what she wanted, but I was still mad about being bound to the chair, so I blankly returned her stare. Juliana uttered an unintelligible noise of frustration, withdrew a gun from the back of her jeans, and shot out the camera.

"Goddammit, Sara, use your magic to open up the data panel," she shrieked while I stared at the remnants of the camera. "I swear, you're as thickheaded as your stupid brother."

"Hey," I said, rising from the chair as my plastic bonds fell to the floor. "You take that back."

Juliana stared at the plastic cords. "You could have left at any time."

"What, and wreck our awesome plan?" I strode over to the data panel and waved my arm. Prompted by my magic, the access door slid open, and I was confronted with a million blinking lights and switches. "What is all this?"

"This is where the Institute for Elemental Research's files are stored," Juliana replied. "Everything that was done to Max, and to the rest of the Elementals, is recorded here."

I stared at the contraption. "So we shouldn't break this."

Juliana shook her head. "No, that would be bad." She stepped forward and began entering codes, her fingers a blur over the keys.

"Do these files include everything that was done to you, too?" I asked.

She faltered, then her fingers resumed their fluttering over the controls. "Like I said . . . everything."

"Why didn't you ever take them before?"

"Only Langston knows the code to open the panel," she replied. "He's not really the sharing type."

"I think I'm starting to hate him as much as you and Max do."

She stared at me, her eyes hard. "No, you don't." A small cartridge popped free. Juliana grabbed it and slipped it inside the inner pocket of her leather jacket. "Let's get out of here, before they figure out where we are."

"Um, don't they already know?" I asked, looking at the remains of the camera.

"Actually, they don't," she answered, and I caught the smallest hint of a smile on her lips. "There are five interrogation rooms identical to this one. I rerouted the video feed from this room to the one furthest from here. Then I disabled the door mechanisms along the only corridor that accesses this room. I also looped the recording of you sitting in the chair. It'll take them a while to figure out what room we're really in, and that we've left it."

"Max wasn't kidding," I said. "Your superpower really is your mind." I looked around the room, my gaze stopping at the single door. "If you disabled the door mechanisms, how are we getting out?"

"Simple." Juliana flipped a switch next to the panel and a trapdoor opened, revealing a set of stairs that led to a tunnel. "We take an alternate route."

"Why isn't there any metal here?" I asked. The closest metal I could sense was in the building's outer structure. "It's like the Institute all over again."

"The short answer? Langston's terrified of Max," Juliana replied. "Ever since you wrecked the Institute, Langston has been convinced that Max was plotting his murder."

"He's not wrong." I trailed my fingertips along the pea-soup green walls. "Do all of these places have tunnels? And how do you know which way to go?"

"Every location is identical, right down to the paint on the walls and the linoleum on the floor," Juliana explained. "Mike prefers to use his imagination for twisting bodies and minds, not interior decorating."

The fact that we were walking down a spacious, well-lit corridor in a Peacekeeper facility was somehow creepier than if it had been a packed dirt tunnel. I kept expecting armed guards to jump out at any moment. Based on the way Juliana held her gun at the ready, so did she.

"I've never seen you with a gun," I commented. "When did you learn to shoot?"

She paused, then spoke slowly. "It all started when I was ten. That was the year Mike put his hands on me at a family barbecue. After my parents screamed at each other for a day or two, my mother signed me up for self-defense classes. When Mike found out, he told my dad that a few punches and kicks wouldn't stop him. The next day, Dad took me shooting."

"I'm sorry."

Juliana looked at me and shrugged. "Don't be. Mike's an evil, evil man. He'll get what's coming to him."

We came to an intersection, and Juliana stopped. "You take the west tunnel. It will get you back to the surface. I'm going east."

"We're splitting up?"

"West will take you right to the main entrance. Your family is stationed on the hill above," she explained. She withdrew the data cartridge from her jacket. "Give this to Max. Tell him it contains the records from the Institute, enough to convict Mike and more."

I grabbed her shoulder before she could take off down the other tunnel. "Wait, where are you going?"

She didn't turn to look at me, but she didn't shrug my hand off either. "I'm going after Langston. Even if I don't make it out of here, the data needs to. The world needs to know that Mike's a monster."

"If you don't make it?" I countered, and I knew I was probably talking too loud. I didn't care. I tried to pull her around, but she stood her ground. "Juliana, this is crazy! What about Max?"

Juliana jolted out of my grasp. "Max would understand," she said. Then she pulled back the safety on her gun and started down the east tunnel.

"I can stop you!" I called after her.

She didn't hesitate. "You won't."

She was right. I stared at the data cartridge in my hand, the tiny plastic and wire component that could end the nightmare that Elementals had been living in for decades.

"I'm coming back for you!" I yelled, my voice echoing against the tunnel walls. "You're no traitor, Juliana Armstrong! You're my best friend, and *I'm coming back for you!*"

Her only reply was silence.

I turned toward the west tunnel and put one foot in front of the other, trying not to think of what awaited Juliana in the other direction. It was only a few minutes before I heard footsteps coming toward me. I flattened myself against the tunnel wall, wondering if I should hide and hope whoever it was didn't notice me, or if I should leap out and attack. I'd just decided on the offensive when my brother came into view.

"Max!" I exclaimed as I stepped away from the wall.

"Sara!" He pulled me into his arms, one of those awkward big-brother hugs that squashed the breath out of me. "You okay?"

"Yeah, Langston just tied me to a chair and hit me with a metal paddle thing," I replied. He released me and I glared at him. "You knew about the drugs?"

"Don't be mad at Jules," he warned, which was admission enough for me. He glanced around, then asked, "Where is she?"

"She went after Langston," I answered. "I wanted to stay with her, but she insisted on going alone."

"Goddammit," Max growled as he smacked the wall. I grabbed his sleeve just in time to keep him from bolting off after her.

"She also wanted me to give you this." I withdrew the data cartridge from my pocket and set it in his palm. He turned it over a few times, fingering the shiny black case.

"Is this what I think it is?" he asked.

"It's the records from the Institute," I replied. When Max smiled and shook his head, I asked, "How did you even know that? It's not labeled."

"Jules always said she would use these records to put Mike in prison for a thousand lifetimes," he explained, almost wistful. "It was one of her goals, back then. One of *our* goals."

"You two had a lot of goals?"

"Yeah. No. Well, two big ones. The first was to stop Mike."

"And the other?"

Max closed his fist around the cartridge. "Get far, far away from the Institute and live our lives together."

"You're both out, so that goal's accomplished," I posed. "Go, get her out of whatever trouble she's in. Then we'll nail Mike with that data, and you two can dream up some new goals."

Max moved to put the cartridge into his jacket, then reconsidered and handed it to me. "Get this to Dad."

I nodded. I didn't like that he was going after Juliana alone, but I wasn't about to stop him. "Portal out and get help if you need it. Don't be a hero."

"Sounds like a plan. Hey, Micah's on the roof fighting the Inheritor of Air."

I swatted Max's shoulder. "You're telling me this now?"

"Lay off," he said. "Listen, go fifty meters, then take a sharp left. The service elevator will take you straight to the roof." He squeezed my elbow. "Good luck, sis."

I punched his shoulder. "Go get your girl, cowboy."

"We are so lame."

We laughed, then went in opposite directions.

I ran the fifty meters to the elevator, then stood in the carriage for the interminably long time it took to reach the roof. When the doors opened, I burst out of the elevator, ready to rescue Micah from whatever horrible things Auster was doing. If that windy creep thought he was hurting my husband, he had another thing coming. As it turned out, I didn't have to be worried about Micah.

He was standing at the crest of a metallic mountain, which was an amalgam of whatever nearby metals had answered his call. The Inheritor of Air was clear on the other side of the roof and was using tiny whirlwinds to throw all sorts of garbage at Micah. I crept along the roofline until I was beside my husband.

"My beloved." Micah leaned over to kiss me while simultaneously shielding us from a barrage of debris. "I trust your brother's foolish plan has left no lasting harm?"

"Max means well," I said, skipping to the side to avoid a shower of gravel. "That's Auster?"

"Yes. Juliana was correct about his disloyalty to his own kind." Micah crooked his finger and peeled up a section of the roof. He flung it at Auster.

"Have you ever fought an Inheritor before?" I asked.

"A few," Micah replied. "Why?"

"You're doing a good job."

Micah glanced at me and smiled. Auster used Micah's distraction to his advantage. A gust that hit with such force I could see it blew up and hit Micah in the chest, sending him skidding to the edge of the roof.

My head snapped around and I glared at Auster. No one messed with my Micah.

I reached for my Elemental abilities, but they were still out. *Thanks, Max.* I slid back the door to my old magic, and I asked what it could do against wind. A picture formed in my mind, and I grinned.

"Wind," I called, and Auster's tiny whirlwinds and hurricanes left him. They danced around my feet, kicking up mini dust storms. "Micah, are you all right?"

"I am." Micah got to his feet and drew his sword. "How did you do that?"

"Old magic."

"Excellent. Bring the traitor here."

I sent one of the whirlwinds to fetch their former master. A moment later, it dumped Auster in a heap at our feet. "What have you done to my ability?" Auster demanded.

"Your winds?" I crouched before him and showed him the gusts and gales dancing upon my palm. "They're mine now."

"But I'm the Inheritor," he spluttered.

"Hey, I'm an Inheritor, too," I said. "Metal, specifically, but other Elements like me, too. I mean, they *really* like me, but my other abilities are what grabbed your winds. What *you* are is a traitor."

Auster started to say something, but I sent a gust to steal his breath. "Listen, we don't want you. We want Armstrong, and you're going to take us to him."

Auster blanched, then looked behind me and grinned. "Looks like he's already here."

I turned around and saw Eddie, the fire made we'd rescued a few days ago. He was wearing Peacekeeper fatigues and had flames dancing down his arms.

Next to him was a company of soldiers led by Mike Armstrong himself.

24

Max

I jogged down the tunnel. I wanted to run but wasting energy when a fight's imminent is a bad idea. The tunnel curved, and when I came around the bend, I saw Juliana a few paces in front of me. She was walking slowly against the wall, her gun up and ready.

"Jules," I called. "Sara showed me the data."

"What did you do with it?"

"Nothing yet. Sara's bringing it to Dad."

She glanced over her shoulder and nodded. "Good."

I caught up to her and peered down the tunnel. "You think Langston's down there?"

"I have no idea if he is or not," she admitted, "but I have to check. He needs to be stopped."

"You've got that right." I stepped in front of Juliana. When she tried moving around me, I put my hands on her shoulders. "I'm going with you."

Juliana gave me a sad smile. "There's no reason for both of us to fall into his trap. Go. Save the data."

"You think this is a trap?"

She shrugged. "It's Langston."

"All the more reason for me to go with you." I slid my hands down to her elbows and squeezed. "I told Sara that getting the data and exposing Mike was always one of our goals."

"Yeah? What did she say to that?"

"She said that I should help you get Langston so we can think up some new goals. Maybe ones like we used to have about a life on the outside. Together." Juliana's cheeks darkened. She stepped back and lowered her gun.

"C'mon, baby, let me help you."

Juliana glanced up, fire dancing in her eyes. Then the floor opened up beneath her. She didn't even have time to scream.

I fell to my knees and pounded on the floor, punched it, pulled with my ability, but whatever trapdoor had taken Juliana from me had not only shut me out: it wasn't metal. I could have portaled after her, but my portals needed a location to lock onto, and without knowing the layout underneath the tunnel, I risked landing on a wall or a drinking fountain or worse: a body.

I slammed the floor one last time before crumpling to my hands and knees, blubbering. Goddamn

Langston for taking my tear ducts. Tears released endorphins, and I could use a few thousand of those right now.

Shit. I gritted my teeth and forced myself to take a slow, deep breath. There was a way out of this. Even though I couldn't follow Juliana, I knew someone who could. I portaled out of the tunnels and came out standing in front of Dad.

"I need an earth mover and Ma," I demanded as he stumbled back into a resistance aide. Heh. I hadn't gotten the drop on the old man since I was ten.

Dad steadied himself, opened his mouth, then closed it when he saw the expression on my face. He nodded, then murmured something to the aide, who went scurrying off. His hands clasped my shoulders. "What has happened?"

"There's an extra layer to this place," I explained as I grabbed a map and a pencil. "Juliana and I were in the tunnel here," I paused and marked the location, "when a trapdoor opened beneath her. Oh, and Sara has the Institute records. Remember to ask her for them." Dad nodded just as his aide returned. She was followed by a girl that looked to be about twelve years old.

"Max, this is Lil," Dad introduced, motioning toward the girl. "She is the strongest earth mover we have."

I nodded, biting my tongue so hard I could taste blood. Then I remembered Illyana, the fire Elemental

I'd done time with in the Institute. She hadn't been much bigger than Lil, but she packed a mean punch. I looked the girl dead in the eyes. She didn't even flinch. "Lil, you up for scoping some tunnels?" I asked.

She snapped her gum. "Sure."

"Awesome. Where's Ma?"

Dad gestured toward the battle. "Leading her redcaps, of course."

I sized up the chaos. "Come on, Lil," I said, heading toward the fighting, pleased when she didn't hesitate. "I'm taking you to meet my mother."

We plunged through the battle, dodging Peacekeepers and the made and Ma's crazy imps. Ma herself was perched atop a pile of rubble, her shield dented and her face and arms streaked with blood. By the look on her face, I knew that none of that blood was hers.

"Ma, you gotta portal me to Jules," I pleaded. Then I gave her a quick rundown of what had happened in the tunnels, including my meetup with Sara.

"What of her?" Ma asked, nodding at Lil.

"Lil's here to learn the tunnel layout and report back to Dad," I replied. "I just need you to get us in."

"Would you like a redcap to accompany you?"

I glanced around at the bloody berserkers. "Ah, thanks, but it's a confined area and all," I replied. "Might do more harm than good, you know?"

Ma nodded, then placed one hand on Lil's shoulder and touched my forehead. "Think of her," she said. I closed my eyes and pictured Juliana as I last saw her, eyes wide as she fell into the trap and away from me.

When I opened my eyes, Ma, Lil, and I were standing in a corridor outside what looked like an ordinary office door.

"Juliana is inside this room," Ma explained. "I thought it best to give you the element of surprise."

"Oh, Langston knows I'm coming," I muttered. "Thanks, Ma. I'll take it from here." Ma teleported out, and I turned to Lil. "As soon as you to learn the layout, report back to Baudoin. Got it?"

"Already got the layout," she replied matter-of-factly. "You need help in there?"

"Nah," I replied. "I've got a score to settle."

"Alrighty, then." Lil disappeared down the tunnel, and I looked at the door. A second later, I kicked it in.

Langston was on one side of the room, leaning against a desk. Juliana was on the other side, her hands up—two Peacekeepers had guns trained on her. I noted that every piece of furniture in the room was made of wood or plastic, as were the walls and floor. The Peacekeepers' belt buckles and the eyelets on their boots were hardened resin; even Langston's watch was plastic. Langston had gone all out for this trap.

"Mr. Corbeau," Langston greeted. "I finally met your sister earlier. What a lovely girl she is. Your family is truly remarkable."

"You all right, Jules?" I asked.

"Still with that abominable nickname," Langston drawled as he shook his head. "Why corrupt a name as beautiful as 'Juliana'? It's rare for one's given name to match their beauty, but clearly it has, in Ms. Armstrong's case."

I clenched my fist. "Talk to me, Jules."

"She can't," Langston said. "I'm sorry, did I not explain that?"

I looked at the bug-eyed bastard for the first time. Langston was dressed to the nines as always, today in a perfectly pressed white shirt and dress slacks and loafers so shiny I could see my reflection in them. His sleeves were rolled up and his collar was open, but he wasn't wearing his usual gold chain. Too bad. I'd been dreaming about strangling him with it for years.

Beneath all the expensive clothes, and the half-pound of gel he used to slick back his hair, Langston was nothing more than a coward. I saw him for what he was when he first came to the Institute. He'd been both frightened and awed by our abilities, but instead of trying to understand what we could do, he sought to control us.

Langston had never controlled me. Even after all he'd done to me, and the way he'd made Juliana suffer to make me comply with his experiments, he never broke me.

He won't break me today.

"What did you do to her?" I demanded.

"I haven't done anything to her. Not yet, anyway. What I have done is make it clear that if she speaks, I will kill her. Notice the guns? Unlike you, Ms. Armstrong knows not to doubt me."

I reached out with my ability and learned that the guns were also plastic and loaded with plastic bullets made from a special polymer Langston had developed so he could shoot me and make it hurt. Langston was an accomplished scientist and engineer, and he carried a hell of a grudge, but his biggest failure had always been underestimating me.

I felt around the room and located a few specks of metal; a single thumbtack and a few discarded staples. It was enough. I sent the metal toward the guns and had it breach the outer casings. In a few minutes, the metal would lock around the plastic gears and totally disable them. I wanted to immediately rub it in Langston's face, but no one needed to know about my trick except me. For now.

I kept searching the room and the adjoining tunnel for metal. Suddenly, my ability swept toward Juliana. She'd hidden a second gun in an ankle holster, and the goons hadn't found it.

It looked like me and Jules might have the upper hand after all.

"What do you want, Langston?" I demanded.

"What do I want? Many things." Langston steepled his hands and pressed his fingers to his lips. "Right now, what I would really like is to leave this place, unpursued by you and yours."

"And if I give you that?"

"You get to live," Langston replied. "Ms. Armstrong gets to live, too. Of course, she'll be coming with me."

"And if I say no?" I pressed.

"You die, I still leave, and Ms. Armstrong still accompanies me," he replied. "What will it be, Mr. Corbeau?"

"I'm going with option three," I countered. "Jules leaves with me."

The Peacekeepers' guns cracked apart and the pieces clattered to the floor. Langston stood up, staring at them.

"So much for your 'no metal in the room' plan," I added, grinning.

He still looked smug. *Great.* "You of all people should know that was a ruse," he sneered. He grabbed a white plastic gun that had been lying on the desk blocked by his body and fired at Juliana. He had lousy aim and the bullet missed by a mile. I grabbed one of the metal-tainted guns and sent it flying into his gut.

"Option four," Juliana announced from behind us, drawing her own gun. "*You* go down instead."

She fired, striking Langston's right leg just above the knee. She aimed to fire again, but one of the goons slammed his elbow into her face and she went down. I knocked the goon out and knelt beside Juliana.

"Talk to me, baby," I said, taking her face in my hands. "All teeth present and accounted for? What year is it?"

She sat up and rubbed her temple. "Max, shut up," she replied. *I guess that meant she was fine.* Juliana looked across the room and swore. "Langston's gone."

She was right; he'd slipped out during the scuffle. There were only two exits. Juliana and I had been blocking one, so we left the unconscious goon where he'd fallen and went after Langston through the other door. It was a straight tunnel with no offshoots, which was good. What was not so good was that we should have had been right behind Langston, but he was nowhere to be seen.

"There must be a hidden exit," I muttered. "No way he had that much of a head start on us."

"Mike's not big on trapdoors." Juliana trailed her fingertips along the wall. "That tells us two things."

"Oh? Such as?"

"One, Langston designed this area of the campus, if not the whole place," she replied. "Two, he has some form of surveillance that's undetectable, at least by you."

I felt along the edges of the tunnel with my ability. There were several metal devices, but none were similar to a camera or audio recorder. "I don't feel any surveillance."

"And I don't see or hear any, yet he knew when I was standing on that trapdoor." Juliana tapped the wall, then got down on her hands and knees and pressed her ear to the floor.

"Are the floors spilling their secrets?"

"Maybe." She rose up on her knees. "Can you locate any pressure sensors?"

I shook my head. "I can feel some wiring, but nothing more."

"That doesn't mean that they're not there," Juliana said. "Remember those rubber and plastic sensors Langston rigged up for Greta?"

I remembered them all too well. The sensors were used to monitor how much raw tonnage was added to Greta, a stone Elemental. Langston wanted to know how much weight she could handle before she broke. Eventually, he did know. She did break. "Yeah."

"Langston designed those sensors with as few metal components as possible. He was afraid you'd disable his equipment to save Greta," she added.

"He was right." I reached out, got a lock on the wires. "So, what do we do? Rip the wires out?"

"I have a better idea. Let's follow them to the control room and find out what's really going on here."

We followed the wires through the tunnels, my ability leading the way. At first, it led us down an offshoot, the first we'd come across, and we ended up at a dead-end near the outer edge of the campus. No big deal—turning around was easy enough.

Not long after we turned around, we found a blood

trail on the floor; unlike Langston, Juliana had aimed true and injured him. Based on the amount of blood, it was a good hit, which meant he probably wasn't moving too fast.

The trail led Juliana and me to a set of double doors that were nearly identical to the entrance to the laboratory at the Institute for Elemental Research. Inside the Institute's lab, I'd been nothing more than a specimen, poked and prodded, drugged to the edge of insanity, and damn near dissected. I was not looking forward to seeing what was on the other side of these new doors. Anyone with half a brain would have turned tail and run.

My heartbeat was so loud in my ears and heavy in my chest that I had to wonder if Juliana could hear it. I glanced over at her. Her back was straight, her fists clenched, her mouth a tight slash across her face. Bad things had happened to her at the Institute, too, but she was here and ready to fight. The least I could do was fight with her.

"Want me to go in first? Scope out the place?" I asked.

Juliana took a steady breath. "We should enter together. If you find a gun, can you grab it for me?"

"Will do." I set my hand on the door. "Let's do something heroic."

I pushed the doors open and felt my heart rate ratchet up. This lab was set up just like the one in the

Institute had been, right down to Langston's torture devices. There was even a man-sized plastic chamber fitted with electrodes.

What is he doing here? The lights were dim, and there was no one in the control room. No one I could see, that is.

"This is weird," Juliana murmured. "Even for Langston, this is weird."

"Should we get out of here?" I asked. Then I felt something. "There's a crap ton of metal behind that door," I said, pointing to the entrance in question. "If it's an armory, I can get you a gun."

"Preferably a loaded one."

"You are picky." I paused. Something was off. "That really is a lot of metal for a place like this."

"How so?"

"You find those amounts in a forge. Even armories don't usually have that much."

She nodded, and we moved toward the door. "Can you tell what kind of metal it is?" she asked.

"Of course I can," I replied. "Almost all of it is iron."

"You mean steel?"

"No. It's the pure element, not an alloy."

Juliana halted me with a hand on my arm. "Can you feel any aluminum? Chrome? Nickel? Molybdenum?"

"There's traces of other metals, but no significant amounts."

Juliana chewed her lower lip.

"Why?"

"Firearms aren't made from pure iron. Almost nothing is, at least not in a lab."

"Then why is Langston hoarding iron?"

The door blew open, the force of the blast sending both of us back, skidding across the linoleum floor. When the dust cleared, I saw the source of the iron: Ferra, the Iron Queen.

I grabbed Juliana's hand and portaled us out of there.

25

Sara

"Hi, Mike," I said. My voice hardly wavered, which was amazing. There had to be a hundred Peacekeepers behind Mike, and all of them were armed to the teeth. I was more worried about Eddie and the white-hot flames dancing across his body. "Remember me? Juliana and I went to school together. It was a while ago. What have you been up to these past few years?"

"Of course I remember you," Mike replied. He was wearing a modified combat helmet that had wires trailing to a battery pack attached to his belt. It looked exactly like the schematic of the Dreamwalker helmet Juliana had shown us at the manor.

"Micah, the helmet," I whispered.

"I see it," he reassured me under his breath. "Fear not, our shields are strong."

"Sara, I've been looking forward to seeing you again," Mike continued. "Now that you're here, we have two Inheritors present, with a third on the way."

I stilled. "Third? You mean water or earth, right?"

Auster bared his filthy teeth. "What fun would those elements be?"

"Whose son are you?" Micah demanded. Mike opened his mouth, but Micah pointed at Eddie and said, "I am not asking you. I am asking him."

The flames lengthened along Eddie's arms. "You don't know my parents, but I believe you've met my sister."

"Sister," I repeated. Then I remembered. Ayla, Oriana's current favorite, was the Inheritor of Fire.

"Eddie's not one of the made," I said, remembering his bleached-out orange hair. "He's an Elemental, Ayla's brother. It's why he's the only fire that survived."

Micah's eyes narrowed. "Oriana will pay dearly for this."

I heard yelling coming from the main building. Max and Juliana were running toward us.

"Oriana betrayed us!" I called out to them and to all of our forces as they clashed with the Peacekeepers. "Eddie is Ayla's brother!" Around us, Elementals and those of old magic gasped at the accusation, turning to try and catch a glimpse of Eddie.

"We have bigger problems," Max yelled back to me as he ran. "Ferra's here!"

My breath caught. "That's not—"

The words died on my lips as Ferra, the Iron Queen I'd hit with a magical wave and watched rust into bits, crashed out of the door that Max and Juliana had just passed through.

"How is this possible?" I demanded.

"Langston retrieved all that was left of her," Juliana explained. "He's been trying to reanimate her ever since!"

"Shit." I scanned the area and saw Mom in the thick of the fighting. Her gaze immediately locked on Ferra, and she commanded the redcaps to advance.

Behind us, Dad saw everything from his surveillance outpost. He looked from us to Mom. Then he dropped a portal and stepped out next to Micah.

"And now we begin the true fight," Micah declared.

"Leave Ferra to me," Dad growled. "I do have business with her."

I opened my mouth to protest, but then Micah and Max suddenly grabbed their heads and fell to their knees.

"What's wrong?" I went to my knees beside Micah, felt his forehead. "Wait, is it the helmet?"

"It must be," Juliana said, pointing at Mike's headgear. "They're at close range, so they're getting the full brunt of it."

"Why isn't it affecting Sara?" Dad asked.

"The deadening drugs," Juliana explained. "There hasn't been enough time for them to wear off. If you can't dreamwalk, the helmet can't hurt you."

Suddenly, everything fell into place. "Is that why you injected me?"

"Yes," Juliana replied. "I wanted to give some to Max and Micah, too, but Max didn't get enough for three doses, and he didn't have time to get more. That, and we needed their Elemental abilities."

She gave me the drugs to help me. Micah put his hand on mine. "You . . . have an advantage," he rasped. "Use it."

I nodded and squeezed his hand, then stood. Mike's brows lowered beneath his helmet. He reached up and adjusted some controls. I glanced around and saw others clutching their heads; Mike must have increased the helmet's range. He also increased the intensity, judging by the way Micah doubled over in pain.

I heard Juliana cry out; Max had fainted. "We've got to get that helmet off of him," I shouted.

"Agreed," Dad said, then a metal door landed next to him. It was followed by a railing, which he caught with his ability before it could do any damage.

"But first, Ferra needs to go," I told him. "She's all yours."

"You get that helmet off of Armstrong," Dad agreed. "We may need Max and Micah to stop Ferra."

I bit my lip; leaving my husband and brother defenseless wasn't my first choice, but Dad was right. We needed them to defeat Ferra.

I took a few steps toward Mike. "I think your helmet's got a glitch," I taunted.

"Does it?" He readjusted the controls. Out of the corner of my eye, I saw Max convulse. I didn't dare look at Micah. Instead, I focused on the line between Mike and Max.

Mike ordered Eddie to toss a few fireballs at me. I held up a hand, but my Elemental abilities were still blocked by the drugs. I reached for my old magic instead, and the fire extinguished mid-flight, but there, in the smoke, I saw it. The energy that arced between the helmet and Max, the computerized waves that were attacking my brother's brain. As I concentrated on that line, the energy solidified and coalesced into a single glassine wave.

I snapped my fingers, and the wave shattered.

I glanced at Max; he was still unconscious, but the convulsions had stopped. I turned toward Micah and gasped. He was flat on his back, blood trickling from his ear. Worse, I looked beyond Micah and saw dozens of others in a similar state.

If I snapped the strands one by one, I might not save them all.

I decided to save Micah first and then work my way through the rest, when I remembered his words: *You have an advantage. Use it.* And I realized that he hadn't meant my old magic.

He'd meant the Raven's feather.

Dad had been adamant that we bring the Raven feathers with us. I'd balked at first; the feathers were precious, and we didn't want them damaged in battle. But Dad had insisted, which meant that he, Max, and I carried three magical boosters with us. Would they be enough?

Only one way to find out.

I withdrew the feather and held it before me. "Energy! Reverse!"

The strands of energy recoiled, snapping back from their victims. They hovered in place for a moment, then changed their course and bombarded the helmet.

Mike screamed and pulled at the helmet, but it wouldn't come off. His entourage tried helping him, but he fell to the ground and I lost sight of him. I moved forward, but Ferra blocked my way.

The Iron Queen was taller than I remembered, but she still had the same lank, steel-gray hair and was wearing the same trashy chainmail shirt and skirt. Unlike the confident, if corrupt, ruler she'd been, this Ferra had the jerky movements of a marionette, and her eyes were clouded over.

I backed toward Micah and Dad. "Something's up with Ferra," I told them quickly. "She's like a zombie."

"Zombies need to be controlled," Juliana mused. I scanned the people behind Mike and saw a mage close enough to exert his will onto Ferra. I wondered if he'd done the same to the made.

"Sleep!" I yelled, and the mage fell to the ground. I couldn't believe that worked.

"Ferra still advances," Dad yelled, snapping me back to reality. "Sara, the mage was a ruse!"

I held up the Raven's feather, hoping it had some juice left. "Ferra, obey me! Stop moving!"

Ferra halted, then her head swiveled around toward me. Her mouth stretched in a rictus grin, a line of drool escaping the corner. "Sar . . . a . . . "

I backed toward Dad. "I—I don't think it worked."

Dad reached his arms overhead, then flung a mass of metal at Ferra. The metal twisted itself around her until it resembled a beehive with only her head exposed.

She laughed. Then she stood, and the metal shattered around her. Dad hurled the railing back toward Ferra and knocked her flat on her back.

A bee landed on my nose; the queen of the hive had come to lend assistance. "Can you distract the rest of the mages?" I asked, since I still didn't know who or what was controlling Ferra.

The queen zipped away, her swarm of bees a dark cloud behind her. They descended on the mages, who were soon busy ducking their heads and futilely swatting away the bees. I hoped none of the bees got hurt.

"Sara!" Dad yelled. Ferra had gathered the metal shrapnel and flung it toward us.

The shrapnel stopped in midair. Micah had rolled onto his belly, his arm outstretched as he kept the metal from landing on us.

"One feather is not enough," Dad roared, brandishing his own Raven feather like a sword. More metal landed around Ferra's feet and she wavered, then burst free from the shards and bellowed.

"*Max!*" I shrieked. "Max, we need your feather!"

Juliana shook Max's shoulders, begging him to wake up. His eyes opened to slits and he coughed. "Wha—"

"Max, feather, now!" I shouted.

Groggily, Max crawled toward Dad and me. He sat leaning against my leg and held his feather toward Ferra. The Iron Queen slowed to a halt, the metal shards heaped around her like a snowdrift. Then Mom appeared above Ferra and cracked her on the head with her sword's hilt. The Iron Queen swayed, then dropped like a stone.

"We had her under control," I said to Mom.

"Can't be too sure with that one," she countered wryly. She backed away from Ferra, her sword at the ready. "Give her an order."

"Ferra, sit up," I said. She sat up. "Ferra, smile." Ferra smiled.

I shuddered. Maybe we should have let Mom finish her.

"Great, we made a zombie Elemental," Max said. "Now what do we do with her?"

Micah got to his feet. "I have an idea. But . . . for the moment, she will need to be contained."

The dust cleared, and we took stock of what we'd done.

At some point, Jovanny had contacted a few friends of his that were members of the almost-ousted Mirlander government. A few hours later, a military company arrived—*actual* military, not the Peacekeepers that had been terrorizing Elementals for the past few decades. Since most Mundanes had grown to resent the Peacekeepers as much as Elementals did, they were glad to help.

"Is he alive?" asked one Captain Brennan when she saw Mike. A portion of Mike's helmet had melted onto his face and neck, and he had burns that ran from his head down over his torso. The first responders had been shocked at the extent of his burns and had put him in a medically induced coma. "And what happened to his face?"

"He's alive," I replied. "As for his injuries, that's an interesting story. What Armstrong really wanted was to be a Dreamwalker, so he studied them for years."

Brennan raised an eyebrow. "Studied?"

"Observed, chopped up, preserved in formaldehyde," I ticked off. "You name it, he did it. Anyway, he learned enough to build this helmet." I pointed to the mass of melted plastic and electrodes on the ground next to Mike's gurney.

"I'm taking your word for it that that's a helmet," Brennan replied with a grimace, nudging it with her toe. "So, what happened?

"Armstrong used the helmet to incapacitate any Dreamwalkers on-site," I answered. "We were able to reverse the helmet's energy and direct it back to him."

Brennan nodded. "Dreamwalkers are real, then?"

I slid my gaze toward her. "I suppose anything's possible."

Brennan shook her head, then called for the medics to move Mike to a field hospital. I left her to it and walked toward Max and Juliana. They both looked awful; Max's skin was still ashen from Mike's Dreamwalker attack, and the entire left side of Juliana's face was black and blue, blood crusted along her jaw and neck.

"What the hell happened in there?" I demanded, looking between them.

"Langston," Max replied through clenched teeth. "He got away."

I nodded. "We'll find him."

Juliana met my gaze. "We will."

"Micah and I will help however we can," I told them both. "But before we go after Langston, we need to deal with Oriana."

As soon as the Mirlanders had the site under control, we assembled and portaled back to the Otherworld, and found our biggest casualty of the day: Silverstrand Manor had been razed to the ground. There were streaks of gold among the silver, proving Oriana's forces were responsible.

"Oh, Micah." I looped my arm with his and leaned against his shoulder. "I'm so sorry."

"As long as we both still breathe, we will have a home together." Micah cupped the back of my head and kissed my hair. "I built this home, and I will build us another. Let us find the silverkin."

We picked our way among the rubble while Mom's redcaps swarmed the estate searching for gold warriors. They found a few stragglers and brought them to Dad to be restrained with the other prisoners. While they sorted things out, Micah and I went to the gardens. There, we found the silverkin.

The gardens were also destroyed, but the silverkin had formed a perimeter around Sadie and Selene's graves. The little guys stood shoulder to shoulder with their silver spears thrust outward, a living metal fence protecting what actually mattered.

"Shep," I gasped, sinking to my knees in front of him. "Thank you."

Shep pressed his forehead against mine, then motioned to the rest of the silverkin. They broke formation and immediately started clearing out the manor's rubble. I watched as they sorted through the scorched remnants of our home. The immensity of what we'd lost sank in—the memories we'd made in those rooms, the time we'd shared with each other in those walls, now so much dust.

My voice came out shaky and wet. "Micah, there's nothing left."

He shook his head. "Of course there's something left." He wrapped an arm around my shoulders, the other gesturing toward the trees. "We have our orchards, our land, and our family. The manor was naught but a structure. We will remake it, you and I, as a haven for our family."

"A haven," I said, rolling the word around in my mouth. "I'd like that."

Micah smiled at me. "Good. Before we commence rebuilding, we do have business with Oriana."

My heart hardened at the thought. There'd be time to mourn later. "Yes, we do. Let's get the prisoners on the metal pathway and get this over with."

Micah and I arrived at the Gold Court ahead of the others. We'd planned everything out down to the smallest detail, and the results would be simple: Oriana was going to be dethroned, and I would take her place.

"This isn't something I ever wanted," I told Micah, my feet having turned to lead at the sight of the golden palace. "I've never wanted to be in charge of anything, much less an entire realm."

"Perhaps this is not what you wished for, but it is where your path has taken you," Micah replied. "I must say, when I was younger, I thought I'd spend my life as a soldier, as my father did before me. I never imagined I would have a wife, much less a human wife." He kissed my knuckles. "And look how happy I am that my life did not turn out as I had anticipated."

I smiled at my silver elf. "You'll help me, right?" I asked him for what had to be the hundredth time.

"I will do anything you require of me. Now, come, beloved. Let us, as you say, get this over with."

We weren't surprised to find the Gold Court defended as if Armageddon was imminent, with scores of gold warriors standing at attention outside the walls. What did surprise us was the sight of Rukmini, the Gold Queen's general, standing beside the main entrance.

"Did you get demoted to doorman?" I asked. Rukmini scowled at me, then turned his glare toward Micah.

"What is the meaning of this?" he demanded. "You dealt my men and me a grave insult. How dare you set foot in the Gold Court?!"

"And good day to you," Micah responded. His cheerfulness made Rukmini's scowl deepen. "May my wife and I petition you for an audience with the queen?"

Rukmini's brows lowered. "The last time I encountered you, your wife referred to Her Highness's golden form in a most vulgar manner," he recounted, dour. "That was not proper."

"Actually, I said 'ass,'" I clarified. "I was referring to Oriana's shiny gold ass. So, can we come in?"

Rukmini opened his mouth, probably to tell me where I could put such requests, when he noticed something behind me. "W-what is the meaning of this entourage?"

I glanced over my shoulder. The redcaps were fanned out behind Micah and me, with fresh blood dripping down their caps and their iron pikes glinting in the sun. In the midst of them towered Ferra.

"The redcaps are escorting a few prisoners. Can we come in as invited guests, or do the redcaps need to take down a wall?"

"I think not," Rukmini began, then I raised my hand and swept him aside.

"He bored me," I explained with a shrug, sending a tendril of magic toward the gold warriors to ensure they'd remain stock-still. The redcaps could handle them, but having fewer opponents to deal with was a win in my book.

"Me as well." Micah extended his arm. "Shall we?"

I placed my hand in his elbow. "We shall."

Micah and I entered the Gold Court, much to the shock and amazement of those inside. It was Micah's turn to ensure that the solid gold men remained immobile while I took care of the Elementals and other creatures. Our plan relied on catching Oriana unawares, which meant we couldn't have anyone running through the halls squawking about me or Micah or the redcaps. Definitely not the redcaps.

Every creature we passed looked at Micah and me as if they'd seen ghosts.

"These people are amazed that we're still breathing," I murmured. "Her plan really was to kill us."

"And for that, she shall be held accountable," Micah replied.

After an uneventful walk through the Gold Court, we entered Oriana's throne room. The queen herself was alone, reading a scroll while seated on her throne. The blood drained from her face when she saw Micah and me, alive and kicking.

"My queen," Micah greeted. "I trust you are well?"

"I am," Oriana replied, as flustered as I'd ever seen her. "Micah, forgive me, but I was not expecting you."

Ayla appeared from behind the throne. Flames licked up her arms and wove through her hair.

"Forgive us for our unexpected intrusion," Micah continued, drawing on all his courtier's skills. "But we do have an urgent matter to discuss with you."

"Do you." Oriana's gaze went to the entrance, but no one was there. "Where is my guard? Where is Rukmini?"

"We relieved him of his duties," I said. "Ayla, how are you?"

The Inheritor of Fire turned to me. "Where is my brother?"

"I didn't know you had a brother. Wait . . . yes, I did."

I snapped my fingers, and Dad and Max portaled into the throne room. Between them was Eddie, bound from shoulder to knee in copper and silver chains. Ayla screamed and moved toward him, but Micah made a cutting motion and kept her on the dais.

"Do you recall when I asked if you knew what metal can do to fire?" Micah asked. "Here is a taste of what I can do."

"What is the meaning of this?" Oriana demanded. "Why have you captured Ayla's brother? Micah, after all you've done to me—"

"All *we've* done to *you*?" I shot back. "Eddie was working with Peacekeepers in the Mundane realm. He was helping the people that kill Elementals for fun. So was Ayla."

Ayla lifted her chin. "You cannot prove that!"

"I don't need to," I countered. "Auster has already told us everything. We also found records and video surveillance of your meetings with the Peacekeepers. And we know that everything you did was on Oriana's orders."

Elementals from the rest of the Gold Court had been slowly filtering into the throne room. As I levied accusations against Oriana, the crowd's whispers became a dull roar. Oriana looked around the room and panicked.

"I know not what Ayla has done!" Oriana cried. "I am not a party to her betrayal!"

"Ori!" Ayla shouted. "Do not betray me, too!"

"Don't worry. You two can share a dungeon." I glanced behind me and saw that the Wood Witch had arrived, with Shelliya and Ash flanking her. Also present was Aregonda, wearing a splendid copper crown and green dress. On her arm was the Raven in his human guise as Bran. Since he couldn't hold his corporeal form for long, it was his astral self, the edges of his being pulsing like a heartbeat. Behind them were dozens of copper Elementals and scores of those beholden to old magic. Mom entered the room with a flourish and nodded toward me.

"The redcaps have taken the court," she announced. "Sara, it is time to pass judgment on the queen."

"Oriana, we have deemed you unfit to rule," I began. "You have committed treachery against your own kind. You have not ruled with your people's well-being in mind. You have used the throne as a way to carry out personal vendettas. We rescind your right to rule."

"You cannot!" Oriana shrieked.

"We can," the Wood Witch said. "You forget, little witchling, that Elementals were born of the old magic. We are your elders."

"You also forget that Elementals had a royal family long before gold became the dominant metal," Bran said. "I was there, and I remember."

"We of copper forgot nothing," Aregonda said. "We of copper remember, and we know that this generation's Inheritor of Metal is the rightful queen."

I laced my fingers with Micah's.

"The Inheritor of Metal is dead," Oriana challenged. "Or so I was told. Did you lie to me?"

"I did not." My voice cracked. Micah squeezed my hand, and I started again. "I did not. The last Inheritor, my sister, Sadie Corbeau, has passed. Before her death, she arranged for the Inheritor's power to be sent to me."

Oriana opened her mouth, but I held up my hand. "That is not all."

Her eyes narrowed. "What else have you done?"

"I am no longer just an Elemental. I also possess old magic, and those of the old ways have pledged themselves to me."

"You seek to take my crown?" Oriana snarled.

"No. I seek to destroy it." I turned toward my mother. "Now?"

"Aye, now." Mom clapped her hands, and Ferra appeared in the hall. A moment later, the redcaps swarmed into the room and toward the throne. Oriana screamed, but the imps never touched her. Instead, they surrounded her, their iron pikes aimed at her throat. Ayla tried to intervene, but Micah kept her immobile.

Mimicking my mother, I clapped my hands. Oriana's crown flew from her head to my hands. I held the crown aloft for a moment, then crumpled it into a golden ball.

"No!" Oriana cried as she fell to her knees. "Ferra took everything from me! My crown is all I have left! Now you've truly taken all that's dear to me."

Ayla gasped, but I ignored the fire Elemental and approached Oriana. The redcaps parted, and I crouched down in front of her.

"I get it," I said matter-of-factly. "You were desperate to keep your crown, and you really wanted my sister's pledge. When she refused, you resorted to threats; when threats didn't scare us, you moved on to lies and deceit. You formed alliances with my enemies, all because you were scared you'd end up back in Ferra's oubliette. I understand why you did what you did."

Oriana blinked. "You do?"

"Of course I do. I can even forgive you for most of it. At times, I've been pretty desperate myself." I rose and looked down on the former queen.

"But your actions led to my sister's death. And I will never forgive you for that." I turned on my heel and told the redcaps, "Put her and Ayla in the dungeon. Then sweep the grounds for gold warriors. The Gold Court ends tonight."

We didn't raze the Gold Court to the ground as Oriana had done to Silverstrand Manor. Instead, we reduced the palace to little more than a golden guard shack keeping watch over the oubliette and its two residents, Oriana and Ayla. Ayla kept trying to burn her way to freedom, but I'd layered the walls with an enchantment that doused even the hottest flame. That, coupled with the redcap guards Mom had stationed there, meant those two weren't going anywhere.

Ayla's brother, Eddie, was also in a dungeon, but not a nice one like the golden oubliette. In a rare moment of solidarity, Mom and Aregonda had permanently dampened his flames to no stronger than a match-stick's and sent him to tend the fires at the Seelie Court. When Eddie had threatened escape, Mom swore to him that if he attempted fleeing, she'd remove his fire altogether and leave him with the Unseelie.

No one's heard a peep out of Eddie since then.

Someone else who wasn't going anywhere was Ferra. None of us understood how Langston had revived her, but he hadn't managed to save her shrewd mind or her biting wit. While that made her less of a worry, it also made her rather inconvenient. We'd ended up sending her to Ash to help him around the forge.

"I hope she doesn't cause any trouble," I said to Micah as we left Ash's blacksmith shop. Ferra had been happily tending the fire in between stacking raw metal for processing.

"I'm sure Ash can handle her," Micah replied. We strolled through the Whispering Dell, the villagers calling out greetings to Micah and shooting me side-ways glances. Him, they were used to. As for me, any goodwill I'd earned as Lady Silverstrand was super-seded by the fact that I'd dethroned Ferra, and now Oriana.

"So much is different, and yet so many things are the same," I murmured. "Everyone knows I'm in charge now, but I don't know if they'll ever accept me."

"These things take time," Micah replied. "One of copper has not ruled for many generations. I have no doubt that once word of your compassionate heart and just hand spreads far and wide, your people will come to love you."

I smiled up at him. "You say the best things."

He smiled back. "I only speak the truth."

Something that was taking quite a bit of time was rebuilding Silverstrand Manor. We were using the same layout as the prior manor, only this time it wouldn't be solid silver. I could finally add that copper roof I'd been dreaming of, and a glorious copper stair-case that led to the upper floors.

"The copper needn't end here," Micah commented. We were inspecting the eastern wing, which over-looked the gardens. "This is your home as much as mine. More, it is our court. It should reflect your metal as much as mine."

"I know." I traced copper spirals onto the silver wall. "But I don't want us to be just copper and silver.

I want everyone to feel welcome here; Elemental and Mundane, old magic and new. We're going to try to be better than Oriana and the Elemental Court."

Micah wrapped his arm around my shoulders and kissed my hair. "We *will* be better. Of that, I have no doubt."

"I know just where we can start." I unwound myself from Micah and tugged him toward the library. "Right here." The silverkin had rescued almost all of Sadie's books, and I was determined to create the library she'd always wanted.

"Sadie's dream was to have a huge free library." I stood in the middle of the room and stretched out my arms. "She had already curated and organized the collection. Now all we have to do is throw open the doors and let people know that it's here. Our court can be more than someplace people go to make requests or pledge loyalties. It can be a place where people come together, to learn and grow."

"Look at you," Micah murmured, his lips quirking into a proud smile. "My copper girl has become a copper queen."

I smiled back at him. "My mom's the queen in the family. I'm more of a copper princess."

26

Max

I never thought I'd see the day when I'd be spending the majority of my time sorting through paperwork.

That'd been my life for those few weeks after we'd taken down the Peacekeepers: first, filling out the forms I'd needed to recertify myself as a citizen of Pacifica, then jumping through a series of bureaucratic hoops to get a government job. That's right—I got a real job, working for my father on his latest pet project. I didn't have a full idea of what this job entailed just yet, but it was cool. I'd figure it out.

Something else I needed to figure out was how to track down my old buddy, Langston Phillips. After we'd handled Oriana and gotten Sara her rightful crown, I went back to Peacekeeper Central and found the tunnel he'd used to escape. I'd even found a few more of his files, including some of his personal notes.

What I *hadn't* found was an address, or even a hint of a location where he might be hiding out.

It's all right. I'll find him. And this time, I'll have help.

Pacifica was in the midst of a series of special elections at this point, being that their former frontrunner was incapacitated and also happened to be a treasonous bastard. While the bureaucrats sorted out the elections, and officials at the military hospital kept Armstrong under lock and key, Dad and Jovanny put together the Elemental Relations Bureau. With their help, I would find not only Langston Phillips, but all the Langstons out there in the world. We would make Pacifica safe for all beings, even if I had to hunt down every bigot myself.

That was all work for the future, and I still had things to do in the present. Since I now had a salary, I'd celebrated by making the biggest purchase of my life, a purchase I never thought I'd make. When you spend nearly half your life as a government prisoner, you don't do much planning for the future. But the ink dried on the contract, and the funds had been exchanged; the deal was as done as it was going to get. As I slid the last document into its folder, there was a knock at my door.

"In," I called. I glanced in the mirror over the desk and saw Sara enter the room.

"Max, she's leaving," Sara prompted. I started to ask who she meant, but I already knew the answer.

Juliana was leaving, because she didn't belong in the Otherworld. For that matter, neither did I.

Sara shoved her hands in her pockets and looked at the floor. "You should go talk to her."

"Think so?" I asked, turning to face her.

"Yeah." She scuffed the rug with her toe. "She doesn't like portals, and you can help her over."

"Good idea." I grabbed my leather jacket and raked my fingers through my hair, then walked down the hall to Juliana's room. Since her door was open, I didn't bother knocking. Instead, I leaned against the doorframe and watched her shove things into a backpack. A full duffle bag was on the floor near her feet.

"No goodbyes?" I asked. She jumped, then turned to face me.

"I've already said goodbye to Sara and Micah, and I left a note for your parents," she replied. "The silver people even packed me a lunch."

Wow. She said goodbye to the silverkin, but not to me. I decided that she was saving the best for last and said, "Well, let's get going. I'll take you through the portal."

"You will?"

"Sure. I know you don't like portal hopping." I hefted the larger of her two bags onto my shoulder. "Are you all set?"

She glanced around the room. "Yeah. Let's go."

We walked down to the metal pathway, and I held

out my hand. When she looked wary, I explained, "We can take the metal pathway to the static portal."

"Um, I've never been on one of these pathways," she explained, hesitant. "And Micah gave me a few portals."

"Save 'em," I suggested. "The static portal's a smoother ride than the made ones. It'll be easier on you. And let me tell you, traveling by metal is doing it in style." I grinned and held out my hand. She hesitated for another moment, then slid her fingers between mine.

"All right," she agreed. "Let's go."

We stood there, smiling like fools. Then I stepped onto the metal pathway and pulled Juliana along with me. I had just enough time to hear Juliana's yelp. An instant later, we were at the edge of the Whispering Dell. The pathway ejected us, and Juliana fell against me.

"You okay?" I asked.

"That was insane," she muttered. She glared at the pathway for a moment, then realized that her arms were around my waist.

"We'll go through the portal this way," I told her as she tried pulling away. "It'll be calmer for you."

Juliana gave me a look that told me she thought that this notion was bunk, but kept her arm around my waist as we stepped though the static portal. The next second found us standing in the parking lot of Real

Estate Evaluation Services. Juliana started toward the back entrance, away from the building.

"Tell me, Jules, what does the future hold for you?" I asked, falling into step beside her. "What will Juliana Armstrong do with her life?"

Juliana thought for a moment. "I'll check in with my mother, make sure Corey's doing okay, then I'll get a place. And a job."

I didn't want to bring him up, but I had to know. "You don't want to go after Langston?"

"I do. I really do, but I also want a life. Mike and Langston have monopolized my life since I was sixteen. I need to take some time for me."

"I get it," I replied, and I did. "After Sara busted me out, I ran myself ragged in the Otherworld. At the time I couldn't have explained why, but now I know. I was finding myself." I snorted, and added, "I'm pretty lucky Micah didn't kill me."

"Were you sowing your wild oats?" Juliana asked, fluttering her lashes at me.

"I did not sow one single oat," I replied. "What kind of work do you want to do?"

"Good question," she replied. "Maybe I'll go to school instead of getting a job, finish my degree."

"Northridge's kind of far from Portland."

Juliana shuddered. "I think I'd rather move on to a new school, one where no one knows me. Or my uncle."

"I approve of that plan." I grabbed Juliana's elbow and steered her toward my left. "Let's take this street."

"Why?"

"I want to show you something."

We walked for a time, making small talk. Eventually we were on a street lined with town houses, and I stopped us both in front of number twenty-six.

"Here it is," I said, sweeping my arms wide.

"Here what is?" Juliana asked. I draped my arm around her shoulders and pointed to the front door. It was white, but I was planning on painting it royal blue.

"This is mine," I explained, unable to keep my pride from seeping into my voice. "I bought it this morning."

"You bought a house?" she gasped, twisting around to look at me.

"Yep, got me a place in the city." I tucked a dark curl behind her ear. "Think you'll be sticking around Portland?"

Her dark eyes found mine and I almost forgot to breathe. "I'd like to."

We stared at each other, me coming up with, and immediately discarding, a million lines. *Aw, the hell with it.* Despite the small amount of common sense I'd been born with, I pulled Juliana close and kissed her. Damn it all if she didn't kiss me back.

When we pulled away, I said, "Maybe I'll call you sometime."

She quirked an eyebrow at me and grinned. "You don't have my number."

"Think I can't find you?"

She laughed, and I kissed her again, a bit deeper. *Okay, a lot deeper.*

"I think you could find me anywhere," she said against my lips.

"You know it."

I kissed her a third time, then she finally pulled away. "I've got to get going," she explained, biting her lip and motioning over her shoulder. "Visiting Mom and all."

"Moms are important," I assured her. Juliana nodded, then headed down the street.

"Jules," I called. "You need anything, I'm here."

She turned around, walking backward. "I know."

"You need me, I'm here."

She grinned. "I know."

I smiled back, then walked up the concrete steps to my town house. As I coaxed the lock open, I mulled over my new life. A simple life. For the first time, I had my own place. My own home. Juliana would be staying near Portland, and she knew I was here for her. She wanted me here for her. And neither of us were trapped anymore.

The locks tumbled open, and I walked into a place that was mine.

I didn't know what the future held, but for once, I knew it would be good.

EPILOGUE

Sara

It was done.

It had taken weeks longer than anticipated, but Micah and I had finished rebuilding Silverstrand Manor. I took responsibility for any and all delays, because I couldn't allow this iteration of the manor to be anything less than perfect. The manor was more than our home; it also served as the Elemental Court, as a free library for all, and as Sadie's memorial.

"It's perfect," I breathed, awestruck. Micah and I were standing on the lawn in front of the main entrance. Wide copper steps framed by silver balustrades led to copper doors set in a silver arch. Silver walls covered in climbing roses and ivy—both gifts from the Wood Witch—wrapped around the property, and the whole of it was topped with a gabled copper roof.

"It surely is." Micah stood behind me and wrapped an arm around my shoulders, and I leaned into his chest. His other hand came to rest on my belly. There was no baby yet, but that was all right. We had plenty of time.

"Do you think your family will visit often?" he asked. We'd created a separate wing for my parents, complete with a mobile command center so Dad could run the newly minted Elemental Relations Bureau from the Otherworld. The solar array Micah's father had set up behind the orchards had been destroyed by Oriana's goons, but Dad had sourced state-of-the-art replacement equipment. Max and Juliana had helped set everything up, which meant that Dad had the most futuristic office in the Otherworld.

As soon as Dad's office was up and running, Max installed an electric lamp in the library. If Sadie's soul really could visit us, she'd know we were thinking about her.

"I hope so," I replied. "Dad and Max are pretty going to be pretty busy, and Mom needs to look after the Seelie Court, but I'm sure they'll make time to visit."

"Soon enough, we'll be busy with our own court." Micah rested his chin on the top of my head. "Are you ready?"

"I am."

We both turned, and I dropped the enchantment that had hidden the manor while it was under construction. Scattered across the meadow were my people—Elementals and Mundanes, those of old magic and many of copper—waiting to stroll through the grounds, browse the library, or come to me for advice.

This wasn't the life I'd anticipated, but it was the life I had. I laced my fingers with Micah's and squeezed his hand.

"Let's do this."